When We Argued All Night

ALSO BY ALICE MATTISON

NOVELS

Nothing Is Quite Forgotten in Brooklyn

The Wedding of the Two-Headed Woman

The Book Borrower

Hilda and Pearl

Field of Stars

SHORT STORY COLLECTIONS

In Case We're Separated

Men Giving Money, Women Yelling

The Flight of Andy Burns

Great Wits

POETRY COLLECTION

Animals

When We Argued All Night

A NOVEL

ALICE MATTISON

HARPER ◖ PERENNIAL

NEW YORK • LONDON • TORONTO • SYDNEY • NEW DELHI • AUCKLAND

HARPER ● PERENNIAL

HarperCollins books may be purchased for educational, business, or sales promotional use. For information please write: Special Markets Department, HarperCollins Publishers, 10 East 53rd Street, New York, NY 10022.

FIRST EDITION

Designed by Michael Correy

Library of Congress Cataloging-in-Publication Data is available upon request.

ISBN 978-0-06-212037-3

12 13 14 15 16 OV/RRD 10 9 8 7 6 5 4 3 2 1

In memory of Rose and Julius Eisenberg

and for Nina, Henry, and Jesse

Contents

PART ONE

What Does Anyone Accomplish?

1

The Whistler
1936

—I hate to see . . .

No conceivable point taking off his shoes here, here being a splintering wooden step off a small slanted screened porch. Rocks and pebbles on the downward slope toward the lake, roots of trees.

—I hate to see (Artie sang) *that evening sun go down.* He sat down and took off his shoes anyway, first one—experimentally, wiggling his toes—then the other. He left the shoes on the step.

—I hate to see . . .

His hot, itchy black socks. Stuffed them into his shoes. Stood up carefully. The rocks hurt Artie Saltzman's feet, but the dirt and pine needles between his toes felt good. He breathed air that didn't smell of city. Halfway to the lake—small, round, ringed by mountains—he stopped, undid his belt buckle, his pants (was he doing this?), then took off all his clothes, bending awkwardly to get his pants and his shorts past his feet. Artie took off his eyeglasses and rolled up his clothes around them, put a good-sized rock on the bundle. A shiver skidded down his back, his tush. Such a dope, he looked around, but nobody was there except Harold, way out in the lake. Who would be there?

—We can get in a swim before it's dark, Harold had said. Immediately naked, unexpectedly substantial, he was on his way into the lake before Artie had put down his suitcase and wiggled the cramp out of his fingers. Now Harold swam smoothly from right to left, twenty feet from shore. Though Artie could beat Harold easily at handball or punchball, and less easily at tennis, Artie could not swim.

—*I love to see.* He sang again. Tree roots under his arches: pain mixed with pleasure. *That morning sun come up!* An old gray wooden boat was tied to the dock, making a rhythmic bump when the water shifted it. He made himself walk all the way into the lake, singing, trying and failing not to stiffen, wince, and hesitate. The water was cold.

—*St. Louie woman!* This he shouted.

Not that cold.

—*With your diamond rings!* He splashed into the water. He was wet, naked and wet, Artie Saltzman in the Adirondack Mountains with his friend Harold Abramovitz—they'd met in third grade; they were twenty-six—in 1936, with no girls (no, the girl who came to mind simply didn't count), no money, but a week off and a cabin in the woods that belonged to somebody whom Harold knew—how did he invariably get what he wanted?

Artie's daughter Brenda—born five years, more or less, after this splash—would notice that when her father sang *I hate to see that evening sun go down*, he followed it with a silence and then, *St. Louie woman, with your diamond rings.* Brenda couldn't tell whether the lines belonged to one song (and what was in his mind between them if they did?) or two songs that he associated, nor whether the third line he sometimes sang, about the morning sun, was his own invention. She did not ask. Only in adulthood did she hear "The St. Louis Blues."

T he lake was socked in with Christmas trees now blurred with dusk and Artie's nearsightedness. No other houses that he could see. No beach, just a cleared space, a few tree stumps. Now that he was wet, he stood looking around, scooping water and tossing it at his shoulders, and the lake lapped his waist. Harold doubled back, swimming a different stroke, maybe a sidestroke, his face away from Artie, his thick yellow curls dark with water. All at once Artie was angry that he couldn't swim. Maybe he could swim after all, maybe desire was enough. He thrust himself forward, whipping his head from one side to the other, his eyes squeezed shut, thrashing his arms and legs. Careful not to go too far but not careful enough. When he tired and stood, he gulped water, choked, scrambled toward shore. Harold had not seen.

They'd taken a bus from the Port Authority, the very building where, on the tenth floor, Artie had clerked ineffectually for the WPA until June, when he'd been laid off. Shirkers and agitators will be dropped first, Ridder had said, announcing the plan to end ten thousand WPA jobs, so soon after the whole program—hiring people on home relief—got going. The administrator's announcement, of course, led to picketing, seizure of the offices, police, all that fun. But though he was again unemployed, now Artie had time for a week in the mountains, and Harold, who still had a job, had finagled time.

Harold had decreed they would buy groceries in Albany: beans and wieners, soup. Uneeda biscuits, Artie had added. They'd hitchhiked (long waits, short rides) the rest of the way, standing with their thumbs out, each with a valise and a grocery bag.

Now it was starting to get dark, and insects kvetched and fussed. Something splashed, far out. Harold lumbered into the shallow water near Artie, his big thighs shoving water, his privates wrinkled with cold. Let's piss in the lake, he said.

As they faced the lake, elegantly pissing, side by side as in a rite that would ensure their safety and prosperity, the purity and health of the issue of their loins—and while Harold reached to shove Artie's shoulder, saying, Son of a gun! to celebrate their achievement—came the tentative sound of a motor. The cabin was on a twisty driveway, and the sound was nearer than the road. It diminished, then grew stronger.

—Jesus Christ almighty, said Artie the Jewish atheist, as they heard a car stop just beyond the cabin. He started picking his way toward his clothes, but Harold walked deeper into the lake, until the water was up to his chest, and stood with his arms stretched wide, casually scooping water, eyeing the cabin and the dirt driveway behind it, where a black Packard was just visible. The engine ceased and doors slammed. Voices. Two young women, one with an orange scarf around her head, appeared at the side of the cabin as Artie yanked at the roll of his clothes and first snatched his glasses out of trouble and onto his nose, then made a quick decision to skip his underwear and try to thrust his legs into his pants, something difficult to accomplish standing up and with wet legs. Brenda and her younger sister Carol would hear this story many times: So I'm thinking, who the hell are these dames? Did Harold set this up? And he's out there bouncing up and down in the lake and smiling.

—Hello? Then more loudly, Hello? The young woman who'd spoken, the one in the orange headdress, was amused, but also something else. Excuse me?

Artie at last worked his second leg through his pants until his foot came out the other end. Buckling his belt, he set off toward the women bare-chested, determined to step forcefully but mincing over rocks and roots.

—What are you boys doing here? said the woman as he approached. She had dark reddish hair under the scarf, which she snatched off, raking her hair straight back from her head with arched, strong fingers, lining it up against its will. She had not said, What are you doing here, Jew? but Artie flinched as if she had, as if she'd been close enough to see his circumcision.

—What the hell are you talking about? Artie said. We have permission from the owner! We were invited! Still in the lake, Harold was now a dark lump, useless. Artie tried to remember the name he'd mentioned. Gus. He said, Gus said we could definitely use the house.

—Gus is my father, said the woman who'd turn out to be Myra, whom Artie would always feel he understood better than Harold did, because of the advantage of this conversation while the great Harold Abramovitz, reader of Hawthorne, Emerson, and Henry James, had stranded himself in the lake.

Brenda and Carol would ask, each time, How did Harold get out of the water? But the point was that Artie had to solve the problem himself. It became clear, as he and the young woman yelled, that something about Gus embarrassed her, even if he was her father. Noticing discomfort, Artie kept arguing. Nobody in later years could remember more than one significant fact about the friend, Virginia, and they didn't learn it until later. Artie and Myra eventually came to an agreement: after all, they were two men and two women, young, and among them they had, at least now, a house of sorts and a car. The girls (who even had money) drove off, saying they'd return with steaks and liquor. Artie had declared there was room for all in the cabin, an unlikely idea.

When the car was gone, Harold limped shivering into the cabin and began scrambling in his suitcase for a towel.

—What the hell did Gus tell you? Artie said.

—He said use the cabin anytime. So I got him to draw a map. Harold rubbed his legs vigorously, then jerked the towel back and forth across his back.

—You didn't tell him we were coming this week?

—I wasn't sure at the time.

—You never told him?

Harold shrugged and dried his ears. He told me where the key was. What the hell difference does it make? He looked whiny and cold, his blue eyes bulging, his wet curls flat.

Artie didn't answer. Harold had found the key readily, in a crevice in the cabin's stone foundation, inside a metal box that might have contained candies a long time ago.

—I'm hungry. I don't want to wait, Artie said.

—Wait for what? Harold began getting dressed.

—Those girls. They're coming back with food.

—Why would they do that? Harold got dressed just so, like a judge putting on his robes. Artie had somehow known this, maybe from gym in high school. Harold tucked his undershirt into his shorts, he straightened his shirt and smoothed it over his tuchas as he pulled his pants up. He rummaged in his valise for a heavy sweater. The bag mostly had books in it.

—I told them they could stay here, Artie said, leaning in the doorway. Given a wall, Artie leaned.

—You told them they could stay here? We don't want them to stay here!

—Why not? They're pretty. Besides, they need a place to stay, and they thought they were staying here, Artie said.

—They don't want to stay here with us, Harold said.

—What's wrong with us? Artie didn't trust Myra, exactly, but he liked her scrappiness, her shikse sense of superiority. Virginia was quiet and pretty, a blonde.

—There's no room, said Harold. They have money. They'll go to a hotel.

—There's room! And why should they give up if it's their place? The cabin had in it a fireplace, a woodstove, a table, a moldy couch, a sink. Pine walls and ceiling, four windows. Bunk beds in a tiny bedroom. A short distance away, an outhouse. We're in the wilderness! Artie said. There's no hotel!

—Sure there is, Harold said. They won't be back. Didn't you say the name Gus before she did? She said Gus was her father after you said the owner was Gus.

—How did she know Gus was old enough to be her father, in that case?

—He isn't.

—And how did she know enough to ask us who we were? If she's not Gus's daughter, she knows Gus.

But maybe Harold was right. The girl, Myra, could be anyone. She would not return. He was sorry. He was curious. They built a fire, cooked franks on sticks, and heated up beans. As they ate, Artie had an inspiration. He thought for a while, then spoke:

There were two naked Jews in the mountains,
Who decided to try out their fountains.
They pissed in the lake,
A colossal mistake—

—Yes? Harold chewed, waiting. They sat on spindly red chairs at the little table against the window overlooking the lake, now invisible in the dark.

—I thought a last line would come, but it didn't. What rhymes with mountains?

—Accountants.

—Forget it.

They piled the plates in a dishpan. There was a faucet with a strong rope of cold water, but no reason to clean up. I'm glad they didn't come back, Harold said. I need to talk to you. He settled himself on the sofa.

—About what? Artie was on his way to the bedroom. I want to unpack, he said. He wanted the bottom bunk, and if he didn't move fast, Harold would end up with it.

—No, sit down.

Artie stood uncertainly, suitcase in hand, then set it down where he stood, pulled one of the wooden chairs closer, and sat down. Can't it wait? We have a week, for God's sake.

—No, said Harold. Look, I want to tell you first. He stretched his feet out into the room, leaned back, arranged his hands behind his head. It's—well, I guess it's news. I joined the party.

—Holy shit. When? The party? What the hell did you do that for? Artie stood, then turned his chair and straddled it, so its back was between him and Harold. He leaned forward on the chair back, familiar rage starting—maybe because Harold had done this without him, maybe because it was, as so often, bigger and braver and more interesting than anything he did. Maybe because it was stupid. He had been at Communist Party meetings, sure. They annoyed him. If you said something wrong, you had to pay a fine. How could Harold, of all people, stand that? Mr. Independence. How the hell could you join the party? Even here, even in the wilderness, did they have to talk about the state of the world?

—It wasn't a momentary decision, Harold said.

—Momentary decision? When did you ever make a momentary decision? Artie made momentary decisions, Harold never. Just tell me this, he continued. Just for one second, tell me this.

ALICE MATTISON

(His skin felt hot.) When was it proved that taking forever to make up your mind means you decide right?

—Would you give me a chance? Harold said.

—As if I didn't know what you're going to say! The working slobs, the suffering masses . . . Artie shifted his chair and sat on it the proper way, then shifted it again and sat astride.

—And you don't care about that? said Harold, still stretched on the sofa but now gesturing slowly with his hands, those insufferably calm, wide pink hands that, for all his life, Artie would picture when anyone said, about anything whatsoever, Just leave it in my hands.

—What you don't like about the party bothers me too, Harold said. They're bossy.

—Bossy! Bossy! Artie flung his arms out, reaching toward the walls. Those guys are totalitarian. They're like Franco.

—Well, I wouldn't go that far! Harold said. The point is, time and again, time—he erected with his right hand a barrier between one time and another time—and again—he erected a second barrier—the C.P. has been the only organization to step in (Harold's hand cut through his barrier) and speak up (the same hand came down on the other imaginary barrier, smashed it to bits). Nobody else has the guts, nobody else has the drive. Harold's blue eyes bulged more than usual.

—Maybe nobody else cares as much about being the center of attention.

—The Scottsboro Boys. The strikes. The . . . I know, I admit, they're not perfect, of course they want attention, they want members. But we have to choose. We have to make a choice, Artie.

—Oh, don't give me that.

—I don't think—Harold stood—that it's truly principled to watch everything that happens and not take a position.

Artie stood and picked up his suitcase again. You and your fancy principles! All my life I've been hearing about your principles! He turned his back. Then something occurred to him, and he couldn't keep his mouth from smiling. Not just your goddamned principles! Your goddamned assistant principles! I'm going to bed!

—All right, all right, came Harold's voice behind him. Harold's suitcase was already open on the bottom bunk. Some of his clothes and books had been taken out. Son of a gun, said Artie. Son of a gun. Was he surprised? He was not surprised. He opened his suitcase on the floor in front of Harold's bunk, took out his pajamas, and remembered the outhouse. Better to visit it in his clothes, and then figure out how to get into the top bunk. It might be necessary to step on the possessions of the guy in the bottom bunk. Too bad.

—Do we have a searchlight? he called.

—No.

Harold Abramovitz's father sewed linings into women's jackets. On the streetcar or in the street he might point and whisper, asking Harold to notice the faulty construction of a woman's coat, how the lining sagged.

—Pop! Harold would say, For God's sake!

—You should know. Harold would turn his head, as reluctant to be seen staring at a woman as he was determined not to be instructed about the garment trades when he'd decided to become a philosopher.

But even as he shrugged away his father's hand on his shoulder (Look! The sleeve—bunched up, there at the shoulder. Never you should do like that! Rip it out!) Harold felt guilty, because the father's life (how proud he had been when he was promoted to linings, how his eyes hurt at night) moved and troubled the son. His father, a stalwart union member, a socialist, was intelligent. Harold knew that if they hadn't lived in New York—City College was free—he might end up sewing linings too—if he was good enough. He honored those who labored, whom he pictured with stubby bodies, round haircuts, and billowing pants, like Brueghel's harvesters, and he tried to honor his parents, but he couldn't seem to perceive his parents' nobility as clearly as their foolishness and errors. He didn't want to feel superior to people who worked with their hands, but he did feel superior. Nights, he enumerated in his mind his rude remarks and instances of disrespect, but the next day he was again rude and disrespectful.

Then his friend Artie—this was when they were in high school—somehow acquired a used camera. He loved photographing Harold's father, who had sad eyes and a wide, bare forehead. Artie showed up at their apartment on weekends, slouching in doorways and declining Harold's mother's offers of seltzer or a sandwich, until he had the nerve to ask Mr. Abramovitz to move closer to the window. Harold's father was unself-conscious, and posed without altering his expression, as patient as if all the history of Eastern Europe resided in his body.

After high school, Artie took business classes at night and worked in a camera store, getting in trouble for telling customers more than they wanted to know. Harold studied English literature at City College's main branch, uptown. English turned out to consist of what he'd imagined philosophy to be. He made only a little money, delivering parcels for a drugstore, but his parents believed their only child would distinguish himself. Reading Wordsworth's *Michael*, about a shepherd whose son runs off to the wicked city and never returns to help his father finish the sheepfold they had been wholesomely building together, Harold felt guilty, but by this time he'd learned to enjoy feeling guilty, and he envied the great Catholic saints their excruciating and yet welcome sense of sin.

The Depression began during Harold's junior year in college. Artie lost his job and began taking pictures of labor union meetings and political rallies, occasionally selling photographs to a newspaper. One or another of his brothers always had a job, so his family had food. The first time Harold went with Artie to a political rally he was doing his friend a favor by keeping him company, but he got interested. The rhetoric made sense. It had the right mixture of the abstract and the specific for Harold's taste. He liked hearing that all who labored were equal, were comrades. It was what he had tried and failed to believe before, but put this way, it was easy to take into his head and expound sincerely. He was not being asked simply to feel bad that he didn't work with his hands and didn't want to. He could look forward to a future in which those who did that labor were not deprived of their dignity or of just compensation.

Artie stumbled from the back door to the outhouse by means of the light from the cabin. On his way back, he heard something familiar: that car again. At least this time he wasn't naked.

—Hungry? Myra said as she came in. The scarf was gone and her hair tumbled about her face. Thirsty? She was smiling, but she looked worn out, exasperated.

Harold had stood to meet them. We thought you weren't coming.

—Don't tell me you ate! Myra said. Never mind. You're eating again.

—Fine, Harold said. We didn't have much of a dinner. I'm Harold Abramovitz.

Virginia smiled blandly. Maybe, Artie decided, coming up next to Harold, she was slow. What took you so long? he said. Where were you?

—He wants to know where we were, Virginia said to Myra, shrugging in Artie's direction.

—So I hear, Myra said. We had to go all the way to Lake George.

—You know your way around, Harold said. Artie had no idea how far away Lake George was. Far. Harold, who seemed to have changed his mind about the desirability of visitors, made gestures suggesting hospitality.

—I guess you could say that, Virginia said. I guess you could say we know our way around, right, My? Then she laughed. The truth is, we got lost.

Ignoring her, Myra unpacked a paper bag: four steaks, a loaf of bread, and a bottle of bourbon. You provide the vegetable, she said. If you want a vegetable. And where's the fire? You should have had a fire ready.

—She's cranky when she's hungry, Virginia said. Then she added, Well, that sounds nice, which made Artie realize he had begun to whistle, which meant he was feeling unsure of himself. Beethoven. Harold and Myra got the fire going again. Myra yanked open a drawer, took out a knife, and began trimming the steaks.

—You knew where the knife was, Harold said.

—I remembered, said Myra. She didn't just glance at him over her shoulder. She turned so that their shoulders were facing, as if she were playing tennis with him.

—It's true you've been here before.

—I told your suspicious pal. Gus is my daddy.

—Gus never mentioned you, Harold said, and Myra looked at him sharply.

Virginia giggled again. Her sugar daddy, more like, she said.

Harold looked from one to the other of them, startled. He looked at Artie, as if to explain the quick look. I've met his wife. I've seen his kids.

Artie couldn't help it. Isn't monogamy a bourgeois capitalist idea it's high time we threw out? he said, with more nastiness in his voice than he had expected. You can't make an omelet without breaking eggs, isn't that how you fellas put it? Break up some marriages too.

Harold was silent, eyeing the steaks, which Myra now laid across the grate, her back to Artie. Then he said in a low voice, Gus isn't in the party.

—I didn't say he was, Artie continued, the roughness and loudness of his voice still surprising him. I'm talking about your principles, your goddamn principles and your goddamn . . . He stopped. The *assistant principles* joke was not funny enough to repeat.

Myra scurried around, elaborately hearing nothing, and found jelly glasses into which she put generous servings of bourbon and water. They ate the steaks rare. Those frankfurters certainly hadn't been enough. Before the food was quite gone, Harold stood. We're giving you girls the bunk beds, he said.

Artie was partly relieved, partly annoyed. He'd have tried a little something with Virginia, he now decided, if he'd had the chance. Just enough friendliness to make it possible to share a bunk, end to end. But now the girls brought in a couple of bags and shrieked their way to the outhouse, then waved goodnight and went into the bedroom.

Harold gave Artie the sofa, insisting he didn't mind sleeping on the floor. He'd found some blankets. The sofa was bad enough. In his clothes, his pants unbuttoned for comfort, Artie lay down and closed his eyes. His shoulder was cramped. He sensed Harold's wakefulness on the floor below him. At last he began to sing.

One-four-nine is the school for me,
Drives away all adversity.

Steady and true, we'll be to you,
Loyal all to one-four-nine rah! rah! rah!

Harold listened silently. As kids, they'd both gone to P.S. 149 in East New York, but as Harold often pointed out, they weren't kids anymore. Eventually his deeper voice joined Artie's.

Raise on high the red and white.
Cheer it with all your might.
Good old one-four-nine.
Hurrah for one-four-nine rah rah rah!

They fell silent, Harold before the last syllables. Some time later—knowing they were both still awake—Artie thought again of his limerick.

At a mountain lake, as day was dimming,
Two bare-assed Jews thought they'd go swimming.
Then they pissed in the lake
A colossal mistake
For a shark came and gave them a trimming.

—A new low, even for you, Harold said.

On a chilly March afternoon in 1930, when they were nineteen, Harold had skipped a class he considered pointless—the professor's ideas about poetry were jejune—to go with Artie to Union Square, so Artie could photograph a Communist rally on unemployment. Artie liked photographing excited, angry people, and he told himself that one of these days he'd produce a photograph of an important event so impressive that a newspaper would not only buy it but put him on staff. At the rally, the crowd was larger than they'd seen before. Artie and Harold leaned on a tree, not far from the speakers but off to the side. More people arrived, and now they were in the middle of the crowd.

—Would you look at those cops? Artie said. Jesus Christ. He took off his glasses and replaced them, then slapped his head—a habit. He had lank black hair that looked untidy the week after a haircut. Then Artie began slapping his own leg rhythmically, and Harold knew something was going to happen. The speakers began urging the assemblage to march on City Hall and demand to see Mayor Walker. Whistling, Artie went to photograph the nervous cops who massed near the front of the crowd, and Harold watched him make his way through the throng and slip sideways up to them, crouch to get the angle he wanted, and shoot. Nobody seemed to notice. Since their childhood, Artie had known how to deny his presence with his slouch and shrug, his skinniness, the flat hair on his narrow skull, as if he was invisible or the color of leaves and shadows. Harold knew that he himself gave just the opposite impression. Strangers in the street sometimes seemed confused, as if they thought he was approaching them specifically. In school, teachers called on him when he hadn't raised his hand, or they looked at him expectantly. Question, Mr. Abramovitz? a professor might say, though Harold was just listening.

Artie returned. He said, They've got people from City Hall up there, maybe the chief of police. He moved away again, into the crowd. Harold watched three women near him cheering lustily, then laughing as if they were pleased simply to be making this noise. The next time he saw Artie, he was photographing three men who looked confused, maybe arguing about whether to stay or leave. Artie seemed interested in the trees near these men, maybe the look of the ridged bark with these gesturing arms and open mouths superimposed on it.

ALICE MATTISON

The mood of the crowd changed. The leaders asked everyone to march to City Hall, and there were cheers. Harold was afraid, but he wanted to march. He was tired of being an observer. There was sudden movement, shouting: the police were charging, and some of the crowd surged against them, while others tried to run away. All at once it was impossible to go in any direction, and Harold saw a man knocked down by a policeman's baton. Others tried to help him or keep from stepping on him, and batons hit them. Harold, shocked, found himself walking *toward* the police, inserting himself between people as if he had business in that direction. Right in front of him, a cop kicked a young woman in a long dark coat. She seemed stunned. Given no time for thought or fear, Harold reached his arms and big hands toward the woman, seized her by the shoulder, unceremoniously pulled her to his chest, then pushed her behind him as the cop charged.

To his own astonishment, Harold waved his arms in the air, his hands gyrating of their own accord, and he began to scream and shriek, high-pitched oohs and ays he had never heard himself emit before. The policeman swatted at his hands with his stick, and Harold felt a strange pain outline his right hand and arm. Behind him, the woman cursed the cop. Putting one hand on Harold's arm for support, she hiked up her skirt and kicked the policeman. She kicked again and he staggered backward. Harold pushed her ahead of him into a space in the crowd. Soon they were crying and shuffling, holding hands. The part of the crowd they were in was not trying to make its way south toward City Hall but east along Fifteenth Street. He and the woman came to a street in which the crowd was sparse enough that they could set their own pace. Her hat was gone and her hair blew over her face. His overcoat was open and torn, and his face was covered with mucus. He was crying. He touched his cheek and felt blood.

They stopped, became self-conscious, looked at each other, and stopped holding hands.

The woman said, How old are you? At the time it seemed like a natural question.

—Nineteen, said Harold. How old are you?

—Twenty-seven, said the woman. Are you from the Bronx?

—Brooklyn. Now they were turning aside to part, but Harold didn't want to. He was sick with fear for Artie but curious about this woman who had touched him so intimately. Wait, he said. My name is Harold Abramovitz.

—Belle Kantor. Do you have paper? I'll give you the address where we meet. He had a squashed notebook in his pocket, a pen.

Coffee, in the morning, made Virginia talk. Harold had found an iron frying pan and was frying eggs they'd bought in Albany. Virginia was from Schenectady and so was Myra, but Myra had gone to college—Vassar, that fancy girls' school—and Virginia had not. You boys been to college? she asked. Sometimes Artie couldn't stop himself with the rhymes and songs. This time he chanted something he'd heard around the campus at City.

> *Jacob, Yitzhak, Abraham and Sam!*
> *We're the boys that eat no ham!*
> *Where we come from . . . don't remember.*
> *New York City College. Yay!*

—Oh, stop it, said Harold. He was dressed, but his curly hair was tousled, making him look like a big baby. He was grumpy.

Virginia considered. You mean you don't remember the words or you don't remember where you come from?

ALICE MATTISON

—I don't remember the words, Artie said. He couldn't help laughing.

—And you eat wieners, which is the same as ham. She had twisted her hair up.

—Not necessarily, Harold said.

Myra was walking behind Artie toward the old couch, where he sat back, his legs stuck out into the room. He had his shoes on but hadn't tied the laces because he planned to change his socks as soon as he had some privacy. Artie rarely drank coffee, but he'd taken some just to warm up, and he was trying to look as if he liked it. Myra said sarcastically, Not necessarily! She touched Artie's shoulder and gave him the sort of half smile people give when they've already agreed together to make fun of a third person. She was smoking a cigarette. Since he and Myra had not had an agreement to make fun of Harold, tacit or otherwise, Artie was surprised. Flattered, maybe. Myra was pretty, with her dark red hair. Her smile scared him, but her breasts were perky. It would be too much to touch her ass, though that came to mind—it was small but well shaped. He lifted his coffee mug in her direction, with what he hoped was a slightly conspiratorial smile.

—So that means you're Jewish? Virginia said, hunched at the table over her coffee. You're both Jewish?

—You don't like Jews? said Artie.

—Leave her alone, Myra said.

—I was just curious, Virginia said.

—Can't be too careful, Artie said. That's how they feel in Germany. Nothing against Jews, just keep an eye on them.

—It's not funny, Artie, Harold said.

—I'm not against Jews, said Virginia.

Harold said, Did you know Jewish doctors in Germany had to turn in their licenses?

Virginia said, I don't pay much attention to the news.

—Oh, my God, Artie said. For Christ's sake.

—Would you stop it? Myra said. Leave her alone. Something seemed to travel through her, starting with the hair or the nose, which was prominent though not Jewish-looking, and out her long fingers. I think I'll take a walk, she said. And in moments, she was gone.

Artie was curious. What did she mean? he asked Virginia. Leave you alone? There's something wrong with you?

—Maybe she thinks there is, Virginia said. She went into the bedroom and emerged in a white bathing suit, then added her heavy brown sweater. She had on shoes but no socks. She went outside, and Artie saw her go down to the lake, where there was a patch of sun.

—So how would the wise Communist Party direct us to spend our morning? he said to Harold, who was busying himself with the tin mugs and unmatched plates. Shall we organize the local bears?

—Very funny.

—What's Myra mad about? Artie said. He was looking around for trouble to make—he knew it. He felt a certain malaise. He was cold; he didn't want to flirt with the girls, though he wouldn't have minded if they flirted with him; he didn't want to go into the water; and at the moment he couldn't remember why this week in the woods had seemed like a good idea. When Artie felt that way, he started up with somebody; he always had, stirring up quarrels among his brothers—he had four—as a child. Trouble was a good way of staying interested and awake. But this time, before he could get seriously interested in annoying Harold, he remembered something: the dilapidated, oarless rowboat he'd seen the day before. He went for his camera. The sound of a tree branch scraping the roof had interrupted his thoughts and changed his mood. Hell, they were in the woods! He should take pictures.

ALICE MATTISON

—I hate to see . . . He hustled to the shore—avoiding Virginia, who sat on the ground, her knees drawn up—and photographed the rowboat, the shadow of the boat on the shore, the shadow of the seat on the bottom of the boat, the weeds beyond the boat. He was trying out a lens he'd bought just before losing his job. When he had money, he spent it on his camera. Better a camera than a woman. After he took pictures, he circled the outside of the cabin and saw no oars. He put his camera into its case and slung the case across his chest. Then he took the thickest, largest stick he could find and (again avoiding Virginia) climbed into the boat, whistling, untied it, and pushed off. He saw Myra return from the driveway and go into the cabin. Whistling and poking at the bottom of the lake with his stick, soon he was afloat.

Harold had been born in summer, only a few months after his parents arrived in New York, and as an infant he slept in a wooden box his mother had used to bring clothing and blankets on the long journey across the ocean. Every morning she put the box near the window so the baby could strengthen in sunshine. Harold remembered, with nostalgia so keen the memory came to him as a taste, cool and milky—vanilla—the pleasure of lying on his back, his limbs at rest, comfortable in every part of his body, watching something flash and flash again in the sunlight outside the window. When he'd told his mother this memory, at ten, she said it was not possible. Harold had grown quickly, and at six months he'd outgrown the box. Besides, by then it was winter, and the window was drafty. A baby could not remember what happened before he was six months old, Harold's mother said. She could not read or write, but she remembered everything anyone had ever told her, and spoke, her blue eyes bulging like her son's, with the certainty and clarity people would later notice in Harold. They would assume he'd picked up the tone at City College, but he had begun talking that way when he spoke only Yiddish, having conversations with his mother. He was content not to argue with her on the topic of early memory. Harold—called Hesh until he started school and the teacher chose *Harold*—knew what he knew. The memory—it made his salivary glands tingle—and the loss of that exquisite comfort as he grew older, informed whatever Harold would eventually do. It didn't make sense for Harold to join the Communist Party: he was elegiac, not radical, but Harold loved fairness as others loved risk or drama, and it was only fair to join with those who stood with the oppressed, whether their reasoning was crude or not. Harold Abramovitz had sought the risk of becoming a Communist, though he looked down slightly on his comrades and they knew it. Brenda Saltzman, many years later, would comment that Harold Abrams—by then he'd have changed his name—had joined the Communist Party as an actor might try out for the role of the tragic hero. That morning at the house in the Adirondacks, long before Brenda's birth, Harold wanted Myra and Virginia to leave so he could talk Artie into understanding why he'd done it. Artie was hard to convince, and Harold—since third grade—had never been able to give up the challenge of convincing Artie. He wanted nothing but to renew the argument.

Neither Harold nor Artie got over the effects of the riot in Union Square. Harold had intermittent pain in his right hand all his life, and occasionally he was unable to control the movement of his thumb. It spoiled his already weak tennis game. The Communists had shown him why the workers must revolt on the same day they'd made it impossible for Harold to sew, no matter how much respect he had for his father. In addition to English literature, and with the same conviction though not the same pleasure, Harold began reading Marx and Engels and attending meetings at the address Belle had given him, even when they bored him.

The afternoon in Union Square changed Arthur Saltzman as well, though unlike Harold he didn't often mention it years later; Harold always did, remembering the one time in his life when he screamed. Artie was not injured, but his camera was smashed and then lost. As shocked as Harold was at the cruelty of the police, Artie remained angry mostly at particular policemen, whom he remembered and described. The one who brought his club down on Artie's camera was fair-haired, with a narrow face not unlike his own. The sight of police attacking unarmed citizens, some of them women, some just people trying to run away, astonished him, and it aroused in Artie an anger that could at times be attached to anything at all.

—But what did the Communists expect? he'd ask, even years later, telling his children the story. What did they *think* would happen? He would glare at Brenda and Carol as if they were the heedless Communists. He conceded without discussion that the protesters were mostly right and the government mostly wrong, but surely everyone knew that, and figuring out in just what way they were right or wrong didn't interest Artie. He'd always been instinctively for the powerless, the losers.

He couldn't afford another camera for a long time, and he was left with a grudge he'd never live past, never see around, and soon couldn't explain. He began to feel as if he'd always been angry: angry was what he was, angry at humanity's capacity for rage, at his own capacity. And angry at humanity's stupidity, which made him begin, at nineteen, to laugh bitterly in a way that would eventually infuriate his wife and frighten his children. Unlike Harold, he didn't tell stories about the protest, except for one that he'd learned not firsthand but from the newspaper. A policeman had stopped Mayor Jimmy Walker on his way into his office that day, not recognizing him, and asked where he thought he was going. The mayor replied that six million people expected him to get to work. What Artie liked—or hated—was that even though he was mayor, Jimmy Walker couldn't count on being recognized and respected. Nobody was dignified. Everyone was a fool. The mayor was stopped from going into his own office by a stupid cop; another stupid cop smashed skulls; a third broke Artie's camera. The afternoon didn't make Artie hate cops forever, but it made him think that cops were stupid, and since cops were just people, people were stupid.

Despite the Depression, Harold got his degree, and eventually the night courses added up, and Artie did too. He worked in another camera store. It closed. He wrote freelance stories about sports and continued selling photographs. At a paper, Artie met an editor who needed a book reviewer, and he thought of Harold. Harold began reviewing, then briefly had a reporter's job. That ended, but when the Federal Writers' Project began, he was hired.

Roosevelt's Works Progress Administration was offering white collar jobs to people on home relief, so Artie, who lived with his parents as Harold did, took an apartment for one month and applied. He couldn't be on relief if he lived at home, and he couldn't get a WPA job unless he was on relief. The investigator's nosy questions enraged him even though he was lying, saying his parents had thrown him out. He got one check, was hired as a clerk in the WPA offices, and celebrated by buying a suit for work and a new lens for his camera. Then he gave up the apartment and moved back to his room at home. He hated the job, but he was glad to have a job. For several months he was bored and obstreperous. Then he was laid off.

Meanwhile, Harold wandered the city to contribute to a guidebook about New York and in spare moments wrote gritty poems in his reporter's notebook about scraps of garbage on city streets and ill-fed cats and children. He'd been going to C.P. meetings off and on since he'd met Belle Kantor at Union Square. After the meetings, he and Belle lingered over nearly empty cups in the Automat, talking about whether the Soviet Union could carry off socialism or about their own lives. Belle's thick brown hair wouldn't stay where she put it, and in her loosening bun and old-fashioned clothes, she looked like Harold's idea of an idealistic European revolutionary. Her husband was so busy with party business she rarely saw him, but because she was married, Harold and Belle assured each other that they were not in love. They allowed themselves to clasp hands across a table on which drops of cold coffee hardened.

Sometimes Harold talked about his friendships with other women. He knew Belle disliked this, but she didn't admit it, and he couldn't stay away from the subject. Harold didn't join the party until six years after he met Belle. He wasn't certain enough or pure enough. He loved literature too much and believed what it implied: all life is interesting, even life made possible by capitalism.

What made Harold join was a conversation with his father, who admitted that as a young man he'd wanted to be a rabbi or a Hebrew school teacher. But I couldn't go to school, he said. Money was everything.

At last Harold understood. Money was everything; the leisure to read books was stolen leisure. The New Deal gave people hope, but only a revolution would make a big enough difference. He approached the group's leaders.

—Finally? they said. They laughed at him, but they accepted his dues.

Now Harold was alone in the cabin with Myra, who had returned from her walk as he was trying to clean the iron skillet, and had gone into the bedroom. Virginia sat on the lakeshore waiting to be loved. Artie, the last time Harold had checked, was fooling around with the busted rowboat. Harold thought he heard thunder. He tidied restlessly, though that was pointless. The place was appealing but not clean. The walls were wooden planks, and the floor was also wood, with years of ground-in dirt. The skillet was greasy and rusty and would stay that way. The windows were dirty. But Harold liked the cabin. He was impatient for Myra and Virginia to leave so he could get a book and sit on the dilapidated sofa. He was reading Henry James's *The Portrait of a Lady*. His suitcase was still in the bedroom, with all his books in it.

He looked out the window. Virginia no longer sat on the ground outside, and he didn't see Artie or the boat. He'd noticed oars behind the cabin that morning. Probably Artie had found them and taken Virginia rowing.

He knocked softly on the bedroom door. Myra? he called. I just want a book from my bag.

There was no answer. He knocked again, then opened the door.

The bedroom was narrow, not much longer or wider than the bunk bed. Opposite the door was a wooden chest of drawers, with Harold's battered suitcase on top. He saw nobody.

—Myra? In the bottom bunk was nothing but an army blanket, left haphazardly on the bare mattress. In the top bunk, a dark shape. He tiptoed across the room and opened his suitcase, regretting the sound of the spring releasing the catch.

—Can you help me? said Myra, sounding different: not mocking.

—Myra? Harold said once more. What's wrong?

—I'm frightened. Virginia went off somewhere.

Harold looked over the iron rail that would keep a sleeper from rolling out of the top bunk. Myra lay with a blanket pulled up to her chin. Her hair was loose on the pillow and on her face. Without thinking, Harold reached to smooth it and position it behind her ears, then pulled his hand back. But he'd touched her hair, which was soft, like a child's.

—There's nothing to be afraid of, he said. Was she worried about the woods? About bears, or—he didn't know what animals might live in these woods.

—I need Virginia, Myra said.

—Why? I think she went rowing with Artie.

—That's what I pay her for, staying with me, Myra said.

—You pay Virginia?

—I'm the one with the money, Myra said, with a low laugh. And she's the one with the brains.

—I doubt that. What do you need her for?

—I promised my parents, she said. They worry about my nerves.

Harold looked at this woman with her red hair. He thought she probably could be talked or joked out of these nerves. So that's what this is, he said, this huddling in the bed? Nerves?

—I had a dream, she said.

He did and didn't want to find out what she'd dreamed. Myra had been dressed when they ate breakfast, but the arms holding the blanket to her chest were bare. She seemed newly awake, rumpled, more attractive than before. Harold was additionally shocked that Gus had carried on with a woman who had nerves, but his discomfort made him want to help Myra. Gus wouldn't leave his good wife and sweet children for her, he was sure of that. He felt sorry for Myra, and that made him desire her. Pity gave a gleam to the otherwise ordinary, giving it possibility. And since Harold secretly despised—very slightly—those he pitied, pity made moral action *less* essential, a relief in his rigorous life.

He folded his arms and pressed them against the iron railing, ducking his head to smile down at Myra. What sort of a dream? he said. He sounded condescending, and winced, but Myra didn't seem to mind.

—Oh, ugly things, ugly things, she said promptly.

—What would you do if Virginia was here?

—You must think I'm a baby, Myra said. She propped herself on an elbow, holding the blanket so it covered her breasts. She seemed to be naked. She was silent, then said, Oh, she just listens, talks, maybe rubs my neck.

So Virginia was a paid companion who was supposed to pretend to be a friend, even a dependent friend.

—Would it help to hold my hand? Harold said. He unfolded his arms and placed one hand—large, pink, steady—on the edge of the mattress. Persuading Myra to get up and dress would be best, but he would prefer this to happen without dissipating the intimacy in the room. He said, Where are your clothes?

Myra jutted her chin toward a tangle of clothing at the bottom of the bed.

—Shall I wait in the other room while you get dressed? Then we can go for a walk. He didn't want to leave the room. Again, he heard thunder. Maybe Myra was afraid of thunderstorms.

—Just hand me those things, would you? Myra said, and with some embarrassment Harold grasped the tangle and pulled it toward her. She held up a brassiere. She had become a child, with no sense of propriety. It was alarming but oddly attractive. What a funny garment, she said.

Harold turned to the open suitcase teetering on the chest of drawers and began self-consciously arranging the items inside:

ALICE MATTISON

socks, pants, books. He'd been foolish to think he could read so many books. The suitcase had become heavy during those hours of hitchhiking. He said, I don't know why I thought I could read so many books in a week! He sounded phony.

There were scrambling sounds from the bed. I'm coming down, Myra said. There's no room up here to get dressed.

Immediately he heard her move. Part of her—her buttocks?—brushed his shoulder. Now he was trapped in the small, dim bedroom with a naked or half-clothed woman behind him. The space between the wall and the bed was so narrow, he couldn't leave without squeezing against Myra.

She took her time. Harold, who rarely tried anything with women, knew he seemed so assured that he'd look foolish if he made a move that wasn't just right. He often envied Artie's boy-ishness and suspected that his friend—with his shrugs and whis-tles and confusion—had done more with girls than he had. Now he didn't know whether Myra was flirting, making fun of him, or just getting dressed in her own way.

—My father says I'm high-strung, Myra was saying. I love thunder, though. Harold wasn't sure he loved thunder. It seemed to be getting louder.

At last she reached around him and put her hands on his eyes. Okay, turn around! Of course she was wearing the same clothes as before: a gray skirt, a blue sweater, and heavy socks. Her red hair was pretty. As he made up his mind not to take any chances with her, he put his hands on her shoulders, or his hands put themselves on her shoulders. Strands of hair caught under his hands.

—Ooh, what are you reading? she said, shaking him off and pushing past him.

—Never mind, he said, and closed the suitcase with *The Portrait of a Lady* still inside, a scrap of paper marking his place.

Scribners had brought it out—part of their reprint of the New York Edition—and Harold had saved up for it.

—Let's see if it's raining, he said. I don't know what's become of Artie and Virginia. He put his hand on her shoulder again, turned her, and ushered her into the main room of the cabin.

—I don't want to go outside, she said. I don't really like it here. His desire had turned to discomfort. He went out alone.

It was windy, blowing from behind him across the lake. He didn't see the boat. A thought he didn't like approached his mind, and he deliberately didn't think it. Harold walked slowly around the cabin, but if Artie and Virginia were nearby, he would have heard their voices. He had an image of them lying on a simplified forest floor—the stage set of a forest floor—rolling and grappling in passion. He wondered if Artie had discovered that Virginia was a paid companion. On the side of the cabin—the side with the bedroom window—was an ell, because the bedroom was not as wide as the house. Leaning against the wall in the ell was a rusted iron shovel, and behind it were the two oars Harold had noticed before.

They weren't much, as oars went. They had no pins, nothing to fit into oarlocks, but a skilled rower could manage, balancing them on the side of the boat. Probably Artie couldn't row, but that was irrelevant because Artie had not taken these oars. Harold continued around the cabin, back to where he'd stood facing the lake. The thought he'd rejected returned, an image more than a thought: Artie, the day before, struggling to swim, choking and sputtering. Harold swam with his eyes open and missed little.

It started to rain and lightning flashed. He knew he should stay away from the water. The boat was definitely gone. He searched the lake, now gray with raindrops, and at last he thought he saw the boat across the lake, far from shore and empty. Harold called, Artie! Virginia! He tried to call loudly but could not do it. Except for that rally in 1930, Artie did the shouting. He considered discussing the problem with Myra but didn't want to. He wished for binoculars, then knew he didn't need them. Nobody was in the boat. In the wind, Harold took off his pants and shirt and shoes and socks, and waded into the lake in his shorts. With rain falling into his open eyes each time he turned his face to breathe in, he began his angular, reliable crawl, elbows wide, in the direction of the boat. Cold and fear made his breath catch in his throat. He gave great gasps. In his mind he saw his mother weep and shout. He was terrified of the lightning but equally afraid of what might have happened. Artie's mother and his mother wept and shouted together. I had to try and save him, he explained in Yiddish to his mother as he swam. I knew it was too late, but I had to try and save him. He said it in Yiddish, in English, in Yiddish again to both mothers. After a while the use of his muscles and the rhythm of the stroke eased him slightly, and he breathed evenly. He didn't ask himself how he proposed to find Artie if he wasn't in the boat. He would be in the boat, huddled against the bottom. Or he'd be shouting from the nearest shore, singing something ridiculous. Or dog-paddling near the boat, and Harold would tow him back.

This trip was Harold's doing. He knew Gus and saw a possibility when Gus said he owned a little cabin. Harold had read Thoreau. He was trying to live like a nineteenth-century person in America, not one of the shouting, crowding immigrants who were his people. Gus was not Jewish: a newspaperman who'd once been Harold's editor, he was a sturdy, offhand Irish guy whose family ran a business he didn't want to work in.

Distances look shorter over water. The lake was not big, and Harold was ordinarily a tireless swimmer, taking regular breaths each time his left arm cleared the surface of the water. Yet this swim took a long time. He stopped and paddled to rest and look around. The boat was closer. It was definitely a boat. The storm was letting up, but he still saw lightning and heard thunder. He still saw nobody in the boat.

He was stupid, that was the trouble with Harold Abramovitz. For all his brilliance—he knew he was brilliant—he was stupid. It was stupid to risk his life for his boyish, exasperating friend. It was probably stupid to become a Communist, and he suspected that others at meetings found his earnestness comical. Not all of Harold's ideals were Communist ideals: he cared too much for the particular person. He would keep his ideals all his life, he knew. He was tired. He wasn't swimming well. He'd been stupid to think he could easily swim to the boat, rescue Artie, who could not even dog-paddle, and maybe drag Virginia in by the hair at the same time.

But now, at last, his arms aching, he was at the boat. He grasped the gunwale and pulled himself up, and the boat tipped toward him. Nobody was lying in the bottom. The shore closest to the boat looked almost as far away as the shore he'd just swum from, and nobody waved from the edge of the water. He turned to swim back to the cabin, but his arms ached, and now the wind was against him. The rain caught in his throat, and tiredness made him take a breath at the wrong time. He made himself slow down and hang, resting, his arms loose, until he caught his breath. If Artie was underneath, he was dead, and Harold knew no way to find out. He continued to hear thunder.

Artie had some trouble poking the boat away from the shore with his stick. It looked like rain but maybe not yet. For the second time in two days he took off his shoes and socks outdoors. Then he rolled up his pants, so he could step into the water and push the boat off again as it bumped its way along the shore, past the cabin and beyond it, along the side of the lake that was roughly parallel to the road. Frogs he never noticed until they jumped, splashed into the water at his approach, and Artie tried to remember if he'd ever before seen a living frog. For a minute he'd thought they were big bugs. He couldn't have said what he was looking for, but as he slogged, poled, and dragged his boat along the shore, his camera bag still bumping on his chest, he liked the intense feeling the dense trees gave him, as if they were dangerous, or in danger. The air had become heavier, grayer.

—*You had better reconsider,* he sang, to the tune of a line in "The Battle Hymn of the Republic." Then he remembered what the line came from. It was a song the protesters had made up, trying to prevent the layoffs from the WPA project where he'd worked. The boss was a bad man named Ridder. Poling his boat, bumping the shore here and there, Artie sang the whole thing, timing the phrases to fit the rhythm with which he jabbed the pole at the lake bottom.

> *Here's our answer Mr. Ridder,*
> *You had better reconsider.*
> *Stop the layoffs, Mr. Ridder,*
> *Or [waving his stick in the air] we'll get rid 'er you!*

The layoffs in question—of clerical workers—had not stopped, and Artie was among those laid off, but Mr. Ridder, the administrator, was gone. Only last week—Artie had plenty of time now—he'd participated in yet another demonstration, the death watch for Mr. Ridder, when the demonstrators lay on the ground around his car.

Something caught his eye. Farther along the lake, past a tangle of water lilies that kept snagging him, was some scrap or rag, something white that didn't belong. Soon—as he tried to make his way to the white scrap, at last having a destination—

he got tired of the boat, which was sloshing with water anyway. The edge of the lake was so dense with reeds and bushes that he couldn't walk along the shore to see what the white thing was. He yanked the boat up a little way, so it would stay put, tied his shoes together with their laces and draped them around his neck. He felt like a donkey with the shoes bumping against the camera case, but he began to wade toward the scrap of white, using his pole as a walking stick and continuing to sing with occasional winces and stumbles. His pants were getting soaked. He was having a wonderful time, and when, years later, he'd tell his children the story of the cabin, he emphasized this outing: the boat, the frogs, the weeds, and the water. Forever he would advocate going outside and getting your feet wet, would always see himself as an outdoorsman, while other people—especially Brenda and Carol—might need to be reminded that nature was just out the window.

The white scrap was Virginia's bathing suit. She was sitting as she'd sat near the cabin, knees drawn up, watching him.

—Whatcha doing? he said.

—Just looking. She clutched her sweater. Now big dark gray clouds moved across the sky. The wind was stronger, and maybe its direction had changed.

—How did you get here? You're dry.

—I walked from the road. There's a path.

—You just took a path into the woods? he said. He'd been congratulating himself on his affinity with the wilderness, but he wouldn't have done that. He was envious. But he said, You could have gotten lost but good.

—Eaten by bears, said Virginia.

It was the first lightness he'd seen in her. Mind if I join you? he said.

—There's no room, said Virginia. This was true. The path

she'd taken was almost closed in by reeds on either side, and it ended at her rock. He stepped around her and sat down on the path, turning up the soles of his feet to dry them. He plucked a long blade of grass and laid it across his lips, trying to make a noise. Artie had fooled around on a lot of instruments, some in high school, where he'd played saxophone in the band, and some in music stores.

—What's it like to live in New York? Virginia said. He ignored her. He was trying to figure out why she irritated him. You're an attractive girl, he said after a while, wrapping his blade of grass around his fingers, weaving it among them, shredding it, then plucking another. There's nothing wrong with your looks, he continued.

—But? said Virginia. There's something wrong with the rest of me? She stood up. Then she gestured in a way he hadn't quite noticed before, except that he had: it was what had made him dislike her. It was a little flutter of the fingers, all ten, a deliberately foolish gesture of incapacity. It seemed to say, How should I know what you mean? and for a second it made him dislike her again, but then it almost made him love Virginia because he could help her.

He could show her what she was doing, and then she'd stop doing it, and though he'd never see her again—she wasn't his type—other men would be drawn to her. Artie was now sprawled on the ground, leaning on his elbows, looking up at Virginia, her legs and thighs followed by her body and head—which was far away, and not a large head to begin with. He scrambled to his feet, his damp pants catching and releasing, and seized both her hands like a suitor.

—Look what you do! he said. Look! I'll show you what you do, and you'll stop. You're not really dumb; you're just pretending to be dumb!

—So just because I'm getting paid for this, you think I'm dumb?

—Getting paid? For what?

—For this. She gestured—the lake, the sky. It thundered, and they both looked around. You think I'm not as good as you?

—I don't know what you're talking about, Artie said. I mean what you do with your fingers. Look. He imitated the gesture, wiggling all his fingers, but that wasn't exactly right. He couldn't quite reproduce it.

Virginia said, Why would I do that? You just think I'm stupid because I work for Myra.

—You work for Myra? he said. Doing what?

—Never mind, she said, and began running along the path to the road. She was quickly out of sight, but then he heard her shout. He put on his shoes and socks and followed. When he caught up to her, ten feet from the road, she was on the ground, saying, Don't touch me, don't touch me. She'd tripped and fallen headlong, breaking a fingernail and scraping her knees. Look what you did to me! she said. And I'm so cold! He helped her stand up and put on her sweater, still trying to explain what he'd meant. Now it was raining.

—Will you stop it? she said. She said her foot hurt and leaned on him. In the rain and thunder, they began the slow walk back to the cabin. She wouldn't talk, and Artie was freezing, but he didn't care. Artie loved self-discovery, and he decided that he'd discovered something about himself when he'd noticed Virginia's habit. He could tell people truths they didn't know, and that would be fun. Artie Saltzman, he said to himself, you were born to teach.

Harold swam back across the lake into the wind. His arms were tired, and he did the sidestroke instead of the crawl.

As he stroked, he went back and forth between thinking it was the worst day of his life and thinking again that he was stupid. When he stumbled from the water, after a long, long time, the storm had ended and the sun was out. He saw no one. Then he noticed that the car was gone. He picked up his wet clothes and went inside in his dripping shorts. Artie was asleep on the sofa in the fetal position, his chin hidden in a blanket. It was not the worst day of Harold's life. He was only stupid.

He started to walk toward Artie in his clinging underwear, to kneel at his side and take him in his arms like a child, but stopped himself. In the bedroom, he put on dry clothes and a sweater. As he pulled his arms through the sleeves, he noticed a sheet of paper on the floor at his feet. It might have been left on the suitcase. He remembered that he had left the suitcase closed, but now it was open. The paper was a note, in large well-formed handwriting.

Dear Harold,

> I'm sorry we have to go. Artie doesn't know where you are, and Virginia is anxious to get on the road. I'm borrowing *The Portrait of a Lady*. You brought so many books, I guess you won't mind.
> I enjoyed meeting you and hope you feel the same. Thank you for being kind when I was down in the dumps.

> Very truly yours,
> Myra Thorsten

Under the name was a Manhattan address.

A narrow stripe of rage, jagged like the lightning bolts that might have killed him just now, began in Harold's stomach and traveled to his fingertips. He did not lend books. He had not brought too many books, whatever he'd said earlier. And *The Portrait of a Lady* was not only the book he was in the middle of but a valuable and important one. She had gone through his suitcase. The woman was unaware of anyone but herself. Yet underneath his anger—there was no time now to figure out how this could be—Harold felt something else: he was glad he'd have a chance to see Myra once more, to explain to her the many ways in which what she had done was wrong. Meanwhile, he walked into the living room. Wake up, he said. Wake up, damn you. It seemed he might cry.

—What? Artie looked around, then dropped his head again and burrowed more deeply into the smelly sofa.

—Wake up. Wake up, damn it. I just nearly died because of you.

—What are you talking about? Artie said.

—Where are those women? Harold said. What'd you let her take my book for?

—What book? said Artie. They left. I had enough of those dames. Tonight we can sleep. At least they didn't eat up all the eggs.

He stood. He was in his underwear, and wet clothes were in a pile beside him. His suitcase was near the sofa, and he pulled out clothes and put them on. But we have to eat hot dogs instead of steak.

—Don't you realize what you did? Harold said, wondering what exactly Artie had done. I thought you drowned. I swam all the way out to that boat.

Artie had forgotten about the boat. Where is it? he said. He led the way outside, in his socks. What do you mean you swam? Wha'd you do that for?

Harold could not explain. He pointed until Artie saw the boat. He didn't want anything to do with Artie. He wanted to go inside, lie down, read, but he didn't have his book, and Harold hated to put a book aside before he'd finished it. Even if he didn't like a book or couldn't understand it, he read all the way to the end. And he would stay in this cabin for a week, as well, whether it was what he had imagined or not. And in a way it *was* what he had imagined. It was wild. It was even dangerous. It was cold. Maybe he should have come alone. He had an idea about Henry James. But he knew he would never have come alone. This awareness made him angrier than ever.

—The boat was gone, he said. The oars were still here.

—What oars?

—Never mind what oars. I could see the boat in the middle of the lake. I couldn't see you.

—You thought I drowned? What the hell? Why would I drown? I was right here.

Harold had started back to the cabin, but he turned, his blue eyes bulging. You were not right here! You were not right here!

—Well, sure, not all the time. But now I'm right here.

—What were you doing? Shtupping that pathetic woman in the woods?

—What? That crazy dame? I had to carry her back here in the rain! I had to listen to her! Do you know Myra pays her?

—Never mind, said Harold. Yes, I know. He walked back into the cabin. Artie picked his way down to the shore and stared at the boat. How the hell did it get across the lake? How would they get it back? This was the part of the story his children would be left with. How would they get it back? Because they never did get it back.

2

Henry James and the
Communists
1936–1939

1

When Myra Thorsten drove away from Gus Maloney's cabin in the Adirondacks with Harold's copy of *The Portrait of a Lady*, he was so upset he scared himself. He had thought about making love to Myra, but brooding on the porch after corn flakes for lunch, he imagined himself hitting her, though not in the uncontrolled, frightening way the policemen in his memory of the Union Square riot still beat women, all but smashing their faces to pulp. In his fantasy, Harold solemnly administered punishment to Myra in a decadent ritual in which she accepted her shame for borrowing a book without permission, and he pronounced sentence, then stepped toward her to carry it out, wielding a shadowy weapon—perhaps a thin cane—which he applied, not hard but firmly, to her shoulder as she bent her head, to her outstretched hands with their polished fingernails, and finally to her buttocks in its snug skirt, as she turned and bent humbly, her hands on her knees. What he imagined embarrassed and aroused him but made him less angry, and he began to notice the smell of the pine trees. Birds' cried and a sound made him think a car was coming again, but it was the wind in the trees. He left the porch, stooping to gather brown pine needles and crush them in his hands.

The weather warmed up, and in the days that followed they sat reading at the edge of the lake, going into the water when they were hot. Artie learned to float. They hitchhiked into Schroon Lake. Harold made notes for something, maybe an essay.

Back in New York, he delayed getting in touch with Myra. He borrowed *The Portrait of a Lady* from the library and finished it, horrified but impressed when Isabel Archer, James's bright, lively, innocent American heiress, returned to her evil husband at the end, though she could have gotten away. At last he wrote Myra a note. He wondered if the book would arrive in a package but discovered that he preferred a meeting.

Weeks passed. He decided she'd given him a false address. Then a postcard came, setting a time and place: a bar and grill near Grand Central Station, a Saturday night. Harold took the subway from East New York, where he and Artie still lived, and arrived early, but Myra was already in a booth, wearing black gloves and drinking what looked like bourbon, her red hair under a small black hat. Her purse, a black pouch with a metal clasp, was on top of the book. The table did not look clean, and it was difficult for Harold to refrain from snatching the book even before he sat down.

Myra raised her glass in greeting, flicking an ash from her

ALICE MATTISON

cigarette, and he slid into the booth with its sticky table, opposite her. She wore bright red lipstick. She had on a stylish gray jacket. A white blouse gleamed from under open lapels.

—Aren't you drinking? Myra asked. She'd dressed carefully; apparently she cared how he saw her. He reluctantly turned his back on his book, went to the bar, and bought a bourbon and water. Almost before he was seated and reaching for his own cigarettes, Myra lifted her glass again, touching his, and began to talk. I can't stand it that she goes back to him, she said. What's *wrong* with her?

Harold lit his cigarette. He put his hand on the book, moving her purse slightly. It had not occurred to him that Myra would read the book, much less have an opinion about it. He was charmed, though he disagreed. He tried to explain what he believed to be true about James's ending: that in making Isabel Archer return to her husband after being away (she had turned down estimable suitors to enter a disastrous, imprisoning marriage), James considered her heroic, not weak—someone who had learned to confront evil.

He tried to explain. If James thinks she should stay away, what is the book *about*? Why would it end just there? What has she accomplished?

Myra scoffed. What does anyone accomplish? She should have stayed away. She could manage.

In college, they did not speak as if characters in books could have chosen to do something else. Harold couldn't think how to explain that this wasn't the proper way to read.

Now Myra took the book (Harold winced but didn't stop her) and began flipping through it. She'd left bits of paper as bookmarks. At least she hadn't written in it. He *hoped* she hadn't written in it. She turned pages vigorously, weakening the binding. She asked questions, pulling her gloves off and putting them on again. What does he mean by this? How can you like an author who'd write something like this? At last she admitted she liked *The Portrait of a Lady*. She couldn't stop reading it. What else do you recommend? she said.

Harold liked being an expert. *The American*?

—Can we talk about it after I read it? Myra said. He hadn't had the chance to scold her for taking the book in the first place. Somehow that incident had become fixed and could not have taken place in any other way, although Isabel Archer, in the book, might have behaved differently if only Henry James had had Myra to consult.

As they stood to leave, Harold said, Do you have a job? Where do you work? Something about the way she picked up her bag and straightened her jacket made her seem like a working woman. He hadn't thought of her working, as if she were a child who would naturally be cared for by others.

—Of course I have a job, Myra said. She was a commercial artist and worked for department stores. I'm good, she said. I'm in demand. With her long right hand, she swiftly drew a series of curves in the air. She smiled at him. He understood her stylish clothes. She was in the business—it had nothing to do with him.

Harold agreed to meet and talk about *The American*. As he made his way back to Brooklyn with his book—Myra refused to be escorted, and he wondered if she was meeting another man— he scolded himself for an assumption he'd made about her. He had believed that a woman who'd have an affair with a married man couldn't be intelligent enough to argue, even erroneously, about Henry James. In the coming days, he stared at the elegant shapes of clothes in newspaper ads, the long sweeping skirts and narrow busts, wondering if he could detect Myra's hand.

2

When Artie applied to teach in the WPA adult education program, he claimed proficiency in photography, journalism, and current events, and was hired, that September of 1936, to teach two afternoon classes in an elementary school in Queens: English conversation for the foreign born. Artie was of several minds as he traveled through Queens to meet his classes for the first time. Since the day in the mountains when he noticed what Virginia was doing, he'd been sure he should teach. At the same time he thought he might be a fraud, only pretending to be a teacher. In the camera store, people had walked away from his explanations. He had not made Virginia listen. In the third place, if he was a fraud, he was proud to be putting something over on the people who'd hired him. He took an elevated train, then a bus. He wore his only sports coat and a fedora, and he carried a briefcase his elder brother had lent him. Inside was nothing but a pad of paper and a few pencils.

The first class had twelve students, mostly mothers who were free while their children were in school. Some attended this very school, and when a child's voice could be heard, the mothers sat up straighter. Current events seemed like a good reason for conversation, and Artie began talking about what he'd read in the newspaper on his way to the school—progress for the Spanish government against Franco and the rebels, a display of military might in Germany, a march by Father Divine. The young mothers were quiet. The school did not use this classroom, up on a dusty, warm third floor. Artie liked its smell. He stood at the front, his hat and briefcase on the teacher's desk, and twirled chalk in his fingers, then dropped it. The windows were open, and fresh air stirred the hair of his twelve students, most clustered near the front. The desks were small, and some students stuck their legs into the aisle. A woman let a shoe fall from her foot and ran her stocking foot over the old wooden floor, as if feeling for splinters.

Artie asked questions. His students knew that FDR was running for reelection, and they considered him a good man but could not say why. Some were not sure who was fighting whom in the Spanish Civil War. They did know about King Edward VIII of England and Wallis Simpson, the divorced American he was in love with, as well as Bruno Richard Hauptmann, who had been executed for the kidnapping and murder of the Lindbergh baby. After Artie thought to ask about the king and his girlfriend, they became less shy.

The one man in the class, who reminded him of Harold's father, was happy to talk. He spoke slowly, with a heavy Eastern European accent, explaining the fighting in Spain sadly and patiently, as if he described battles taking place outside the window while he watched.

When the class ended, Artie had an hour off. The classroom was lonely and he went to talk to his supervisor, a woman a little older than he, Beatrice London. Your name gave me the best idea I had, he said, walking in on her. It wasn't true, but why not say it? She was a small woman with tight brown curls, sitting at a desk that filled the office, and she started when he spoke. He'd forgotten that he moved silently. He said, London made me think of England, and England made me think of King Edward and Wallis Simpson—my ladies knew more about that than anything else.

Beatrice London looked at him soberly under her hair, then smiled. I hope you can get them away from that kind of subject, she said.

On the contrary, said Artie, pleased with himself. Making students feel they already know something about the subject at hand is the best way to prepare them to be receptive to learning. He had not known he possessed an educational philosophy. Beatrice London bent forward a little, her chin protruding. He found himself whistling. I just thought you might have something you wanted to tell me, he said. Instructions.

—No, said Miss London.

The second class was full of talkers, some who barely understood English. The old man with the accent, unaccountably, was in this class too, so Artie didn't feel that he could bring up exactly the same subjects. But after a while he ran out of others, and the man was again happy to tell the group about the rebels in Spain and how Hitler and Mussolini supported them and the Spanish loyalists opposed them. This group didn't need to be told.

Another man stood and, with expansive gestures and little English, denounced Roosevelt—in the pay of the capitalists—while a man who seemed to be Italian shouted that Roosevelt was the only person who cared about him and his family. Others shouted. Artie clapped his hands, stamped his foot, and shouted, Gentlemen! The two men stopped, apologized. They sat down and faced front. One folded his hands on the desk.

—Why did you sign up for this class? Artie asked them. He said it with exasperation as well as curiosity, though he was pleased that this group was wide awake, but the students considered the question appropriate and the women raised their hands. So I can become citizen, they said. So I can talk grandchildren. The group resumed talking and arguing. Artie didn't think their English would get better, since they didn't listen, but he liked them. Each had come to a truce with the English language, and that was enough. They were all older than he.

Instead of going home when it was over, he went to Harold's, though he didn't have his camera with him. Harold was not home, but his mother gave Artie a glass of seltzer and then a bowl of soup. When Harold arrived, they ate again, and Harold said he'd walk Artie home. He was excited about a meeting he'd attended, a woman he'd talked to.

—You're such a fraud, Artie said cheerfully. You don't give a damn about suffering people.

—Just stop it, said Harold. His voice shook. Artie knew he had gone too far. Of course Harold cared. Artie wanted to talk about his classes, but in the right way. Being a teacher should seem significant, not just something he could get paid to do. But he said, Nah, you're just looking for girls. What happened to what's her name—Belle? Did you give her back to her husband?

Harold didn't answer, and they walked in silence. It was dark. Darkness was interrupted by places where streetlights gleamed through rustling leaves. After passing under a light, they'd be back in darkness, as if the night itself encouraged them to pause and reflect privately. Artie began to whistle.

—What's that? Harold said.

—What's what?

—What you're whistling.

—I think it's Mozart, Artie said.

A block or so later, Harold said, Every few days there's something in the paper about Jews in Germany.

—Not today, Artie said. Speech by Hitler. Women should stay home and make little German babies instead of going to work.

—If you'd looked closely enough, you'd have found the Jews, Harold said.

—Yeah, Artie said, what is it with us Jews? Anybody looking for somebody to kick around? Here we are! All set. Then he said, But what are your pals in Russia doing about it, huh?

—What's Roosevelt doing, for that matter?

—Roosevelt has other things on his mind.

—Winning the election? said Harold. He doesn't have much to worry about.

They came to Artie's house. Sometimes they walked past it, circled through the neighborhood more than once, but now Harold seemed anxious to be by himself. As he turned back, he said, Remember that girl, Myra Thorsten?

—What girl? said Artie. The dame at the cabin?

—I saw her.

—You saw that girl? The one who took your book?

—Well, I had to get it back, Harold said. We had a drink.

—Stay away from that dame, Artie said. Harold was already moving away, and his wide, solid body was a dark shape, his face obscured by shadow but his pants and shoes easier to see in a puddle of light. Harold kept his shoes clean and polished. The laces were tied evenly.

—I can see she's a handful, Harold said. But she had some ideas about the book. She's no dummy.

—Stick to the smart little Reds, said Artie. Harold waved and started walking.

Artie continued teaching adult education classes, mostly at night, at the same school, paid by the WPA. Twice he taught a photography course. If you had ten students, you could run a class. More often it was English composition or conversation, and sometimes the same students came term after term. A young woman memorized verb tenses and vocabulary words, turning in pages of homework in pencil, making herself complete every exercise in the textbook. Artie sometimes corrected her errors. Sometimes he didn't. The loose-leaf pages, heavy with pencil marks, made him sad. Miss Kowalski's hands must have been damp with sweat as she clutched the pencil, and the pages were stiff, as if they'd been moist, then dry, more than once. Maybe she cried over them.

Beatrice London remained the supervisor. Artie got used to the sight of her moving quickly through the corridors, always with her curly head thrust slightly forward. She ground her heels into the floor. She was mildly attractive, with a conscientious look, and was careful not to be informal with the teachers she supervised. Artie decided she would like being encouraged to make friends, so he asked questions about lesson plans, and she frowned and answered, then sought him out again to give a fuller answer. She grew friendlier. One night he made a joke with her: he told her she should get ten cents less a week for wearing out the floor with her heels. Miss London ignored that and stayed away from him for a while.

One evening, a year after they'd begun working together, it was raining, and Miss London and Artie happened to meet on their way into the building. Her umbrella had broken and her hair was wet and hung over her face. Artie, wiping his glasses on his handkerchief, bent his knees so he'd seem short and pulled his own hair forward, then walked past her the way she walked, looking down at the floor and coming down hard with each foot. Hey, Bea! he called. She had a stiff way of holding her hands at her sides, and he imitated that as well. It was just a few steps in the corridor, and later Artie swore to Harold that he was the one who looked silly—nobody would even know he was teasing her.

—Teasing? Harold said. You can be rough.

—It was nothing, Artie said. After that, Beatrice London began complaining to Artie when his class made too much noise. He'd write a topic on the blackboard—*The New Deal isn't working*, or *Women should have jobs just like men*, or *Communists should be thrown in jail*. He'd point to someone in the class, who had to start arguing for or against the proposition. Whatever opinion was expressed, Artie opposed it. If a second student disagreed with the first one, he might switch sides—something his students considered magical; they couldn't do it—or he might point to the first student and make the two of them argue. Others would leap to their feet to join in. Teachers complained that shouting came from Artie's classroom, and now and then a student went to Miss London to say Artie had taken some outrageous position in class. One evening, when a fistfight broke out between an Italian man and a Russian Jew, a woman rushed out and phoned the police. A cop appeared in the doorway, and Artie said, What the hell are you doing here? and would have been arrested if the teacher next door, an older guy, had not persuaded the cop to forget it. Beatrice London made Artie sign a long description of this incident.

She'd do anything to get me in trouble, Artie said, after telling Harold this story. It was another of their late walks, this time in the fall of 1937. Harold had recently moved to a small apartment in Manhattan. Tonight he'd somehow gotten free tickets to a play, and Artie had come into the city to meet him. Afterward they had coffee. But Artie got angry when Harold first mentioned Beatrice London, and Harold wouldn't let him get away with it. They had been asked to quiet down, then to leave. Ridiculous! Artie said as they made their way out. They walked. When Artie was bored, he stopped to take a photograph, using the light of a street lamp, trying to pick up the shimmer of a puddle.

Now he had returned to the subject. She'd love to get rid of me, he went on. But she's too timid to do anything.

—She might work up her courage, Harold said.

Artie said nothing for quite some time. Then he looked up at the sky, as if for approval, and recited:

A fella who taught for a living
From Labor Day right past Thanksgiving
One day went too far.
He's as dead as the czar!
If only he'd had a misgiving!

—That's not as bad as some, Harold said.

—And the joke is, said Artie, It's all because she thinks I'm good-looking. She's in love with me.

—That would make it worse, Harold said.

3

Harold would finally marry Myra Thorsten in 1943, and during the intervening years he considered himself someone women laughed at or pitied. Still, once he had his own place, he felt he should seduce them, making this decision all but grimly. One afternoon he invited a young woman he had met at the Forty-second Street library to have a sandwich with him. Working for the Federal Writers' Project, he spent many days in the main reading room. The woman's name was Mary, and she was an assistant to a historian. At a delicatessen they ate corned beef sandwiches and sour pickles. Mary told stories about her family; there were uncles younger than their nephews, and each story included two or three characters named *my cousin*. At first he listened, enjoying it. Then his impulse was to convince her that her opinions were wrong. Nobody had such simple motives as she ascribed to her relatives—but he stopped himself: what mattered was taking her to bed. Someone as muddled as Mary would forgive his awkwardness or would not even notice. He invited her to his apartment, a few blocks away.

ALICE MATTISON

She hesitated, then agreed. She had a habit of looking up at the ceiling when asked a question and then smiling before speaking. It might have been either annoying or adorable; Harold determined to consider it adorable. As he brought her into his apartment, he remembered that his bed was unmade, the room was cluttered, and he had nothing to offer but coffee. They talked, and he took her home.

The next time—having made the bed and bought a bottle of liquor—Harold stood, crossed the room, and laid his wide hands on Mary's shoulders so heavily she flinched. He expected her to laugh or be offended, but she didn't laugh, and they went to bed. It was clear to him that Mary had lost her virginity earlier, and he wondered if it was as obvious to her that he had not. Maybe one of the uncles or nephews had taken advantage of her. Maybe she was relieved to be approached by someone who bought her a sandwich and touched her gently.

Harold thought of himself not as a good lover but as an emergency lover: someone who could perform if preferable men were unavailable, a kind of understudy. Even if Mary didn't laugh openly, he assumed she laughed when she got home, laughed when telling the story to her girl cousins. It was embarrassing, but he'd learned that to become the kind of man he wanted to be, he had to endure embarrassment. He spent another evening with Mary, this time including a movie in between the sandwich and the sex, and again Mary didn't laugh. But Harold was bored with her, and since his purpose had been achieved, he couldn't come up with the wish to see her again. Surely she wouldn't mind: her interest in him was charitable. He was startled when he received a letter from her a month later, asking if she'd done anything wrong, apologizing. The letter confused him, and he didn't answer it. He decided it was a kind gesture, designed to make him feel as if he'd dropped her instead of being dropped. Of course, in a sense he *had* dropped her, but only in a sense.

Some women said no to Harold, but more than he expected said yes. They did not laugh in his presence. He reflected that there must be even worse lovers around than he, whom women did laugh at openly.

He noted that the women he approached were rarely Jewish. He felt more Jewish, himself, as years passed, and spent gloomy hours wondering exactly what he'd be doing at the present moment if he lived in Germany. The women he dated were surprised when he told them that Jews were no longer permitted to attend German universities or that their passports had been made invalid. One woman's face took on an abstracted, spiritual look, like Joan of Arc's, when he told her about a story he'd seen in the *Times* that week—it was March of 1938, just after Hitler had annexed Austria—reporting that in a few weeks Germans would vote in a plebiscite. Naturally, Jews would not be permitted to vote. Voters would be asked a question Harold had memorized: *Are you German, do you belong to your Germany and its Adolf Hitler or have you nothing to do with us?* He waited for a reaction, but his date seemed too stunned to reply.

Then she reached across the table; they were having coffee in a little place not far from the Metropolitan Museum. Harold felt a momentary triumph when she touched him, then was horrified to feel triumphant and pulled his hand back. Deriving personal benefit from her outrage at Hitler was a trick as contemptible as the tricks of the Nazis themselves. He would have nothing further to do with this woman; she was a decent person and he didn't deserve her.

4

Unlike Harold's girlfriends, Evelyn Shapiro truly didn't count, according to Artie, who had been taking walks and eating ice cream with her for years. He'd never bought her more than a soda. Evelyn, whom he'd met in the neighborhood, had graduated from Hunter College at the worst of the Depression and could get a job only in her uncle's shoe store. You'd be surprised how many people have ugly feet, she said to Artie. Bumps, corns, squashed toes.

—Don't they wear socks?

—Not for fancy shoes.

The store sold good shoes and Evelyn got substantial discounts. Artie liked the way her legs looked in high heels with little straps, but he also liked taking long walks. When Evelyn said her feet hurt, he teased her, offering to buy her shoes just like his own. Except for her shoes, she was practical, with wavy hair and a round face. Her big breasts made Artie sick with longing, but that was late at night on the sofa he slept on in his parents' crowded apartment, where his married brothers got the bedrooms. When he was with her, Evelyn's breasts were under blouses and jackets. He'd often rest an arm on her shoulders and even stroke her neck, but that was all.

One summer night Artie and Evelyn walked all the way to the reservoir in Highland Park, past the tennis courts where Artie spent Saturdays and Sundays if possible. Then they walked around the reservoir and back home, stopping for ice cream cones. Artie began complaining. Beatrice London had threatened to give him fewer classes to teach in the fall. He couldn't get away from her. The ice cream was spoiled by anger, and before he finished his cone, he dropped it.

—I don't like it when you shout, Evelyn said, elaborately stepping around his cone on the sidewalk, continuing to lick hers. She always bought maple walnut.

—Who's shouting? said Artie. I'm not shouting.

—You've been shouting for twenty minutes, said Evelyn. I'm not your supervisor.

—And it's a good thing, too, Artie said.

She stood still and then turned toward him, suddenly looking younger. Now that her cone was gone, she stopped to lick her fingers, one at a time, between sentences, but it made what she said, for some reason, more serious. I'm tired of you and your yelling. I'm tired of you and your banging on tables.

—What tables? He was frightened. Was she tired of him, himself?

—Anywhere there's a table, you bang on it. You banged on the table in my house last week. My father thought you were yelling at me. He almost threw you out.

—For Christ's sake, I wasn't yelling at you! Artie said. He's got nothing to do but listen to us?

—I'm his daughter, Evelyn said. She was quiet and Artie whistled. They walked.

—So you're tired of me, is that it? he said then. You want me to stop showing up? Is that what you have in mind?

—I'm not tired of you, Evelyn said. I'm tired of spending my time deciding whether the head of the WPA is the stupidest man in the world, or somebody in Washington, or the editor who wouldn't buy your pictures.

—He should have taken them! said Artie. I've never heard anything so stupid in my life.

Evelyn stopped walking. She said slowly, Yes, I guess that editor is the stupidest. He's been the stupidest man in the world three times in the last two weeks. That has to mean something.

Artie stood under a street lamp and looked at her. He looked down at the sidewalk and began to whistle. Come on, he said then. He stopped to pick up something he caught sight of in the dark. It glinted. It was a key, an old key, and he slipped it into his pocket, in case he wanted to take a picture of a key. When she started walking again, he put an arm on her shoulders, not squeezing but resting it there for a moment. She shook him off. She meant it. Other times when Evelyn had yelled like this and laughed at him, he had stopped calling or coming by for a while, and maybe he'd do that again. He didn't need her.

5

Myra Thorsten grew tired of Henry James after making it all the way through *The Wings of the Dove*, annoyed when the lovers—who had deceived a rich, dying woman so she'd leave them her money—didn't marry at the end. They did wrong, Myra said, but it won't help to waste the rest of their lives feeling bad.

—Do you think they go to bed? Harold asked. James had included a scene that didn't quite say it.

—Of course. It was the summer of 1938, and they were sitting on a park bench outside the Central Park Zoo, having a rare outdoor meeting.

He tried to argue that the betrothed couple couldn't marry, explaining that for Henry James, moral questions took on life, that characters might spend their lives in response to what had happened earlier, living with an absence.

—You mean James thinks not doing something is something to do? said Myra. Just being good?

—Knowing what's true, more than being good, I think, Harold said.

—Well, I don't agree, Myra said. He was beginning to wonder, himself, whether knowing what's true was something to do. Henry James would have been astonished to discover that Harold Abramovitz compared his own membership in the Communist Party to Lambert Strether's renunciation of marriage and happiness at the end of *The Ambassadors*. The party had begun to seem like something required of him. He was quiet at meetings, though he argued vociferously for communism among his friends and relatives, who dismissed him with the same gesture: they flopped their right hands over and down, as if they flung off something slimy.

—You know, we could go to the lake, Myra said now.

—What lake?

—Gus's cabin.

—Oh! he said. Myra read not minds but the edge of minds. She knew he had not stopped thinking about the cabin in the mountains. Harold had known her now for two years but had not been to bed with her. Myra was too scary. She'd know too well what he was thinking. Myra would laugh.

—Do you still know Gus? Harold said. The thought was distressing, but the thought of the cabin was exciting. He stood up and she stood too. They entered the park and began walking.

—Of course I know him, said Myra.

—But how is that possible? Harold said. You're not still . . . you know?

—What do you mean, how is it possible? said Myra. There are lots of ways to know people. Maybe he'll let us go there. I can ask, at least.

He wondered whether she meant she spent her time with him differently—having renounced him, perhaps, imitating the characters in James despite her protestations. He wanted to go. He didn't want to quarrel.

—He'd lend it to us? he said. Or he'd be there?

—I'll find out.

Harold didn't want to be the guest of the man who had had an affair with Myra—of the man and his wife. But the cabin was too small for guests, as they'd proved when they'd been there. He couldn't stop asking questions. You mean you're friends? Does his wife know about you and Gus?

—I'm tired, Myra said. They sat down on a bench near the boat pond. Children brought toy boats to float in the pond, and nursemaids looked after the children—even now, even in the Depression, people had nursemaids or might be nursemaids. He speculated on whether nursemaids would favor a revolution.

—I don't know if she knows, Myra said. It's not a thing we discuss.

—But how can you be her friend?

Myra ignored his question. Look, I'll ask him, she said. Then she added, I wonder what she gets paid—tilting her head toward a uniformed woman. She could be mean to the kid and nobody would know.

Her mind went from topic to topic, sometimes responding to something he hadn't yet said. Myra seemed to have no preconceptions, and she hadn't worked out a set of ideas or ideals in advance, so she might think anything about anything—Gus, Henry James, the women in the park, who might be oppressed working people and might be Cinderella's stepsisters. She didn't think in categories and didn't seem to have an inward list of ideas she believed. Harold had made up his mind about so much: he envied her freedom of thought. He felt old. What would it be like to read a newspaper with that kind of freshness, without ready opinions about Roosevelt, about Hitler and the Jews, about the threat of war? Surely Myra knew she was against Hitler. The Germans had gone from harassing Jews and depriving them of rights to dispossessing them, settling them in concentration camps. Wouldn't Myra know right away that this was wrong? She didn't look at each story about Hitler with an open mind, surely, curious to see if this time, perhaps, he'd make sense? Of course, her feelings weren't just the same as his—she wasn't Jewish. And sometimes—was there a thrill to this or only the curiosity that arises from repulsion?— sometimes there was the tiniest hint that, long ago and out of earshot of Harold or anyone like him, she might have been part of some nasty conversations about Jews. No, Myra was no more anti-Semitic than any other gentile, but surely they all—well.

The point, though, had nothing to do with Hitler and the Jews. It had to do with sex. The point was that if Myra saw a man and wanted to sleep with him, she did not flip open a book of personal rules that included *Stay away from married men*, or any other kind of men, because she had no book of personal rules. And everyone else seemed to have one—tattered, thin, half-forgotten, but available.

—Do you do that often? Harold said.

—Do what? The sun was warm here and she sounded sleepy.

He hesitated. Do you take many lovers? he asked.

—Well, what business is that of yours! said Myra, jumping to her feet. She sounded more playful than angry, but as they continued to walk, she said, more quietly and slowly than usual, You think I'm a slut, don't you? And suddenly her tone was ugly. All you think about is the suffering masses. Contemplating my disgusting little life makes you feel pure! It gives you a thrill to think about people like me—well, that's pretty despicable, don't you think? You don't have the nerve to live your own life, you just like scaring yourself with mine!

Her words wouldn't stop. Harold was strangely elated, then troubled. He thought she might be right. He was stodgy and stupid, and of course women—he'd known this forever—laughed at him.

—Myra!

—I don't know why I waste time with you and your stupid books. You're so superior, but what you know isn't everything!

—I know that. I'm not superior. The path they were on had taken them out to Fifth Avenue again. As she spoke, he felt thick—physically thick—muffled in his clothes and his fleshy body, kept from thinking or acting. How could someone like him presume even to think about people who worked with their hands, people like his father—to think about what they needed, what society should do for them? He stared at Myra. He had not looked at her, not really, in all this time they'd been sitting and walking side by side. Her hair was cut shorter lately. She wore a brooch at the neck of her white blouse. She squinted because it was late afternoon and she faced west, toward the park. Her squint made her face seem childlike.

—You're good. You're serious, he faltered.

—Serious? You're damned right I'm serious, Myra said. She glanced at her wristwatch. Late, she said. So long.

—Wait, said Harold.

—I have to go, she said. She touched his arm as if to get a faster start, crossed Fifth Avenue against the light, and hurried down the cross street. Harold watched her go, then walked north for no reason, turned, turned again.

6

One night Artie said, Enough already.

—Enough of what? It was November, still 1938, and he and Harold were walking fast after a quick supper at an automat, walking to the next subway stop because they were in the middle of an argument.

—Enough of this women laughing stuff.

—But I just told you, Harold said. She ran away.

—Who cares? The meshuggeneh shikse! Let her run, Artie said. First you take advantage of a girl, then you dump her, and finally you figure out that everybody should feel sorry for you. It's disgusting.

—That's not the way it is, honestly, Harold said.

—Yeah, I know, I know. They were quiet for a block or so, as often happened when they disagreed.

—Did you see, Holland may take some of the refugees? Even more predictably these days, after silences Harold talked about Germany and the Nazis. Before he'd begun worrying about the Jews, it had been Spain, and Harold's shame that he didn't want to enlist. My mother would die if I enlisted, he had often said. But that's no excuse. Half the Abraham Lincoln brigade is guys whose mothers feel just the same way. The truth is I don't want to.

Artie hadn't wanted to either, but he didn't feel ashamed of not wanting to.

They came to the station. Artie had to go to Brooklyn, and Harold lived a few stops downtown. It's late, Artie said.

—I'm going to keep walking, said Harold. Talking about women, Artie had gotten nowhere with him, as usual. Everything came back to the Jews in Europe. As Harold turned away, his shoulders sagged and he looked older than he was, and for a moment Artie wanted to run after him. For a man who hadn't put a prayer shawl around his shoulders since his bar mitzvah, Harold was obsessed with being Jewish. Harold—and his whole family—could think about frightening subjects longer than Artie or any of his brothers or his parents. Enough, his father would say, if someone began talking about Hitler. His mother would weep and run from the room, and his father would say, You have to upset her? But when Hitler's speeches were on the radio, the whole family listened.

As he rode over the river to Brooklyn, Artie's mind returned to the subject of women. Harold thought Artie attracted women without trying, while he had no success. But Harold's life was full of women, while Artie had—well, he sort of had Evelyn, but that never went anywhere. If his supervisor had once liked him, the feeling had turned to hatred. Staring at his own reflection in the train's dark window, the lights of the city behind his own narrow, bespectacled face, Artie understood for a moment that he'd caused Beatrice London to hate him. He should stop teasing and challenging her, if it wasn't too late. He knew he wouldn't stop, just as he knew that his various brothers wouldn't change in one way or another, and the thought made him sad.

It was Beatrice London's fault, anyway. He had to get away from her, even if that meant being alone in a classroom with kids all day. He had no idea what you did with children, though he'd gone back to City College and daydreamed his way through some ed courses so he'd be qualified for a regular teaching job if he could get one. He was twenty-eight: he should get a real job, find a real girl, get out of his parents' apartment. But that was another sad thought. He liked slouching around with a camera, playing a little handball in the park on weekends, listening to music or walking the streets with Evelyn—or alone, whistling and daydreaming. Women in daydreams were easier to manage, and he hadn't seen Evelyn since their argument about—whatever it had been about.

But a few weeks later she called him and they walked. The weather was cool, and they followed their cold-weather routine; the walk would lead, eventually, not to ice cream but to tea in the kitchen of Evelyn's parents. Excited to see her, Artie had much to tell: at the last minute—right at the start of the new school year—he'd been called to teach seventh-grade social studies. The classroom maps were from before the world war, and the principal didn't like him, but the kids were funny and he was done with Beatrice London forever. I can't learn all those kids' names, he said. I call them all Johnny or Sadie.

They reached the two-family house where she lived, but instead of leading him inside, Evelyn dropped to the porch steps. She ran her hands through her hair and said, Do you think you might want to get married?

Artie sat down. Something went through his body as if he'd swallowed a fishing line with a hook attached, but it was not exactly painful. A hook made of metal so bright it seemed sharp, though it was not sharp. He began to whistle. After a while, he said, Why do you ask?

—Somebody wants to marry me. I'm twenty-seven. There comes a point. But if you want me to, I'll say no.

She wiggled her shoulders as if to say six of this, half a dozen of that, but her voice betrayed that the question was not casual.

—Say no, Artie said. Who is he?

—A nice person. He's becoming a pharmacist.

—A pharmacist, Artie said, somehow expelling the syllable through his nose. A pha-ah-ah-ah-armacist.

—Artie!

—So you're proposing? he said. He stuck his finger in her side. Her blouse felt stiff to his finger, but under it her body was soft. Sometimes when he put his arm around her, steering her or agreeing with her, he moved it from her neck to her back. He knew Evelyn's back, even the bump where he could feel underwear, better than her side or her front. Now she pulled away, ticklish. He poked her again. You're proposing? he said again. I have to tell my children their mother proposed to me? That's the sort of woman you are? Why didn't you tell me? All these years I've wasted on a woman who proposes!

She stood up, leaned over him, and placed her hands around his neck. I strangle people, too, she said.

What came to Artie was the song from the WPA protest, which he often sang for no reason at all. As he sang it this time—

gasping, as if being choked—he found he could alter it for the occasion:

Here's your answer, Mr. Ridder,
You had better reconsider,
Stop the strangling, Mr. Ridder,
Or I won't marry you!

They were both virgins. Every touch was exquisite.

7

Harold didn't see Myra for four months after she ran away from him. He knew that Myra didn't quite believe other people's feelings mattered, but he had liked trying to become the exception. He missed her. She read the books he proposed. They had moved on from Henry James to Edith Wharton and newer authors—W. Somerset Maugham, Aldous Huxley. Myra read childishly but eagerly and passionately. But she was unprincipled, Harold reminded himself, not truly serious. His comrades at party meetings would disapprove of her.

Harold had always been unsure as a Communist Party member—unsure before he joined, no less unsure now. But he could prove to those who were confused why the Soviet stand on some issue was correct, why as Americans they should support it. He could argue forcefully for positions he didn't quite believe in. He resisted handing out leaflets or ringing doorbells to recruit new members, but he wasn't the only one. What his heart had told him in the first place, though, it continued to tell him. It might not make sense to sit in meeting halls so long his backside hurt from the wooden chairs, or in somebody's living room until late at night, trying to make a distinction among positions that seemed all but identical. But the Communists were right about the struggle of the workers, and though his socialist parents scorned the party, Harold thought it might well be true that only the discipline and theory of communism could free people like them. The Communists were right about his father, and even if they were wrong about the revolution—Harold was never certain that a revolution was imminent in the United States, never even sure that what had been accomplished in the Soviet Union was as good as people said—they were right about what the right sort of revolution would lead to.

For three years Harold had been a bad Communist. He was not personally bringing about any sort of revolution. He could no more do that than he could make women love him. But he attended meetings, he wrote leaflets—even if he didn't distribute many of those he stuffed into his briefcase at the end of the meeting—he marched on picket lines and appeared at rallies and protests, aware at all times of his body, which was too dignified, unable to recede into a group. After a meeting he might even go out somewhere for late-night coffee and more talk. Eventually he forgot himself in the pleasure of using his brain.

One winter day Harold received a square envelope in the mail with Myra's name on the flap in back, and he waited a bit before opening it. It was an invitation—in an Art Deco design he liked—to a cocktail party. For a moment he thought he wouldn't go, but only for a moment. The good design reminded him of the ways in which Myra was reliably smart. She had a telephone, and he had to go to a candy store to phone and say he was coming.

On the day of the party he dressed carefully and arrived on time. Myra's black dress was tight at the waist, with a wide skirt and a swoosh of shiny fabric at the neckline. She brought Harold a martini and introduced him to her friends. He had known her for three years but had met only Virginia, who wasn't at the party and had never been mentioned after their encounter in the mountains. But here was a crowd: older than Myra, substantial, managing cigarettes and drinks while talking.

As always, Harold was conspicuous, and a man and woman began asking him questions. They were skeptical but intrigued to learn he worked for the Writers' Project. Harold had written part of the section on Negro Harlem in the New York City guidebook, and the man wanted to know whether Negroes answered his questions. When they moved on, Harold thought he'd go home rather than try to start another conversation, but Myra came over and linked her arm in his. I can't do this, she whispered, smiling falsely but sounding frightened.

—Do what?

—Have this party.

—It's fine.

—I'm going to start crying, she said. Get rid of them.

—Get rid of them? How could I do that?

—Do something or I'll start screaming, and they'll think I'm crazy, Myra said.

—All right, Harold said. Give me a chance. Go get more ice cubes.

Myra obeyed. He walked to the drinks table and poured something into his glass. He couldn't think how to make people leave unless he walked up to each of them and quietly asked them to do so, which would be unpleasant, might not work—and would make them think Myra was crazy. He sensed that she was really just trying to make him do what she asked, and he couldn't help liking that.

—What did she say? said a woman's voice at his elbow. She was fast-moving and small, with sharp elbows. You've never been to one of her parties before, have you?

Harold introduced himself.

—I'm her cousin, said the woman. She needs to eat.

—What? said Harold, but he was grateful. He followed Myra into the kitchen, where she was already weeping. Is there food? he said.

—People don't care about food at a party like this.

—I care, said Harold. Myra had no food. Let's go buy some, he said. Where's your coat?

—If I put on my coat and leave, said Myra, they'll all leave.

—Isn't that what you want? He persuaded her to get her coat, and he put on his own.

—Are you going? said a man standing near the door.

—Shopping for food, Harold said. Back in a minute. He held Myra's coat for her and they left.

—Let's not go back, she said.

—I think we'd better, Harold said. Where's a delicatessen? She lived in Greenwich Village, a few windy blocks west of Washington Square.

—Oh, who cares about those people? she said. I don't even like them. At this point Harold became so confused that he had to stop walking, stand still, take long breaths, and try to know what he thought.

—Come home with me, he said then. Myra had never been in his apartment. It was dirty and messy. I'm going to cook some eggs, he said when they got there. They ate eggs and went to bed for the first time. It felt right to take her under the rumpled sheets, to stroke and kiss her limbs, her neck, and the back of her head where the hair began. They made love and he turned aside, then turned back and began stroking and touching her again. He'd never felt such tenderness toward another person. The bones stood out on the nape of Myra's neck, and it seemed as if he could snap them. He was ashamed to have such a thought, and he kissed her generous breasts and her flat belly. She stayed all night.

After that, every week or so, Harold took Myra to dinner (he remembered the lesson of the party and tried to make sure she ate, but often she scarcely touched food), and sometimes to a play or a concert at Lewisohn Stadium or the City Center. Then they went to his messy apartment and spent the night. Harold didn't tell his friends he was seeing her again—not his friends in the party, not Artie. In Harold's imagination Artie told him that Myra was spoiled and selfish, giving him one of his quick, thick-browed glances, his mouth moving as he whistled. Harold preferred Artie's other look, a still, surprised searching look from behind his glasses. It came when he wanted to photograph something but hadn't yet seen how, or couldn't return a shot in tennis he had been sure of, or hadn't yet thought of a joke or a limerick. But he and Artie didn't see each other much during the winter of 1939—Artie was busy—and when they did, he didn't mention Myra.

In the spring, she offered again to ask Gus to let them use the cabin. He didn't like thinking of Myra and Gus in those bunk beds or maybe on blankets on the floor. But he wanted to go back there, as if he'd left an idea under a rock between the cabin and the lake, almost three years ago, and might find it again. He had lost the essay he'd started that week. When he thought of going to the cabin with Myra, she wasn't exactly present—maybe driving around looking for steaks and liquor again.

In July, they went. Harold couldn't yet drive, but Myra borrowed a car, and Harold liked watching her drive, with the window open and a scarf blowing across her face. She promised to teach him how. They stopped for groceries and arrived in the dark. As before, Harold was entranced by the smell of the woods, the quiet. He was surprised to see changes in the cabin:

there was a double bed in the main room now. Fully dressed, they tumbled onto it, grappling and kissing. He was freer than in his apartment. They pulled off their clothes, and he grasped her buttocks, her arms, squeezing her flesh, reveling in the touch of her. They were children in a make-believe house. To his surprise, the thought of Gus—the hint of the presence of Gus—made it better, as if Harold had won some sort of contest, just being here with Myra, and Gus had lost. Harold scolded himself for his usual belief that everything was complicated and hard.

In the morning he woke up first, dressed, and went outside, tense with excitement. He began walking. He always had paper and pencil in his pocket, and before long he was resting one foot on a rock, leaning on his thigh while making notes. He had more to write about than what his various assignments—book reviews, essays for the guidebooks he worked on—gave him a chance to say. What he wanted to write had something to do with his father, something to do with books. The moment when characters in literature saw something larger than themselves thrilled him (the same moment that still, despite everything, excited him at party meetings). He returned with a little plan for an essay. He'd seen this coming and had brought some books: Hawthorne, Stephen Crane. Myra was still asleep.

When they went swimming, Harold was surprised to see two cabins across the lake under the trees. A long dock stretched into the water. He saw no cars or people. Myra nodded when he pointed. Did she already know? Harold wanted the cabin and lake to be his secret. Myra returned to the book she was reading, by Pearl Buck. As he had imagined, she was not quite present at the cabin. She slept, or stared at the lake with a book in her lap, or read. Now and then she became needy and weepy, but Harold was used to that and he liked cheering her up, coaxing her to eat. It was a game, if a slightly embarrassing game. By the end of their few days, he had a draft of an essay, written at the table in the main room.

8

A rtie and Evelyn were married in August 1939. It took them a while because they both lived with their parents and couldn't afford an apartment. Twice during those months, Evelyn broke it off. You tire me out, she said. Both times, he waited a few days and called, and they went to the movies, or took yet another walk, or found a time when they could be alone in her parents' place or his, where they kissed and groped. Meanwhile, Artie took the exam and got a regular teaching job, not just a WPA job, and with the extra money they were able to rent an apartment. By then Hitler was threatening Poland, playing with the French, defying the British.

Artie and Evelyn arranged to be married in a rabbi's study. Artie borrowed a suit from one of his brothers, and it was too large. His head looked small between broad gabardine shoulders, and his rumpled hair and wild eyes, behind his glasses, added to the impression that he'd spent some time lost inside the jacket and had only just managed to emerge with his face at the front.

Only their families were at the ceremony, but Evelyn had sisters, and they put together a nice spread at her parents' house, so friends could come too. To Artie's surprise, Harold brought Myra Thorsten. He hadn't mentioned her in a long time, and at first Artie didn't recognize her. He was additionally confused when Myra took his face in her hands and squeezed it, shaking her head in disbelief, as if she knew him well and could scarcely credit their present situation. Artie, Artie, you were the one I liked first, she said.

—What's this Artie, Artie? he asked Harold when they found themselves alone in the kitchen.

—She's good for me, Harold said. I think too much.

—What's wrong with thinking?

—Do you know what just happened? Harold said.

—Sure. I got married. Artie leaned back against the windowsill in his in-laws' kitchen. He liked that sill: it was higher than some, and he could rest his behind on it, stick his legs out, and perch, half-standing, dancing his feet in time with his whistling. He'd done it many times, but now he did it married, and that was amazing.

—Stop whistling, Harold said. You haven't heard a radio. I know—you didn't have a chance.

—What's going on?

—Hitler and Stalin, said Harold, and his voice cracked, then got oddly high, almost a falsetto. He was enunciating carefully, like someone who knows he's too drunk to speak. One of Artie's brothers had poured Harold a glass of schnapps, but that wasn't why. Hitler, Harold said, and Stalin . . . have signed a nonaggression pact.

—What are you telling me? said Artie. What?

—My friend. Don't, Harold said. His voice was stronger. Von Ribbentrop is in Moscow. He flew there—his car, with the swastika, passed under the red flag. They agreed to divide up Poland.

—Well, well, said Artie. Well, well.

—Don't, Harold said.

—What's going on? Evelyn came into the room. She wore a light gray suit. Artie had stopped by in the morning to walk her and her family to the synagogue. Not a long white dress and a veil? he'd said, when he saw Evelyn. I don't rate a long white dress?

—You rate anything, Evelyn said seriously. She had looked straight at him and kissed him. No joking, Artie, no joking.

And Artie had teared up, kissed her back. No joking, he said. That was all the wedding they needed, but they'd gone through with the rest of it.

The suit was pretty and showed off her breasts. Evelyn put one hand on Artie's arm and one on Harold's. They'd met a few times. Is something wrong?

Artie said, It sounds like Harold's Soviet friends may have let him down. It sounds like things aren't quite what we thought over there in Europe. It sounds like our highminded Communist brethren . . .

—Stop it, Harold said. I've already had an argument with my neighbor. I see him at meetings. He says it's a trick, nothing to worry about. But I'm finished. I'm finished. He began to sob, and for the second time that day, Artie had to point out to himself that sometimes foolery and whistling and teasing aren't enough. He said awkwardly, You want to bring Myra to dinner, come. We're married—we'll have a kitchen, a table. Just a couple of blocks from here. We bought a table, right, Evvie? Right? We can make dinner for my old friend?

—Of course, Evelyn said. Come soon.

Artie couldn't resist. My formerly Red friend. My sadder but wiser friend. Evelyn put her hand over his mouth, and Harold looked her full in the face, Artie noted, as if he'd never seen her before.

—Your friend Myra, Evelyn said, using her head to point to the living room, is talking to my sister. She might be feeling shy. Go stand with her. Harold left the kitchen, not saying anything more.

—And you—you go talk to my father, Evelyn said to Artie. Tell him . . . what? Tell him I'm beautiful. Artie didn't think she was beautiful at that moment. He thought that despite the suit she was a little funny-looking but in a way that delighted him. She was the funny answer to a secret riddle. Whistling, he walked up to Evelyn's father and said, You raised a bossy woman.

—You never noticed? said his new father-in-law. You maybe blind or something?

—Stalin made a pact with Hitler, Artie said. They're going to divide up Poland.

—And throw away the Jews, said Evelyn's father. Throw them away.

3

Drives Away All Adversity

1940–1945

1

Pregnant, Evelyn banged pots and wept at what she heard on the radio, cooking barefoot because all of her many shoes now hurt her feet. Artie didn't know if she was angry at Hitler today or at him. He had had no idea about marriage—no idea that a woman who was humorous and resourceful when they took a long walk might not invariably be humorous and resourceful. But also no idea about sex. Evelyn loved sex, and though she had been a virgin until their wedding night, she was not shy or modest. Artie was shy for about a minute. Then he discovered that sex was the best possible way to play, to fool around. He made love, Evelyn said, like a monkey, and he said, So that's where you are when I can't find you—with your boyfriends in the zoo.

Yet one startling afternoon, Evelyn screamed at him—with no affection in her voice—not for being messy or careless, which he knew he was, but for being fussy, which he was not. And even if he had been, why was fussiness something to scream over? He had corrected her grammar.

—You could be drafted, she said now, turning from the stove. She wasn't angry with him: she was frightened. Then she said, They wouldn't let you do *that* in the army! He was helping her cook dinner, trying to peel a potato in one long strip. She took the potato out of his hands and did it quickly.

—I won't be drafted, he said.

—What's so special about you? Her voice sounded as if she did consider him special, and he took that in.

He said, We're not going to war. Harold had been arguing with him about this. It was well into 1940 and Europe was bloody.

—We're going to let them die there? Evelyn said.

—They won't die. But they were dying. Is the baby moving? He liked to put his hand on her belly and wait for movement. She nodded, abandoned the potato, raised the hem of her maternity smock, and laid his hand across her middle. He felt her skin, her blood coursing and lunch digesting, and his child. He said, He's not kicking, just moving this way and that way.

—That's right.

—So you're such an expert, he said, which way is he facing? She guided his hand. This is her backside.

—Her? Her little tuchas, he said. I'll give it a squeeze.

—Artie, she said. Artie. I think there's going to be a war.

Brenda Saltzman was born a stubborn and cranky girl with a square face and sparse light hair in January 1941, a few months into the bombing of London. The United States was still at peace. A long, difficult labor wore out Evelyn, and Artie disgraced himself, screaming at nurses, terrified and furious. When he wasn't allowed to be with his wife, he was sure she had died. He saw Brenda for the first time through a window into the nursery as she lay crying in a bassinet. A nurse picked up his daughter, but she wouldn't stop yelling. Her cries delighted her father. He liked her.

But two weeks later, Evelyn shouted, How should *I* know what to do? when the baby—in her bassinet in the kitchen because they had so few rooms—wouldn't stop crying and go to sleep. You figure it out, if you're so smart!

She went into the bedroom and closed the door. The crying became louder. Artie wondered if music might soothe a baby. He went into the kitchen, picked her up, and tipped her against his shoulder. He put his finger into her hard toothless mouth because he liked the way that felt, and rubbed her gums. He took her into the living room and began dancing to the music on the radio—Duke Ellington. Brenda yelled hard—her face was dark red—but maybe she'd like different music better. He turned off the radio with his free hand, then put Brenda down on the rug on her back, and began looking for the record he wanted: Villa-Lobos's *Bachianas Brasileiras* 5, a piece of music so strange—wordless, gorgeous wailing over the sound of cellos—that it might sound normal to a baby. He hurried to put it on the turntable of the Victrola.

When Evelyn came out of the bedroom, Brenda was still screaming, while Artie held her and danced a slow, creative dance to Villa-Lobos, oohing along with the ululations on the record. What are you doing? she said.

—We have to be patient.

—Why don't you give her a bottle? Evelyn said, though she herself had insisted the baby couldn't possibly be hungry.

—She's not hungry, Artie said.

—How do you know? You're in her mind? Evelyn had become solidly round with pregnancy, and that or something else seemed to make her move more directly than before, as if she hurled her weight against obstacles. She flung herself into the kitchen, and he heard the sounds of warming up a bottle. Brenda continued screaming, and Artie took her into the bedroom to remove the evidence of his failure. Without taking off his shoes, he lay down and arranged Brenda facedown on his stomach, pulling the bedspread over both of them. The baby's chest heaved rapidly against his and he was overcome with joy. He rubbed his hand down her bony back and rear end, singing his old school song, while Brenda's saliva soaked his shirt and he smelled urine from her leaky rubber pants. Her cries were softer.

> *One-four-nine is the school for me*
> *Drives away all adversity . . .*

Evelyn came in, moving more slowly now, testing the milk on her wrist. She put the bottle down, picked up Brenda, and took her to the waterproof pad on the dresser.

—Poor baby, Evelyn whispered, as she unpinned the diaper. Artie turned on his stomach and hid his face. He wanted his life back: his funny wife with the jiggling lump in her belly, his own competence. He was a teacher, but he couldn't teach his daughter how to be a person.

—I'm not mad, Evelyn said, but she sounded mad. He got up and went for his camera, which was in the living room. He'd piled his photography equipment on a chair when Brenda was born. It had been in a cabinet in the bedroom, but they needed the space for her clothes and diapers. He'd already taken many pictures of her. Now he brought his lamp and set it up. Evelyn was sitting on the bed, holding the baby and feeding her the bottle, but when he came in with the lamp, she watched him set it up and then heaved herself and her daughter up and went into the living room. When he came in, she was on the couch, still feeding the baby. You don't want me to take your picture?

—The light will disturb her.

—You want to comb your hair? Evelyn had always loved having her picture taken. You're so beautiful, he said. Her wavy hair was rumpled, longer because she didn't have time for a haircut. You don't *need* to comb your hair.

Evelyn stood, handed him the baby—who began to cry again—and wept against his chest. I don't want a baby, she said. I don't mean that. I don't mean that.

—Should I stop taking pictures? Artie said. It was unthinkable.

—I don't want you developing them in the apartment. She stopped crying and stepped away from him. You're locked in the bathroom for hours. The smell, the chemicals. It's not good for her.

He'd known this was coming but also had not known. But she's so pretty, he said. Your parents like the pictures.

—Don't make me decide now, Evelyn said.

Two weeks after that, she did decide. Artie had set up his lights and tried to get Brenda to follow his hand with her eyes, taking picture after picture. Her changing face fascinated him, its unmediated honesty. But Evelyn didn't trust him unless the baby was smiling. Brenda knew how to smile now but didn't do it often.

—It's not just the space or the smell, Evelyn said, walking into the living room from the bedroom, where she'd been folding laundry, as if picking up on a conversation they'd been having a moment ago. I don't like the mood you get into. I don't like the way you get when they don't turn out the way you want.

—For crying out loud! Artie shouted, so loudly that Brenda started to cry. Would you stop it? he shouted—at the baby. He'd never before shouted at the baby.

—Be quiet! Evelyn said, and snatched Brenda up. I have to say this. I've given it a lot of thought—

—All right, I'll just go. I see where this is going, Artie said. He folded his tripod and unplugged his lamp, with its clean smell of heat and light that he loved, put his precious camera into its case, then bundled everything in his arms. He had much more equipment—he developed and printed his own pictures—but this would make his point.

—Where are you going? said Evelyn.

—What difference does it make? Artie said. His arms were full, but it was winter. His coat was on a chair, and he managed to stuff it under his arm and walk out of the apartment, leaving the door open. Oh, for God's sake! he heard her say. He expected Evelyn would follow, but as he ran down the steps, he heard the door close behind him. He stopped in the lobby to reorganize, trembling, and put on his coat. He had no hat or gloves. There was no time for this—he had papers to mark and lesson plans to write. He could dig his keys out of his pants pocket and go back upstairs or even ring the doorbell, but he began trudging toward the elevated train that would take him into the city. He didn't know what he'd do with all this stuff if Harold wasn't home.

Harold had rented his second apartment, on an undistinguished block in Murray Hill, for one reason: the front windows. He had one room on the second floor of a brownstone—two stories up from the ground, up staircases diminishing in grandeur—with a bathroom made out of a former closet and kitchen equipment in an alcove. The front windows weren't as large as the ones on the first floor, but they were large enough, and the apartment faced south, so in winter the sun warmed and brightened it. On Saturday afternoon Harold was drinking coffee he had just percolated, sitting opposite a woman buttoning her sweater. She'd come in from the bathroom, where she'd retreated to dress. This was the first time he'd seduced her. A week earlier they'd struck up a conversation at an art gallery and had met by arrangement at a different gallery earlier that afternoon. Her name was Naomi; she was bright (and Jewish) and she had turned out to be a virgin. Naomi wasn't especially pretty, but she was honest and funny, with a worried crease between her eyes that smoothed out when she wasn't nervous and thus gave Harold an interesting challenge. He was feeling kindly, elderly, and erotic. Naomi, with no experience, apparently considered him a dignified, confident lover. Now he was being charming on purpose, listening with sympathy to a story she was telling that she'd begun an hour earlier, before he'd interrupted her with a hand that lingered on the center of her back for quite some time before it moved farther. Because she was so smart (she taught French in a public high school in a rich neighborhood in the Bronx), he could be himself. If he didn't call, this woman would write no pathetic letters. Virgin or no, she took her coffee black and drank it with her feet drawn up under her, telling him how she'd gotten lost in Paris when her aunt and uncle gave her a trip to France as a graduation present. At the thought of Paris, her eyes grew large, as if she was stretching the lids up so as not to cry, and he knew they'd have talked about the war, but the doorbell rang and the crease returned between her eyes. Her eyes were blue, like his, and close together.

Harold considered not answering the door: he could signal Naomi to be quiet and not move until they heard departing footsteps. The visitor was right outside—the downstairs door was never locked. But nobody as suave as Harold was pretending to be would be afraid to answer a door. He rose, frightened but interested to know what would happen if Myra was his guest. But it was Artie, his arms full of photography equipment.

—What are *you* doing here? Harold asked, making his voice jocular so Naomi wouldn't worry.

—That's a fine way of saying hello, said Artie, crouching to set his bundle on the floor. Sorry to interrupt. He nodded curtly in Naomi's direction as he stood, his possessions clattering as they settled.

—What's this stuff?

—Can't you see? Two cameras in cases, a tripod, a lens in a case, a light on a pole, and a screen to focus the light. Any further questions? Artie remained standing between them. Harold had closed the door and was now perched on the bed. He was glad he'd made the bed while Naomi was in the bathroom. He didn't feel like inviting his friend to sit on the edge of the bed next to him, and Naomi was in the only chair. Artie's long, thin face was tense, his cheeks sucked in as if he was ready to whistle at any moment, his heavy brows squinting with outrage over his glasses. Harold murmured their names, and both guests nodded. How's the baby? Harold said then.

—Evelyn threw me out.

—Really?

—She said I can't keep this stuff at home. Apparently she's the president now. I thought we reelected a guy named Roosevelt. Artie sat down on the rug, leaned over on one hand, and let his legs sprawl to his side. He took up most of the room. Can I have coffee?

Harold stood and so did Naomi. You don't have to go, he said.

—I should do some things today. She followed him into the alcove with her cup and saucer and set them down. Then she touched his arm, and he stopped reaching for the coffee pot and kissed her quietly on the mouth. I'm sorry, he said in a low voice. I'll see you soon. He brought her coat from the hall closet and held it for her, then saw her out to the landing.

—And what was that all about? Artie said when the door was closed. He had moved to the bed, where he sprawled as he had on the floor. He had a cup of coffee with no saucer and he'd already drunk half of it.

—Don't put your shoes on the bed, Harold said.

Artie kicked them off. All over with Myra? he said. I can't say I'm sorry.

—You don't know Myra, and you have a superficial idea of what she's like, Harold said.

—It's not over? You're skipping out on her? Artie finished his coffee and began twirling the cup between his hands.

Harold had lost all his confidence. We don't have a formal arrangement, he said. We're not *promessi sposi*.

—Ooh la la, Artie said, his usual response to any foreign word. So that gives you the right to lure little girls into your cave? Did you tell this Naomi about Myra?

—I didn't do anything wrong, Harold said.

Artie said nothing. His silence was more effective even than his sarcastic speech, and Harold had an uncomfortable sense that something he had believed to be true was not true. He even glanced around as if Naomi might not have left after all. Sometimes, in the shower or late at night, Harold understood that the game he played was indeed a game: he pretended he did no harm to the women he slept with, that he was such a clown, such an oaf, that at best they pitied him. But this was pretending. Then the thought passed.

—Myra's not the girl for you, Artie said.

—Why, because she's not Jewish? Because her family has money?

—Myra's trouble, that's why, Artie said. You don't want to spend your life with Myra, and that's why you run around with all these Naomis. Tell Myra good-bye and keep Naomi. I like Naomi.

—You don't know a thing about it.

—I have eyes, Artie said. There's a lot I could tell you that you need to hear.

—Such as what? Harold said mildly. Don't you think you'd better solve your own problems first?

—Such as your job.

—My job? Harold still worked for the Writers' Project, though many people had been let go.

—I'm telling you, there's no future. Sooner or later you'll not only be fired, but you'll be in the paper as a Commie Red.

—I told you, I tore up my membership card.

—You think anybody will care about that? Artie stood, put his cup down in the alcove, picked up a kitchen towel, and began playing with it, twisting it and snapping it loose. He said, You think the American people are going to check the expiration date on your membership card? This stuff is getting worse and worse, this Dies and his committee. You don't need it.

—I don't want to teach children, Harold said. He knew what Artie thought he should do. He wanted to teach, but in a college. He wanted to get a doctorate in English literature. He couldn't teach until he'd done that.

—What's so terrible? Long vacations, you're home early, the kids are funny.

—I don't think so, said Harold.

—*I don't think so,* Artie mocked, making the words sound weak and uncertain.

Myra had made the same suggestion. You like the sound of your own voice, she had said. If you teach, you'll hear it all day long. Nobody had much respect for him, Harold reflected, but remarks like that kept him with Myra. This Naomi—all these good women. They didn't have the nerve to say things like that.

—I'll think about it, he said, feeling as if by some kind of elaborate logic he owed it to Naomi, the teacher he'd just seduced and would probably never see again, to think about teaching. He could take education courses at night. It was true that the Writers' Project wouldn't last. He stood up. I'll see about it, he said.

—You won't be sorry, Artie said.

—I said I'll see about it. Now what about all this stuff? He pointed.

—Just for a week or so, until she calms down?

—You want to leave it here? For God's sake!

—What's so terrible? I didn't bring the baby and leave *her* for a week.

—What's she like?

—Come see her. She's smart. She's driving me crazy, but she's smart. Artie replaced the kitchen towel on the table, furled into a long cloth tube. Come back with me. Come eat with us.

—You're in the middle of a fight.

—Evelyn will be nice if you come with me.

—It's trouble for her.

—She won't care. What's trouble? Another plate? I'll set the table. I'll wash the dishes. Come on.

They left Artie's beloved photography equipment in a tangle on the floor and took the subway to Brooklyn.

2

On November 25, 1942, the *New York Times* reported that Dr. Stephen Wise, the chairman of the World Jewish Congress, had confirmed that half the estimated four million Jews in Nazi-occupied Europe had been exterminated. The story was on page 10. Harold had bought the paper on the way to work, read the first pages, and put it aside. He picked it up that evening to read on a subway ride to Brooklyn.

Artie's photographic equipment had now been sitting on Harold's floor for more than a year and a half, and Harold had phoned to complain about it. He didn't complain, but he did mention it to Evelyn, who had answered the phone. She invited him to dinner. She liked him and often invited him. On his way, Harold read the story about the Jews.

—My God, he said to Artie and Evelyn, carrying the paper in, folded back to page 10. My God. He had intended to demand the retrieval of Artie's belongings once he was there, but now that he'd read the newspaper story, his wish to clear his floor had become selfish and trivial. He put down the paper to take off his overcoat. Brenda stood in her overalls in the middle of the room. She had a chunky, square face and her lips looked as if she might cry or complain, but she was quiet, holding something. When Evelyn turned away with the coat, Brenda came toward Harold and held it up for him to see. It was a stuffed horse. Is that your horse? he said.

—Baby, said Brenda.

—Your baby.

They sat in the living room. He lit a cigarette and Evelyn brought him a drink. When he tried to talk about the story, Artie and Evelyn shook their heads and looked shocked but wouldn't speak. Brenda was surely too young to understand, but they didn't seem to want to talk in front of her about such a thing. Evelyn was pregnant again, and when Harold spoke of the newspaper story, she put her hand over her protruding stomach.

—We haven't seen you, Evelyn said. It had been a few weeks. You're all right?

—I was rejected, Harold told her. Pearl Harbor had turned war and the draft from discussion into fact—as if frightening figures on a movie screen had stepped into the theater, three-dimensional. Artie had expected to be rejected because of his nearsightedness, his fatherhood, or both, and was glad about it. Death? he had often said to Harold. Who needs it?

But Harold had always told himself he'd go and fight. True, since the day the police had beaten him up in the Union Square riot in 1930, his right hand trembled at times and became weak. Sometimes it hurt. His hand made him drop things and kept him from doing anything precise—he couldn't have drawn the fine, shapely lines in Myra's illustrations, even if he had the talent—but he could almost control it if he tried. He hadn't thought it would keep him out of the army. He'd imagined being drafted, even enlisting. Then, when the war started, he was startled to find himself hoping to be rejected: afraid. Soon enough, he'd received a draft notice, but he failed the medical exam. His hand was too disabled. He thought he might have exaggerated the weakness on purpose. Were the doctors smart enough to detect that kind of deception? He was afraid to be a soldier, but when he'd received his 4-F notice, he'd been depressed for days. He'd told few people he'd been turned down, not Myra.

—That's *good* news, Artie said.

Harold shrugged. Not really.

—You've got better things to do with your life, Evelyn said.

—But with this going on? Harold pointed at the newspaper.

Artie waved his hand dismissively, but Evelyn nodded.

A few weeks later came a front-page story. The members of the United Nations had issued a joint declaration protesting the Germans' cold-blooded extermination of the Jews. This account was full of detail. Jews were taken to camps in Poland; nobody returned. Healthy people worked as slaves, and the rest were systematically exterminated. The United Nations, the paper reported, was making plans to bring the perpetrators to justice—which wouldn't bring dead people back to life, Harold pointed out. This time he said it to Myra. The story was two days old when he met her in the garment district on a Saturday. She had to see someone in an office. Harold had waited in Herald Square; he liked watching the iron statues on the big clock that had recently been installed there. Mechanical men lifted their arms and struck, and their hammers crashed against the big iron bell. At last Myra came along, annoyed at her assignment. A few days earlier, he had finally told her he'd been rejected from the draft. I assumed, she had said.

They went to see *Casablanca* for the second time. The war was going badly in real life, and the movie first cheered Harold, then depressed him: the French national anthem, the courage of the characters, his own cowardice. Later, they sat in a luncheonette and he began to talk about the extermination camps.

—Do you think it's true? she said. Her lipstick was a new color, darker, and it or something made her skin look dark and flushed, healthy with purpose but a little brutal. She rarely read a newspaper.

—Of course it's true. They've been investigating for months.

She considered. She had ordered only coffee—though he urged her to eat, as he always did—and had drunk it quickly, getting lipstick on the rim of the cup, and now she took out her compact and lipstick, blotting her lips on her napkin, stretching her mouth open and then pressing her lips together like a fish. Harold watched her, sipping his coffee and eating a cheese danish. He didn't like the way she repaired her lipstick, but he wanted to see her do it.

—Do you remember how I used to get? she said now.

—How you used to get? You mean, upset? When you and Virginia—

He wasn't sure he was allowed to speak of it. Sometimes, even now, she'd panic as she had at the cabin, but she never referred to these episodes later.

—When we met, she said.

—I remember.

—Well. That's the kind of thing I'd think about. You know.

—What kind of thing? He didn't know what she meant.

She sighed, putting her compact and lipstick into her purse, closing the clasp with unnecessary attention.

—That's what I used to think about. I didn't know how to stop. People killing other people. Not like wars, but just like this. Deciding to kill people and doing it. Maybe smiling.

He put down his cheese danish. What made you think things like that?

—How should I know? Maybe I read something when I was a kid, heard something. Scary stories. Most kids laugh.

He had so many questions he couldn't speak. He wanted to know what her thoughts were like, why she couldn't stop, how it was for her—for a woman—to have these thoughts.

—So I know it's true, she said. People can do that. Hitler—he's not like one of the bad guys we have around here, you know?

—No.

What did he want to say? He had to say something large and loud to Myra Thorsten, but they were in the third booth of a crowded luncheonette, with people at the counter, people walking by. He had half a cup of coffee left and part of his danish. His fingers were sticky. Will you marry me, Myra? he said.

—You mean that? She had reached for her bag again, and she held it in front of her like a shield, or as if she displayed it.

He didn't know if he meant it. They'd known each other for more than six years. He kept returning to Myra. He loved taking her to bed, but just as much, he loved waking up, late on a Saturday or Sunday afternoon, to discover she was gone, and he was free to think of other women, other people, other topics. His parents were baffled that he'd know a woman as American as Myra.

They left the coffee shop and walked holding hands, his sticky hand in hers. They scream at me all the time for seeing you, she said.

—Who screams?

—My mother, my sister. My father doesn't know I sleep with you. He'd kill you.

—Really?

—He might. Or he might kill me.

—They don't trust me?

—They say you'll never marry me.

Harold had often thought that he would never marry Myra, but it was new to consider himself a potential villain for that reason. The idea pleased him, but he was offended, though they had guessed right about his intentions. Of course, he never intended the drama of abandonment they apparently believed possible of him—and now he couldn't say just what he had thought would happen. Myra would get tired of him and disappear—that must have been it.

—They don't care that I'm Jewish?

—They figure you'll make money.

Instead, weeks after their wedding, early in 1943—it seemed to happen immediately, as if a dress, a dinner, bridesmaids (Myra's two cousins, including the one who had spoken to Harold at the party) had been lined up waiting—Harold lost his job. He couldn't find steady work as a reporter. If he hadn't been married, he'd have gone to graduate school at last and become an English professor, making a scanty living writing reviews and freelance stories, but now he finally took the exam to become a teacher. Meanwhile, they lived mostly on Myra's earnings. When they married, he'd given up his apartment (he didn't know what Artie did with the cameras and tripod, when at last he had to insist they go) and moved in with Myra, whose place in the West Village was slightly bigger. But now they couldn't afford even that. On a tip from somebody, Artie found them an apartment near his own in East New York. Artie, with his years of marriage, his children—Evelyn had given birth to another girl, Carol—seemed older, though he'd always look boyish compared to Harold.

—We can play tennis again, he told Harold. I'll show you a thing or two. Suddenly Harold was living a mile from the neighborhood he'd grown up in, teaching in a nearby high school not very different from the one he'd attended. He'd attempted to flee into Manhattan—into adulthood—and had been captured and returned.

3

On a Saturday afternoon, Artie stayed home with Brenda, who was taking a nap, while Evelyn took Carol along in the baby carriage to the grocery store. It was spring 1944, and when Brenda woke up, Evelyn instructed Artie, he should take her outside. Evelyn's hair was pulled back with barrettes, and her eyes looked large and weary. He maneuvered the carriage down from their second-floor apartment while she carried Carol. When he heard Brenda talking to herself a little while later, he went into the children's room and found her sitting up, frowning deeply. She put up her hands to be lifted, and he took in her urinous baby smell. She was trained but often wet the bed. He changed her and gave her a snack, but he wasn't wearing his shoes and didn't feel like the major nuisance of getting himself and Brenda out the door, so he decided to teach her to play golf, showing her how to use her push toy to knock small toys into a box he placed on its side in the kitchen doorway. Brenda was entranced. She shoved things with the push toy, yelled I win, I win, and ran back and forth, becoming wilder. Artie found her delectable, with her disorderly light brown hair flying, her clothes hanging out, her voice loud. She had a bellow and she indulged in it now. They ran together. When she fell, he picked her up and pretended to eat any part of her that might have been injured, each limb, her neck, her ears. He set her down again. He was tired, and now it seemed that Evelyn should come home, but not much time had gone by.

—All right, you play now, and I'll watch you, he said, and lay down on the couch with his book.

Soon Brenda began to scream in a different way, more frantically, with abandon. At first, Artie put down his book and watched her, taking even more pleasure. But then she picked things up and threw them—first a magazine, then some mail, then the book he'd been reading. She hurled the book, then dove after it, and tore the page that came to her hand, holding up the torn piece of paper and laughing.

—Wait a minute! Artie shouted. What's the matter with you? He was screaming as if she were an adult. Why are you tearing my book? Do I tear your books? Brenda started shrieking, and he turned away disgustedly, half intending to find one of her books and tear it, to show her how much she wouldn't like that.

He picked her up roughly. She was wet with tears and needed to be changed again, because he'd forgotten to take her to the toilet, and her shoes were untied. She did not stop screaming. What, are you stupid or something? he said. What do you think will happen, you do things like that? He smacked her backside.

A moment later, Evelyn came in carrying Carol. What's going on? she said. The people downstairs complained about the noise. What is *wrong* with you? What did you do to her? She picked up Brenda and held both children, and now Carol began to cry.

—Your back will hurt, he said, but she carried both girls into the bedroom. She'd left the carriage and groceries downstairs, so he went down and lugged them up, and then he put the perishables in the refrigerator, but he was too angry—with all of them—to put the rest away, so he waited resentfully in the living room until she came through alone, on her way to get a bottle for Carol.

—Maybe you want to call the cops on me, he said then. Maybe you think I'm dangerous! Send me to prison. It'll make a good story in the paper. Give the downstairs people a little more to think about. He picked up the cheap camera he used these days for snapshots and walked out of the house. How he missed developing pictures—the smells, the suspense, the strange surprises. He'd sold all that equipment without saying anything to Evelyn.

Home was not easy, but in the classroom the unexpected only inspired Artie. The riskier the better. He could not discipline his seventh- and eighth-grade social studies students because they knew he was amused by bad behavior. Eventually, though, he'd lose his temper. Once, he kicked his metal wastebasket around the room, scattering papers and causing a terrible banging, scaring the children. They quieted down, and the look in the girls' eyes made him uncomfortable. But when he told them that maybe their teacher was dangerous and they should call the cops, they laughed, unlike Evelyn, who didn't speak to him all day after he said that. The children liked his whistling and his games. Artie devised games to teach everything, managing to use his outdated maps to let them see how badly the Allies were doing in the war, then how things began to improve. Children would play General Eisenhower and Winston Churchill deciding what to do, and once he chose someone to play Hitler, but the boy refused and Artie didn't push it. He never concealed his own opinions except as a trick. But he encouraged the children to disagree with him and held debates that got louder and louder, until the bell rang and the kids said they had to go to math, while Artie wanted to keep arguing.

4

Harold came home one evening, late in 1944 when Myra was a few months pregnant—he had found time despite teaching to write a book review, and he'd just turned it in—to find Gus Maloney in his living room. He hadn't seen Gus since long before the war. Harold had known him as a newspaperman, but Gus had left his paper to work in a family business not long after Harold and Artie borrowed his cabin in the Adirondacks. When Myra, now and then, mentioned Gus, it was with irritation, possibly fond irritation.

—Gus has no sense of direction, she said once, when they were looking for an unfamiliar place.

Another time she said, Gus doesn't eat chicken. Have you ever heard of someone who doesn't eat chicken? They were eating chicken—or, Harold was eating chicken. Myra was rarely observed to eat. Her remarks made it seem as if Gus might be waiting just outside the room, and indeed, now he had come in. He sprang to his feet to shake Harold's hand and give him a slap on the arm that made him think Gus had been in the war. He stumbled slightly as he sat down again, and it turned out he'd served in the Pacific, had been wounded and discharged. His arms and legs were long, and he seemed ready to spring up again, despite the limp, to do what Harold couldn't. Harold became intensely conscious that Myra and Gus were a couple of goys while he was a Jew, as if they'd have ways of deceiving him he couldn't begin to imagine. Gus was lanky, craggy-faced, older than Myra and Harold, with graying hair he flung off his forehead with a careless gesture.

—We were talking about the cabin, Myra said.

—You still own it? Harold said, remembering the silence and the smell of the woods. It was several years since he and Myra had been there, and again it had seemed unreachable, maybe because Myra didn't mention it and Harold, always wondering about Gus, couldn't.

—More than ever, Gus said. It's mine since my father died. I have some plans for it, and I thought it might hold a sentimental value for you too. He cleared his throat. Since I take it that you met there.

Harold didn't answer. He was taking off his hat and coat. Gus kept talking. For what he called a pittance, Harold and Myra could become part owners of the cabin. With some money, Gus could enlarge it and put in a bathroom.

—Nobody can go there often, Gus said with a broad gesture. There's no point in just one family owning it.

—We don't have a car, Harold said. What Gus was proposing would put him permanently into their lives, but they'd also have the cabin.

—The bus goes pretty close now, Gus said quickly, while Myra said, You know my father would let us use his car.

Harold hung up his coat, leaving his hat on a chair, and considered coffee or whiskey. Myra had offered nothing. She was deep in their most comfortable chair, her legs drawn under her, looking sleepy. She disliked pregnancy.

Harold said, What does your wife think about asking us into this deal? He lit a cigarette, then became uneasy—Myra said smoke nauseated her—and stubbed it out.

—My wife? Gus said. She thinks it's a good idea.

Pouring drinks, Harold kept his back to Gus. Well, we don't have any money, he said. We can't consider it. He found himself angry that he couldn't own the cabin or some of it, while he was simultaneously angry with Gus for making the proposal. He'd always been suspicious of Gus and now found himself wondering whether Myra's child was his own. But he loved the cabin.

—Not for me, she was saying. He handed a glass to Gus and took one. Myra said, Maybe my parents would put in some money. It would be nice for the baby. She spoke, as she occasionally did, in a slight falsetto, and when she did, there was trouble. When they were alone, she'd tell him four or five things he already should have done that he'd never thought of—bought her a present or told her not to wear something she had decided was unbecoming. She'd become more and more outraged, then would weep for hours, no matter what he did.

Maybe her parents already knew the whole scheme. We'll talk about it, he said. What did I hear about you, Gus? You're in business?

—Funerals, said Gus.

Harold needed to go outside and walk. Funerals! He wondered how long it would take to walk all the way to the reservoir in Highland Park. It was a bleak spot, an enormous angular stone bowl of dark water with a fence and a treeless cobblestone path around it. From it one could see distances. Gulls flew from Jamaica Bay to the reservoir, if rain threatened, and settled on the water. Harold got up, hitching his trousers self-consciously, and stood near the chair on which he'd dropped his hat. Out of the corner of his eye, Myra, in her dark green robe, had grown sharper, more alert. Why was she entertaining a visitor in her bathrobe? Well, since her pregnancy, she often worked all day in it, making drawings in bed of models and clothes she'd seen only once—clothes that wouldn't fit her now. Once a week she'd dress in stylish maternity clothes and take her portfolio into the city.

Sometimes, after she'd criticized him, Myra cried and said, I know I'm impossible. I don't want to be impossible! Harold, don't let me be impossible! He'd take her in his arms, soothe her, talk to her in nonsense syllables, offer to open a can of soup, but she'd shake her head. The chair with his hat was as far away from her as he could go.

5

When Harold heard that President Roosevelt had died, in April 1945, he surprised himself by crying, though he'd often quarreled—sometimes out loud, in one-sided arguments—with Roosevelt. He had turned on a radio and was caught by surprise. It was another shock, after the shock of seeing the films of concentration camp survivors a few weeks before. Myra came running with the baby when she realized that Roosevelt was dead—with their long, skinny son, their floppy baby, whom people tended to hold horizontally, so he seemed less organized than the usual compact infant squashed comfortably against an adult shoulder. She'd insisted on calling him Nelson, a name that sounded pretentious to Harold. Now she was speechless, then distracted, saying they had to go see her parents, who had never been enthusiastic about Roosevelt. She went to get dressed, scattering hairpins, then changed her mind. They stayed home, and she squeezed against Harold on the sofa. Nothing is the same, Myra said.

Evelyn Saltzman was devastated, weeping over her daughters and then handing Carol to Artie so she could cry in private, which meant in the bathroom. Artie was upset too but didn't say much. He distracted Brenda from the sound of Evelyn's sobs by carrying her around the house on his shoulders, neighing and clutching her feet, trotting and even galloping, though she was afraid and after a while begged him to stop. But Artie neighed louder and ran faster, not wanting to think too hard about the ways in which time had passed, the man who seemed as if he'd be president forever was dead, and Artie himself had turned into an adult, despite everything. He felt sure he must be a boy still, but there was so much evidence to the contrary, more every day.

4

When We Argued All Night
1951–1952

—Beatrice London, Harold said, swinging his arms as he walked, when Artie couldn't guess who of all people was teaching in Harold's school. A jolt of irritation passed through Artie before he remembered who she was. The three kids ran ahead of them on the bumpy hexagonal paving stones of the paths at the Central Park Zoo: Brenda, sturdy and yet unsure, self-consciously pumping her arms, her thin curls tight against her head; Nelson, almost as tall as Carol, his feet flopping as if his ankles had no bones; Carol, who seemed like a different kind of kid because she was not awkward. Artie quickly, superstitiously, counted them, though Beatrice London was not a kidnapper or a dangerous zoo animal possibly out of its cage, just the grouch who had been his night school supervisor.

Now she taught homemaking at the high school where Harold taught English. I recognized her name right away, he said. She's pretty. I imagined a gnome, with her nose touching her chin.

Nelson was afraid of the seals and couldn't stay away from them, yet wherever the children led them, they came back to the seals—Artie was sure Nelson made this happen—and he would cry. Now his head was down and his nose dripped. Brenda kept walking, but Carol took his hand. One seal sat on an exposed shelf, another slithered out of their dirty pool. Sea lions, were they sea lions, not seals, and what was the difference? Artie could imagine being afraid. Not afraid that they'd hurt him, afraid of the way they flopped. Maybe Nelson feared turning into a seal.

—Did she recognize *your* name? Artie didn't remember speaking of Harold to Beatrice, but he might have. He had tried to make friends. Let's buy them Cracker Jacks.

—Cracker Jacks would spoil their lunch, Harold said. Artie thought he might buy Cracker Jacks anyway.

It was September, and they'd been teaching for a week, after the first days of putting their classrooms in order and dealing with the demands of 110 Livingston Street. The kids were back in school too: Brenda in fifth grade, Carol in third, Nelson in second, though he seemed like a baby. Harold was silent now and Artie whistled.

When they left the zoo, Brenda glanced over her shoulder at her father, then climbed a heap of glacial boulders near the path. They sat down on a bench to watch her. Nelson hit Carol's leg and she hit him back.

Artie was annoyed with Harold for telling him in his superior way that he'd discovered Beatrice London, sweetly teaching homemaking. Harold had a way of implying that Artie made enemies needlessly. Nelsy, he said, let's have a race. See if you can beat me.

—I can't beat you, Nelson said.

—Maybe you can, Artie said. You're not like your father. He's a terrible tennis player. But maybe you can beat me at running.

—Cut it out, Harold said.

Carol walked slowly in Brenda's direction. She wore a blue cotton dress, and her head, above it, was small and cute.

—Come on, Nelsy, Artie said.

At last Nelson stood up to have a race. Artie chose the starting line and the finish, a bench a little distance down the path. Carol, Artie called, you're the referee. Make sure I don't cheat.

Carol smiled and waited. Artie did cheat, starting to run when Carol had called, On your mark, Get set, but not yet, Go. She had paused to let him, since he always did it. She shouted, You cheated, Daddy, you cheated!

—You got me, he said. Nelson didn't comment. He didn't get into position to run or even face front. Carol said, Go, and it took Nelson a while to get going. Artie couldn't run slowly enough to let Nelson win. Harold had taught the boy *nothing*! Artie loped to the bench when Nelson was halfway there. If it had been Carol, he would have staged an elaborate fall to let her get ahead of him, flopping on the ground, shocking passersby. But he stretched out his arm and touched the bench, yelling, I won, I won! He danced a little. Nelson stopped and put two or three fingers into his mouth.

—Nelson, Harold called.

Brenda came running from the rocks. Jumping off the last rock, she fell. She scrambled to her feet. Stop it, she screamed as she reached her father, crying and pounding his arm with her fists. I hate you, Daddy, I hate you.

—Where did you come from? Artie said. Nelson understands—boys have to learn, win or lose.

—I hurt my knee, Brenda said.

—Hurt your knee? You can't think of anything to say, you figure out you got hurt.

—I—don't—do—that! Brenda screamed; she shrieked. She sat down on the paving stones and pulled her skirt above her knee. It was bleeding. He's just a little kid, she sobbed.

Harold, still on the first bench, stood up. Let me see, Brenda. Ignoring his own child, who still stood with his fingers in his mouth, Harold went to Artie's daughter and reached out a hand to help her up. Brenda seized it, pulled, and with the momentum of rising fell forward, in tears again, against Harold's body.

—Would you just stop it? Artie shouted. She was too old for this. Adolf Hitler rose from the dead and killed you, is that the trouble?

—For God's sake, that is *enough*! Harold said. These are *children*. Come on, Brenda, let's go back to the zoo. You can wash your knee in the ladies' room. Carol will help you, won't you, Carol?

He was crouching, now, his legs straining his pants, examining Brenda's knee. There's a lot of gravel, he said.

—Oh, for heaven's sake! Artie said. He came up to them and brushed the gravel off Brenda's knee with his hand. I'm taking you home, he said.

—It's an hour on the subway, Harold said. Everyone's hungry. What's got into you?

Beatrice London. Artie couldn't stop. Well, you and your pathetic kid can go and dine in that case. Artie seized Brenda by the shoulder, knowing Carol would follow, and strode south to the subway.

Years earlier, Brenda's father had taken her to Central Park, also to the zoo, but by herself. Her mother had wanted Artie to stay home. It had something to do with a promise. Brenda didn't like hearing her parents shout.

They walked from their house to the elevated train station, but when they had climbed the steep staircase, Artie said, Did you bring money?

Brenda said, You brought money.

—I've got money for myself, said her father. Where's *your* money? He put a coin into the slot and went through the turn-stile. Brenda stood crying on the other side.

—You didn't bring money? he called. I guess you'll have to go underneath. Brenda was supposed to pay. She was six. The woman in the booth could see them. If she didn't pay, she could go to jail.

—Sometimes you have to be an outlaw, her father said. You're a city kid. Do what it takes.

An old woman came up the stairs, glared at her father, and put in money for Brenda. She took Brenda by the hand and led her through. The woman said, I don't know what that was all about. Little girl, is this your daddy?

—Yes, Brenda said. The old woman left them and went up to the FROM CITY platform, where she stared at them across the tracks. They climbed different stairs, under a sign reading TO CITY. Her father laughed. Little girl, is this your daddy? he asked her several times that day. Little girl, is this your daddy?

Today, Harold felt soft and firm at the same time, and fall-ing against him was like falling onto a bed or sofa, something else that was soft but would not give way. And when Brenda fell against Harold—she was almost too full of joy, too embarrassed, to let herself remember—he put his big hand on her shoulder. It was as if he said, I know, I know, and that was the look on his face when she turned, while her father steered them away. Harold stood still, looking after them, and Nelson had moved to the edge of the grass and stood with his back to them.

She was too old to cry in public, but she was more angry with her father than ashamed of herself. She was ashamed of him, as if she should have been able to keep him from taking advantage of Nelson. She'd learned early, playing with Harold's son, that you didn't take advantage. The girls in *Little Women* would not have done so either, and if they had, their mother would explain to them kindly that they must not.

The subway was far. Nobody spoke. Then her father said, *There once was a dad and his daughters . . .*

Long silence followed. Carol knew about limericks but couldn't make them up. But she was always ready to forgive. She tried, *They went to the zoo . . .*

Of course Brenda could make up a second line that would work with her father's, but she resisted as long as she could. Carol said again, *They went to the zoo . . .* Uh, *It was true . . .*

—Oh, for heaven's sake, Brenda said. That's not the way you do it. She recited:

> *There once was a dad and his daughters*
> *They were eight, and ten and three-quarters.*

She said it gruffly and hastily, suppressing the rhythm and her smile.

—*Very* good! Artie said, and Brenda knew that for once he had not succeeded in coming up with his own line. He quickly thought of the rest, though:

> *They went to the zoo*
> *Where they danced with the gnu*
> *And were interviewed by the reporters.*

—Get it, Caroly? he said, reaching to tickle her. Gggg-nu? What's new?

—I'm hungry, said Carol.

—There's a Schrafft's around here, Artie said. We'll have waffles.

Harold got to know Beatrice London when they were both assigned sixth-period cafeteria duty. Kids eating in sixth period had been made to wait too long for their lunch, and Harold—who had patrolled the cafeteria at all possible hours—thought sixth period was the most difficult. Being extra hungry made them more willing to throw food or fight.

Beatrice London was not a union member or at least not a member of the Teachers Union, which Harold belonged to. He had friends in the Teachers Guild—which had broken away from the Teachers Union because they believed it was dominated by Communists—who said they didn't think she belonged to that either. She was a tidy woman with small breasts and a little frown. She seemed old-fashioned: maybe she wore her skirts longer than other women did, or maybe it was her hair, which was short and curly and made her look naïve, like a girl in a musical comedy who misjudges everything in the first act but gets the man in the end.

He tried to remember just what Artie had said about Beatrice London, what his grievance had been. He probably expected her to find him delightful, and instead Beatrice had found him confusing. Walking in the aisles between the dirty tables in the cafeteria, her skirt swinging a little, her hands stiff at her sides, fingers spread as if she was afraid of touching something, Beatrice London was visibly conscientious, and maybe that was what seemed old-fashioned. Harold wanted to befriend her.

One day, easing from his end of the long room to hers, he said, I hear you teach home ec.

—That's right.

—What's it like, just teaching girls? Do you miss the boys?

She didn't stop her slow march, and he scrambled to walk next to her. She looked toward a table of boys as if she was only just now noticing boys. They were a little raucous, and Harold touched the nearest one on the shoulder, smiled, and said, Just keep it down, fellas.

—I have brothers, she said. I'm used to boys.

—My wife is having a baby, Harold said. We have a son and I'm hoping for a girl.

—That would be nice.

He gave a casual wave and returned to his end of the room, striding purposefully, as if he'd detected incipient trouble, but feeling uncomfortable. She was shy.

A week later, a food fight broke out at her end of the cafeteria, with the usual accompanying rumble of onlookers stamping their feet, and he hurried over. Before he arrived, Miss London clapped her hands, and when she was ignored, she walked between the disruptive boys. A handful of something brown landed on her back, and the boys quieted. Instead of scolding them, she made them stand at the side of the room. You too, she said to several other boys, who apparently had smiled—Harold couldn't tell. They were mostly Negro boys. She marched them into the kitchen, the brown stain noticeable on her white blouse, and then led them out again, each bringing a dishrag. Under her eye, the boys cleaned most of the cafeteria and were still cleaning when the period ended.

—Down on your hands and knees, Harold heard her say. A cafeteria worker came over with a mop, but she waved him away. Harold had gone back to his end of the room.

Later, one of his students said, That home ec teacher.

—Yes?

—She allowed to do that?

—I don't know, Harold said. He made up his mind to speak to her. She knew too well how to be cruel, but that was more reason to confront her, to help her. A new teacher could get into the habit of cruelty, and then she would be stuck.

Taking the train into the city one afternoon instead of going straight home, Harold found Beatrice London sitting opposite him, the *New York Times* folded in front of her with the crossword puzzle on top, a pencil in her left hand. He moved across to sit next to her.

—You're a lefty, he said.

She looked up, slightly alarmed. Harold Abramovitz, he said. Sixth-period lunch.

—I recognized you, she said. He glanced at the puzzle. He knew an answer, but some people didn't like help. She moved her left hand so it blocked the squares she'd filled in. Then she said, I've been wanting to ask you something.

He was pleased.

She said, Do you have a friend named Arthur Saltzman?

—Yes, yes I do! said Harold. It would give them a connection, and maybe he could go from talking about Artie to talking about dealing with obstreperous kids. Maybe she'd say what she hadn't liked about Artie, and he could reassure her. Artie wasn't easy, he could say truthfully, but he was worth it. He meant no harm. She might say Artie had teased her, and he could tell her about times when his friend had teased him. He could describe the recent time in Central Park when Artie had gotten Nelson to race and lose—but no, that would be *too* bad.

—What's he doing these days? Beatrice London asked.

Harold mentioned the junior high where Artie taught social studies. He said, He's quite a guy.

—He certainly is! said Beatrice London cheerfully, but then she stood up, putting her folded newspaper into a large purse. My stop. Nice to see you! and as the train doors opened, she hurried out, her head down, her free hand held stiffly, bent away from her body.

Artie preferred teaching current events to the established curriculum, and his students knew all about the investigations of Communists in the city schools, among other subjects, but he taught the expected units when pressed by his chairman—who liked him—on New York history or the five boroughs. He'd taken his classes to explore Staten Island and the Bronx, places they'd barely heard of. Once he failed to count and lost a child who lingered in the Museum of the City of New York when the rest of them had left. The boy asked directions, and when they got back, he was waiting on the front steps of the school. Artie hadn't missed him. He blamed the children, and after that assigned buddies, and yelled at the group if they lost track of their partners.

—That's not my job, he said, keeping track of you kids. My job is knowing and thinking. How am I supposed to keep you straight, just a lot of interchangeable children?

He'd test them. Okay, you, he'd say suddenly. Who's your buddy? Gary? Okay, which one is Gary? The kids teased him for not knowing their names and sometimes insisted they were who they were not. Once a class almost convinced him that a stranger was Gary.

Artie didn't remember their names, but he knew each child and worried about them until Evelyn knew them all too, though not by name. They'd be the Boy with the Dead Mother or the Girl Who Flunked Spanish. As Brenda grew older and learned to read, she had insisted that her father should learn the names of the children. She read his roll book and learned them herself. Naturally, Artie made it a game. Who's the kid who got sent to a psychiatrist? he said once.

—Lydia Maturo, Brenda said promptly.

—Artie, she shouldn't know that! Evelyn said. Nobody should know that! Carol's listening too.

—My kid has sense, Artie said. She won't go all over the neighborhood, talking, and if she did, what difference would it make? Lydia Maturo doesn't live around here. Carol is playing with her dolls—she's not paying attention.

B renda knew that Carol always paid attention. If you ever meet someone called Lydia Maturo, Brenda told her sister when they were alone, don't be surprised if she seems crazy. Someday there might be reason to use this piece of information. It could somehow help Brenda rescue Carol when a problem came along that Artie and Evelyn couldn't solve. Brenda knew that her mother often cried in the bathroom. Evelyn criticized Artie when he left his things around, told Brenda secrets, or didn't mark his students' papers until late at night.

Brenda thought it was unimportant that her father did these things. Her father could speak in the voice of a horse, and for years Brenda had not been certain that an invisible horse named Prancy didn't live under their kitchen table. Artie could sing and whistle and make up limericks; she herself had known how to make up a limerick since she was four. He had opinions about everything, from what her teacher did to what the president did. Sometimes he got so angry with the government that he screamed at her, his eyes flashing, as if it were all her fault.

As Brenda grew up, she tried to understand why her interesting father was boring, while her boring mother was interesting. Brenda would rather walk around the block with her mother than have an adventure with Artie, even though Artie's adventures involved distant subway lines, dusty museums, obscure parks with names he made up, like the Forest Primeval. When he got angry with her, they both shouted. Other people might notice, but only she was ashamed. Brenda valued her father's praise more than her mother's, though she never could learn anything he taught her, like tennis. His eye on her was thrilling. But even when Artie was angry, he was tiresome, and she eventually decided it was because though you couldn't guess in advance what he'd think up, once you knew, you knew what he'd say about it, and he'd insist so hard there was no room for conversation.

When Harold first became a teacher, he had avoided looking into his students' faces, especially the Negro children's faces. Boredom and hostility are easy to detect. He looked over their heads or out the big windows at the side of the room. When he joked, nobody laughed. By the end of each day his hands were covered with chalk dust, and when he smelled it on his body or clothes, he doubted everything he'd believed about the power of literature and his own power to teach it. He wanted to be a professor, teasing out the meaning of Hawthorne and James with graduate students. Instead, he taught *Green Mansions* and *The Mayor of Casterbridge*, books that existed only to be taught in high school.

One evening he was on the phone with Artie, who was telling a long story about his own students. Harold was bored but prolonged the conversation to avoid helping Myra with Nelson. He felt disloyal to his wife, his child, his friend, his work. For a man with a hardworking conscience, he noticed, he rarely did the right thing.

—So the little bastard stepped on my foot, Artie said. Still hurts.

—Why did he step on your foot?

—What I was just telling you. Unresolved conflicts with the bourgeois classes. He said he tripped.

Harold pictured the boy. Then he realized he was picturing not a stranger but one of his own students, a small, muscular Negro kid whom the others respected, though he was short, because he was fast and powerful. Artie's student was younger, of course—different from the boy Harold was thinking of, whose name was Elwin Hunt. But Harold continued to think of Elwin, lithe and swift—unlikely to trip over anything—tripping over Artie's foot, almost dancing onto Artie's foot.

—This kind of teaching, Harold said slowly. This kind of teaching, it's the most important thing there is.

He forgot Artie in the imagined sight of a boy he had been unwilling to look at but had apparently memorized, Elwin with his short legs and big feet and unlikely speed, his ears—the boy had big ears on a small head. Ears sometimes grew first.

—What are you talking about? Artie said.

—I'm doing what I should be doing, Harold said.

—And you think I'm not? Artie said. I told you to get a job with the Board of Ed for years. Now you're giving me a song and dance?

—No, no, Harold said. I was thinking aloud.

This was the work he was supposed to do, this was the work that joined his love of literature with his miserable greed for social justice. He got off the phone doubting himself. Maybe he'd be just as afraid on Monday.

He was not. He began to like the people he taught, these creatures between children and adults. He began to type stories and essays he found for them onto mimeograph stencils, then run them off. He learned how to get the mimeograph machine to work without tearing the stencils. By his second year he was famous for it: they'd call him when the machine jammed. He joked and cajoled his students until they cared about what he'd found.

Harold joined the Teachers Union, though everyone knew it was full of Communists, and he talked Artie into joining as well. The TU worked in the Brooklyn streets with poor kids, worked on integration, worked on civil liberties. The Teachers Guild, he said to Artie—the tamer union—was more interested in pensions.

The first time Artie went to the cabin without Harold—Harold and Myra now had part ownership and encouraged him and Evelyn to go—he made up his mind to learn to swim. Evelyn could swim a little, but though she loved the sounds and smells of the woods, she didn't like having to cook in the makeshift kitchen, and she seemed to hold the lake responsible. She took a brief, hasty swim each warm afternoon, as if it were required, then didn't get wet again. Artie, one eye on the girls, watched her while she splashed a few feet, out where the water came up to her neck. She made more noise than Harold did when he swam and produced more foam. She thrust her head in its white rubber bathing cap back and forth.

In anticipation of this week in the country, Artie had taken a book about swimming from the library, and he tried to persuade Evelyn to read it. Her sense of humor had become more acid with motherhood, and the way in which she found Artie's suggestion funny hurt his feelings.

—Okay, he said, you're the expert. I merely note that you can't swim ten yards without getting tired.

—I merely note that you can't swim at all, she said. So Artie decided he could teach himself to swim without getting the book wet, not an easy proposition. He forced himself to walk quickly into the cold lake because Evelyn was watching—or maybe he could even be seen by one of the people in the few quiet houses that now were spread around the lake—and leaned forward, gingerly putting his face in the water while holding his breath. Eventually he learned to turn his head to one side to take a breath and let it out under water. He dared to open his eyes. He practiced the flutter kick while holding onto the dock, to which a canoe was now tied. By the end of the week he could propel himself a few yards through the water.

The following year Artie and Evelyn paid Harold and Gus to

rent the cabin for two weeks in July, and that became their habit. Brenda especially loved it—well, they all loved it, but Brenda would disappear, walking as far as she dared, returning late, or she'd go into the woods with a book and not be seen for hours. Evelyn had learned to drive and announced that she'd never liked swimming in the lake, with its rocks and weeds. Schroon Lake village, a few miles away, had a sandy beach with life-guards. Artie insisted there was nothing like swimming in front of the cabin (I can dive from bed into the water! he said, though he couldn't dive), but on warm afternoons Evelyn slowly drove the girls down the long driveway and onto the paved road to Schroon Lake. She unfolded a canvas chair and watched Brenda and Carol, who ran in and out of the water and splashed around under the lifeguard's eye. Later, they walked up the hill, back to Route 9, and bought ice cream.

Harold, who could go to the cabin whenever he liked—he and Artie both had cars now—found that he disliked being there with Myra and Nelson. They seemed to pick the hottest days of the summer for their vacation, and though it was cool at night, the days were slow and lazy, the hum of insects reproachful. Myra loved sleeping in the sun, getting browner, and Nelson, as he grew, carried rocks into the water and brought them out again, but Harold wanted to walk long distances, wearing out his restlessness so he could write. A few times he went alone, in fall or spring, for a weekend, and then the cabin was all he had dreamed of, except that he felt guilty for leaving Myra alone in the city with Nelson. Sometimes the shouts of children from houses across the lake made him look up from his book and think wist-fully of his own child, who was more baffling and troublesome than children ought to be. Sometimes a fisherman's motorboat interrupted the dense, layered quiet, but then the quiet returned.

By the fall of 1951 Harold had long since learned to relax in the classroom, looking from one student to another, watching them think, watching them for the fun of it while they wrote or thought up answers to his questions. He caught himself making unconscious, habitual gestures, the kind students notice and laugh at, but he didn't care. He tapped his chalk excitedly on the blackboard, making little dots, and the students joked about how many little dots they'd earned. This year another kid had big ears: Kenneth Duggs, tall and difficult, bright, with small, tight features. Sometimes their noses grew even before their ears, but Kenneth's nose hadn't grown yet, and maybe it would stay as it was, made tiny by his ears. He had a dark-skinned, tense face that sometimes forgot itself and looked curious. Harold couldn't resist the curious ones.

One Saturday, early that fall, a police car moved on a group of boys loitering late in the evening, some on the sidewalk and some in the East New York street, and Kenneth Duggs was struck by the car—knocked over so his head hit a fire hydrant. He died later that night in the hospital. Harold would never find out if his nose would have grown, if he would have suppressed or indulged his curiosity. A student phoned him late that night. Awakened, astonished both by the news and the child's willingness to phone him, he began to cry. He put on his clothes, his hands shaking, and drove through the dark streets to the corner where a crowd was gathered, almost outnumbered by police cars. Harold stood at the edge of the crowd, in tears, for a long time. He saw no one he knew.

The papers carried the story the next day. The officer said he hadn't seen Kenneth with his dark skin and dark clothing, but witnesses said the street was bright with streetlights and headlights, and there was no reason for the car to move forward, certainly not so fast. On Monday, older teachers put their arms on Harold's shoulders and told him not to let the kids talk for too long about Kenneth's death. There was a ceremony in the auditorium, and Harold also went to the funeral, in a Negro church. The other teachers were almost as upset as Harold, but when neighborhood protests and marches kept happening—people wanted the officer brought up on charges—most of the teachers avoided the subject. Harold and his students talked of little else. They marched, they spoke out in impromptu meetings at churches. He found himself talking to their parents, drinking coffee in their kitchens. Harold was horrified and thrilled. The chairman of his department heard what he was doing and urged him to stop. I respect you for this, he said, but it's not a good idea.

Harold thanked him and went on to the meeting at the church, where he'd already agreed to speak, but he knew what the chairman meant. When Artie heard about it, he was exasperated.

—I'm taking a chance, yes, Harold said. But the boy—the boy is *dead*.

—Oh, stop sounding superior, Artie said. With your nefarious past . . .

—They don't even care if you've got a nefarious past, Harold admitted, once they get interested.

—So you need to be a hero?

Since the passage of the Feinberg Act by the New York State legislature two years earlier—subversive persons were to be eliminated from the teaching profession—the Board of Education had been investigating and firing teachers suspected of Communist ties.

Artie kept talking, moving on to the question of what Harold should say if he did get called in. Look, you quit the party years ago. Tell the truth, if anybody asks. You joined and you quit.

—It's not that simple, Harold said.

—Of course it's that simple. You wouldn't be a fool and take the Fifth, would you? Let some kind of crazy idealism ruin your life? People who do that have a death wish.

—Stop it, you don't mean that, Harold said.

—Of course I mean it.

Harold sighed. Why did they have to discuss this? You mean I'd name the people I knew? If it happened to you, you wouldn't do that.

—Of course I would, Artie said.

Harold knew he should get off the phone. Myra, heavily pregnant with their second child—and always testy because she didn't want to gain too much weight and ate as little as she could—was demanding tearfully that Nelson get out of the bathtub. If she got upset enough, she'd frighten him. He said, Nobody's asking me anything at the moment.

Teachers were accused of perjury if they denied membership in the Communist Party. If they admitted it, they were asked to name other Communists they'd known, and they were fired if they didn't. Harold knew quite a few teachers whom he'd known years ago in the party. He finally hung up. I'm going out for a paper, he called to Myra, and put on his coat, though he could hear Nelson crying now. Outside, feeling in his pocket for change, he found himself walking not toward the newsstand but toward the station. No, that made no sense. He went home without a paper, let himself in, and offered to read to Myra. She lay flopped on their bed, almost on her face, her dark red hair scattered, her belly to one side—it aroused him, the look of her big belly—and her nightgown hiked up around it. He read Edna Ferber aloud, starting at the top of the page where she'd left a bookmark. Harold had a girlfriend, but he had managed not to go and visit her.

Harold had been faithful to Myra for two years. One of the two women he was seeing at the time of his marriage worked at a magazine where he sometimes wrote and delivered book reviews. He was relieved when she changed jobs and he no longer knew her. The other was Naomi, the French teacher. She had found out soon enough about Myra and didn't mind seeing him anyway. But a few weeks before his wedding, she put a stop to it. I draw the line, she said.

Two years later he called her. She'd met a man, but when he proposed marriage, she had stopped seeing him, and whenever Harold turned up at Naomi's apartment in the Village and asked for tea or a drink, she let him in. She looked older, still with a tense line between her eyes, and it was hard not to rub it away with his thumb. Sometimes he did. Naomi was unshocked by sex but surprised, each time, at how pleasurable it was. I don't see why people think they should do this with only one person, she said, in bed one afternoon, a rainy afternoon when Harold had come from the library. We don't talk with just one person. We don't eat with just one person.

—So you no longer draw a line, Harold said.

—Yes, I have become depraved. You must lead your life as seems best to you.

On the way home he'd pick her hairs off his clothes. Naomi shed.

Myra accused him of sleeping with other women, becoming hysterical, but she'd always done that. Artie, who knew some facts, was disgusted. Harold had always suspected that Myra continued to see Gus Maloney, and he minded less than he thought he should. He liked knowing the cabin was his—almost his—so much that he didn't care what it took to have it. Myra didn't go there with Gus, he was sure of that; now and then she was mysteriously elsewhere, but only for a couple of hours. People need to live, Harold said to himself. He didn't have daydreams of being with women—women were a responsibility—but of being alone at the cabin, writing and reading and taking walks, looking up to watch a bird or a boat, looking down again at a book.

*A*lger Hiss, Harold wrote on the blackboard in his large loopy handwriting. This was a class of juniors—Kenneth's class—and all he was sure about concerning the day's lesson was that he would not talk about Kenneth. Underneath *Alger Hiss* he wrote *Whittaker Chambers*. Which name sounds like the bad guy? he asked. The class had been discussing *A Tale of Two Cities*. Harold wanted them to think about words themselves; he talked about the taste of words, and the kids laughed tolerantly. He made each of ten students read the famous first sentence of Dickens's novel aloud: *It was the best of times, it was the worst of times, it was the age of wisdom, it was the age of foolishness, it was the epoch of belief, it was the epoch of incredulity* . . . Meanwhile, Harold pounded out the rhythm on the desk and shouted the repeated words. When he began listing the characters, the students were quick to see that Jerry Cruncher and Mr. Stryver resembled their names, but it was harder for them to hear anything in the names Charles Darnay, Sydney Carton, and Madame Defarge, even though Harold stretched it out ominously—Madahhhhme Defahhhhge . . .

So he wrote *Alger Hiss* and *Whittaker Chambers*, not sure how much the students would know about them, and asked his question.

—But that's not fair! shouted Harvey Edelstein, the shortest boy in the class and often the hardest to teach because he knew so much and couldn't keep quiet. Harvey had no sense of nuance. He waved his hand back and forth, supporting his raised arm with his other hand, leaning forward at his desk.

Harold didn't want to talk about the innocence or guilt of Alger Hiss and Whittaker Chambers, he wanted to talk about their names, about the emotional effect of sound. But he couldn't control the boy. His hand still raised, Harvey said, It's unfair because you mean Hiss sounds like the name of the bad guy, just because when you hiss, that means something is bad—but Hiss isn't guilty. Chambers is the bad guy, Hiss shouldn't be in prison right now!

—Do the rest of you know what he's talking about? said Harold with a sigh. He put it as briefly and objectively as he could, explaining that Whittaker Chambers was someone who admitted that he used to be a Communist and claimed first that he knew Alger Hiss, and then that Alger Hiss was not only a Communist but a Soviet spy. He mentioned Hiss's position in the Roosevelt administration. He decided to leave out the Pumpkin Papers (though Chambers's concealment of papers that allegedly incriminated Hiss in a hollowed-out pumpkin was a delicious piece of the story), and just said that Hiss had insisted he wasn't a Communist or a spy, that he was tried twice for perjury, and that the second time he'd been convicted and sent to prison.

—Now, the learned Mr. Edelstein, Harold continued, gesturing grandly toward Harvey, has anticipated my admittedly lame point, which is that the name Hiss sounds bad. Maybe that's too simple an example. Hisssss, he said. He wrote *onomatopoetic* on the board. And doesn't Chambers sound good? Chaaaaymbers, he said, Darnaaaay. Doesn't the sound give you a confident, happy feeling? Some students looked interested, others confused. Whittaker! Harold said then. Could a bad guy be named Whittaker? Whittaker, whittaker, whittaker—it sings!

—So you think Whittaker Chambers is right because he has a nice name? Harvey said.

—No, Harvey, Harold said, his chalk pointing straight at Harvey's bright brown eyes. I think if they each had the other's name, Harold said, Alger Hiss would be a free man today.

One of the front-row girls giggled. But then he wouldn't be him, he'd—

He could not make himself clear today! I mean, he said, the

man we call Alger Hiss would be free if his name was Whittaker Chambers. The jury had to decide who to believe, and they couldn't believe a man with a name like Hiss. It's deep in our consciousness—the lying serpent in the Bible.

In fact, this was Artie's argument. Artie was the one in love with the names. Both Artie and Harold assumed Hiss was innocent—everyone they knew thought Hiss was innocent—but Harold was more likely to blame the guilty verdict on the benightedness of the American public and the craziness of the congressman who'd made it his cause, Richard Nixon.

—But, Mr. Abramovitz, do you think Hiss is guilty? Harvey Edelstein asked now.

—That's not for me to say, Harold said, and the bell rang. The class filed out. He was free this period—the fourth—and would sit at his desk and eat the lunch he'd brought from home. He started to erase the board as the woman who taught next door stuck her head in.

—What did you think of that memo? she said.

Harold shook his head. The assistant principal was an old reactionary, and this woman—a union member like himself—was infuriated by his insinuations and demands, and she liked to relieve her rage by analyzing his awkward sentence structure. Harold had only glanced at this latest note to the faculty.

—Alger Hiss! she interrupted herself. What the hell are you teaching?

Harold looked over his shoulder at the blackboard. Dickens, he said. It all made sense—one of the kids even thinks I'm a Commie hunter.

—Erase it anyway, she said.

—That's what I was doing. As he turned to erase the board while she glanced again at the offending memo, she said, Been meaning to tell you something. Speaking of Whittaker Cham bers. I heard you've been making friends with his female counterpart.

—Heard from who? said Harold. He was alarmed at the word *female*. Could she somehow have heard about Naomi? This teacher was a nice married woman. She would hate him.

—London? she said. What did I hear—you're in cafeteria patrol with her? Be careful.

He relaxed. The home ec teacher? She's one of those sweet women who's going to turn herself into a little despot because she's scared to be nice. I'm just trying to give her a little advice.

—I wouldn't be so sure she's a sweet woman, his friend said. There are some bad rumors around.

Was Beatrice London a famous loose woman? Did Harold's friend think he'd seduce the likes of Beatrice London? It was absurd and annoying. He sat down and took out his tuna sandwich, and she said, Got to talk to the office about a kid, and hurried away.

To Artie's surprise, Evelyn decided to invite Harold's family to come for supper on a Saturday. He didn't like Myra and he knew Evelyn didn't like her either. But Evelyn thought she should invite them, and when Evelyn thought that, things happened. It took a few tries to set the date, and by the time they came, Myra was almost ready to give birth. Evelyn made a roast. Myra came into their apartment a little ahead of Harold and Nelson and sank into the chair near the door, rubbing her belly. She said, I thought we might have to cancel, but it was a false alarm. Then Harold and Nelson came in, holding hands and looking around shyly, as if they were both six.

Myra looked good—stylish, no less, in a loose brown coat— even though she was nine months pregnant and was leaning sideways in her chair in an awkward way. Evelyn! she said in a firm voice, deeper than the voice Artie remembered. It's good to see you. Thank you for inviting us.

Politeness was big with Evelyn, and Artie knew that direct thank-you would look classy to her. Evelyn liked finding reasons to think well of someone. She stepped forward in her apron and leaned to kiss Myra's cheek. Together, they made a soft, pretty shape.

—So Nelsy, what's new? Artie said to the little boy. Sit down, sit down. It was a couple of months since their race in Central Park, and he wondered if Nelson remembered.

—For heaven's sake, take their coats! Evelyn said, and everyone stood again. She gathered the coats and thrust them into Artie's arms.

They had no hall closet. He laid them on the bed. Evelyn self-consciously offered drinks, and Brenda stood in the doorway, with Carol behind her, looking at Harold and Nelson, who were still squeezed close together, with Nelson leaning on his father's legs.

—You girls want to show Sir Nelson some of your stuff? Artie said.

—I want to stay here, Brenda said.

—Sir Nelson! Carol liked that. She ran into their room, emerged with the checkerboard, and set it up at Harold's feet, explaining as she worked. Nelson was prevailed upon to play, leaning against Harold's well-polished shoe.

—So, Nelson, Artie said, are you for the Dodgers? What about that game? Tragic! He meant the play-off game with the Giants, which the Dodgers had lost at the last minute.

Nelson didn't answer, but after a while he got interested in the checkers game and bounced on his knees with pleasure when he took Carol's checkers. When they lost interest in winning, they made piles of checkers, then knocked them down. Then

Myra heaved herself to her feet and brought her drink into the kitchen, and Artie said, What happened at the church?

—The meeting about the cop? I went.

—What's going to happen? Artie said.

Harold shrugged. Probably nothing. It wouldn't bring Kenneth back anyway.

—So, in that case, Artie said, what are you knocking your brains out for?

Harold turned his glass around as if examining it for defects, then sipped. I couldn't tell you, he said.

—You're crazy, Artie said lightly.

—Let's forget it for one night, Harold said. Brenda, what are you doing in school these days?

—Just regular, Brenda said.

—She's in a play, said Artie.

Brenda said, I'm Benjamin Franklin. It's about the Declaration of Independence.

—Do you mind playing a man? Harold said.

—The whole thing is dumb, said Brenda, but speaking of school reminded Harold of his recent efforts to teach *A Tale of Two Cities*. His students, he told Artie, had thought Sydney Carton was a fool to die for Charles Darnay. Especially because it was the guillotine, he said.

—I'd rather be in a play about that, Brenda said, and left the room, following Evelyn and Myra into the kitchen.

She had to force herself to leave the room. She wanted to stay and figure out a way that Harold would hold her as he had in Central Park, the day he had a fight with her father. Today, Nelson had leaned against him as if he was sure Harold's legs would not move, and that was something to envy, though she would not want to be Nelson, and not just because she'd have to be six again. Since that bad day at the zoo, Brenda had a story she told herself late at night. She ran away from someone evil, who chased her. Harold waited, his arms wide, and Brenda ran into them. He closed his arms around her and walked to a river, then carried Brenda across. The water came up to his knees and then his waist. On the opposite side, Harold sat down and Brenda leaned against him.

It was more painful to talk to Harold and know that maybe he wouldn't pick her up and carry her across that river—maybe he'd be too busy with Nelson—than to walk out of the room. But walking out of the room was not a simple matter.

In the kitchen, her mother snapped the tips off string beans at the table while Myra slouched against the wall. So he broke it on purpose? Myra was saying.

—Not exactly, said Evelyn, glancing at Brenda. No, not on purpose.

—Then what? Myra said, but her mother didn't answer. Would you like to help, honey? she said. She gave Brenda the bowl of string beans and began taking plates out of the cupboard. The good dishes were on a high shelf.

Adult conversation was sometimes mysterious, not because she didn't understand but because Brenda didn't know why it mattered or how it could possibly not matter. Adult unhappiness—she came to the word *unhappiness* only for a moment, then forgot it—was unlike her own. Brenda felt so different from the two women in the kitchen that it seemed she could laugh or cry and they wouldn't notice or wonder why.

She asked Myra, What are you going to name your baby?

—It's a secret, Myra said.

—Why? She had a feeling it hadn't been a secret until she asked. Can I guess? Will you tell me if I guess?

—Can she go play? Myra said.

—I want her to help, her mother said. So she stayed but didn't try to guess the baby's name. Her mother didn't care about the string beans—she could have done them in a minute. Maybe she liked to show Myra that Brenda helped, or maybe she didn't want to hear what Myra would say if Brenda went away. Brenda tried to think how to find out what that was.

Then Myra said, Harold said he lent Artie that record. I'm supposed to remember to ask for it back.

—I didn't mean he broke it on purpose, Evelyn said.

—Oh, I know. I know what you mean.

—He could have . . .

—I know.

—They have a funny way of being friends, Evelyn said.

—I know, I know.

Brenda let the bowl of string beans fall on the floor, not quite on purpose, so as to see what that would be like. It did feel like something her father might do.

—Oh, God, I don't have another vegetable, her mother said.

—Wash them off. Myra roused herself in this emergency, and when Evelyn had picked up the string beans and brushed them off on her apron, Myra put them into a strainer and washed them thoroughly. The incident woke Myra up. She said, When I was a kid this kind of thing happened all the time, and your floor is cleaner than ours ever was. Don't worry about it, Brendy.

Evelyn stopped what she was doing and watched Myra wash the string beans, flicking each one quickly between her long fingers. She said, When you go to the hospital, I'll take care of Nelson.

—I wasn't worried, Brenda said. She liked being called Brendy. Her mother didn't like nicknames, but her father sometimes said Brenny. I have to go to the bathroom, she said then, and used that as an excuse to go into the bedroom and read until it was time to eat. Carol was still playing with Nelson on the living room rug. They were now building something using checkers, Tinkertoys, and their shoes and socks, while the fathers shouted about McCarthy, a name she heard often. The broken record, whatever it meant, seemed to have been forgotten. Harold didn't notice her walk through the room. Having him sit on the green squashy sofa in her house, his big hands on his fat knees, was unbearable.

Harold's parents were supposed to take care of Nelson when Myra had to go to the hospital, but when she went into labor, his father was in bed with a sore throat.

—Evelyn offered to keep him, Myra said. She was repacking the bag she'd already packed for the hospital, leaning forward at intervals and holding her belly. She looked scared, young without makeup. It was Saturday morning, and she'd begun having contractions in the night. Harold was scared too. He hadn't been this scared when Nelson was born, but he hadn't known how important—if difficult—Nelson would be. Now he worried about all three: Myra, the baby, and Nelson, as if the poor kid had to go and be born a second time.

He disliked leaving Nelson with his parents; the boy puzzled Harold's mother, and that made Harold feel responsible. Harold was angry with Myra daily but had never been angry with Nelson. Myra hated having Nelson lean on her constantly, but Harold liked having that loosely jointed body pressed into his own—and yet it made him uncomfortable, as if children weren't supposed to love their parents, which was absurd. He knew he resisted Nelson.

When he dialed Artie's number, Evelyn answered and readily agreed to have Nelson stay with them. She said, He can sleep on pillows in the girls' room, and Harold said no, he'd pick him up in the evening, before going home himself. Spending the day away from his parents would be hard enough for Nelson.

Off the phone, he called, Come on, big boy. Uncharacteristically, Nelson had been playing alone in his room. You're going to visit Carol and Brenda.

—You too? Nelson said, coming out with a toy truck in his arms.

—I've got to take Mommy to the hospital. Today's the day when you get a little brother or sister.

—I don't need one, Nelson said.

Harold looked at his rumpled son. He was tall for his weight, and his clothes were invariably too short or too loose, though Myra tried, spending more than Harold would have thought necessary. Today his pants were too short and were also twisted in an odd way. Don't you have a belt? Harold said, picking Nelson up and trying to sort him out. Let's bring some toys.

Nelson agreed to go to Carol and Brenda's house when Harold emptied the briefcase he used for teaching and put toys into it. The boy looked comical tugging the thing. Harold hurried him into the car. When he drew up to the curb in front of the two-family house on Van Siclen Avenue where Artie lived, he beeped the horn lightly, rather than take the time to go in. Myra was in the passenger seat, her head down. She hadn't spoken since they left the house, except to say "Damn it God damn it!" a few times. He lifted Nelson out of the back seat and set him on the curb as Evelyn came out. She looked as if she had something to say, and Harold tried to think what he'd do if she'd changed her mind, but she said only, Hi, Nelson. She straightened up, looked hard at Harold, who was setting the briefcase on the sidewalk next to Nelson, and then said, How's Myra?

—Is something wrong? Harold said.

—It can wait. Go.

—I want to go with you! Nelson said, clutching his father's leg. Evelyn looked at Harold, who was helpless. She pried Nelson's hands off his leg. He'll be fine, she said. We bought a television set. He can watch with the girls.

Nelson was screaming as she carried him inside, leaving the briefcase on the sidewalk. Harold didn't want to lose it. He'd been using it since college. He was annoyed with himself for thinking of something so trivial with his new child on the way.

—Harold! Myra said sharply, and he put aside thoughts of Nelson and his property. They had to drive over the river—the hospital was in Manhattan.

H arold and Myra's new child, Paul, wasn't born until one in the morning, and Nelson spent the night at Artie and Evelyn's, in Carol's pajamas. Evelyn scolded Harold on the phone for not putting anything but toys into that bag. Of course they had retrieved the bag. This was in the first phone call, when it was ten o'clock at night and there was no baby and Harold couldn't leave. This possibility had not occurred to him.

Evelyn said, He's already asleep. I talked him into it.

—Is he all right?

—He's all right, she said. Things aren't so good here, but he's fine. I won't lie to you and tell you he ate anything but mashed potatoes.

After he got off the phone and was stuck in the waiting room again, Harold remembered the way Evelyn looked when she came out of the house all those hours earlier; something was wrong.

At last a nurse brought Paul to him. Harold took the new boy in his arms, looked at his creased, mottled face, and experienced unalloyed joy for the first time in his life. He would still love Nelson. He would not love him any less, and he did love him, if with backward, upside-down love. Paul was not superior to Nelson—he was a shriveled blob of a kid at present—but Harold (oddly, he thought of Kenneth Duggs) had somehow learned to care when he should care. The kind nurse sneaked him in to kiss Myra, but after that, Harold had to tell someone, and he called Artie from a pay phone in the hospital lobby. This time he answered. We have a son, we have a new son, Harold said, choking back tears.

—You woke me up, Artie said.

—I'm sorry. I had to tell you.

—Nothing wrong with girls, Artie said. Harold could hear Evelyn in the background saying, It's a girl?

—No, Artie said, now to Evelyn. Not a girl. Another boy. Nothing wrong with our girls. He's showing off, having boys.

—Give me the phone! she said, and her voice became loud and happy. Harold, honey, that's wonderful! A boy! Everything's all right? Forgive Artie, he's upset, but he'll be fine.

—I won't be fine, he heard Artie say. Harold didn't have time for one of his friend's elaborate grievances. Of course there was nothing wrong with girls—the point was, Paul was a healthy baby. Harold had thought he wanted a girl, but he now knew that Paul was the baby he had wanted. He felt an ease he didn't recognize, walking to his car and driving through the dark streets, which seemed simpler: supernatural traffic engineers had widened and straightened them in the hours Harold had been in that waiting room. It was easy to travel home, and he parked on his silent block, where everything looked subtly different.

The next morning Harold woke up later than he'd intended and drove straight to Artie and Evelyn's. Maybe he'd just visit Nelson; maybe he'd bring him along. He wondered if Artie might come with him and stay with Nelson in the waiting room while Harold went to see Myra. Maybe the nurses would let him sneak Nelson in.

Brenda opened the door. Congratulate me, Brenda, I'm a daddy again, Harold said, and held out his hand. Brenda took it. Her hand quivered in his, and he had a sudden sense of her distinctness as a person, her keenness. And here came Nelson, laughing because Carol was holding him back. He fastened his arms around Harold's leg.

—We're in the kitchen, Evelyn called. She was reliably friendly, which made Artie easier to take. She was not pretty, and that made her seem even more trustworthy. Her eyes were too close together, but they looked straight at Harold. Sit down, she said. How's Myra?

Artie was at the table with coffee, buttering a roll, scattering crumbs. Harold sat, pulling Nelson onto his lap. Artie looked down at his coffee, and so Harold looked again at Evelyn. To his surprise, she looked away. What's wrong? he said. What did my kid do?

—It's not your kid, Artie said. Look at this. He stood up. Ev, where's that letter?

—In the living room. Just tell him.

—All right, I'll tell him. I got a letter.

—A letter?

—From the Board of Ed.

—From the Board of Ed? said Harold, baffled, and then he understood. It couldn't be. It was terrible—how could something terrible happen today? He put Nelson on the floor and put his hands on the Formica table as if for balance. Artie, he said. Then, They called you in?

—In three weeks. The assistant superintendent.

—Oh my God, Harold said. Oh my God. What are they going after *you* for?

Teachers were made to come to the Board of Education and were asked if they belonged to subversive organizations. Artie could truthfully say no, but then he'd be asked if he knew other teachers who were Communists. If he refused to answer either question, he'd be suspended. Next came what they called trials, and the teachers were fired.

Harold had thought it wouldn't happen to Artie, it wouldn't even happen to him. There were so many lefty teachers, mostly Jews, City College graduates like them. Everyone knew Communists in the thirties, when joining the party hadn't been extraordinary. He and Artie weren't officers in the Teachers Union. There was no way even these fanatics could hunt down everyone in the school system who had Communist sympathies or who knew Communists, and it had seemed probable that he and Artie—especially Artie—would be overlooked. He couldn't imagine what had brought him to their attention.

Nelson climbed back into his lap, and Harold put his arms around him, rocking him gently back and forth. He had to get to Myra. Artie glared. His black eyes glinted with rage, and he tore his roll into pieces and rolled the pieces into crumbs. Then Artie shoved the crumbs toward the center of the table and put his face down and sobbed.

—Don't, Harold said.

—I'm not going to save your ass, Artie said. He was crying like a child, and Nelson whimpered. Artie stood. His face was red and his black hair flopped on his forehead as it often did. Wait a minute, he said, and hurried out of the kitchen.

—Daddy? Nelson said.

—What is it, honey?

—Did Mommy die?

Harold stood. He carried his boy to the window that looked out on the ordinary Brooklyn street, where a car drove by and a man walked a dog. No, baby, no, Mommy's fine. We'll go see her in the hospital. You know you've got a brother?

—What's his name? Nelson said.

Harold heard water running in the bathroom. Paul, he said.

—Will Paul take away my toys?

—No, baby, Paul can't play with toys yet. Don't worry about your toys.

—I brought the truck and Laddy and the horse, but I forgot some other toys. Can we go home now?

Artie came back. His face looked damp and his hair was slicked down, which made his nose look big. I gotta talk to you, he said.

—Come to the hospital with me, Harold said. I was going to ask you—if you'd stay with Nelson while I go in. I don't think they'll let me take him into Myra's room, but maybe if he just sees the place, he'll calm down.

Artie looked suspicious. I'll ask Ev, he said, and left the room again.

—Let's pack my toys, Daddy. Nelson had climbed out of his arms and tugged him toward the children's room, and Harold followed awkwardly.

—I told you, you'll talk to the union representative, he heard Evelyn saying. They were in their bedroom. Don't just assume—

—He wants me to come with him, Artie said.

—Where? To the hospital?

—I could stay with the kid when he goes in.

—Go, Evelyn said. Together, you'll figure something out.

Brenda was reading on her bed. She looked up and then down again at her book. Mind if I come in? said Harold. He pointed. The floor was strewn with toys.

Carol began filling Harold's briefcase with Nelson's belongings. As Harold shifted on the linoleum, trying to help, he realized that Artie was behind him in the doorway, whistling, and though Harold couldn't see him, he knew that Artie stood with his arms folded, rocking back and forth over the wooden door-sill. He whistled an insistent jazz melody.

In the car they discussed the best route to the city but then were silent. A gritty, cold rain began to fall, just frozen enough to make a click on the windshield. In the backseat, Nelson sang, inaudibly at first. Then Harold heard some of it:

> *I went in the car because Mommy died*
> *Mommy didn't die, she didn't die*
> *I went in the car because the baby died*
> *I went in the car because Daddy died*

Artie said, Look here.

—What?

—Time after time I told you joining the party was asinine. Now, just because I know you, I have to lose my job?

—You won't lose your job, Harold said. He hadn't seen the letter, he found himself thinking, and for a moment he found himself wondering why Evelyn and Artie would invent such a story when only his baby mattered.

—It's not right.

—Look, it's a mistake. Probably somebody else with the same name. The union will figure it out, Harold said. You never fooled around with this stuff—this is crazy.

—The union isn't going to solve it. I don't know how this happened, but you know as well as I do there's only one possible outcome where I don't lose my job.

—Which is? Harold resisted the temptation to look at him. He was a careful driver.

—Which is simple. Which is that I tell them I wasn't a Communist, and when they ask, I say I know someone who was and his name is Harold Abramovitz.

Harold's hands clenched on the wheel. You could lie.

—Lie about what?

—Tell them you were never a Communist and you don't know anybody who was ever a Communist.

Artie gestured so wildly that Harold was afraid he'd grab the steering wheel. For crying out loud! he said. You want me to perjure myself? How many people in this city know I know you? They probably already know you were a Communist, or they'll find out from some other sucker. The only way to save my job is to tell them the truth, and Harold, I love my job. Again, he sounded as if he might sob. They were nearing the approach to the bridge, then they were on the bridge, and Harold looked around for something distracting.

—I'm a good teacher, Artie said, as the skyline, gray in the weather, opened around them: its chaos and charm, with boats and the Statue of Liberty to one side, and before them the irregular shapes and shades of gray of Manhattan's haphazard architecture, the simplicity of the Empire State Building. Artie went on, It's the only thing I'm good at. He paused. I'm sorry.

Harold drove over the noisy floor of the bridge and into Manhattan. If that's how you feel, he said. Harold loved his job too, and now he had two children, and Myra couldn't work with a tiny baby in the house. If he lost his job she'd never forgive him; he couldn't imagine what she'd do. Myra thought people who cared too much about politics and ideology were fools. She'd leaned into him the night before, when he'd finally been allowed to go to her. I wanted a girl, she said. Harold knew that was true, but she'd never said it before. Did you see the baby?

—He's perfect, Harold said. He'll make everything good. Now as he drove through the quiet Sunday streets, he tried to regain the sense of being complete that Paul had bestowed on him. To his surprise, he found he could. His life would go well no matter what happened. Artie, he said. We won't let this make us enemies. You do what you need to do.

—Don't give me that, said Artie.

Myra missed Nelson—they wouldn't let him in—and worried about Paul. She no longer minded that he wasn't a girl. A nurse had tried to persuade her to breastfeed, and the suggestion made Myra frantic. You don't want me to do that, do you? she asked Harold, and he didn't know what the right answer was.

—He'll be fine, whatever you do, he said. The baby—heavier than Nelson had been at birth, and round where Nelson had been elongated—slept sturdily, his thumb in his mouth.

Myra said, The doctor said it's unusual that he learned to suck his thumb in the womb. He's smart.

Paul might or might not be smart, but Harold admired his capacity—even before he saw light and people, before he knew what he was—to figure out what his body could do for him. He wondered if Paul had also masturbated in the womb.

During the elevator ride back to Artie and Nelson—an interval between Myra's fretful delight and Nelson's anxiety, Artie's rage—Harold had a free moment, thinking of nothing but the numbers of the floors, and something made him think of the woman who taught next door to him. She had said Beatrice London resembled Whittaker Chambers. That was how she'd gotten to the topic of Beatrice London. Beatrice London wasn't a sexual threat; that wasn't what she meant. Beatrice London was an informer. He'd heard of them—former Communists who named names and sometimes made claims that were completely fabricated. Beatrice London could have told the Board of Ed that Artie was a Communist just because she had never liked him. And Harold himself had provided Beatrice London with the information she needed: that Artie worked for the school system.

Sitting in the waiting room, Artie—who was still reliving the Dodgers' loss to the Giants in the play-off game for the pennant—tried to explain the Dodgers' lineup to Nelson, leading up to the decision to pitch Ralph Branca, who gave up the winning home run to Bobby Thomson. He couldn't tell if Nelson understood. Nelson stared at him, his nose running. Artie looked up and saw Harold coming from the elevator. As his friend took out his handkerchief to wipe Nelson's nose, Artie stood, said, So long, fella—touching the boy's shoulder—then, to Harold, I'll take the subway home. He turned toward the door, buttoning his coat. Harold called after him, but he kept going, out into the street.

At home, Artie walked into the living room, sat down, and picked up the paper. Evelyn was startled when she walked through the room. I didn't hear you come in! How's the baby?

He didn't answer and didn't say anything more that day, even when Evelyn got angry or when Carol made a joke of it. Daddy, I'm going to jump out the window if you don't tell me not to, okay? Well, I guess you want me to jump out the window!

Brenda, who understood more, pulled her away. Artie was too upset not to scream and shout if he spoke, but he also found not speaking an interesting game. He'd have to talk the next day at school but maybe not until then. Evelyn stopped speaking to him when he didn't answer her, but she put food on the table.

Walking into his school the next day, he looked at the ordinary, ugly reminders that this was a New York City public school: the warning against trespassing signed by William Jansen, Superintendent of Schools (who was caught up in the investigation of suspected Communists and Communist sympathizers, and had questioned the first accused teachers himself); the tiled corridors with signs denoting the basement as an air-raid shelter; the clock and window pole in his classroom, with a hook at the end; the big windows with their many panes. The American flag hung on its pole near the door, and at the shrill sound of the bell, children appeared, walking close to the walls on either side of the corridors while teachers stood in the center.

Artie wordlessly accepted a parent's note explaining a child's absence, then handed over the bathroom pass, also without speaking. He'd have to lead his pupils in the Pledge of Allegiance—someone might notice if he didn't—and he thought he would scream if he had to start speaking by asserting his fidelity to a country about to betray him: to mistake his stubborn, cynical, unsentimental but undeviating loyalty for disloyalty, for foolishness, for an organized opposition to law that would not have interested Artie, even if he hadn't found Communism boring from the start.

—Rochelle, he said to a girl whose loose-leaf binder had slipped onto the floor, pick up your notebook. He had spoken and could mumble the Pledge of Allegiance.

Two weeks later, and a week before the day he'd appear at the Board of Ed, Artie—who now spoke to his family but became irate if somebody wanted more of him than monosyllabic replies—went to New York to consult with someone from the union, which was providing him with a lawyer. The headquarters was on West Fifteenth Street. Listen, he said to the woman who greeted him, extending her hand to shake his, It has to be a mistake. I'm not a Communist. I was never a Communist.

—I wish I could tell you that's going to make a difference, she said. They talked, and he walked glumly back to the subway. When he changed trains at Delancey Street, he noticed Harold walk onto the train ahead of him. He sat down without seeing Artie, and Artie didn't go over to him. But Harold must have spotted him. As they crossed the Williamsburg Bridge he came over and laid his heavy hand on Artie's shoulder. Are we speaking? he said, sitting down.

The river sparkled in winter sunlight, and Artie automatically noted, through the spotted window behind Harold's head and across the aisle, buildings he looked at whenever he crossed to Brooklyn.

—My friend, Harold said.

—How's the baby?

—The baby is fine. The baby sleeps and eats. The big brother wets the bed, but the baby is fine.

—It figures, Artie said. Where are you coming from? Like him, Harold must have gone into the city after school.

Harold looked uncomfortable, then said, The Forty-second Street library. It was possible—he'd come from the West Side if he got on at Delancey—but the pause made Artie know he was lying.

—Oh, for Christ's sake! he said. You got a two-week-old baby at home—you're playing the field already?

—Don't be silly, Harold said, but he self-consciously refolded his afternoon paper—the *World Telegram and Sun*—pressing the edges crisp as if that was important.

—I know, I know, one of your old pals, Artie said. I'm not accusing you of picking up prostitutes in Hell's Kitchen. Or wherever you guys pick up prostitutes.

—I don't know, Harold said, smiling.

—Oh, go to hell, Artie said.

—I probably will, Harold said. Do Jews believe in hell?

The train crossed the bridge and clattered slowly through Williamsburg. Nobody ever told me, Artie said. My parents were more interested in making a little hell on earth. He was shocked yet again at Harold, at the difference between them.

—I know what you mean, Harold said. For a moment they were silent. The train, which continued to run above the ground after the bridge, bumped to a stop, the doors opened, and people got on, bringing cold air and noise. The doors rattled closed and the train moved on. Artie studied the buildings next to the train: window shades, a plant, sometimes an empty room, once a head and shoulder as a woman turned. They came to Eastern Parkway.

—Mr. Saltzman, Harold said in his deepest voice, Are you now or have you ever been a member of the Communist Party? It was a game.

—No, Artie said, without expression.

The doors opened. People got off and others got on.

—And do you support any organizations that advocate the overthrow of the United States government by force and violence?

—No, Artie said. You know I never did.

—I know, Harold said, in his ordinary voice. Then in the deep voice, And do you know anyone now teaching in the New York City schools who is or has ever been a member of the Communist Party?

Artie paused for a long time. The doors closed. The train pulled out of Eastern Parkway. Yes, he said.

They reached Van Siclen Avenue. Harold would stay on for one more stop. Artie stood up and edged past him. Harold looked up. I think you mean it, he said. I'm not going to blame you.

—Blame me, Artie said, before he slammed his hat on his head, left the train, and walked into the chill of the wind on the platform. Would you just blame me for once, you self-righteous bastard?

You're not thinking, Evelyn said.

—How do you know whether I'm thinking? I think inside my head.

—I know whether you're thinking or not. They were walking from the train station after a visit to Artie's parents on Sunday. He'd barely spoken. The girls, in red boots, walked through puddles ahead of them. This isn't what you want, Artie, Evelyn said. Wind blew in his face. The rain had stopped, but the air was wet and his nostrils hurt.

—I know what I want. His summons to the Board of Ed was now three days away. He had not told his family, though she'd urged him to. His immigrant parents would not understand and would be stricken with woe and fear. Evelyn plodded through the wet at his side, head down, clutching a scarf closed at her neck, an umbrella in her other hand. His mother had offered food, his brothers had argued.

—Artie, she said, you were never a Red. Neither was I. But these people—McCarthy, and these people in New York who are just as bad. They don't understand why people joined the party. You didn't join, but you *might* have. I almost did.

—Well, that's where you're wrong, he said, and his rage made him sound as if she was the enemy. I never put any stock in those fools. Harold and I—we argued all night. They had no common sense. I would never—

—But Artie, Artie, listen, she said. If you had to choose between one and the other—if it was the Reds or these crazy people going after them, if you had to choose, which would you choose? They're not just going after the Reds—it's also the sympathizers. And you and I, we sympathized! We sympathized for good reason. How can you—how can you name names?

—Not like that I didn't sympathize.

—But even so, she said. Artie, you keep saying this and I thought you were just talking, but I'm starting to believe you. You don't want to do this. You don't want to name Harold.

They were almost home. Now it was raining.

—Just tell me you won't name Harold, she said. We'll manage; we'll figure out something. Tell me you won't. Artie was silent. At last Evelyn opened her umbrella and called the girls, and the three of them walked in a huddle, under the useless umbrella, while Artie walked a little apart, getting wet, his hands in the pockets of his overcoat. He could not whistle.

The day he had to go to the Board of Ed, he taught his classes. After school he walked to the train station and made his way to downtown Brooklyn. At the Board of Ed he was shown into the office of an assistant superintendent. A small man who looked as if he might be wearing a wig sat behind a desk that was too large for him. He invited Artie to sit. Artie sat, still in his overcoat.

—I just need to ask you a couple of questions, Mr. Saltzman, said the assistant superintendent.

—Go ahead, said Artie. What did he owe to a man who'd cheat on his wife with two babies at home?

—Mr. Saltzman, are you now or have you ever been a member of the Communist Party? The assistant superintendent's fingers went up and down on the desk blotter, as if he played the same notes on a piano over and over.

Artie felt an immense need to be out of this room, to walk on the street, to whistle. I refuse to answer, he said. I refuse to answer on the grounds that it might incriminate me. I take the Fifth. He tried to remember what the union lady had said. The only way to avoid naming names. I take the Fifth Amendment.

—Very well, Mr. Saltzman, that will be all.

When Harold found out—not from Artie but from Myra, who found out from Evelyn—that Artie had not named him, he walked out of the house at eleven at night, drove to his friend's house, and rang the bell. What do you want? Artie said, flinging the door open.

—It was my fault, Harold said. I know who did it.

—Will you let me sleep?

—No. Harold came in and closed the door behind him, and Artie left the room, then returned with his coat. Let's go downstairs. As they went outside, Artie said, Don't think this means I don't think you're a lying, cheating, stupid fool.

—I'm worse, said Harold, turning up his coat collar. I told that woman you're a teacher. You didn't know I'm as stupid as that.

—What woman?

—The home ec teacher. Harold tried to come up with the name in his agitation. Beatrice London.

—Beatrice London?

—She's an ex-Commie who's an informer. I think she claimed she knew you in the party.

—Oh, for Christ's sake! Not that dame! I couldn't have my life ruined by someone else? How the hell do you know?

Harold told him the story. When he finished, Artie said, You're right, you're stupider than I thought.

—I'm sorry.

Artie was like a teenager beside him as they stood in front of the house—surly, whiny. They're going to suspend me. Then they're going to fire me.

—They can't for a while—there's a lawsuit. They can't fire anyone else until there's a decision.

—So they'll put me in suspense for months, and then they'll fire me. They sat down on the steps. It was freezing. We could go in, Artie said, but they continued sitting there. After a while, he said, She would have figured out I'm a teacher some other way. Forget that part.

Harold shrugged.

Finally Evelyn came out in her bathrobe. Do you guys know it's one in the morning? she said.

—Yeah, Artie said. What's so special tomorrow that I'll miss if I sleep late?

—You still have to go to work.

—To hell with it.

—At least come in. I'll make tea. Harold. Her voice, when

she was upset, had the rhythms of her immigrant parents. Harold followed her inside, and at last Artie came too. Go to sleep, he said to Evelyn. I'll come soon.

Artie boiled water for tea. They didn't take off their coats until they'd drunk it, they were so cold. I've always been a wise guy, Artie said. How was I supposed to know I was making jokes with the devil?

—Because she had no sense of humor? Harold said. Like McCarthy.

When the tea was gone, Harold stood and made more. Have you got anything to eat? They ate peanut butter and jelly sandwiches. Artie cried. He wasn't angry anymore, only scared. It's all I know how to do, he said. I'm a good teacher. I'm such a good teacher.

—I know you are, Harold said. It was getting light when he stood and placed his teacup firmly in the sink. I'm going to take a piss, he said, and get rid of some of that terrible tea. And I'm going home. We'll solve this, my friend.

—I don't think so, Artie said. Harold had moved to put an arm around his shoulders, but Artie shrugged it away.

Artie and six other teachers were suspended from their jobs at a meeting of the Board of Education two weeks later. Harold had gone to some of these meetings because he was a union member, and he'd read stories of others. The board knew there would be protests, and it would schedule suspensions or dismissals last, after many routine agenda items. The union members, in turn, would sit through all of them, but when the question of suspensions was raised—the board always agreed on them unanimously—the union members jumped to their feet and began shouting protests. This board is trampling on the Bill of Rights! someone would shout.

Policemen ejected the shouting teachers, and they screamed, Don't you touch him! We're taxpayers! We own this building!

The cops would herd them toward the doors, and they'd rally and speak outside. Artie had never been to one of these meetings, but everything happened just as Harold had described it. It was announced that there would be trials of the suspended teachers. They'd be entitled to lawyers and to cross-examine witnesses.

The trials didn't happen for many months, until after summer vacation. When Artie's trial finally took place, his lawyer subpoenaed Beatrice London, who described in detail Communist Party meetings they'd supposedly gone to together, cups of coffee afterward, walks to the subway. She made you sound like her boyfriend, Harold said later.

The first week of school, that fall—the sacred week when the first bright leaves appeared and any achievement, whether teaching or learning, seemed possible—Harold, as when he was a boy—organized his notebooks and roll books, putting everything into the briefcase he'd eventually repossessed from Nelson. In his mailbox at school was a letter summoning him to the superintendent's office. There had been spies at the protest meetings, or someone else had named him. He wasn't surprised, but shocked, as if he'd heard of the death of someone he loved whom he expected to die. On the appointed day, Harold went to 110 Livingston Street and pleaded the Fifth Amendment. He was formally suspended the day Artie was dismissed, and dismissed a couple of months later, when McCarthy, in Washington, was at the height of his powers. A year later, Harold and Myra would be the last on their block to buy a television set, so as to watch the Army–McCarthy hearings, the end of the senator's short career.

5

Green Books
1953–1963

1

Singing *I hate to see that evening sun go down,* Artie looked into the window of a music store, like the dilapidated places where he'd once worked, letting kids try out trumpets and cornets they'd never buy until the owner lost everything or fired him. *I love to see that morning sun come up.* This shop was more dilapidated, maybe owned by someone so good-hearted he'd give money for any instrument, starving in there, worse off than Artie. The window was piled with scarred instrument cases, their leather stained and rubbed away: cases for clarinets, flutes, bassoons, no doubt with dull, creaky instruments still inside, sold by some musician or would-be musician who finally gave up— took the office job, married the girl. On top were instruments with no cases at all: blotchy trumpets, greenish and dented, parts of clarinets, dull gray flutes. He was on his way home from work. He'd begun walking down Broadway instead of getting into the subway. He'd walked miles.

Artie had taken a job unwillingly, but he wasn't young. He couldn't pretend his luck would change any day. He worked in Evelyn's uncle's shoe store. His brothers had been too embarrassed to look at him when the Board of Ed fired him, too embarrassed to hear Artie's angry explanations, or just unwilling to let their crazy brother work in their various businesses, in which room might have been found for somebody who could read and count.

Or they waited to be asked, but Artie didn't ask, and nobody came forward except Evelyn's uncle, so now Artie Saltzman, seventh-grade teacher, fitted shoes to the feet of irrational people. Even now, he couldn't resist teaching: he told his customers that women shouldn't wear tight shoes or high heels. Everyone should wear shoes in which they could run, if necessary. Evelyn's patient uncle patted Artie's shoulder and said, She wants size six? Sell her size six.

Artie had played the clarinet as a young man, and he too had sold the instrument eventually. He didn't remember where. It was not like selling the photography equipment. He turned to go away—*St. Louie woman . . .* Then he turned back and walked into the store. It was dark, dusty, and he was alone. He thought he would sneeze but instead, as he stood listening to something, he cried, shedding new tears for the pupils he didn't have, the lost privilege of walking into the teachers' lounge and finding someone to joke with (*What do you eat that candy for, do you know what it does to your teeth?*), arguing with the school secretary about where paper should be stored. The main entrance to the school had a simple decorative pattern of slanted bricks, with no mistakes he'd ever found, and he'd marveled, many a morning, at the care given to add a little style to something that might have had no style at all.

It was some kind of whistle tootling along, playing the complicated ups and down of the baroque music he'd been hearing on the radio. Ah, it was a recorder. The music came from the back of the store. Wet-faced, Artie pushed through a curtain.

The instrument Artie bought that day from Frederick, the man in the dark store, was a soprano recorder. But the soprano was squeaky, and he moved on to an alto, even though he had to learn a whole new fingering. The second time he came to the store, he signed up to take a few lessons. He had found what he wanted.

—Not the same key, Frederick repeated. He was a distinguished-looking man, unlike the battered creature—a match for the instruments—whom Artie had expected. Looking at a C on a page of music, Artie arranged his fingers on the holes of the alto where they'd go for a C on the soprano.

—No, no. The C is now an F.

—Be quiet a minute, Artie said. When he finally caught on— the C was now an F!—he was so pleased he had to teach someone to play.

The recorder was a wooden cylinder with a line of holes on top and one hole—for the thumb—underneath. The soprano was shorter and thinner than the alto. They came apart, and the top of the lower part had waxed thread spooled tightly around its neck, so it wouldn't shift when it was fitted inside the upper part. It was important to wax the threads at stated intervals. A long thin brush, cotton thread looped around stiff wire, cleaned spittle out of the instrument when you were done playing. Artie practiced scales and exercises. There were trills and mordents— ornamental flourishes for which the musician played extra notes above and below the notes on the page: lore nobody else knew.

When he began lecturing about the recorder at family dinners, his relatives thought that he meant a record player, but the recorder was an ancient instrument. Ancient or not, it drove Evelyn crazy, and he liked to practice in the kitchen. On her way from the stove to the refrigerator, she tripped on the spindly metal feet of the music stand. She sent him into the bedroom, but the music stand seemed to walk back when she wasn't looking. And sometimes she listened, saying, That's pretty.

When their father brought home a second music stand, Brenda and Carol removed the music books, notebooks, and pencils that had rested on the first stand's lip, then dressed the metal contraptions in hats and skirts, and marched them three-leggedly around the house. Evelyn got home late these days, and the girls were alone after school. She'd taken a job keeping records in a home for the aged, and she was also taking a course on how to do it.

Brenda preferred being at home without her parents in the afternoons. It was restful. She and Carol watched anything they liked on television or they listened to the radio. What interested Brenda was the Rosenberg case, which her parents refused to discuss as too upsetting for children, though Brenda was twelve and considered herself an adult. She followed every detail of the trial and discussed it with nobody but Carol, who had nightmares but loyally wouldn't say what they were about. These people who seemed as if they might have been Brenda's aunt and uncle were going to be electrocuted.

Artie yelled when he found his music on the floor, then told them he'd brought home the second music stand so he could teach Brenda or Carol to play the soprano recorder he had stopped playing in favor of the alto. Carol offered to learn. Brenda disliked the squeaky sound but didn't want her father and Carol to know

ALICE MATTISON

something that she didn't know, so she hung around while Artie showed Carol how to read the notes and where to put her fingers. Later, Brenda practiced until she played better than Carol did. Carol quit, and now the challenge was to learn more quickly than her father. Soon Brenda—who couldn't always explain or alter an intensity that took shape inside her—could play all the songs in the beginners' book. She couldn't overtake Artie because he delayed teaching her some things. He believed that the best way to learn was to practice the basics, not to add new skills until the old ones were mastered. Brenda learned trills but not mordents, and she never learned the alto, so it remained mysterious to her how F could be C or the other way around. Her father was soon playing music he borrowed from the public library, flute and clarinet pieces he somehow figured out, playing in the kitchen after supper, while the rest of them cleaned up and tripped over him.

Everyone connected with the Rosenberg case—lawyer, judge—had a Jewish name, Harold noted. The Rosenbergs' lawyer tried to delay their execution, which was scheduled for a Friday night—after the start of the Jewish Sabbath—so the judge had them killed before sundown. Ethel Rosenberg had resided in Harold's mind for months, and as he walked through the dusty city in June 1953 on his way to hand in a book review or get an assignment, he seemed to experience her terrified obstinacy. Her brother had betrayed her—her *brother*.

When Harold lost his job, he had changed his name to Harold Abrams. Someone else—someone wider, bulkier, harder to spell, and closer to immigrant awkwardness—had lost that job. For months after he was fired, Myra wept and slept, neglecting the children, while they lived on savings and money from her family, plus the few dollars he made from writing. He roamed the city, dropping in on Naomi, or sat restlessly in the library, trying to write and looking at job ads. But one day Myra had a mysterious errand in the city, and came home to announce that she'd been hired for a lucrative commercial art job. Harold began staying home with Nelson and Paul. On the Friday on which the Rosenbergs would die, Harold stayed outside, pushing Paul in his carriage, keeping away from the radio. At three, he picked up Nelson at school, and they went to the playground. By the time he reached his apartment and snapped on the radio, the Rosenbergs were dead. They'd had to shock Ethel three times to kill her. Myra was home and in the bathtub. It was late.

Nelson, hot and overtired, began running back and forth through the house saying, Is she dead? She's dead. Is she dead? She's dead, and Harold realized he'd forgotten him and had walked straight from the door to the radio, picking up Paul as he did so, not remembering he had another son.

—Are you tired? he called to Myra, pausing in the bathroom door.

—It's hot, she said.

Harold changed the baby and Myra came into the kitchen as he started supper. Paul was in his bassinet in the doorway. As she eased herself, in a summer robe, into a chair, Nelson leaned silently against her and she shrugged him off, then touched his arms and shoulders and forehead. Go wash your face, Nelson, she said. You're overheated. Then she said, I'll make supper.

Harold agreed, though sometimes he regretted agreeing. Supper would taste better, but she was tricky when tired. Retying the belt of her robe, Myra took his place at the stove. Nelson, who had not washed his face, followed. Did you make money today? he asked her.

—Don't stand near me, Myra said. She was getting ready to cook lamb chops. You'll get burned.

—Why did they kill those people?

—What people? Myra studied the cans on the shelf.

—On the radio.

—Nobody got killed, Myra said.

Nelson resumed leaning against her. He said, They did get killed. He had a way of leaning against her right arm that made her shake him off like a fly.

—What did they do? Nelson said. Did they burn up? The radio said they got killed.

—I didn't realize he was listening, Harold said.

—What's he talking about?

—The Rosenbergs.

—Oh, my God, Myra said.

—What, Mommy? Nelson said. What did they do? Did they take people's money?

—He thinks people get electrocuted for bank robbery, Myra said. Honey, nobody died, they just put them in jail.

—But the radio said.

—These are bad people, Myra said. They did a lot of bad things, Nelse, but they didn't get killed. Nobody got killed.

—But bad guys get killed, Nelson said. He sat down on the floor, his back to Myra, and leaned forward, his hands clasped behind the back of his head, his head down. It was something like the posture Harold had been taught to enforce during Take Cover drills, when the children were supposed to get under their desks—as opposed to ordinary air-raid drills, when they sat on the corridor floors.

—And . . . these . . . people . . . got . . . killed, Nelson said, bobbing his head rhythmically.

—Nope, Myra said, now at the sink. Didn't happen.

—Myra, Harold said.

—When he's older, she said. You should hear my father on this topic. Couldn't happen soon enough. Sing Sing?

—What? Harold said.

—They did it at Sing Sing, didn't they?

—Come on, Nelson, Harold said. Let's give you a bath.

When he thought later about evenings like that, he didn't remember Nelson eating in his pajamas. He often carried or walked him off or, when he was old enough, urged him to take a bath on his own. Nelson liked baths, and sometimes they'd forget and find him in a cold tub, his skin wrinkled, an hour later or more, playing with the assortment of toys and household objects he took with him. Did he never return and eat? Did Harold not notice? He'd discover gaps like this when he described the children to Naomi.

—You want kids, he said to her one night, when she'd asked him whether Paul had begun to talk.

—I have kids. She meant her pupils. She had a childish body for all her passion, straight and firm, and season after season she wore the same navy blue skirt. Now she leaned toward him, her hair pulled up in a ponytail, as if she was a high school girl, her shoulders square. They were eating spaghetti and meatballs at a little place in the Village that Naomi liked, drinking red wine. Harold couldn't feel guilty for sleeping with Naomi—he simply couldn't, though he did feel guilty for not feeling guilty—but he felt guilty for eating in restaurants when Myra was home with the children, scarcely eating at all. A year after losing his job, Harold was studying for his doctorate in English literature at Columbia, and now it was easy to meet Naomi after classes.

She twirled spaghetti on her fork, forgetting Harold in the task, that little frown line steady between her eyes. Naomi often startled him by looking older than she did in his imagination. She had to be thirty-five or more by now; he didn't know how old she'd been when she sat in his apartment weeping over the occupation of Paris.

When she twirled her fork, she thought only of the fork—or of the fork and Paris—but not of him, not of any man. She didn't play the game other women he knew played, that sad game they always lost: waiting for a man to do what they wanted him to do. Naomi risked her youth, her time, her body—and that was what you had to do if you didn't play that game and if you were a woman: you risked being single, childless, and middle-aged.

—You don't mind that I treat you this way, he said. The candle on their table, in its chianti bottle, lit her face. I think you don't mind—is that right? He meant to sound admiring, not rude, and he gentled his voice to make that clear, but she wouldn't play *that* game either.

She cut her meatball with her fork and ate before looking up. Mind your buying me dinner? No.

—That's not what I mean.

—Mind that you married Myra instead of me? You deserve each other.

—But *your* life? What kind of a life—

—I'm going to France in the summer, she said. I'm going to stay in a chateau and speak French all day.

—I didn't know, Harold said.

—I'm sure the effects of the war are everywhere, but at least now they can have people come and stay. She spoke as she always did of France and the French, with respect and restraint, and maybe as if she had to think twice to speak English when talking about France.

—You didn't tell me.

—Oh, I wouldn't have left without telling you, she said. You can come to the ship with a bottle of champagne. Yes, it's a terrible life. She laughed. Then she said, Nobody in my family marries. I've told you that. She finished her dinner—she always cleaned her plate—and folded her arms on the table, wineglass in hand.

—Somebody must.

—Well, my parents married, but their brothers and sisters still say it was a mistake. She frowned. I don't mean a problem; I mean an error. They walked into the Municipal Building looking for a bathroom and, by mistake, went to the room where the clerk who performs marriages sits, so they had to get married.

She could go on this way, making up stories about her relatives, who sounded like rabbits or field mice in a Beatrix Potter story, with little harmless arrangements and childlike ideas of what adults do. She would not—*would not*—turn the conversation to Harold's failings, Harold's troubles, Harold's boring, lumpy burden of grief at how badly he'd managed his life. A conclusion, anyway, at which she scoffed. You wanted to go to graduate school, she would say, you're in graduate school. You wanted to bed a sexy French teacher, you got that. You know just what you're doing.

2

When Evelyn Saltzman had been in college, she didn't know what work she wanted to do, and then it was the Depression and she sold shoes. What she was good at, Artie knew, was knowing what had to be done immediately and what could wait. Of course, the bastards at the home where she worked weren't slow to discover that Mrs. Saltzman, who was hired part-time to keep records, also knew when to start planning the fund-raising dinner.

—They're not paying you for that, Artie said, when she came home late and tired. Evelyn ignored him, and soon she had a full-time job.

—It's up to you, Artie said when she told him her new salary. But don't tell me it's because I complained about money!

—Did I say that? said Evelyn, and went into the bedroom to take off her shoes. He followed. They still found sex a fine game, but even with the door closed, she wouldn't do it when the girls were awake.

She wore her hair pulled back with two barrettes and had never stopped having the look of a girl who might giggle or run away if you surprised her. Artie sometimes put down what he was doing and stared, watching Evelyn walk through a room, looking as if anything at all might be in her mind—something amusing, something easy to think about. When Artie noticed that look, he promised himself never to yell at her again, and one night he made up a limerick for her.

There once was a guy with a wife.
They had plenty of trouble and strife
But her hair was so curly
Although she was surly
He loved her for all of his life.

—Who's surly? Evelyn said. Anyway, it's wavy, not curly. She was piercing potatoes with a fork, preparatory to baking them, and she pretended to throw one underhanded at his head. Artie waited for Brenda to come home, to recite his limerick for her.

Brenda was late. It was spring 1956, she was in high school, and she had stayed after school to try out for the tennis team. She didn't know much about tennis because what she did know, her father had taught her, which meant that she knew one thing well. Brenda still played the recorder and had even gone with her father to a meeting of the American Recorder Society, at which an auditorium full of recorder players—brandishing their soprano, alto, tenor, and bass recorders—played music together. Brenda tootled along on her soprano, biting the inside of her cheeks to keep her mouth from opening in laughter at the sound she and her earnest neighbors produced.

He'd never taught her the alto recorder, never taught her the trickier ornaments on the soprano, and in the same way, in tennis she'd learned nothing but a basic forehand. But it was a lovely forehand. She practiced in the park, batting balls against the handball courts after school. A good forehand might impress the coach, who would teach her the backhand and how to serve. How hard could it be?

Artie had laughed when she mentioned at breakfast that she'd be home late because she was trying out for tennis, and his laughter made her lose her temper. Then she cried.

—It's about time you learned to be realistic about what you can do and what you can't, he said, ignoring her tears. That made her sure she couldn't do it, but now she couldn't back down. And she hated to give up her image of herself, darting across a court, slamming a ball—backhand—just over the net, as a stymied opponent scrambled for it.

Brenda knew it would be better not to pay attention when her father criticized her, better to feel angry instead of ashamed. But she could sustain her anger only so long, and when she was alone after an argument with him, she frightened herself with imagined rituals of worthlessness, torments inflicted on herself, not by her father but by godlike authorities. Alone in the bedroom she shared with Carol, Brenda might conclude that she ought to be killed or turned out to starve. Her father didn't say it, he didn't think it, but something in his ridicule met something in Brenda that consumed his laughter with terrifying eagerness. Her mind turned on her, and her thoughts were too big for her head.

So she had to try out. And anyway, what could the coach say that would be worse than the cruel, laughing voice she sometimes heard as she deposited coins to ride the bus, or tied her shoe? It spoke inside her ear—not her father's voice, not anyone's—high-pitched, not quite clear.

Brenda didn't make the team, but her forehand got her into an advanced after-school class that the coach, Mrs. Broward, said was another way of making the team. Mrs. Broward was short, powerful, and blond, not young but younger than Brenda's parents. When she volleyed with Brenda—leaning forward, positioning her racket and grinning, then meeting any ball without stretching—Brenda felt protectiveness coming toward her, along with the tennis ball and, to tell the truth, a hint of disdain. A couple of girls had crushes on Mrs. Broward and informed the others of the progress of their passions, but Brenda hated the word *crush* and would never have spoken of the yearning delight she took in the coach, who sometimes dug in her pocket, thrusting her hips forward slightly, to ease a man's handkerchief from the shorts that hugged her thick midsection. Her voice was critical but never sarcastic. Someone said Mrs. Broward had once sung in a Christmas show in the auditorium, and Brenda would have given much to have heard it.

Her father was not surprised that Brenda didn't make the team—after all, she didn't know how to play tennis. At supper, he detailed all she didn't know. Brenda sometimes went along on a Saturday or Sunday when Artie met Harold to play. She'd watch or take her racket to the handball court and practice. Artie would interrupt his game with Harold, which he nearly always won, to go over and give her some pointers.

—Leave her alone, Brenda heard Harold say, the second time he did this. She has a teacher. Let the teacher handle it.

—What does that dame know? Artie said. He and Harold rarely talked about anything but tennis these days.

Mrs. Broward didn't teach as Artie did. Her after-school class learned forehand, backhand, and serves, all within a few days. Brenda stood to demonstrate service with an imaginary racket, flinging her arm at the kitchen ceiling.

—This is asinine! Artie shouted, and Brenda burst into tears.

—Artie, said Evelyn.

—Artie, Artie, he said, imitating her. Every time I give these kids something to think about, something to consider, it's Artie, Artie. What's wrong with letting her see her teacher isn't God in heaven?

—Mrs. Broward is an excellent teacher, Brenda said, though she didn't know if Mrs. Broward was a good teacher or not.

For a year, Artie heard about the after-school tennis class and Brenda's beloved Mrs. Broward. When Brenda came to the park, he could see right away that her form was lousy. One night when he got home from work she was arguing with Evelyn about how to cook meatloaf. It's disgusting, Brenda said.

—You've eaten it this way for years, Evelyn said.

—It should be crisp, Brenda said.

—For God's sake, now what? Artie said. She wants caviar?

—I'm having a conversation with Mother, Brenda said, *if you don't mind*. It ended with her refusing to eat anything but toast and jelly, which she prepared ostentatiously, several times that evening, crunching the toast crudely.

As Artie and Evelyn were turning off the television and moving toward bed, Carol came out of the bedroom. She said, Brenda got thrown out of the tennis class.

—What are you talking about? Artie said.

—She said she could come home earlier now, and I said, Did you quit tennis, and she said, Not really.

—Not *really*! Artie said.

—Leave it alone, said Evelyn.

Artie ignored her. Brenda! That dame threw you out? What happened? He strode into the girls' bedroom without knocking, something they made a fuss about. Brenda was in bed, but he could see she was only pretending to be asleep.

—Tell me what happened!

—Would you leave me alone?

—She threw you out?

She sat up. If you must know, yes, Mrs. Broward said I'm out of the after-school class.

—Did she give a goddamn *reason*? Did she offer the slightest *explanation*?

Brenda started to cry. Leave me alone. I stink, that's all. Forget it.

—For crying out loud, Artie said. I'll go talk to this Mrs. Broward with her fancy ideas and total incapacity for education.

Brenda leaned forward and screamed, *Don't you dare!* Then she said. It's not her fault. I can see I'm no good.

—Well, whose fault is that? If the pupil can't learn, the responsibility goes to the teacher. You wouldn't have found *me* telling some kid he can't learn! I just tried a little harder. He was leaning in the doorway, getting interested. Carol was in bed, and now Brenda lay down and turned her back to him under the covers. Artie kept talking. One method doesn't work, you try another one. I should have talked to her a long time ago.

Brenda had pulled her head under the blankets.

Carol said, Daddy, Brenda doesn't want you to say things like that.

—And what do *you* know? Artie said.

—Artie, come to bed, Evelyn was calling.

There once was a guy with three women, Artie said. *There once was a guy with three women . . .* Oh, to hell with it.

He had worked out the limerick by morning. Hey, Bren, he said, how about this? Brenda was eating corn flakes and hadn't yet spoken.

He recited,

There once was a guy with three winnimen
As delicious as sugar and cinnamon,
But they cried all the time
Though he plied them with rhyme
And sooner or later they DID HIM IN.

—For God's sake, Brenda said. At least she'd spoken.

—I'm taking the morning off and coming to school with you, Artie said.

—You are not.

—Of course I am. What kind of a father— He didn't finish the sentence. Brenda stood up, her cereal half eaten, and left the room. Before he knew what was happening, she was gone, not saying good-bye.

Artie could find the goddamn school on his own. He put on his tie and called the store to say he had to talk to one of Brenda's teachers and would be late. Evelyn asked what was going on, but he didn't say anything, and she was in a hurry herself.

Artie walked into the first school office he saw, hat in hand, and asked how to find Mrs. Broward. The building smelled so much like a school that he was shaky, though it didn't particularly resemble the junior high where he'd worked. He was directed to another office, where the dean of students decided they'd go and speak together to Mrs. Broward, and sent for Brenda as well.

In Artie's mind Brenda was a child, but as he sat in the dean's office, nervously waiting, he heard steps that sounded familiar but sounded like a woman, and when he turned, Brenda looked different. At home her gestures were histrionic, chosen to communicate outrage as often as not, but here she had the efficient, sturdy walk and movements of a short woman going about her business, expecting to be left alone. Seeing her father, she stopped and said, Oh, for heaven's sake, what is this all about? She told the dean that she understood perfectly why Mrs. Broward had dismissed her, that she didn't mind, and that she was more interested in other activities.

—What activities? Artie said.

—I haven't decided yet.

The dean, who was pleased to have a parent taking an interest, led the way to the girls' gym, where Mrs. Broward was teaching a large phys ed class. Through an open door Artie glimpsed long rows of girls in green uniforms doing jumping jacks, and the dean asked them to wait while he went inside. Brenda wouldn't look at Artie. Then the dean returned with Mrs. Broward, a stocky woman, not much taller than Brenda, in a white polo shirt and white shorts.

—Bren, she said, you know why I cut you from the group, don't you?

—I tried to tell him, Brenda said.

—It simply seems to me, Artie said, in what he knew was a loud voice that seemed to get louder when he tried to modulate it, It simply seems to me that if a pupil has trouble learning, that's the signal for the teacher simply to redouble her efforts. This is your failure, not my daughter's.

—No, Mr. Saltzman, Mrs. Broward said. Sorry to put it this way, but other girls are better. I don't keep anyone in that class for long. It's onto the team or out of the group. Mrs. Broward looked straight at Artie as she spoke, then took a step in his direction, raising one arm and holding it, palm down, just above his own arm, as if she owned the space between them and reserved the right to touch him.

Artie didn't know he was going to do it, and his right arm moved, in response to the movement of her arm, before he spoke. It swung backward as if to meet a good shot with his forehand, and he said, Don't you touch me! and then—to his horror, as rage seemed to course through his body so he felt all his veins and arteries at once—he delivered a blow to Mrs. Broward's white-clad shoulder that knocked her back against the tiled wall. She fell to the floor.

The dean sprang between them and grabbed Artie by the wrists. He struggled, he heard a sound that was Brenda shouting, and then he understood what had happened, and stopped moving, and began to sob.

—I lost my job, he said through sobs, so nobody heard him. I know how to teach, but they took away my job.

Brenda knelt over her teacher, looking like a child after all. She turned and said to her father, I will never speak to you again, and helped Mrs. Broward stand and walk away.

The dean led Artie to his office, where the police interviewed him, then brought him to the station house. Mrs. Broward had said she would press charges. Artie could go to prison. After some hours they sent him home with a summons, which he showed Evelyn. She was too embarrassed and frightened to speak.

For many weeks Artie did not shout. He called Harold, did not tell him what he'd done, but picked a fight with him. Forget the tennis, he said. I can't have a decent time, you're turning into such a snob—telling me how to teach my kid, sounding like a fancy professor.

ALICE MATTISON

—That doesn't make sense, Harold said.

—Well, I'm so stupid I don't go to Columbia, so I don't make sense, Artie said, and hung up.

But he wrote Mrs. Broward several letters of apology, and in the end she decided not to press charges. Brenda blamed herself for the whole incident; she shouldn't have loved her teacher.

3

Myra left her job and became the art director of a glossy women's magazine Harold had seen in supermarkets, but of course never read. Now she was paid so much there was not much reason for him to work. He stopped feeling that he was depriving his children of shirts and raincoats to feed his craving for literature. As a graduate student, he taught composition, and he continued writing reviews and articles: his professors said he had an ideal life. He wasn't ashamed of being a man supported by his wife, and Myra liked having more money than he did—it was always helpful when Myra liked something—but Harold thought his father, who had died recently, would have been ashamed. Sometimes he seemed to catch the old man watching him sorrowfully from a point just beyond Harold's peripheral vision. A few times he turned swiftly, looking for him, and then winced to picture his big blond self whirling.

He missed Artie. Myra had found out from Evelyn that Artie had gotten into real trouble. Of course, he didn't want Harold to know. Harold's life had only improved with the loss of his job. Artie's was harder. Harold waited. He felt clumsy, angry with Artie for his childishness, angry with himself for being unable to help.

During most of the year, Myra didn't read books, only magazines resembling the one where she worked. Harold felt guilty that their life had deprived her of reading, what he believed in most: as if the wife of a divinity student had no time to pray, he told Naomi. Myra insisted she didn't miss books, which made him feel worse. When he'd first known her, she'd read incessantly. Now he closed the bedroom door in the evenings and stretched out on the bed with his notebooks, reading and rereading books he'd loved for years—he had started his dissertation, on Henry James—while Myra watched television. Once a year they spent as many weeks as she could take off from work at the cabin, and then she did nothing but read, looking up dazed at times, not quite recognizing him. The look of her face then—the unplanned simplicity—stopped his heart. She'd sit in a canvas chair at the lake, always with more than one book beside her, in case she got tired of the one she'd begun. Before their trips, she gathered what she called green books—books to be read, apparently, when surrounded by trees—and there would be a pile of books in the trunk when they drove north, mostly new bestsellers, sometimes older books she mysteriously deemed green. She would never read Jane Austen in the mountains, she said, as if anybody could see why, but F. Scott Fitzgerald qualified. The distinction had nothing to do with urban versus rural settings; he thought possibly it had to do with sexual openness, but he didn't ask.

At the cabin—which Artie no longer rented for a few weeks each summer—Harold and the boys swam or put together jigsaw puzzles, or they drove into Schroon Lake. Myra looked up and waved when they drove off. It was 1961, the summer when Nelson at fifteen grew taller than his mother, and he finally stopped mashing himself into her body when she'd let him. Harold didn't notice until weeks had passed and he realized he had stopped hearing Myra tell Nelson to leave her alone. Harold was always trying to make friends with his older son, as if Nelson was somebody else's child he thought he should know better.

Paul, at ten, was easier—blunt, critical, funny, not polite, but so confident it seemed his rudeness was not that of an impertinent child but of an adult caught in a child's body, unfairly expected to suppress adult opinions. Harold needed to look away when Paul scoffed at Nelson, who was so much taller—a thin, rangy kid with hesitant gestures, looking down at Paul and then away when Paul spoke, rarely answering. Nelson was afraid of insects. He took hours—literally hours—to work up the nerve to walk into the water and get wet, yet he wouldn't stop trying, standing all afternoon in water up to his ankles. Nelson liked small objects—toys when he was small, little trucks and plastic animals and things he found in the house: a cap of a lost pen, rubber bands, boxes that had held matches. The inside slid into the outside. Now his toys claimed to be functional, but he still fiddled with small objects: a souvenir key ring, combs and scissors that folded into themselves, in case you ever needed a comb or a scissors.

One hot August morning that summer, Harold made his way down to the dock early, with his coffee and James's *The Golden Bowl*. Eating in the cabin was easier these days, now that it had a real kitchen. Myra's father, who liked to fish, had done most of the work himself. He and Gus seemed to be friends, and Harold wondered what they knew about Myra that he himself didn't know. His father-in-law felt proprietary about the cabin, and Harold, who had contributed little money, couldn't object to his plans. Now the old man had said he was going to cover the rough pine walls of the main room with what he always spoke of as decent paneling, as if the present boards, which Harold loved, were obscene. The old bedroom had become an open hallway that contained a rickety red table with a phone on it and had three doors. Two led to dark but cool bedrooms, the other to the bathroom.

Harold's father-in-law had bought the lots on either side of the house when a developer subdivided them, and Harold was grateful. Now ten or a dozen houses stood on the lake, fishermen used boats with outboard motors, and occasionally children played wild games in the evening, rowing into the lake and shouting. Once or twice, Paul joined them. But often the other houses were empty. This morning the lake was still, and he saw nobody. The evergreens that ringed the lake—he'd never found out just what kind of trees they were—were so dark their green was almost blue.

Harold had explained the topic of his dissertation to Artie as *What are Jews for in Henry James?*

—For? What are Jews ever *for?* Artie said cheerfully. Many people think Jews are no use at all. He'd had nothing to do with Harold for two years. Then he had phoned and suggested they meet to play tennis. Harold understood that he was supposed to act as if this was nothing special, and he immediately agreed. After a few weeks of tennis dates, Evelyn had suggested that the two of them take Paul and Carol—who were still willing to go—to a museum or the zoo, and they went to the Hayden Planetarium. Walking to the subway that afternoon, Artie had asked, So what ridiculous topic did you pick to write about? and that was what led to his comment on the use of Jews. It was winter and the wind was blowing into their faces. Harold, who still wore a fedora, was clutching it. Artie was bareheaded.

At the time, Harold had ignored what Artie said, but now he realized that the usefulness of Jews was exactly what he was writing about, though he didn't think he could call his dissertation—or the book he was already imagining—What Is the Use of Jews?

The Golden Bowl was one of several James novels in which lovers can't afford to marry and do harm to naïve rich people so as to get money. He was fond of this pair, the Italian Prince Amerigo and the American Charlotte Stant. Without revealing that they are in love with each other or are even more than just acquaintances, the prince marries Charlotte's best friend, an heiress, and later Charlotte marries this woman's father. And then the old lovers must deal with constant proximity—they don't plan to cheat. Harold, sitting on the dock with his feet in the water, opened *The Golden Bowl* to the page where Charlotte and the prince have a moment alone, and Harold found words he loved: *they could breathe so near to each other that the interval was almost engulfed in it and the intensity both of the union and the caution became a workable substitute for contact.*

The Golden Bowl was a green book, most definitely. He looked up at the lake. Once, he and Naomi had met by chance in the street. They spoke without touching, and then she turned her head in the direction she was going. A few hairs that had come loose from her ponytail curled against the back of her neck, and he raised his hand, which just grazed the side of her ear.

But not touching—and not speaking and not knowing exactly what's going on—can take characters only so far, and that was when Jews became useful in Henry James, if not in real life, or so it seemed to Harold. In the book, several Jewish characters—or people who look Jewish—take small actions that set the plot in motion. (James wrote of these Jews with faint distaste, and that horrified but fascinated Harold.) And when the young heiress outgrows her stupidity and finally figures out what's going on, she learns about her friend and her husband's past from a Jew, a dealer in antiques.

Where would the plot be without Jews, and where would James be without Jewish biographers and critics? But would the Columbia English department, with its sole Jew, consider Harold's question worth asking? He believed that in James, Jews were good for saying what nobody else would say, but then what, then what?

The screen door behind him slammed. He turned his head, one finger in the book, to watch Myra step firmly in his direction. She carried two hardcover books with colorful jackets. Halfway to the lake, she detoured to loop onto her arm the back of her canvas chair, which she moved each night to a spot that got sun in the morning, so dew or rain would dry by the time she came out. She came more awkwardly after she picked up the chair, the faded yellow canvas slung on her left arm, the books held in her right. She wore a black bathing suit with a white terrycloth jacket, and her red hair, roots showing a little since she bothered to look her best only when she was working, fell in waves around her head. When the sun grew warmer, she'd return to the cabin for a big straw hat. She came to the edge of the water and put the books on the dock while she set up the chair. They were *Lady Chatterley's Lover*—only recently legal—and *Justine*, the first volume of *The Alexandria Quartet*. She set up the chair, wiggling it to make sure the legs were evenly set into the ground. Then she retrieved her books and sat down. She didn't open them, and Harold didn't speak.

Myra drummed the heels of her hands on *Lady Chatterley's Lover*, as if imitating a fanfare, and laughed a little, perhaps at her gesture. Harold, she said, I'm in love with someone.

4

Brenda twisted her knee stepping from a train onto a subway platform on her way to work in 1961, the summer she was twenty and had just finished her sophomore year at Hunter College. She went down on all fours, a little too close to the edge of the platform, as the train moved out behind her, and a man reached to steady her. Careful, he said, supporting her arm with a firm hand as she stood. He was maybe in his thirties and wore a jacket and white shirt but no tie, and he somehow resembled her father's friend Harold Abrams, though this man looked Chinese. It was the slope of his shoulders that recalled Harold, a combination of claiming quite a lot and modestly denying it, built into the shape of his body. She didn't think this clearly until later.

Brenda went to Hunter College because it was free. It felt like a continuation of high school with no men, but she liked having a reason to come into the city every day. She was majoring in math, but it was too hard. The summer job gave her a different reason to come into Manhattan. She liked the anonymity among people, the warm, gritty breeze off the Hudson.

The man on the train platform looked at her with frank laughter, as if to say, Look at us, touching when we don't know each other! and Brenda was surprised too. She laughed back, feeling her mouth open wide and her big teeth protrude—Brenda was appalled at the size of her teeth—though her knee hurt and it was hard to walk. Her hands were dirty from landing on the platform.

Brenda had been in love four times, twice with teachers—both women—once with the man who supervised her work in the college bursar's office during her freshman year, and once with a boy in high school who didn't like her. She had never been touched by someone she was in love with except inadvertently.

She'd dated and kissed boys in high school but didn't like it when they touched her. So she had little experience of the welcome, deliberate touch of a man's hand. This man said, Take your time, and Brenda felt something like an expanding balloon in her chest. Together, they started up the stairs to the street.

—Don't you have to go to work? she said.

—I work odd hours. His jacket was clean and somehow fragrant, even in the subway. My name is Douglas, he said. Where are you heading?

—A couple of blocks from here, Brenda said. The company she worked for supplied clothing manufacturers with buttons and hardware, such as hooks and eyes and snaps, but Brenda rarely saw the objects themselves except in storefronts in the neighborhood, where there were many such companies. She dealt with pieces of paper.

She thought she could manage on her own after a minute, but she liked climbing the grimy stairs with Douglas, in pain but not agony, looking down at chewing gum wrappers. He might be dangerous: he wasn't hurrying to work, and he used a full first name by itself. She thought a normal person would have said either *I'm Doug* or *I'm Douglas X*—but she was interested in putting herself in possible danger, figuring she'd escape just in time, waiting to watch herself do that.

When they reached the street, Douglas said she should rest her knee, and they went into a luncheonette and ordered coffee. Brenda watched herself curiously, as if she were watching a movie. He offered her a cigarette and she took it. He said, Are you a student?

Douglas said he tutored people applying for citizenship. I make it easier, he said. Papers. He didn't have a foreign accent, but his speech seemed slightly formal, and he said he'd come to this country from China as a baby. She began talking about her classes, and he asked intelligent questions. After an hour, he said, I think we should go to my apartment.

It was as if the decision was already made. The apartment was a block away, in the opposite direction from the office. Again, Douglas supported Brenda on the stairs. She followed his lead. Inside, without discussion, he removed her clothing, one piece at a time, led her to a clean bed, and kissed her cheek. He helped her onto the bed and began stroking and rubbing parts of her body vigorously, and then at last he undressed, turned aside to put something on his penis, and entered her. She had never done it before. She had tried to imagine it. How did the penis fit? The penis felt big. Brenda didn't go to work. Maybe she never would. In some tentative way, she was pleased with herself.

Douglas believed in good behavior, though she was pretty sure that whatever work he did involved illegalities. The second day, when they met in the same coffee shop, Douglas bought her coffee but then insisted she had to go to work.

—That's stupid, they'll fire me.

—Maybe not.

—Why not? I didn't even phone them yesterday, and now I'll be late.

—Tell them you got hurt. You were at the hospital all day.

—What about today?

—It will be better that you're late, he said, and gave his abrupt laugh again. They'll know you do things your own way. He had a light voice that rose and fell in pitch. She was disappointed, but she needed the money. He walked her to work, and Brenda went upstairs and was not fired. The people weren't interested enough to fire her. She was glad to be meeting Douglas later: he'd want to know what had happened. The woman in charge of her shrugged, and Brenda got back to work. She was not smart enough to be a math major, but she was a genius at

Volkman Trimmings, and that was her only trait there: she was the girl who could add in her head.

She sat before the pile of bills—larger than it would have been yesterday and thus less boring. Her vagina was interestingly sore. She had been a virgin and now she wasn't one. She had allowed her clothes to be taken off in the apartment of a man she had known for an hour. He had not killed her, or seemed to dislike her thick, straight body. It saddened Brenda to recognize in herself something like a wish to be killed, something that had made this encounter possible. But she was pleased as well—eager to know what would happen next.

The boy she'd loved in high school was straightforward and pleasant, and they'd been in honors classes together term after term. When she realized she loved him, she made herself noticeable by starting arguments with him in class. Once she made a class laugh at him, correcting his misconception about the Egyptian seizure of the Suez Canal. She thought he might seek her out for more argument later, but he avoided her.

That day Douglas asked if she'd like to look at pornography with him. The magazine he showed her was stupid. In her fantasies, men asked her to do strange things, but nothing like what she saw in the magazines, which mostly concerned what women wore, tightness and fullness and hidden or exposed body parts. She planned what she'd say—how she'd get out of his apartment— if he asked her to wear something like that. They went to bed as before. He didn't ask. He didn't hold or hug her, and his kisses on her mouth were mild bites. But his firm touch was kind, and this time she felt pleasure.

Several weeks passed. Sometimes Brenda visited Douglas during her lunch hour, thinking she'd go back to work. His eyes lit up with humor. He often held his long, narrow hands up and out, as if to prove they were empty. Usually she didn't go back to work. When she left Douglas's apartment alive and unharmed (everything in her upbringing would have suggested this was unlikely), she found herself nodding briskly on the stairs, and she noted that she nodded the same way when, once again, she arrived at work after an unexplained absence and nobody cared, something else she'd been raised to think was impossible.

It was a hot summer, and in the dead air of the city Brenda was loose, adult. She held herself upright, straighter than usual, as if something inside might tip and spill. One afternoon she argued with Douglas. It was about a plant in his bedroom. She demanded to know why he didn't put it near a window, where it would get sunlight, though Brenda knew nothing about growing plants.

He took her to bed and said politely, Do you think you might like me to give you a little spanking, just because you are such a bad girl for arguing with me about the plant?

Brenda sat up quickly. I don't think so, she said. She was confused and troubled, partly because she thought she might indeed like Douglas to give her a little spanking, but she could never admit that that was so. She dressed and, when he apologized, assured him that she wasn't offended and would come the next day.

When she arrived at work the next morning, her supervisor said, Never mind, just go to the office and they'll pay you what they owe you. After that, Brenda had no reason to be in that neighborhood and, belatedly, she didn't want to be. She told her family the trimming company didn't need her anymore. Douglas had known her last name, but she hadn't told him her father's name or where they lived, so he couldn't look her up in the phone book unless he was prepared to speak to many Saltzmans and Salzmans.

With three weeks until school was to begin, Brenda spent a few days at home, restless and bored, alone all day. Carol had a babysitting job. Now the city felt intolerable. She thought of the cabin in the Adirondacks, where she hadn't been for years. She knew she'd feel better if she could be somewhere where she could think, and she asked her father if he thought Harold would let her go to the cabin for a few days.

—All by yourself? he said. What do you know about a place like that? There are things you have to know. The stove.

—I might call him, she said.

—He has no time for us! Harold was busy, she knew that. The last time he'd been in the house, he'd explained the book he wanted to write. But she didn't need his time. It took a few days to work up the courage to phone him. She imagined herself telling him the story of Douglas, gratefully accepting his inevitable disapproval and careful advice—but she wouldn't do that.

Brenda felt worse about the breakup with Douglas than she expected to, better about her lost virginity and how little she had to give to lose it. He always used condoms, and she had just had a period, so that was all right. What seemed most remarkable was the size and unmanageability of the person she had discovered herself to be—her recklessness—as if she'd planned to be a dog or a cat and found that she'd become a rhinoceros.

She didn't know when she'd find Harold at home, and she didn't want to talk to Myra. At last, one evening, she went for a walk after supper and phoned his number from a pay phone. Harold answered, and she asked if she could use the cabin for a few days—if nobody else was there. Maybe there was some painting or cleaning he wanted done?

He paused. Nobody's there, he said slowly. My father-in-law was there, but he's gone. But how will you get there? Do you have your license?

She had her license, but her father would never lend her his car. She would take the bus to Schroon Lake, she said, buy groceries, and find someone she could pay to drive her to the cabin and come back for her when it was time to leave. I bet there's a taxi service, she said confidently.

—The phone in the cabin is connected, Harold said. If something goes wrong, call me. She realized he was hesitant not because he thought she'd harm the cabin but because she herself might come to harm, and she almost cried.

Brenda arrived in Schroon Lake late in the afternoon, and it took several hours to find someone who'd drive her to the cabin. Before inquiring, she'd bought groceries, so she walked up and down the main street several times, her suitcase in one hand and her bag of groceries in the other, before the man in the liquor store offered to drive her when he closed up shop. He wouldn't take money. By the time she arrived, it was dark and her bag of groceries was damp from her sweaty arm.

—You're sure the lights work? the man said. I'll wait while you try the lights. She knew where the key was hidden, in a crevice in the stone foundation, in a Band-Aid box. The lights worked, and she heard the man's car as he returned to the main road, the sound diminishing down the long driveway.

She put down what she was carrying and looked around. She hadn't been to the cabin for eight or nine years. There had been improvements, of which she disapproved. The old pine boards had been covered with highly varnished paneling, still smelling of newness. But she could still take in the real smell of the place: chill, mustiness, the woods. She heard the lake slap the shore. She crossed the screened porch, opened the door to the swirl of moths, and tried to make her way to the lake in the cold darkness. She returned for the flashlight, found it in its old place next to the sink, and succeeded. At the lake, she turned the light off. She was cold and hungry. She could scarcely believe she was there, and through her own efforts. She heard katydids: it was late summer, but they were still sounding three syllables. The solid arcs of the mountains were visible against the sky until the half moon went behind a cloud. She saw a few stars, but many clouds. She crouched on the damp shore.

Surrounded by mountains, she let herself know what she felt. In the dark, as she hugged her bare arms, her detailed and un-ready self took its place like a giant puppet in the air, hurrying into an adulthood for which she seemed to have had no prepara-tion. Brenda had managed childhood, even the weeks when her father lost his job, by means of a slightly stupefied steadiness. She was intelligent, but her intelligence felt slow-moving, clumsy, easy to put aside. She did what was necessary, did not ask much of herself, taught herself not to notice the effect on others of what she did, and had told herself that was all right because she was a child. She understood, crouching—then sitting—on the damp ground, that she had believed there was only so much harm she could do to others or to herself, just *because* she was a child. She couldn't help her father but couldn't hurt him either.

Now she understood that she could do harm. Worse, part of her wanted to do harm, sought harm and punishment and shame, as if only those exercises could sufficiently explain or respond to events and people as they were. Thinking about the summer that had just passed, Brenda didn't sense in herself the capacity to choose, or even to know, whether she would do harm—to herself or to others—or not. She might have destroyed her parents' lives by being murdered in Douglas's bed. She might have insulted Harold when she phoned, turned him against her forever; it was as likely as the pleasant exchange that had taken place. For a long time she sat on the cold shore of the lake in the dark like an exile, growing colder and colder in her sleeveless city blouse, thinking the same series of thoughts about herself, hoping to come to a different end. She was immense: dangerous. It was exciting; it was terrible. At last her mind moved to another topic, and she stood awkwardly—that knee was still a little sore—and stumbled into the cabin to heat a can of soup, open a beer, smoke a cigarette.

5

H arold had figured out that what Jews were good for was saying what others wouldn't say, and he continued to hold that view even though when Myra said she was in love, sitting on her canvas chair in her sunglasses, looking not at him but at the glittering lake—which took in all news and still looked serene—Harold quickly said, Well, that's not a conversation I feel like having! Gathering his belongings, he returned to the cabin, though he was the talkative Jew and she was not. He blustered through the rooms, making noise that caused Nelson—asleep on the living room couch—to stir. Then he went back outside and down to the shore, where the shimmer of heat was already dizzying. Is it Gus Maloney? he said.

—Well, of course not! said Myra.

He went back inside. Without inviting either boy to come along, he drove into Schroon Lake for the paper, his hands trembling on the wheel. They were still trembling when he paid for the *Times*, and he stood in a hot parking lot, greedily taking in the news, forcing himself until he was thinking of nothing but the news and what it implied. The story that interested him most these days was the Eichmann trial in Israel, and the paper that day reported that the evidence phase was done and the court would pause for a couple of weeks. Harold had read everything, watched the highlights on television, listened to the radio.

He got back into his car with the newspaper, thinking of Jews in Henry James and Jews in the life of Eichmann—anything but thinking about Myra—and drove some miles out of his way before returning to the cabin.

And even when he'd had time to think about what she said, even then he couldn't think about Myra. She drove him mad—she was selfish, unpredictable, critical, then suddenly charming and talkative, friendly. They rarely made love, but when they did, it remained a thrill. He knew there was something wrong with Myra. She was almost never seen to eat, though she cooked. She'd smoke and watch him and the boys eat, then she'd leave the room, and later he couldn't say when that had happened. He didn't know why she had said she was in love with someone, whether it was true. He found he was terrified that if he asked a question, she'd leave him. Months passed and speaking became less possible.

Aren't there Jewish writers for you guys to think about? Harold's closest friend at Columbia asked, one evening that fall, speaking thoughts Harold had entertained as well. He was a Negro named Austin Granger, with whom Harold sometimes shared supper in a neighborhood place before they both taught late composition classes. Austin was writing about Richard Wright and Langston Hughes. You make yourselves miserable, he said. Henry James or T. S. Eliot, one or the other! That's all you Jews look at! Your literary gods are a couple of anti-Semites. You're trying to join the aristocracy.

—I never was accused of that before, Harold said, though he had been. I lost my job in the public schools for being a Red. He didn't miss his high school job more than occasionally. It was almost worth it, bragging about being a victim of oppression.

—You're no Red, Austin said. You're an aristocrat. He had

said much the same when they picketed Woolworth's together a couple of years earlier, eagerly joining student sympathy picket lines that supported the lunch counter sit-ins in the South. The two of them marched for an hour or two.

—You and I, we don't belong in the streets, we belong in libraries, Austin had said then, including himself that time. Now, when he asked about Jewish writers, they were making their way back from supper, in the early dark, to their seven o'clock classes. They began talking about Philip Roth, Bernard Malamud, and Saul Bellow, why Harold admired them and why he wanted to write about Henry James anyway. It was October and raining lightly, and Austin was wrapped in a big rain cape that made him seem mysterious. He tapped Harold's shoulder in farewell, on his way to his own class, and Harold made his way through the corridors to his classroom. The heat had been turned on, and there was a pleasantly indoor smell. The weather and the season promised time for reading and writing, reasoning silently and aloud, and though Harold's freshmen weren't true intellectual companions, they were bright and interesting. He loved his joking yet serious suppers with Austin; they both loved their work too much to say so aloud, but their passion for what they did was in the space between them at the table.

A folded note was Scotch-taped to the door of the classroom with his name on it: Call your wife, it said. Harold's throat tightened. The note was from the department secretary. He excused himself to the three students already present and hurried to the office. From a phone on someone's desk, standing, he dialed his house and heard Paul's hello.

—Mommy called? Harold said.

—She's not here, said Paul. His voice was squeaky with anxiety, and Harold became frightened. What's going on?

—Nelson did something, Paul said. I don't want to say . . .

—He's in trouble? Nelson was in high school, and there had been conferences with concerned teachers. He wasn't disruptive, they were assured, but inattentive. Harold and Myra had nodded in rare unanimity. Nelson was inattentive.

—He's in the hospital, Paul said. Then, in tears, Daddy, he tried to get killed.

—Oh my God, Harold said. His own voice rose in pitch, and as he experienced the sensation of being separate from his body, he also sensed two people behind him in the office stand up and turn in his direction as if to catch him when he fell.

—He's not dead, Paul said, and sobbed again. He'd never been home alone before and explained through sobs that he'd volunteered to stay and wait for Harold's call.

Harold said, He'll be all right, sweetie, I promise. Don't worry.

But how could he know? After their conversation was over, Harold realized he should have told Paul to go to a neighbor's. He should also have asked what exactly Nelson had done, but he didn't call back. He sent the secretary to dismiss his class, raced to the street, and as he searched for a taxi, he found himself, irrationally, worrying primarily about Paul, alone where criminals might break in, where he might take it into his head to imitate his brother, whatever his brother had done. Jostled from side to side on the wide seat of the taxi—fancy but shabby—he settled into his real trouble: his boy Nelson, his first boy, his darling son whom he'd never known how to love.

When Harold finally saw Myra in a hospital waiting room on the floor where he'd been told he could find Nelson, she was smoking and crying, a closed magazine in her lap. What if Nelson was now dead? As he went to her, he suddenly thought of her lakeside confession—or boast or point of information—from three months before. It was absurd that he had been unable to speak of it. He looked right and left as if he expected to see another man hurrying to comfort Myra, a man in a well-fitting suit who'd lean over her solicitously, the smoke from their cigarettes mingling over their heads. She was alone, and Harold dropped his briefcase on the floor—the same briefcase in which Nelson had carried his toys when Paul was born—sat beside her, and put his wide hand on her knee.

—What happened? he said, and was surprised at his voice, which sounded old and almost foreign, almost his father's voice.

She wasn't startled, and she turned and fell against his chest, sobbing. He'll be all right, she said, he's going to be all right.

—What did he do?

—Oh, Harold, she said. He jumped in front of a train.

Nelson had tried to get himself killed by the IRT at Union Square, jumping off a platform after an afternoon spent somewhere in the East Village. He'd been seen, alarms raised, the power turned off. The train stopped. Irate transit workers had rushed to him and yanked him back to the platform. He had a broken leg and bruises from the jump. After a short stay in a medical ward, he'd be sent to a locked psychiatric unit.

Harold, as the hours and days passed, could not stop thinking about what might have happened—what Nelson had planned—and could not bear to think about what might have happened. *Why* was almost beside the point.

Jumping from a subway platform was such an easy, obvious way for New Yorkers to die that it was unthinkable and unspeakable, and for the first days and weeks the primary effort of them all—parents, relatives, doctors, and nurses—was to look past Nelson's act and only at the bruises, the broken leg, as if he'd fallen when out for a walk. Harold could not ask why, ask himself or Nelson or anyone, because the answer had the coming train in it: it was what Nelson had chosen to accept, the train reaching his body. Or had he been so sure he'd be rescued? How could he have been sure?

Harold abruptly led a new life, rushing back to the university only when he had no choice. Nelson, in lank hospital gowns that bared his thin chest and tremulous neck, wouldn't answer his father's questions or agree or disagree with his speculations. Unlike everyone else, Harold couldn't stop beginning sentences that would include the coming train, but even he couldn't bring himself to finish them. When he was with Nelson, he did most of the talking. He had something to say to Nelson, something to say at last. The choice for suicide, Harold believed, was dignified and honorable—a choice, but a wrong choice. To choose death was to decide that life—the bargain offered human beings—was not worth it. Suicide wasn't Harold's choice, or the choice of the writers he loved best and believed in. Harold felt that if he explained to Nelson that suicide was an honorable choice, he could then persuade him that it was a choice he should not make, that the arguments of those who rejected suicide were better than of those who believed in it. *Live, it's a mistake not to,* James's Lambert Strether had said, with touching awkwardness.

—James doesn't mean *Live as opposed to die,* Harold explained, in Nelson's hospital room, but live *fully,* don't deny oneself intense experience. But the other view, he repeated, the defense of suicide, was a view. Eventually, he hoped Nelson would read some of the authors who had espoused and others who had denied this view. (Would it be dangerous for Nelson to read authors who espoused it, and who *were* they, anyway?) As father and son, perhaps they could soberly make the decision to reject this view.

Nelson didn't reply. Myra smoked and looked angry—or sometimes scared. Paul stood and stared out windows, his back to whatever room they were in. He seemed older than he was.

Paul was the one who'd say, as the three of them walked from the train station to their apartment, Is there anything in the house for supper? Should we pick something up?

Nelson's psychiatrist was a thoughtful Jewish man who looked as if he might have enjoyed talking about literature, but he was not interested in discussing suicide as a philosophical position. From Harold and Myra he wanted to know details about Nelson's childhood: toilet training, schoolwork. Harold said, Nelson's different from everyone, hoping for some ordinary back-and-forth discussion.

—How do you find Nelson different, Mr. Abrams? asked the doctor.

—That's not true, said Myra, and the doctor swiveled in his chair to face her. He's not different from everyone, she said. He's like me.

—In what way?

Harold chided himself for expecting a psychiatrist to talk like a dinner guest, then realized that the dinner guests he was imagining were no more real than the psychiatrist of his fantasies, the man who would exonerate Harold and Myra while restoring Nelson to something he had never been. The dinner guests were in books, and so were the psychiatrists.

—I'm of no use to my sons, he said to Austin Granger.

—Oh, look here, Austin said, looking uncomfortable. He was younger, unmarried, the son of a bus driver who was as baffled about him as Harold's father had been about Harold's desires and choices. Sometimes Harold and Austin seemed a generation apart, and their racial difference made Harold awkward as well; he wondered if Austin blamed him for discrimination and Negro poverty. Would a Negro boy be thrown in jail, not sent to a hospital, for jumping off a platform and disrupting the trains?

It was a relief that Nelson was in a locked ward, but someday he'd be released, and Harold didn't know how he'd stand it, not knowing where his son was at any moment. Nelson was friendlier once he was in the psychiatric hospital. He didn't mind confinement as much as Harold had expected. Maybe he felt safer. Harold dreaded the visits, but going alone, he'd sit on the edge of Nelson's neatly made bed while his son, dressed, sprawled at the other end of it, and as 1962 began, progressed, and ended, they talked about what they saw on the news—the hanging of Eichmann, the death of Marilyn Monroe, the Cuban Missile Crisis.

—I might go into politics, Nelson said once. It seemed an absurd ambition for this silent, brooding boy who couldn't make friends, but Harold was uplifted because Nelson had spoken of a future. He was on medication and grew heavier, which made him seem likelier to live, as if the hospital had proposed to save Nelson by enlarging him, so there would be more to grasp and hold on to.

Harold had been pleased to let Brenda Saltzman use the cabin, but he was surprised to hear from her. He was sorry he hadn't seen a way to ask her about herself and her father. He was sure that at heart, Artie still blamed him for the loss of his teaching job. And Harold was embarrassed at the difference between them. Even if Artie had been exaggerating the one time he said it, it was probably true that he thought Harold was a snob.

Yet after Nelson was admitted to the Psychiatric Institute at Columbia-Presbyterian Hospital, Harold wanted Artie to know all about it, if only so that he'd stop resenting Harold's good fortune. Or because it was important: he couldn't live through something important without Artie. Harold's life now included many more trips on the subway, where he was unable to keep from thinking of Nelson walking closer and closer to the edge of the platform. He was in agony, though also not in agony. He liked the upper Broadway neighborhood where Nelson was, which had vigorous street life, huge fruit and vegetable markets, and cheap discount places. Combining a visit to Nelson with his classes or trips to the library, Harold had more private life. He didn't visit Naomi for months, and then he did again.

Now it was easier for Harold to stop by Artie's shoe store, also on Broadway but closer to midtown, and propose that they go out to lunch. It had been embarrassing—for both of them—to see Artie at work in his tie but no jacket, kneeling to measure women's feet. The first time Artie said he had no time, but Harold tried again and they went to a Chinese restaurant in the neighborhood, where Harold studied Artie's face, bisected by sunlight. Artie danced his fingers playfully in the light, which didn't seem to bother him. He seemed younger than Harold.

—Do you miss teaching? Harold said, after they'd ordered.

—Oh, my friend, it's everything, Artie said, and his face wrinkled as if he would cry. He poured water and tea and drank both. Is that what's bothering your kid? That stuff we went through?

—I don't know what's bothering my kid, Harold says. He says he didn't want to live, but now he does. He makes it sound like nothing much—he didn't want a sandwich but now he does; he didn't want a glass of water.

—Maybe that's what it's like, Artie said. You should have got girls, and I should have got boys. Everybody would have been fine. I don't know what's what with Brenda. Nothing like what you're going through—at least as far as I know. She goes to college, but she doesn't seem interested. He shrugged. A waiter put dishes before them.

Harold felt himself prepare for something, and then Artie said, You still have a lady friend? At last the sun seemed to bother him; he stood and closed a curtain behind Harold, and Harold realized he should have closed the curtain.

When Artie sat down again, Harold said, Yes.

There was a long pause. Maybe it's none of my business, Artie said. I made up my mind I didn't want anything to do with you, the way you live, but maybe it's just none of my goddamn business. What do I know?

—Say what you want to say, Harold said.

—If I'm allowed to say, Artie said, spearing beef slices with his fork (Harold had learned to use chopsticks, eating in little places near Columbia with Austin, but Artie waved his hand at an idea like that). If I'm going to say, then here's what I say. What the hell do you expect your kid to do, knowing his father's treating his mother like that?

—How would he know?

—How would he know? How would he know? I'll bet you twenty Chinese lunches that Nelson knows the whole story.

Harold did not take the bet, and he did not discuss the subject with Nelson, but he made an appointment alone with Nelson's psychiatrist. He said, I thought maybe you should know. I see a woman. Very discreetly.

The doctor asked a few questions, then offered to refer Harold and Myra to a psychiatrist of their own. Do you think it's a good idea? Harold asked. That we see someone?

—For your son's sake? the doctor said. It could be.

—I remembered something, Harold said as he stood and gathered his coat. My wife—well, the summer before last, my wife told me she was in love with someone. The doctor looked up, amused. For months, Harold had thought constantly of what Myra had said, but when Nelson was hurt—and when time passed without anything else from Myra—he had put it to one side, and now it was true that he had not thought about it for many weeks.

The end of term was approaching—Nelson had been in the hospital for a year—and Harold had papers to grade. Over the

Christmas holidays, he was determined to make some progress on his neglected dissertation, but he made up his mind that in January he would suggest to Myra that they consult the doctor whose name and telephone number Nelson's psychiatrist had given him. He wondered if he had to tell Myra about Naomi—to have a reason. He tried not to think too hard about what he would say and concentrated on choosing, well in advance, a date on which to speak.

When the time came, an evening in January 1963, Harold cooked dinner—Myra had come in late—then washed the dishes while Paul did arithmetic problems at the kitchen table. Next, Paul watched a little television, but then he went to bed. Harold had chosen a night when Myra didn't have a favorite show, and when he came into the living room, she was lying on the sofa, a stack of magazines on the rug next to her. He knew she was checking out the competition, looking at layouts and design. Her feet were toward the doorway he stood in. If he were to sit down, it would be behind her.

—My, he said. There's something I want to talk about.

—Talk, she said, continuing to turn pages. He sat, but she didn't turn to look at him.

—I think it might help Nelson, he said, and hesitated. He started again. Dr. Fried thinks it might help Nelson for us to speak to a psychiatrist ourselves, together.

—What us? Myra said. You and me? What do you mean, Dr. Fried thinks? How do you know what he thinks?

—I went to see him, he said.

—Without telling me? Are you trying to turn Nelson against me? You visit more than I do, but I can't do anything about that—I can't leave work. I missed so much time when he got sick.

—Yes, I made an appointment and spent a few minutes with Dr. Fried.

—And what right— Myra sat up and wheeled around, her hands on her knees. What right did you have to do that?

—I think either of us has the right to speak to our son's doctor, Harold said. He heard himself sounding rational in a way that would set her off—it always did. He knew with dismay that he was trying to make that happen.

—And what did you say to Dr. Fried, Myra said, that made him decide we should see a psychiatrist, may I ask? What on *earth* did you say to him?

Harold was silent for a long time. There was an answer that would not be the whole truth but might work. He said, I told him what you said.

—What I said?

—At the lake. The summer before last.

At that, Myra laughed, self-consciously and ironically. Oh, so you were listening! I had no idea you were listening. I thought you had some water in your ear and couldn't hear me! You certainly never have taken any interest in that conversation before.

—I was interested, Harold said. I was interested.

—So let me get this straight, Myra said. You walked into Dr. Fried's office and said, My wife says she loves someone, and he said, Better go see a shrink. Is that what happened?

Harold was silent. He felt a great need to take off his shoes. He knew that if he left the room to put on his slippers, he would not come back. He never took his shoes off in the living room. It would feel immodest, outlandish. He stayed where he was. He should have realized that it would not sound likely that he'd walked into Dr. Fried's office and accused his wife, and slowly Harold conceded to himself that to make that claim would not be fair, would not be ethical. Harold wished to be moral—and usually considered himself all but depraved. Yet that was self-indulgent. He was not depraved, he saw, in a dreadful moment of clarity: he was only habitually selfish. He had not been a good person, but possibly he had changed. Maybe he could be less selfish.

—Myra, he said, and it felt, as he spoke, like the first honest thing he'd said to her since the day they met, I want to tell you what I told the doctor.

—I should hope so, said Myra, but her features narrowed, as if she hoped he would not.

—I know this will distress you, he said. I told him I—I have a mistress. A lover. A woman.

Myra jerked her head back and shut her eyes as he spoke. He didn't know whether she was surprised at what he had said or the fact that he'd spoken out loud. She was quiet for a long time, and he waited. He expected crying, screaming, but no.

She stood up. You'd better sleep in Nelson's room, she said.

—What?

—I'm going to bed. I don't think there's much to be said tonight. I want to make some phone calls before we talk again.

—Phone calls? Harold said.

—My father. To recommend a divorce lawyer. And my father, also, come to think of it, about the other thing. I'm getting the cabin. Leaving the magazines scattered on the rug, with their dazzling colors, their photographs of cold, elegant, powerful women, Myra walked into the bedroom. You can get your slippers and pajamas now, she said, turning. And move the rest of your things to Nelson's room when I'm at work tomorrow. You can take a week if you need it to find an apartment. Paul stays here. I stay here. She'd rehearsed this many times in her mind, Harold understood. Maybe she'd even spoken it out loud. She had been waiting for him to say what he had just said. He gave a wild, wordless cry, reaching toward her. Still, it would have been wrong not to say it.

6

Wake Me When You Leave
1968–1969

Brenda had believed that land, even when it was called flat, was at least a little bumpy. Driving across the country in the summer of 1968 to a job she'd found while trying to prove she couldn't, she was astonished to discover that land may be flat as floors are flat. In the San Joaquin Valley were peach and apricot trees—on peach and apricot ranches (they were called, hilariously, she told her parents when she finally phoned) where trees stood in straight lines. Brenda the New Yorker had not known peaches and apricots grew on trees. Now she couldn't remember how she had thought they grew—on bushes, on vines? Driving to pick up groceries, cigarettes, wine, and beer, waiting for a light to change in the dazzling heat of an avenue straighter and wider than any street in the East, she decided that everything she'd thought a week earlier had been stupid, except she still loved the music she loved, and she still hated Lyndon Johnson and his war. Maybe she was the only person in this valley who felt that way.

But quiet, cool canals—straight rivers—cut through the town: irrigation canals, built before there were houses. One canal was a block from the house where she'd rented a sparsely furnished apartment made from a remodeled, attached garage. You could walk along the levee.

Working in a New York office after she dropped out of graduate school (after she went to graduate school because she hated working in an office), Brenda had begun participating in peace marches, exhilarated to walk down the middle of streets cleared of cars, among people she agreed with, being cheered and screamed at. Her mind had been on public events for once, that spring: the murder of Martin Luther King, the announcement by Robert Kennedy that he'd run for the presidency (Brenda wore a button for him), Johnson's speech saying he wouldn't run again, Eugene McCarthy's campaign. But after a march, with her own skimpy life waiting for her like a neglected pet, Brenda admitted to herself that she was not one of the truly impassioned. If her thoughts about the war were in black and those about the man she was sleeping with were in red, she had more red thoughts than black thoughts. She enjoyed marching too much for someone who was supposed to be angry. Here in California it might be different. In the absence of a private life, this lonely week before her job began, in the absence of hills and curves and maple trees and her parents—and finding herself, for the first time in her life, in a conservative town—she felt new rage about the war and new grief about the death of Robert Kennedy, who'd been shot as she packed her things in New York.

The man she thought about had been her American literature professor, and she envied his life. One night, as they drank red wine in her East Village kitchen while he rolled a joint, he interrupted her complaints, saying, You could teach in a community college.

—Who'd hire me?

—You have a master's.

She had lasted two years in grad school, studying English (she'd long since given up math) like Harold Abrams, whose book about Henry James sat on her shelf. She had read certain parts several times, though not the whole.

—I hate your smugness, she said. First, you get me so worked up over you I quit grad school, and then you blithely tell me I can get a teaching job. He was married.

—You didn't quit grad school because of me, he said mildly.

—How would you know?

It was intolerable that he should get away with this. He'd spoiled her life—oh, she knew he hadn't *spoiled her life*; she'd never felt at ease in graduate school. But he didn't love her and never had. To prove his suggestion was foolish, she borrowed her father's *World Almanac* and looked up community colleges. Then she wrote letters to forty of them, asking for a job. When she waved the stack of denials in his face, he would apologize and leave his wife, or at least help her figure out something else. But one school wrote back with a job offer, and when she phoned to tell her lover, he broke up with her. So here she was, hired to teach English at a public junior college, on her way to buy groceries in a town with peach ranches. She'd been to the college once and had met the department chairman, who smiled tiredly but said little.

Heat collided with her when she got out of the car. Hot weather here was a three-dimensional object—a box of hot dry air with notches for cars and buildings. Contraptions to bring cool, damp air hung on the side windows of people's cars. By evening the weather would be cool. Whenever she went out, she saw the unexpected: Mennonite women in old-fashioned dresses and white bonnets, their hair scraped away from their faces. Men in cowboy hats and big belt buckles, who walked as if they took themselves seriously but would have been comic performers in New York. The veterinary practice was called a Small Animal Hospital, as if somewhere there was a Large Animal Hospital—for horses and cows? Everyone wore light-colored clothing. Checkout clerks greeted Brenda as if they knew her.

The supermarket was air-conditioned, and she liked to go there. When she was done shopping, she studied a bulletin board: tractors and lawn mowers for sale, free kittens. A kitten would be pathetic—the friendless woman and her kitten. But someone offered recorder lessons—even here! Each evening her father still warbled away his grief at his lost job. She still had her soprano recorder and played easy tunes when she was bored with reading. The notice was in large, friendly handwriting. Maybe Brenda could finally learn the alto or the tricks of the soprano her father had never taught her. She missed competing with her father, fighting with him, or touching his head and ears with teasing tenderness now and then: the head and ears of a man who did love her. To give her trip to the supermarket meaning, Brenda dug a pen out of her purse and wrote down the phone number of the person who gave recorder lessons. As she left, a man with dark hair glanced at her. It took her a moment to understand what made her notice him: his hair was longer than the hair of other men here. He had antiwar hair.

The man with antiwar hair answered the door when Brenda arrived for her first recorder lesson with his wife, Lee. He said, I'm Richie Michaels. She didn't say she'd seen him before. Richie was tall and slightly stout, with wide-open blue eyes and eyebrows that seemed higher than other people's so he looked surprised, or maybe he was surprised. She learned from Lee that he was a builder with three crews, and at present he supervised two construction projects: a large apartment complex and a two-car garage he was building on someone's property.

Lee, who had a tangle of black curls and a pleasantly irregular, thin nose, played the recorder—all sizes—so well, Brenda was ashamed of having learned so little and lied when asked how long she'd been playing. Lee made the recorder seem like an authentic musical instrument, not an embarrassing toy. She was from San Francisco, she told Brenda, as if that explained why she might know how to play the recorder. Richie had grown up here in the valley.

—We met at Berkeley, Lee said. Of course it was different then.

She was probably in her thirties. Brenda knew she meant before the Free Speech Movement and antiwar demonstrations, and she wondered which side Lee was on. Her hair was also long. She found a duet for them to play and talked about Brenda's tonguing and phrasing, and Brenda discovered that she and her father had played a Bach phrase incorrectly thousands of times. Lee had a way of exaggerating the movement of her tongue while explaining, to signal her student what to do, which Brenda found sexy. The supple, large tongue, which Lee stuck out to show her—she was not a woman who'd be expected to stick out her tongue— contrasted with the bony nose. When Brenda left, she was a little heady about her new teacher, feeling—in this desolate new land—the beginnings of the kind of crush she hadn't felt since high school, that idealization of a teacher. She went home and drank two glasses of wine, wondering how she'd buy grass here.

The next time, Richie wasn't present, but at the end of her third lesson, when Brenda came out of the den where Lee taught, he was drinking beer and watching TV in the living room and he offered her a beer. She looked at Lee, who nodded, as if she and Richie had been waiting for the right moment to make friends.

The news was on, and Brenda waited edgily. She had seen no evidence of political views in this house, or any views, only some mildly religious embroidered samplers that Lee said her mother had made. She had not seen books—books would tell her what they thought.

Richie said nothing when the war footage was shown, but Lee said, There's a march on the Presidio next month. Want to come with us?

—Protesting the war? Brenda said dully. In San Francisco?

Richie could be sarcastic. No, in Tijuana. What do you think?

She was pleased to be teased. His voice was rough, but Brenda had grown up with rough voices. Sure, she said. She drank two beers with them.

By the time of the march, classes had started, and she was working hard but was excited to leave for a Saturday, riding in the backseat of Richie's white Ford. When they reached San Francisco and found a place to park—the city was unlike anyplace else, with abrupt hills and bright houses—the march had begun, and they joined in where they were. Richie walked along the side, faster than the other marchers, as if he were needed closer to the front. Brenda and Lee followed, Lee holding Brenda's elbow so they wouldn't lose him or each other. The crowd filled the street. Richie looked as if he should be wearing a hard hat, Brenda said to Lee, who smiled uncertainly. She meant that he looked as if he was at work—absorbed, energetic, clearheaded, and wearing dress pants and a button-down shirt, unlike the people around them in patched jeans and T-shirts with messages.

—His cousin died there, Lee said as they hurried behind him.

—*Hey, hey, LBJ, how many kids did you kill today?* the crowd shouted. Brenda found her voice. She felt an unexpected, embarrassing joy: at being where she was, at being with Lee and Richie, who seemed more authentic, less theatrical than the few antiwar teachers she'd met at the junior college. A broad hand gripped her shoulder. Richie had circled back to introduce them to people he knew, and Brenda found herself shaking hands with organizers of the march, who were talking not about the war, the weather, and the size of the crowd, but about which route the police had agreed to, how many speeches they'd be allowed to give at the rally before the crowd would have to disperse, who would be arrested this time. Again, Richie gripped her shoulder, this time to steer her in a different direction. She looked around for Lee. She's coming, Richie said. His big hand tapped the center of her back—one, two, three—as if offering ritual comfort. Then he held her hand for a few seconds before letting it go and leaving her to keep up with him as he settled into the slow steady pace of the other marchers.

She watched little kids with long hair and OshKosh overalls who rode on their fathers' shoulders. People stepped onto the sidewalk to rest, change their babies on a blanket on the ground, breastfeed on wooden porch steps; people hurried to catch up to their friends. *What do we want? Peace! When do we want it? Now! What do we want? Peace! When do we want it? Now!* Someone up ahead asked the questions, and the marchers shouted the answer. The chant grew faster until they were shouting *Peace now, peace now, peace now!*

The march both distracted her from the war and reminded her of the war. It was childish to imagine that wearing jeans patched with peace symbols and shouting would make the war end. She felt ugly, out of place, and complicit in a dangerous, destructive world. Children were being napalmed, and that was her fault because she was an American—because she had fun on these marches, because she came only when she had the time, only when she knew she didn't have to be arrested. If she was arrested, she could lose her job. She wouldn't risk even that.

Lee had reappeared with food. Brenda accepted a half sandwich: ham and American cheese. Glad you turned up, Richie said. He might have meant Lee, who had rejoined them after disappearing, but when Richie spoke, Brenda felt Lee become anxious and decided it was a compliment to herself. All at once she felt powerful, free, able to do anything—able to fight the government, required to fight the government, able to be the government that did wrong. She loved these people, this Lee and Richie whom she'd found or invented in what her father insisted on calling the Wilds of California. She was wild too.

For a few hours at a time, Harold Abrams forgot he had children. His life after divorce didn't feel like a continuation of his old life but like an alternative one, as if he'd returned to his youth and started over. He lived alone in an ungraceful postwar apartment not far from where he had lived before he was married, in Murray Hill. He prospered: he finished his dissertation and became Doctor Abrams (and wished he had remained Abramovitz because Abrams was someone he didn't know). He got a job, and now he drove over the East River every day to teach at Queens College. His book on Henry James was published by a university press and received respectful reviews but did not change the history of thought, even among his friends. Austin Granger—now teaching in Chicago—sent a short but enthusiastic note.

Harold had forgotten that lives take place in chronological order, that one cannot lose one's past. When something reminded him of Nelson or Paul, a muscle in his chest would clench. It might have been easier if he and Myra had divorced when the children were little, when he could have picked them up on a Saturday and taken them to a museum or the circus. Myra said both boys were old enough to plan their own time, so there was no need for a formal visitation schedule: Harold could see them anytime he and they wished. In 1968 Paul was in his last year of high school, living with Myra but planning to go away to college. He agreed to restaurant meals with his father, and sometimes, after a couple of hours, if the service was slow and the food was good, they talked as they used to. Paul was tall, curly-haired, and confident, a happy kid who excelled at debating and was impersonally polite to his father, as he was polite to the judges of debates all over the city.

When Nelson was discharged from the hospital—subdued and timid, after two years away from life—he had gone to a college in Massachusetts recommended by his psychiatrist. But he'd dropped out and now lived in an apartment in the East Village with an indeterminate number of young people. At different times there was no phone, a disconnected phone, or a phone nobody answered. Once, someone answered who had never heard of Nelson.

Harold—this new Harold, Professor Harold—felt better in one way, and it wasn't being rid of Myra, not that he'd ever be completely apart from his sons' mother. Though he was glad to be away from the tiring drama of life with Myra, he missed her astringency, her narrowed eyes, her rare hard-won approval. But now it was easier to think about himself, about his life, as a series of moral choices. Before, he'd lived two contrasting moral lives: he was a good boy, and he was someone who reveled in badness. Asked by a stranger as he walked down the street, he would have spoken for the good old humdrum values. In practice, he considered himself a bastard and took pride in that at times; at other times he sickened himself. He had outgrown his moral code but had no other.

Harold in his solitude set out to learn and practice a new moral code—to find a way to be as good as he thought people should be—and doing so made him want to write about it. He proposed an essay to someone at *The Nation* he'd met in his reviewing days: it would be about political action—including his own youthful membership in the Communist Party—and whether political outrage and activism are invariably meaningless if they are motivated in part by selfishness. If young men protested the war because they didn't want to be drafted, did their protests count? Harold no longer believed in his old self, but he wanted a reason to keep his old politics, which felt more valid than ever as war continued in Vietnam, and as protests against it were considered unpatriotic, while angry students were treated like unruly children.

One Tuesday evening that fall, Harold came home tired after a late department meeting and sat down in front of the news with a drink, breaking his rule, which did not permit him to turn on the television set until he'd cooked something. The news was depressing, and sometimes he would watch something else— anything—to take his mind off it, not eating until nine or ten. The descent of his fleshy rear end onto the sofa cushions was to be avoided. This would matter even more on a Tuesday because he had an early class on Wednesdays and intended to reread the short stories he had assigned. It also would be a good idea to go over the proofs of his essay for *The Nation*, which were due in a couple of days.

The doorbell rang at eight thirty, freeing him to turn off the TV. The garbled, interrupted voice on the intercom sounded like Nelson, and it was indeed Nelson who came uneasily into his father's apartment a few minutes later. Nelson was a darker, narrower version of Paul: thin, loose-limbed whereas Paul was solid—and it was hard not to think of Paul as the standard for young men, though he was the younger brother. Nelson moved at angles to objects, at a slant, while Paul squared himself, walking through the center of doorways and standing parallel to the wall behind him, at right angles to the wall at his side. Harold recognized his own way of negotiating space in the way Paul moved. Now Nelson said nothing after his greeting: Hi. It's me.

—Have you eaten? Harold said. He led the way into the kitchen and began searching the refrigerator and freezer.

Nelson stood behind him. I'm not too hungry, he said.

—Well, I am. How are you? How long is it since I've seen you?

He glanced behind him and saw Nelson's shrug.

Harold found frozen hamburgers and cooked rice and frozen asparagus to go with them. Do you want a drink? he said.

—Milk?

Harold had no milk.

—I'm not too thirsty, Nelson said.

When Nelson had told Harold he was leaving college, he said, I'm pretending all the time. Harold didn't know what he meant and wished he had thought fast enough to ask; he'd never been able to find a way to ask since then. Nelson had said then that he wanted to be an actor, and that actors were better off taking acting classes and going to auditions than getting a degree. Now he'd been in New York for a couple of years. Harold hesitated to ask about acting, but as they ate, he said, Are you still going to auditions?

—I'm kind of busy. But sure, sometimes, Nelson said.

—Busy doing what?

—I was in Chicago. Unbelievable.

—Chicago? For the convention? My God, you could have been killed!

Nelson had a way of smiling with only part of his face. I didn't get killed by that subway train when I was a kid, I'm not going to get killed going to demonstrations. But that's why I came—I mean, to see if you were okay and all that, but I wonder if I could have some money. I had to quit my job to go to Chicago, and he wouldn't give it back to me.

Harold tried to remember if he had known where Nelson was working. Which job?

—It was a good job. The box office at St. Marks. He looked up from his plate and down again.

—Really? St. Marks Cinema? Do you watch the films?

—Oh, man, sure. But he won't take me back.

—I never saw you there, Harold said, but he didn't want to sound as if he doubted what Nelson said. Sure, I can give you some money, he said quickly.

Nelson looked up, with that fragment of a smile again, and down once more. He had hair past his shoulders and the start of a beard, and his face above the beard was marked and scarred. Harold stood and put his plate into the sink, then walked to his son at the end of the table and knelt so as to look at his face. He'd never before done anything like this. Nelson, he said. Why do you look so—so tired, so . . . he didn't want to say *ravaged*. So—not right?

—Do you mean do I take stuff? Of course I do. When I can get it, which isn't often. You need money for that.

—That's not what I meant, he said, terrified not of grass—he'd been turned on by his students long ago—or even of LSD but of heroin. Do you still live in that apartment?

—Sometimes.

Harold felt—because he was kneeling—a sudden new freedom. Nelson, why did you jump in front of the subway train? Why? He didn't even mean the question. He meant, Why can't I understand you?

Nelson stood, so Harold had to get up as well, and led the way back to the living room. He said something Harold didn't hear.

—What? What is it? Harold hurried behind him, not wanting Nelson to leave but worried about his class the next day.

—I said, Did it ruin your life, what I did? They were sitting down now, and Harold was afraid Nelson would lean forward and turn on the television.

—I ruined my own life, insofar as I've ruined my life, Harold said, but I don't consider it ruined. Your mother and I were a risky business from the beginning, if that's what you mean.

—I bet, Nelson said.

—Nelson, why is your face so marked up?

—I got beat up in the street, Nelson said. I was on mescaline, a bad trip. I stayed out all night. Somebody beat me up for my money.

—You're not afraid, Harold said.

—I already died, Nelson said. It wasn't so bad.

—But you didn't die.

—Sure I did, Nelson said. You don't jump in front of a train and live, Dad. He got up and began touring the room—bookcases, windows with venetian blinds. His back to Harold, he said, Anyway, I'll be drafted and die in the jungle, and if that doesn't happen, a hydrogen bomb will get me.

Nelson always had little things—except in the hospital, where they were afraid he'd harm himself with them. Now Harold saw there was something in his hand: a small glass unicorn. He sat back in his chair. You're twenty-three. They're not drafting guys of twenty-three.

—There's no telling.

—And you have a medical history.

—Insanity. That could help. Nelson sat down on Harold's shaggy gray rug and stretched out his arms and legs. Dad, you should have stuck with Mom. She's nuts and now it's all Paul's problem, since I'm also nuts. Paul will be old fast. He's getting gray, Dad, he's turning seventeen and he has a gray hair. He stood again, stared at Harold's books. I've thought of applying for conscientious objector status.

—Are you a conscientious objector?

—Yeah. Aren't you?

At last, Nelson stopped circling and sat down, again on the arm of the sofa.

—Maybe I am, Harold said. The moment was good—the question about himself, the admission about Myra, the unfair pleasure in being Nelson's confidant when it seemed that Myra wasn't. He said, Of course, in the Second World War, you—

—I know, I know.

—Stay here tonight, Harold said, standing. He wouldn't get his work done, but he'd get up early. Or he'd fake it in class.

—No, Nelson said. There's a chick. He shrugged and lingered, looking at the books again. Then he hurried to let himself out. Goodnight. Thanks for the food.

—What about the money? Harold said. Wait.

—I'll be back, Nelson said, but Harold didn't see him for two months.

What little Brenda knew about teaching was irrelevant, except for the familiar form: people gathering at scheduled times in a room with windows on one side, the expectation that somebody would stand in front and speak. One surprise was that the person in front was herself. The students included scared, silent girls; boys who wore heavy belt buckles decorated with rodeo scenes; neatly dressed boys with short hair and button-down shirts, who were often studying to be cops; Mexican-American kids; a few Portuguese; hippies with long hair; Mennonite girls in organdy bonnets; Vietnam vets. The veterans were the best: smart, profane, but ungrammatical. Her classes were elementary, most were remedial, and she saw that her task was to make her students less frightened of reading and writing, maybe less frightened of thinking and talking. When she said it was important to ask questions, a girl raised her hand to ask if she also believed in setting off bombs.

At the first faculty meeting in the fall, a history instructor with a gray beard made sure to shake Brenda's hand, and she saw that political alignments here were clear and fixed. Nearly everyone avoided politics or openly approved of the war, but three or four were the campus radicals, known to everyone. She spoke up during the meeting, finding herself arguing for encouraging the Mexican-American kids to form a club, for the importance of creativity in the classroom, for an uncensored literary magazine. Some older women teachers turned to look at her. Someone said it might be better if new teachers didn't speak.

Brenda was lonely. Her recorder lessons were her only contact with other people except for these teachers and her students. She was one of very few Jews and found herself wondering if there was a synagogue nearby, not that she'd know how to conduct herself there. The second week, one of the long-haired kids asked Brenda if she wanted to be the faculty adviser of a new literary magazine, to be called *Speak Out*, and soon the five kids who came to the first meeting (one an older woman named Grace) were her best and only friends.

Speak Out had no budget, but the students seemed to care more about getting together than having a magazine. They did make signs soliciting poems and stories, and posted the signs on bulletin boards—and then a memo went out to the whole faculty reminding them that only authorized organizations were allowed to post notices on bulletin boards, and the signs disappeared. When Brenda read the memo, she flushed with rage and spent a morning writing back to the dean who'd sent it. Her letter to the dean made him summon her to a meeting, where he shook her hand and assured her he understood that she probably hadn't known the rule. His eyes were perfectly round, light blue, and she tried to think if she'd ever seen truly round eyes before. He was not interested in her arguments about freedom of speech and the educational value of creative writing, and he quickly dismissed her—courteously, as if they had agreed. She called Grace and told her the whole story. That night for the first time in her life she was made sleepless by intense feeling other than unrequited love.

At a bar in Oakland, a boy from the magazine group met a black poet who gave him a copy of a book he'd written and proposed that they invite him to read to the students. Brenda looked over the book, which had been published by a small press in San Francisco. Some poems were about the man's childhood. Hearing them might make her students more confident, writing about their own childhoods. The poet was willing to come for nothing. They had to reserve a room in the student center, and she wanted signs to go up and not come down. She went to see the chairman of the English department, who apparently counted out each Monday how many words he planned to speak that week, put them into a bowl on his desk along with paper clips and rubber bands, and used them up judiciously; during his long silences he frequently reached into the bowl and twisted a rubber band around his fingers or played with a paper clip. She suspected— from a look of pain in his eyes—that in his silence he agreed with her about most issues. In the longest speech she'd heard from him yet, he said the English department would sponsor the reading. A table in the room where the reading took place would have Hawaiian punch, bowls of pretzels, and paper cups on it, and the students would be allowed to put up signs.

—Buy the Hawaiian punch in the morning, he said, as she

thanked him and stood to leave. The ladies in the cafeteria will chill it. Give me a receipt later.

Because she was buying Hawaiian punch and pretzels during her office hours the morning of the reading, Brenda had a conference with one of her weakest students in the afternoon and was late to the reading. The girl was sweet but not quite able to read. Brenda tried to explain sentences, punctuation. When she became worried about missing the reading, the two of them took their conversation to the student center, where they found that the assigned room was full. The poet was already speaking, and Brenda and her student listened from a room just to the side. He read well—intense, angry poems. Brenda had forgotten how many of his poems had "fuck" or "motherfucker" in them, or maybe some of these weren't in the book. Her student listened eagerly. Hearing a poem about a white policeman beating a black man, she seized Brenda's hand. And then—they could hear but not see—there was an interruption. A voice announced the end of the reading, asking the students to disperse. Brenda, her arms and face hot, held her student's hand, and the two of them squeezed through the door at which they'd been listening and into the back of the room. It was the round-eyed dean, and he was closing down the reading because of the poet's language. Not knowing anything but that this girl had to hear poems, Brenda led her student through the crowd to the front of the room, where the poet—tall, dark-skinned, with a big Afro—looked as if he was trying to decide whether to get angry or laugh. Excuse me, Brenda said in a loud voice, when she reached the front row. Excuse me.

The dean turned his round eyes in her direction. Miss Saltzman? A question?

She caught sight of her chairman, sitting with his head down. She hesitated for only a moment. This is wrong, she said. The poet has a right to the language he chooses. He has a right to be heard. The students have a right to hear him.

—This assembly is dispersed, the dean said. This man may not read to this assembly! He looked nervous, and when Brenda continued to argue—The students have a right to hear him!—he said, That's nonsense, and he left the room.

The crowd made an anxious, deep noise. A few students left, gathering their belongings hastily. Then Grace, from her seat, spoke in a clear voice. I'm sorry, she said to the poet. I guess you can't give a reading. But—would you just read a poem for *me*?

—Sure thing, said the poet, smiling, and he read an antiwar poem about a black American draftee. The audience settled and listened. Two black students cheered.

Someone else raised a hand. Would you read a poem for me?

Someone else. Would you read a poem for me?

One night Brenda was cooking spaghetti sauce, shoeless, a glass of red wine at her elbow, when the doorbell rang. It took her a second to identify the unfamiliar sound. She answered the door in her socks, spoon in hand. The door had panes of glass halfway up, and she saw that her visitor was Richie, Lee's husband, looking down at his shoes. Brenda knew that she'd been waiting for this. She opened the door, saying Hi, Richie, and then had a moment of panic, of loss of trust in herself. What if this wasn't Richie but only someone who looked like him, someone asking directions or collecting for charity? But it was Richie, and what was going to happen next would not mean what it would in her life as it used to be, a life in which she didn't march against war or confront the dean.

Richie stepped into the apartment and looked around. Not bad, he said. He took her in his arms, as she wished him to, and nuzzled past her hair to her lips.

—I'm not sexy, she said, through his kiss. She was thick—chunky—with short blond hair that became more straggly if she grew it.

—You're my type.

His smell was familiar. Some previous lover had Richie's smell, and she thought of a woman who'd flirted with her for months but had never come closer. Richie's arms were short but powerful, holding her firmly. She probably should have been offended when he led her to the bedroom—presumably he'd been looking for a horizontal surface when he looked around the living room, but she had no couch—and laid her on the bed without even saying, Shall we do this? But she was only amused and happy.

And then the sex was not what she expected. She had imagined—she had imagined this more than once—brusque, all but rough sex from this practical, straightforward man. But Richie moved in a measured way, maybe following a mental checklist—what to touch first, what to kiss next. She was on birth control pills, but she would have liked him to have inquired or to have offered to use a condom. When he was done, she said, Lee doesn't know you do this?

—She doesn't say she knows.

—You don't talk about it.

—We don't talk about it.

He was acknowledging that he saw other women habitually. That didn't bother her, but something did bother her. It should have been her disloyalty to Lee, but it wasn't, and she swallowed hard as she lay naked on her creased sheets, sweaty in a way she'd been missing. Then she knew: when she'd first seen her, it was *Lee* she wanted to touch—her hair, her neck. Now she didn't even mind betraying Lee. She scarcely knew her, and the recorder was a bit silly, but Brenda would have preferred it if her politics—founded, after all, on notions of justice—made her just.

—I'm a slut, she said experimentally.

—Don't use words like that, please. He stood up and she heard him in the bathroom. He didn't close the door. She smelled the spaghetti sauce, and it smelled burned. Had she left the flame on when she went to the door? Are you hungry? she said, when he came out.

—I ate.

—Do you want a glass of wine?

—No, thanks.

What kind of lovers could they be, if he wouldn't drink wine and talk? He left quickly. The sauce was not burned but congealed. She added water and ate spaghetti with lumpy sauce. She was starving. After she ate, she settled into her only comfortable chair with a second glass of wine and a pile of papers to mark. Now she felt better. As a woman with a secret married lover, even one not quite to her liking, she'd feel more confident in the classroom and among the faculty. She drank her wine and corrected her students' spelling. On the bottom of their essays she wrote encouraging suggestions for expanding and deepening their modest thoughts. One boy wrote about riding bulls. The challenge was to stay on the bull for six seconds. In bed she cried.

When Richie didn't come back, Brenda forgot that she hadn't been sure she wanted him as her lover—of course she did. Three weeks after he rang her doorbell, she stayed late in her office to meet with students. When the last one left, after she'd explained yet again about periods and commas, Brenda sensed somebody in the corridor, and she went to see if a student was too shy to enter. Richie stood near the tiled wall. Are you done? he said.

—You came here?

—This is a better time for me.

—How did you know where I was?

—It's not hard.

He took her hand as they left the building in the dark and led her to his car in the visitors' lot. She was too happy to pull her hand away. He was silent as they drove, then began talking about the war. He'd studied the geography of Vietnam, maybe beginning before his cousin was killed. Richie's political views were without vanity or narcissism: he had no interest in his image, only in ending the war.

It did not seem to have occurred to him that she might have had other plans. They drove to her house. He'd brought a bottle of Scotch, and she drank a little with water in it. He drank it neat and asked for an ashtray. I didn't know you smoked, she said.

—I smoke when I drink Scotch, he said, lighting a cigarette. She smoked too. Lighting up, Richie tipped back his head, then ducked forward and smiled. He looked younger then, with a smile that seemed to ask for approval. His jaw looked less solid, and she could imagine the teenage boy he had been. He drank half of what was in his glass and crossed the room to put his arms around her. He rested there, stood still as if to say it had been a long wait. And it had been. She moved first, turning her face to kiss him, and he turned it back with his hand, which swiveled her chin almost roughly, so she was afraid she'd offended him. She felt something familiar: a fear of giving offense and a loss of capacity to take offense, which seemed to come at the same time with a man. She'd left her car in the lot at the college without mentioning it and would have a long walk in the morning. She was afraid of Richie and excited to be afraid. She felt a moment of nostalgia for her crush on Lee. It would be different with a woman, but then she'd be a lesbian, and surely she was not a lesbian. Anyway, something about this fear was irresistible.

The sex was better this time, and she struggled to come, wanting both to prolong and end the sensation. He seemed to let her come when he chose. Can we talk a little? she said when he stood.

—Gotta piss, he said. He looked at his wrist, though he'd taken his watch off. When he came out of the bathroom, naked, he went into the living room and sat down next to his Scotch. Brenda could see him through the doorway, and she put on her robe and followed. He patted his knee and she hesitated, wishing she had a sofa. She sat on a nearby chair and said, What was it like to grow up here? and Richie became talkative, telling stories of working in the canneries on high school vacations, going to Yosemite, driving out to caves and canyons with girls. Partway through, he left the room and came back dressed but then talked some more. Then he stood, leaned over to slap her thigh, and left the apartment, kissing her on the mouth on his way out.

She tried to think as Richie did about politics and the war. She thought that if she could pay attention to the world, not just to herself, she would be able to put to one side the question of when he'd come back—but she couldn't. For a day she'd hold the thought of his return like a drink she sipped all evening; then it was gone. Her classes distracted her a little. The college administration's repressive politics affected her students every day, and the government that waged distant war showed up in her students' anxiety and silence, and their fear of the draft. She liked these kids and wanted to spend time with them—she was more comfortable with her students than with anyone else in town, including Richie.

She phoned Lee, choosing a time when Richie would surely be out, and told her she was too busy for recorder lessons, and after that she never picked up the instrument.

Richie began to come more often, and she wondered if she'd won out over some other woman. He became more playful, more talkative. Twice he let her cook him dinner. She didn't know what excuse he made to Lee, but it was sweet to cook for him, as sexy as sex. They talked about dogs and cats. Richie and Lee had had one of each, and both had died. It was like the night

ALICE MATTISON

they'd talked about his youth: she never heard him speak for so long except about the war.

Artie was sure Harold needed him more than ever, now that he'd become a famous person, or maybe just a person who seemed famous to the people who already knew him. Artie clipped newspaper articles that mentioned Harold or left them circled in red, the paper folded on the kitchen table. He had seen a fairly decent review of Harold's book and a short article about a panel discussion in which Harold had participated. He had a knack for finding mentions of Harold. Something would make him know he had to read that story and in the tenth paragraph he'd see his friend's name, or pretend name—the name of his successful self, Artie said to Evelyn, now that Harold Abramovitz, the boy he'd gone to school with, had been murdered and thrown in a ditch. Dumps his name, dumps his wife, he said.

—You never liked her, and his name is his business, Evelyn said. Maybe he got tired of spelling it.

—I knew it would happen before they ever looked at each other.

—Knew they'd get married? She was cutting out a pattern on the kitchen table, making something for Carol's coming baby. Carol was married to a law student, lived in Queens, and belonged to a synagogue—which both irritated and tickled Artie. She worked in the city planner's office.

—Get married, get divorced, the whole thing, he said. They wouldn't listen to me, of course. Why should anybody listen to stupid Artie? But look at this.

He'd found an article in the paper about intellectuals who opposed the war, and it mentioned something Harold had published in *The Nation*. The bastard didn't tell me, he said. Now it's probably the next issue already.

Artie found the issue, read the piece—disagreed—and cut it

out to mail to Brenda in California, where she'd moved for no good reason. He didn't call Harold, but Harold called him a week or so later.

I presume, Artie said to him, you are calling to quiz me about your famous article.

—I didn't think you'd see it.

—If you want me to see it, you could send me a copy, or you could at least call and tell me it exists. Yes, I saw it.

—And what did you think?

—A ridiculous argument, Artie said. He tried to remember just what the article had said.

—Well, that happens not to be why I called, Harold said. Do you know what happened to Beatrice London?

Artie, who had been leaning on the wall in the kitchen, said, Let me take this on the other phone, yelling to Evelyn to hang up the kitchen phone. He was postponing hearing about Beatrice London. Whatever had happened to Beatrice London, Artie—who still sold shoes and played the recorder for hours each night—didn't want to know about it.

What happened, Harold insisted on telling him, was that Beatrice London had been sued by someone else she'd informed on, a woman, and the woman—who insisted she had never been a Communist and produced witnesses who had known her well in the thirties, and even known Beatrice in the thirties—had won.

—The mood's different—things are different, Harold said. He kept in touch with people he'd known from the union and had heard all about it.

—So what do you want me to do about it? Artie said.

—Ask to be reinstated.

—I don't see you asking to be reinstated.

—That has nothing to do with it, Harold said. I *was* a Communist. And I wasn't turned in by Beatrice London.

—And teaching in a high school would be a comedown for the mighty Professor Abramovitz, Artie said. Excuse me, Abrams.

—Right. I hire high school teachers to wipe my behind. Listen, you idiot, go down to the Board of Ed and see if you can get your job back. You know you want it.

—Why should they give me my job back?

—Because they'll be afraid you'll sue them. Because they've given five people their jobs back. Don't you pay attention?

—Should I go there or write them a letter?

—Yeah, Harold said, write them a letter. Call me and read it to me before you mail it.

—You think I've forgotten how to spell, crawling around on the floor with the goddamn shoes?

—You never knew how to spell, Harold said, which was not true; Artie had always loved words even more than their meanings. He read the dictionary.

—Who do I write to?

—Everybody. Write to the superintendent, and CC every name you can find at 110 Livingston. I'll call the union and get them to give us a list.

—What did they do to Bea London?

—You called her Bea?

—Beatrice is Bea, no? Used to make her mad. Did she go to prison?

Harold laughed. I don't think so. How are your kids?

They talked for an hour.

I t was Christmas break when Brenda finally got around to reading the essay from *The Nation* that her father had sent her. Her parents had wanted her to fly home for the holidays, but she didn't. Richie had hinted that he'd have more free time because Lee was going to visit relatives.

But Brenda never knew when Richie would come, and she had only one date marked on her calendar during the Christmas season. The *Speak Out* group proposed having a party, and pleased Brenda by wanting her company. Most were estranged from their families or far from home, stranded in this agricultural valley when they'd meant to go either to Los Angeles and become movie stars or to San Francisco, where they'd live in an enlightened and druggy society.

—We could do it at my house, she'd said, and today she was straightening her apartment in readiness. She had an uneasy feeling that the college administration would not approve of this party. But none of these kids were in her classes—well, Grace was going to take Brenda's composition class in the spring, but Grace didn't count. She was older than Brenda. These were good kids, and nobody else would know.

It was a few days before Christmas, and she hadn't heard from Richie for weeks. Brenda had been inside all day; the weather was chilly and raw, and she'd been postponing a trip to the store. It was maddening to care, but if she left she might miss him, and she couldn't leave. She was desultorily straightening her desk when she found the pages torn from *The Nation*. HAROLD, her father had written in red in the top margin of the first page, with an arrow, in case she didn't notice the byline. And near the top, in the left margin, he'd scrawled something else she couldn't read. She carried the pages across the room. Her apartment was warmed by one heater, under a grate in the floor, and the only way to get truly warm in the damp California winter was to stand on the grate, which she did for so long her shoes had developed ridges to match the wrought-iron grille's pattern. She stood swaying slightly and read Harold's essay. *Vietnam and the Graying Radical*, the piece was called.

In the last few tempestuous months, as the inspired and picturesque young with shaggy heads and peace signs have taken to the streets, among the myriad reactions of their elders it would be a mistake to overlook the rueful and perhaps embarrassed look on the faces of older men and women marching beside them—or not marching, hesitating as they slowly lace up cracked walking shoes in outmoded styles that have already tramped many miles.

Now she made out what her father had written next to these words. *What does he know about shoes?* Harold discussed the views of several aging thirties radicals toward the Vietnam war, using their books and articles as well as interviews to discuss first a man in his fifties who now led the peace movement in Cleveland and had been finding something to protest about the American government since 1935; then a professor who'd written books linking radical American movements to those in Europe and elsewhere; and finally a journalist who had renounced his early radicalism and now attacked the Left.

She kept reading, standing, until she reached a more personal passage near the end.

It may be of some use to describe the political and, indeed, moral shifts in thinking of one obscure young radical, who has aged into a less political person—an English professor— but who watches the marches with envy and has tentatively come to the conclusion that it makes sense to participate, his doubts stemming not from uncertainty about this abhorrent war but about the moral validity of protest when protest is sexy, when it's personally useful, and when it's fun.

Now she went into her living room and sat down to concentrate, as Harold described times she'd heard about only from her father. He had grown up the child of immigrant Jewish socialists, he explained, and had been drawn in when he began attending Communist protests and marches as a bystander. *But I have to admit,* Harold wrote, *that I was as entranced by the image of myself—the fervent young radical—as by the ideology I embraced.* There was something Brenda the English teacher didn't like about Harold's prose. She didn't like *embraced.* But she kept reading. She'd always found him irresistible but absurd, absurd but irresistible.

And I also disliked myself and saw through my posturings. I found reasons to tell my friends that I was a Communist, explaining to myself that I told them in order to proselytize, to win converts; but I knew why I told them: because it made me seem mysterious and bold. Women liked it. They'd spend time with me—go to bed with me—in order to talk me out of my politics, or that's what they told themselves they were doing. We were all in a game together, a play.

Later in life, I worked as a New York City high school teacher, only to lose my job when my past connection to Communism—long ago disavowed—came to light. I was guilty then, too, of vanity. I taught, and worked for civil rights, in a poor neighborhood. I secretly told myself I was a hero, but the greater secret was that I was of small or no utility to the people I supported, just someone entranced by the idea of himself.

Brenda, shamed and thrilled, knew what he meant. She thought he should have mentioned his friend, her father, but that thought disappeared in her pleasure. She felt the same way. She too had been a vainglorious fool, standing up for civil liberties and admiring herself for doing it, facing down the evil dean. But Harold continued:

But what I have just confessed is not the whole story, and that's what gives me hope—hope for myself but, more important, hope for the hirsute present generation of advocates for justice, who in their own way are surely as self-conscious, as self-satisfied, and as hungry for the romance of opposition as my friends and I were. I knew when I became a Communist that I was, in part, ridiculous, and I have to trust the person who, even then, writhed with shame in the night but kept his membership card current: if I had not been sincere as well as ridiculous, I would not have joined the Communist Party, would not have remained in it for several years. The party has long since lost its glamour for me, but the reasons I joined were good reasons, and the ideals that made me join are ideals I hold today: justice for the poor, justice for the working man, reward for labor. The Communist Party, it turned out, had no idea how to go about achieving these ideals—and, worse, it was in love with authoritarianism, but its desires were the desires I still hold. I can't, finally, blame myself for joining the Communist Party, however many girls it enabled me to lure into my shabby digs.

This was a new thought for Brenda. Her father had invariably spoken of Harold's membership in the Communist Party as foolishness, and she had assumed Harold had come to agree with him.

I gave up Communism when Stalin agreed with Hitler to share Poland: when they signed a nonaggression pact in the summer of 1939—which did not dismay everyone I knew in the party. Some shrugged, insisting it was a trick, and held out until the terrible revelations of 1956, but to me—a Jew already terrified for European Jewry—having anything to do with Hitler was unthinkable. I was true to what I believed—as I was true, later on, when I taught and tried to help my ghetto students survive (literally—one was killed by police) their difficult lives.

We are lucky enough to live in a country in which protesting is usually not fatal—in which it is often fun and sexy—but when the times command dissent, we must protest anyway. So I raise a glass to the kids who fill the streets today, shouting down this abhorrent war, and sometimes you'll see me in the rear, in those worn-out shoes, trying to keep up with young people spryer than I.

Brenda sat thinking about Harold Abrams and what she had read for longer than she should have, with a party to prepare for. Then, abruptly, she wanted to be outdoors, even if it was raining. She thrust her arms into her jacket sleeves and was out the door before her jacket was buttoned. The rain had increased, and as she drove, the windshield wipers swept noisily back and forth, with a syncopated squeal as the right one, which must have been bent, lagged. The immediate effect of reading Harold's article was to make Brenda generous: she bought more food, more beer and soda than she would have. She seemed to have something to celebrate.

She expected eight or ten kids, but fifteen showed up, one bringing a plate of Christmas cookies in different shapes, decorated with colored sprinkles, and another a dish of guacamole and a bag of tortilla chips. Several brought records. She put on *The White Album* and the students nodded shyly when they recognized the music, as if they had wondered about her taste. She left the beer in the refrigerator and put bottles of Coke out on the table with the food, but after an hour or so, she noticed that beer—her own beer and some in brands she hadn't bought—was on the table. She wanted a beer herself but had taken Coke because she was the teacher. Conversation had begun slowly and shyly, as if they weren't exactly the people they were at school, but now there was more talk, louder when it was hard to speak over the sound of the records—someone had turned up the volume. More people came in and the group divided, so there were several conversations at once. Grace arrived with her husband, a beaming man who looked like a minister. Again, talk slowed, but finally everyone—even Brenda—took beers, and that helped. She forgot to think as a teacher and became a hostess, worrying that her party was boring and stiff. So she was pleased to see young people she didn't know and tried to get them into conversation. Some didn't know she was a teacher, and some were probably her age. One girl said no, she wasn't a student at the JC, but her boyfriend was, and she nodded at a couple of young men near the food table, neither of whom Brenda knew. She smelled a joint, excused herself, and went to speak to Grace. Should I try and stop people from smoking dope? she said.

Grace looked at her in a funny way, and said, It might be too late.

Brenda wondered what Grace's husband thought. What do you do? she said. He wasn't a minister, at least. He sold insurance. I know a lot of these kids, he said. Our kids are younger, but I've seen these around. He pointed. I know that girl. Nice girl.

Grace laughed, but she looked uncomfortable.

—You think I should make them stop smoking dope, don't you? Brenda said.

—Don't go by what I think, said Grace, which was not what she'd have said at school, where she spoke her mind. There was no one else to ask.

Brenda went over to the two boys passing a joint back and forth. I have to ask you to stop, she said.

—Stop what?

—I'll get in trouble with my landlord, Brenda said. Take the dope outside. No, don't. She pictured them smoking—all of them smoking—lined up in front of the house. Just put it away until you're somewhere else, okay?

—Sure, one boy said, but he looked annoyed. They soon left.

Toward midnight, a drunken boy tried to kiss her. You're the nicest teacher I ever had, he said, and then she realized that he was, indeed, her own student: a quiet boy named Neil in the back row of a remedial English class. Neil, honey, no, she said gently, and she was afraid he'd cry.

—Come in the kitchen, she said. Help me make coffee. He was blond, skinny—he probably weighed less than she did—with tight shoulders. In class she had wished she could rub his shoulders and make his neck look less taut, and now she wondered nervously if she'd been attracted to him and if he'd sensed it. The thought embarrassed her and she opened another beer. When she saw three more kids smoking a joint, she didn't stop them. She and Neil made coffee, and she made him drink some. I don't really like coffee, he said. She carried cups and mugs into the living room—she had not thought about coffee and hadn't bought paper cups—and then brought the milk container and sugar. She began throwing out beer bottles. She took the needle off the record on the turntable—Richie Havens—and turned on the overhead light. Only six or eight kids were left, and now they began to look for their coats. A small blond girl threw her arms around Brenda. She was a stranger and had come with two other strangers. I never, never, never thought, she said. When Brenda was finally alone, she was suddenly depressed and didn't try to clean up, but went to bed.

She was awakened by the doorbell, frightened before she was fully awake, as if the ringing was the next event in a bad dream. She never thought of ignoring the bell. The ring was prolonged, and in her dishevelment, blinking and holding her head down because a headache was overtaking her, she struggled into her bathrobe and to the door. It was light out. Her breath tasted unpleasant, and she held her hand to her mouth. Richie stood outside, and if he hadn't already seen her, Brenda might have called an apology and gone back to bed. But her heart was tumbling in her chest as well; she was happy to see him. She'd feared, the night before, that Richie would never come back and that if he didn't, she was somehow not the person she was claiming to be, not the person the party guests thought they were looking at.

When she let him in, he put his arms up as always, but she didn't move into them, embarrassed.

—What went on here? he said. The room smelled of stale beer and crushed potato chips.

—Give me a minute, you woke me up, she said.

—What have you been doing?

—Richie, I need to pee.

—Who was here?

—Students. The *Speak Out* group—you know, the kids who want to put out a magazine. Not all kids.

—Not all kids? In his coat, he began gathering paper plates. Where does the garbage go? he called.

—Stop! Sit down. Let me just wash my face. She went into the bathroom, peed, washed her face, brushed her teeth. She would have liked to shower, but she was afraid he'd leave.

—I'm sorry! she said, coming out. Let me do that. Want coffee?

He shrugged and withdrew to the window, standing with his back to it, so when she looked into his face she could see only shadows and the planes of his nose and chin. It felt as if she would gain points in some game she hadn't agreed to play if she could get him to sit down, that he would gain points if he didn't. She removed the obvious clutter and started coffee.

When she returned to the living room while the coffee perked, he had moved out into the middle of the room. His mouth twitched oddly, and for a moment he looked frightened. Nobody's here? he said.

—What do you mean?

—Nobody's here, I mean—is anybody here? Now he sounded impatient.

—Except us? Why should anyone be here? She looked around. Had one of the kids gotten so drunk he'd passed out? Was someone in the apartment with her?

—I mean, he said, in the bedroom.

She understood. No, of course not. You think I slept with them?

—One would be enough, I presume.

—Of course not! she said. For heaven's sake. I go crazy waiting for you.

—And you know I come when I can. And you take it out on me when I can't, by coming on to one of those students. You said they weren't all kids. Again, she glimpsed that tipped head, the look of someone younger, more unsure—only for a moment.

—I don't do that, she said, but she felt ashamed, as if she had done it, as if what she'd done while simply leading her life— thinking each action was the next logical one—might somehow have fallen into a shape she hadn't planned or wanted.

He'd had a haircut and his hair was shorter this time. Now, she said, you don't look the least bit like an antiwar person. It seemed that she could fix this morning if she could get him to relax his neck, his jaw.

—What are you talking about? I don't look like what I think.

—You had long hair. I thought you were against the war the first time I saw you.

—I happened to like the way I look in long hair, he said resentfully, and I happened to get tired of it. So you don't want to sleep with me anymore because I don't look like one of your scruffy friends?

—Richie, she said as gently as she could. Of course I want to sleep with you. I don't even *have* friends.

—Oh, yeah, so who were you having fun with last night? Your enemies? And obviously you gave them stuff to drink, he said.

Now she was worried. I didn't mean to, she said, but I let them come here, and I bought beer. I thought they wouldn't take any unless they were of age, but things got away from me.

—Got away from you! You didn't *mean* to buy beer, but somehow—somehow or other— His voice rose to a falsetto, *Oh my gosh, I seem to have bought some beer!* In his own angry voice he said, You never were running it. I can see from here you didn't show a goddamn grain of sense! He sounded like a father, not exactly like her father, though it was an accusation her father might have made, but like a father more sure of himself than hers was, one who knew the rules and enforced them. And like the kind of father she knew of but didn't have, Richie stepped toward her, his hand raised, and smacked the side of her head and her ear. How can you be like that? he said, his voice high again now, almost teary. What am I risking, with someone who can't think?

When he connected, Brenda cried out and stepped backward. Her face stung, and the shame was worse, mixing with the headache. Don't! she said, but it sounded more like a plea than a command. She ran into the bedroom and flung herself on the bed, sobbing, and he followed.

—Aah, what do you do things like that for? You think you can come to a town like this and have that kind of party? You haven't noticed how people think around here? I hope what I just did is the worst of it.

There was some solace in giving way to the sloppiness of tears. At last he began stroking her back and shoulders and her hair, and his voice turned soft. It's okay, baby, it's okay. Maybe nothing will come of it. We'll hope for the best. Come on, baby.

She turned, and after a while, she opened her arms to him and felt the comfort of his solid, expressive body. His body was more nuanced, more able to express complex feeling, than his talk. It cherished her convincingly. Lovey, he said, as he was getting out of bed, reaching to stroke her shoulder again. You know why I did that? I had to do it. I had to wake you up. Do you understand?

—Yes, Brenda said.

—Maybe nothing else will happen, he said, and she didn't know whether he meant maybe nothing bad would come of her party—and what would that be?—or whether he meant he might not have cause to hit her again. She pulled the blankets around her, bruised, shamed, comforted, afraid and not afraid. So it had happened.

Harold phoned a lawyer. He had to phone several before he found someone who was interested in taking Artie's case against Beatrice London on a contingent fee basis. Simply writing a letter and asking the Board of Education to restore Artie's job had no effect. Artie had not been surprised—he was almost triumphant—when his letter was answered by someone who obviously didn't know what he was talking about.

—I should change my name, like you, he said, and apply to teach for the first time. Hello, this is Artie Saltz. Can I teach Social Studies? I've heard it's fun. My first unit will be freedom of speech in the classroom.

—You probably wouldn't have to change your name, Harold said. Nobody there would think about who you might be. But if it ever came out, you'd lose your job again.

—I was kidding. It's no fun these days. Kids pull knives on you. Why should I bother?

—You'll never be happy until you do. Harold had no classes that day and had met Artie for lunch at the Chinese restaurant. He was reaching his chopsticks into the middle of the table for shiny eggplant cubes, looking up now and then at his old friend, who still used a fork but who ate a lot and never gained weight, unlike Harold. Maybe fitting shoes all day kept him slim.

—What do you know about happy? Artie said. Living alone in that place—like a doctor's office. Bare, white, and cold. At least when I go to visit, you don't make me wear a johnny coat that shows my tuchas. He pushed his chair back. I don't know which would be worse, teaching or this. My back is a wreck from all the bending in the store. I'll be a cripple before I can retire. I had to stop playing the recorder at night—I can't stand up after a day in the store. But teaching again? All those kids? I'm not the same guy.

Harold thought that might be the truth. Maybe he was being foolish, telling all these lawyers that justice required putting his friend back into the classroom. Maybe it was too late.

Then Artie said, Okay, give me the name of the lawyer. And now tell me, how are your kids? And Harold, do you ever get to the cabin these days? Is it still there?

Harold bent over his briefcase, looking for the notebook in which he'd written the name and number of the lawyer. His head was down, and he was glad Artie couldn't see his face when he mentioned the cabin. Harold had to compose himself before he could speak again. Paul's fine, he said. Writing for the student newspaper. He wants to go away next year—maybe Berkeley. He's caught up in this stuff, but he's not crazy. I think he'll be okay.

—And Nelson? Artie's face tensed.

—The same as ever. He heard anger in his own voice and Artie waved as if to say, Never mind. No, Harold said. I'm not ashamed of him, but Artie, what can I do? He's in the street, in some apartment—I don't know. I'd go back and change everything if I could, but I wouldn't even know what to change.

It was the thought of the cabin that had upset Harold. The lake and the woods around it didn't enter his thoughts for weeks at a time, but when the memory came, it was intense. The cabin and even its surroundings were diminished these days, with those other cabins on the lake. Paul said he was bored when he went with his mother and grandparents, but when Harold thought of being there, it wasn't even the lake and the mountains that came to mind first; it might be walking out of Grand Union with a bag of groceries and across a rainy parking lot to his car. He didn't know why his brain had bothered to keep that memory.

Harold took leave of Artie, urging him to phone the lawyer. That bitch owes you something! he said. He took the subway to Times Square and walked over to the library, the wind puffing out his raincoat as he passed Bryant Park. He was writing an article about Delmore Schwartz. His mood improved. He felt lucky to have the day—it was exam week at the college—to have the city, the freedom to go into the reading room and consult an obscure book, as he'd been doing all his life. He began feeling his usual guilt: Artie's life had been narrowed, not broadened, by their dismissal from the school system. Harold put that feeling aside. He could feel guilty about any number of topics, and what good did that do anyone? He was having dinner with Naomi, meeting her at a restaurant downtown. Naomi enjoyed good food but didn't want more than health required, as she enjoyed other people without craving anyone. He was shy about touching her. She was at ease, watching others and commenting on them. Her heart wasn't constantly breaking and mending, and she didn't have to protect herself. Naomi had the luxury to be clever, to be wise. He could marry her now, but she didn't need him any more than she ever had.

The book he consulted was old, interesting, and useful. He read into the late afternoon, making careful notes on the 4 x 6 index cards he preferred. When he left the library, it was dark. He started walking down Fifth Avenue, then jumped on a bus, but when he got off, close to the restaurant—downtown on the East Side—he realized he was much too early. He'd lost track of the time in the wrong direction, which was a little embarrassing. He was near Nelson's apartment—if Nelson still lived in the apartment—and though he hadn't been there, he thought he remembered the address and had it in the little leather book he carried in his briefcase. He was afraid to ring the doorbell, if there was a working doorbell, but he could walk past the place. The apartment was in a poorly kept-up brownstone, and he didn't know which floor it was on. He felt overdressed in this neighborhood with its shabby, colorful shops smelling of incense: as always, Harold was conspicuous. What if Nelson had seen him walk by his house and keep going? At that thought, he took his address book out to check the address—he was right— and returned. He mounted the front steps and tried all three doorbells, none of which was labeled. After a wait, he heard sounds inside, and the door was opened by a girl with loose hair and overalls.

—I'm looking for Nelson Abrams—I mean Abramovitz, Harold said. Nelson had pointedly refused to change his name.

—Are you his father?

—That's right. I'm Harold Abrams.

—Hi, the girl said.

—Does he live here? Harold persisted.

—Sort of. He's here now.

She led the way up a staircase with loose treads and squeaky boards, to a dark landing, then into an apartment. He was in a living room like various shabby living rooms of his youth, and four or five young people sat on sofas and a bed and on the floor. There were a lot of filled ashtrays. These kids were accustomed to dropping in on one another. It would have been more awkward if he'd tried to set up an appointment. There was insistent music he didn't recognize. Nelson was one of the kids sitting on the floor, leaning back against a sofa, with a gray tiger cat in his lap. Except Nelson was too old to be considered a kid. He looked up and smiled. Dad? He wasn't surprised enough.

—I was in the neighborhood, Harold said.

—Trying to score some good stuff? one of the kids said, and Harold didn't know if he was seriously offering him a deal or not.

—Just in the neighborhood.

—You're not a narc, are you? someone said, then smiled.

The girl made room on the sofa against which Nelson leaned, and Harold sat down.

—Do you know anything about cats? Nelson said. I'm worried about this cat.

—Is it yours? Harold said, looking down at his son's hair. It was an unexpectedly tender view of Nelson. His brown hair was clean.

—I brought him home to feed him, Nelson said. I bought cat food, but he won't eat.

The girl said, He wants to be outside—he's an outdoor cat. He's going to spray too—you know, Nelse, a male cat that hasn't been altered can't live in a house.

—Just giving him a chance for a decent meal, Nelson said. But he won't eat. Maybe Ralph fed him.

—Who's Ralph? Harold said.

Nelson tipped his head back to look at him. He looked better than when he had come to Harold's house. A very cool guy I met, trying to end the draft. He might give me a job, but he can't pay.

—That's wonderful, Harold said, with unconvincing enthusiasm. Volunteer. End the draft. He felt as if he was on display. He asked more questions. Let me know the address of the organization, he said. I'll make a contribution.

—Sure, Nelson said, but kept stroking the cat.

Harold continued asking questions: When had Nelson seen Paul? He didn't remember. Then he described his afternoon at the library. At last it was time to go and meet Naomi. Where is it? Harold said, as he stood. The place where you might work. Where's the office?

Nelson pointed vaguely.

—Downtown?

—Downtown.

—I've got to go, he said.

—You don't think the cat is sick? Nelson said, reaching the animal in Harold's direction.

Harold stood. He reached down to stroke the cat. It was bony. I don't know. Maybe.

—No, you're not an expert on animals, are you? Nelson said.

The girl didn't stand up and Harold let himself out. He was

late now and hurried to the restaurant. His hand felt unclean from touching the cat. No, he was not an expert on animals. He found Naomi at a table in the back. It was an Indian restaurant they liked. Naomi had learned to eat Indian food in England and had introduced it to Harold. She looked up as he came along—amused at what she seemed to see in his face.

—Nelson's all right! he said, with sudden certainty. I found his apartment. It's not so bad—it's an apartment. It's true, he hasn't figured out his life yet, but he's all right.

She looked doubtful, but she smiled and patted Harold's hand—the one that had stroked the cat. He pulled it back.

—I'm glad to hear it, she said.

—You don't think I'm right.

—I didn't say that.

He sat down, and a smiling waiter rushed forward with a napkin and a menu. Naomi was delicately eating the spicy Indian crackers they always served at the start of the meal.

—You think I'm deluded. You're probably right.

—Why should I think that? Tell me about it. He excused himself to go to the men's room. When he came back, his happy excitement was gone. Nelson lived in Harold's upper abdomen—maybe where his diaphragm was. It had loosened, just because Harold had found him and his face looked better, but while he washed his hands, it was as if someone behind him had tightened a band around his body.

On Christmas morning Brenda found a grocery bag on her front step, which proved to contain a bottle of good Scotch, a salami, a book of crossword puzzles, and a handmade bead necklace. The Scotch made her know that this was Richie's present, and Brenda was soothed and cheered by the combination—crossword puzzles because she liked words? She'd eaten much of the salami and drunk some of the Scotch before he turned up again, and he seemed to think she should have kept them for his visits, as if she might have been entertaining other men, not just nibbling salami for lunch.

It was February before he hit her again. In the intervening weeks, Richie fucked her with tenderness and intensity, leaving her spent and joyful. Other times he was playful, staying for a couple of hours to drink and tease. Brenda bought a television set and they watched the news together like married people. Richie speculated aloud about the start of the Nixon presidency. He never said what excuse he gave Lee when he visited Brenda, and she approved of that. Sometimes he was coming from work, and a few times he told her about the projects he had lined up or the ones his crews were working on. She talked about her students and her classes, and he listened, staring as if everything shocked him a little. Youthfulness would cross his face briefly and be gone.

He hit her again on a Thursday in February when the dean had left a note in her mailbox asking her to come to his office a few days later. Richie showed up unexpectedly, late that evening, tapping on the glass pane in the door. Brenda was in her bathrobe. He seized her by the shoulders and began propelling her toward the bed. She was usually delighted by such an interruption of the long evening she'd otherwise spend in her big chair with a stack of papers—it was funny, it was fun—but this time she put up a hand to stop him and said, I need to ask you about something. I'm glad to see you.

—Ask.

She told him about the note from the dean, and his neck stiffened. Why are you asking me?

—I don't have anyone else to ask.

—So you're scraping the bottom of the barrel?

—No, that's not what I mean. You're sensible. You run a business. And you grew up here. Should I be worried?

He glared at her, his arms in a long-sleeved polo shirt—which seemed a little short for his body when he held them at his sides, as he did now—rigid. Isn't it a little late to ask?

—What do you mean?

—You have a wild party, God knows what you do with all these men, you serve booze to underage kids—and then you ask me if you should worry? I don't know what I see in you, baby. You're stupid if you ask that question.

She straightened her bathrobe and tied the belt more tightly. It was light blue, a present from her parents years ago, stained now. She looked dumpy and boring in it, but Richie seemed to have no complaints about her looks. I'm not stupid, she said. She shouted it. I'm not stupid. Now her voice shook. I may be naïve, but I'm not stupid. It was something her father might have said, calling her stupid or, more likely, asking her if she was stupid, if she was pretending to be stupid, or if she thought maybe he was stupid for putting up with her.

She took a step back from him. You may not come here and call me stupid.

Richie swung his right arm back and socked her across the side of her head, socked her again on her shoulder, so she fell to one knee. He stepped back and looked at her. The phone rang. Had the landlord heard something?

She let it ring.

Is it your boyfriend? Richie said, in an ugly voice. Aren't you going to answer it? Answer it.

—I'm not going to answer it. It had to be the landlord, complaining about noise. Everyone she cared about was in New York, and it was the middle of the night there. But what if something was wrong in New York?

It rang and rang. Answer it, Richie said, and she was afraid not to. Her shoulder and face ached and she was crying. She crawled to a chair and supported herself, standing up, then made her way to the phone, holding the edge of a table as she went. It was her father's voice that said, Brenny? Brenny?

The nickname made her miss him even before she knew what was happening. Dad? What's wrong? But his voice sounded happy.

—Wrong? Nothing's wrong. You're an aunt, that's what!

—Carol had the baby? Is everything okay? Carol's due date was weeks off.

—Everything's great. It's a boy—we finally got a boy, not that there's anything wrong with girls!

—And Carol's all right?

—She's fine. She just had it. Lenny called me. Woke us up—I even woke you up, didn't I? You sound confused. I'm your father. I'm a grandpa!

—What's his name? Brenda said.

—I forgot to ask. Your mother's telling me I should let you sleep. Isn't that great?

—It's wonderful, Daddy.

—And I'm getting my job back.

—What? Your job?

Richie wore no coat. Now he turned—she saw him as if he was far away, like someone three or four rooms away in a museum where gallery followed on gallery—opened the door, and slammed it behind him.

—What was that? her father said.

—What?

—That sound. Did you drop something?

—Yes, I dropped something, Brenda said. Daddy, I'm so happy. I'm coming to visit the baby. I'll come soon. She had to climb out of this trouble, this life. She couldn't get on a plane—she'd have a black eye and bruises. But she had to see her parents and her sister.

—What about your job? she said.

—It's a long story. I'll tell you in the morning. I should hang up, in case Lenny calls again.

—Okay. She put down the phone carefully. The papers she'd been reading were scattered on the floor, and she bent, in pain, to pick them up. She wanted her nephew to have nothing like this pain in his life, never for a moment. But she knew that every life includes pain, and the thought that this baby was already destined for trouble and hurt made her weep yet again as she took herself to bed.

She was awakened by a tap on the window behind her, and she knew it was Richie again. The tap was repeated. Aching, she got out of bed. If she turned on the light, he'd see her clearly. She went into the living room, and he must have heard her because she heard him walk around the house and tap again on the pane of the door. She turned on the porch light and, yes, it was Richie. She wasn't afraid he'd hurt her. Something made her want to open the door, something confusing, something to do with the baby, with the thought she'd had earlier that life isn't life without pain.

She opened the door just an inch.

—I'm sorry, baby, Richie said. I am so sorry. I am so sorry.

She let him in. He said, I know it's wrong to hit you. I should not hit you.

—That's right, she said.

—But you'll forgive me, won't you? You're not going to throw me out? I've been walking around town all this time.

—What will Lee think?

—I don't care what she thinks, but you have to love me, he said.

—I have to love you? He had used the word love only once before.

Richie's sturdy body paced through the living room in the dark, where the only illumination came from a strip of light from a nearby streetlamp. He was walking carefully, not to make noise, and that calmed Brenda. He cared about not waking the landlord. I don't know why I did that, he said. I had no call to do that. But, baby, he said, and turned and stopped. Put on the light, would you?

She turned on a lamp, and they sat down. She was cold and went into the bedroom and returned with her blanket and wrapped it around herself.

—I will never hit you again, Richie said, and she knew that was not true. But she waited to see why she was not just throwing him out. But, baby, what we have is not just hitting. And you know, you could hit me sometime too, if you're really mad—I would hit you back, maybe, but—

He paused and she was stiff with horror, expectation, and pleasure.

—Don't you think we're better that we do things this way? Other people are boring, he said.

—Because they don't hit each other?

—Don't you see? he said. We do things in a big way, you and I.

—You mean, Brenda said, you mean we are passionate.

—I mean we are passionate. We take a risk. We live the way people should live. The other people in this town—they don't live like this, and they wouldn't understand. I knew you would. Because you're from somewhere else—I knew that the first time I saw you, in the market. Then when I found out you're from New York, you're Jewish—I knew you wouldn't be like other people, that whatever happened, you'd understand, you'd know it's worth it.

—You think it's worth it to me to be hit if I can be your lover?

—Isn't it? I mean being the kind of people we are.

She didn't have the courage to say no, and she didn't want to say no. She couldn't say yes.

—Maybe, she said.

—Oh my love, my lovey, my loving lovey, he said, and he guided her into the bedroom and made love to her roughly and gently, and spent most of the night. She woke to see him carrying his shoes, tiptoeing out of the room. She felt some satisfaction in what they had, their daring, her own daring, her capacity to see the good in this man. She thought it was funny that he expected her to be open to violence because she was Jewish.

The faculty had an association, and someone represented Brenda when the dean, in April, brought witnesses against her who swore that she'd served beer to students at her party, and that students had smoked illegal drugs.

—Did you see Miss Saltzman smoke illegal drugs?

—I don't think so. The boy who spoke was the boyfriend of the girl who had hugged Brenda and said she never, never, never. What had she meant?

The faculty representative said little and passed Brenda a note that read, *I'm not sure there's much we can do about this.* Brenda, shamed and frantic, knew that what was being tried was her politics as much as anything else, but what could she say? It was her own fault. Grace, at Brenda's request, sat at the back of the classroom where the meeting was being held. Brenda had spoken of her as a friend, though this term she was her student. The classes were going so well she thought maybe she was actually a teacher. Students wrote pages she read with interest and even pleasure. They read poems and stories, and some even wrote poems and stories. Someone wrote a novella. Research papers on Southeast Asia and the wine industry of California appeared, among others, and only one was visibly plagiarized (the student who claimed to have written it copied the words *See Illustration, Page 48* when they appeared in his source). Now, to her surprise, Brenda wanted to stay.

But two weeks later she received an official letter in the mail terminating her employment at the end of the semester in June, and then she wanted to leave right away. She phoned Grace, who drove over to Brenda's house, and they stayed up late, drinking wine and talking about it. Grace said if Brenda left now, it would be disloyal to the students. How much do they have? she said. You'd be abandoning them. Brenda was touched that she left herself out. She'd be abandoning Grace too.

—I'm not abandoning them; the administration is forcing me to abandon them. The administration has decided they're better off without me.

—That's not the way they'll see it. And it's not true. Anyway, you have a job until the end of the term. You'll get paid. Maybe you need the money.

—Of course I need the money.

—Where will you go? Grace said then. I'll miss you. I wanted to be friends—after I get my A. If you don't stay, I won't get it.

—Won't they hire a substitute?

—I'm subversive. Nobody but you would give me an A.

—You've earned an A. You've written pages and pages. You're the only person in this valley who can spell.

It was one in the morning. Brenda had drunk too much wine. Want to spend the night? she said.

—No, thanks. Grace was tall and narrow, with a calm, round face and hair in soft waves down the sides of it. Brenda longed to stroke that hair. Of course, she could trust Grace—one more student being given drink, though a student older than Brenda:

Grace had turned out to be thirty-eight, ten years older. What if you wreck your car on the way home? Brenda said. They won't just fire me; they'll kill me.

—I won't, Grace said. I can't spend the night. I wish I could. Something passed between them so potent that Brenda was scared, and she stood up. I'll make coffee. She found cookies. They each had three or four. They grinned and hugged.

—I'll stay until the end of the term, Brenda said.

Two nights later, Richie beat her up again. This time it was because she was uninformed about the war. She couldn't even remember later what she'd said, something vague about a story she'd seen in the paper. He lectured and lectured and began pacing and yelling and demanding, and working himself up to the kind of frenzy, once more, that made it easy to take her by the shoulders and pinch hard, to thrust his face into hers, to demand again and again that she stop being the kind of woman who doesn't care and doesn't know. You could be better than that! he said. You're not like Lee. He swung at her face and swung again.

Brenda sank to the floor, sobbing, not caring that her face was wet with tears and snot, making no effort to clean herself. You'd better go, she said, when she could look up.

—I didn't mean it like that. I didn't mean to get like that. I'm taking out my rage at Nixon on you. It's a rough world, lovey.

—It's late, she said. They had made love hours ago; it was rare for him to stay so long. He stood up, kissed the top of her head, and left her where she was. Brenda didn't move for a long time. The phone rang and rang, and she didn't pick it up. She hadn't gone to see the baby, but she talked to Carol now and then. The baby was fine. Finally, the ringing stopped. More time passed, and then Brenda stood up and went to the bathroom to wash her face. She sat in her chair for another half hour.

Then she sat down at the typewriter and wrote a letter to her chairman, who had looked at her with increasing sadness. *I'm sorry to let you know in this abrupt way that a family emergency has called me back to New York and I must leave immediately. I deeply regret being unable to complete the semester.* She wrote a note to her landlord, explaining that she would have no further need of the apartment and apologizing for leaving in it a television set that she would not be able to take with her. *Thank you for everything,* she finished.

She began to pack. Imagining her mother observing her, she threw out everything in the refrigerator and wiped it out. She had saved cartons she'd brought in the fall, and she filled them with books. Working all night, she was able to pack her car and leave before daylight, leaving the note to the landlord in his mailbox. She ate breakfast in an all-night place and waited until the bank opened, when she emptied her checking account. On the way out of town she mailed the letter to her chairman. She drove a hundred miles north and put up in a motel for two days. Her bruises ached. The only useful thing she did was reorganize her suitcases so she had to open only one to get the clothes she'd need on a cross-country trip. She slept and cried.

If she hadn't fled, she'd have let Richie in again. She wanted to phone Grace and explain, but she didn't want Grace to know the truth. She was appalled at herself, appalled at the person she was, less and less in control every year, less and less able to find a life. She had never spoiled anything this badly before, and she didn't know how or why it had happened. All she could tell herself for sure was that she was against the war; everything somehow seemed to have flowed from that conviction—and her solitude—but she didn't know why that should be so and didn't regard it as an excuse. She blamed herself for everything.

The motel had a television and she watched without seeing. The second night, she found in her glove compartment the map she'd used the previous summer, driving across the country. She brought it into her room and studied it, deciding to take the northern route east—Route 90—because she knew nothing about the places she'd drive through: Idaho, Montana, Minnesota. Making the decision was the first moment at which she felt able to choose to do something she wanted. The trip ahead of her would be a slow progress through ordinary interactions she would—somehow—not destroy: conversations with waitresses in which she would ask for coffee, conversations with motel keepers in which she would ask for a room, exchanges about the weather with men who worked in gas stations. She trusted herself with nothing more and wouldn't need more. She considered driving on back roads instead of the highway, to make it take longer. She had no idea what to do when she reached New York—which she assumed must be where she was going: driving toward her father's disapproval and her mother's distress. But she would see the baby, Gabriel, for the first time. She had promised to fly east months ago. She had gone shopping and sent him a little red shirt and a pair of baby overalls: at least she had done that.

She spent a couple of days in Seattle, having her ancient Volvo worked on. With her car in a garage, she walked around near her motel, looking at houses, people, and stores. She had no energy to try and find the center of the city, buy a guidebook, go to look at what was there to be looked at. She stayed where she was: she had found a garage and a motel, and at the end of a long walk were a couple of places to eat.

Artie's quest to be reinstated as a New York City teacher ended happily, abruptly, and mysteriously, when he received a form letter from the Board of Education instructing him to report to an office where he'd be required to complete certain papers updating his records. It looked like the letter that might be received by a teacher who was returning after taking time off, he explained to Harold on the phone.

His lawyer had filed papers, written letters, and asked questions, and Artie would never know whether that had anything to do with what had happened. The letter had come the day before Carol gave birth to Gabriel. Wasn't somebody getting born the day I lost the job in the first place? he said to Evelyn.

—Sort of.

—Do you see a pattern here? Artie was elated, giddy. He hadn't called Brenda the day he found out about the job. He was uneasy with her—baffled by her decisions, her life—but the news of the baby made him forget everything else.

Artie was assigned to take over the seventh-grade social studies and English classes of a teacher at a school in Queens who had just gone on maternity leave. When he'd imagined being reinstated, he'd pictured his old school and what he'd feel walking into that doorway with its neatly arranged bricks. His new school was in a postwar building of no particular style, and his arrival there—more paperwork—felt unrelated to the intense events of his dismissal. Nobody seemed to know about that. He was glad. He was simply going to work, but now, he pointed out to his friends and relatives, he no longer had to crawl around on the floor and handle strangers' feet. A few days after he quit the job in the shoe store, he knew how strange—even educational— it had been. There were times when a foot revealed terrible secrets: strange wounds, malformations, obscene ankle tattoos. He knew something he hadn't known before and knew it was something he could not explain, at least not quickly, at least not in a shout.

With astonishment, he heard the way his pupils talked. He'd forgotten, now that his daughters were grown up. At first, these kids seemed different—more knowing, more cynical, older.

Then they didn't. He could still make them laugh by sternly telling them to do something they couldn't possibly do: Girls in the first row, please turn yourselves into butterflies. He still argued with them. Evelyn told him to be careful, for heaven's sake, but Artie had never known how to be careful. He loved the children more than he had before—or more simply than before, as he loved Gabriel more simply than he loved Carol and Brenda: he wanted less.

It tickled him that Brenda had become a teacher because as a girl, she'd insisted there was nothing she'd hate more. All through the spring, he missed Brenda and imagined companionable conversations about their shared profession. How different could their work be? He wondered if he could advise her about problems she faced and wondered what she'd think of his classroom. Brenda had been remote and terse all year, but he wanted to be friends with her; he'd always known that she understood and approved of him, even though they still had fights. Now they were colleagues. One night late in April he woke up thinking about a problem in his third-period class. Artie had developed insomnia in his fifties, a restlessness that made him wander the apartment, staring out of dark windows, picking up books and magazines and putting them down again. At present, he was troubled about two girls in one of his classes. They were smart, and he wanted to reach them in something like the same way he had wanted to reach Brenda. They passed notes and glanced at him defiantly if they saw him looking at them; they whispered in class. They claimed to be in favor of the war and frequently raised their hands to ask how any patriotic person could fail to support the fight against communism in Southeast Asia. And just this morning, one of them had said, But maybe you don't think communism is so bad, Mr. Saltzman? and he felt himself blush as he looked at her.

—I'm asking you to find Vietnam on a map, that's all, he said. In his new school, at least, the maps were more up-to-date than in the school he used to work in—his real school, he called it to himself.

Maybe Brenda would have helpful ideas. It was not the middle of the night in California, only the evening. He liked having an excuse to phone her. He dialed her number and let the phone ring. No answer. He wondered where she might be on a weekday evening.

The next night he tried Brenda again, but again she was not home. The next day was Saturday, and as soon as it was late enough in the morning to call California, he tried Brenda's number again. When did we last speak to Brenda? he asked Evelyn, when again there was no answer.

—Two weeks ago.

—I've been trying to call her and she's never home.

—When did you try to call her? Why didn't you tell me? Evelyn was straightening up after lunch.

—I didn't want to worry you.

She turned from the refrigerator, leaving the door ajar, the mayonnaise in her hand. What are you protecting me from? I have such a good life I've never learned how to worry?

—You do have a good life, he said.

—I do. I have a good job and a grandson, but I wish Brenda was closer to home.

—And a good husband. Who can still do it in bed. Who even has a job you don't have to be ashamed of.

—Artie, I was never ashamed. She went to the phone, and he saw that she knew Brenda's number by heart. Nobody home, she said. It's Saturday. She's running errands, or maybe she's doing something nice.

—Or getting arrested, he said. Marching against the war.

—Not getting arrested, I hope. We'll try later.

She tried every hour. She'd turn away from the phone each time, saying, Look, I know this is silly. She could have gone on a trip. She's a grown woman. She's older than Carol, and I don't worry if I don't know where Carol is.

—You know where Carol is. She's at home, she's at work, she's at the grocery store. Or the shul.

Evelyn didn't answer. She was compulsively cleaning. It's not that, she said. If I couldn't reach Carol, there are ten people I could call who might know where she is—her mother-in-law, her friends. If I can't reach Brenda, there isn't anybody in the world I can call. What is wrong with her, that there's nobody I can call?

A day and a half later—Evelyn was speechless with fear by now, and Artie was considering calling the cops in Brenda's town to report a missing person—the phone was answered. Artie, watching, saw Evelyn's startled face. This is Evelyn Saltzman, she said in her work voice. I'm trying to reach my daughter Brenda.

Artie ran to the bedroom phone. She took off in the middle of the night, a man's voice was saying. I don't know where she went. And I don't know what kind of fishy stuff was going on in this apartment. Have you been calling all day? I kept hearing the ringing. It's an adjoining apartment—I hear everything.

—I'm her mother, Evelyn said. Can't you tell me more? Is her car there?

—Her car is gone, her things are mostly gone, the rent is paid. But she didn't give me notice, she didn't turn off the electricity or the phone. I don't know what's going on, and whatever it is, I don't want to be mixed up in it. Men showing up at all hours! Look, I don't know what kind of people you are, but that's not what I expected, renting to a teacher. Now he was shouting.

—I'm sorry to have disturbed you, Evelyn said, and hung up. Artie ran back into the living room. You should have got his name! You should have got his number!

—Why didn't you? You were on the phone!

—I don't know. I couldn't talk.

—At least we know now she's not lying there dead.

—Is that what you thought? he said.

She sat down, and her voice was weak. Artie, where could she be? Why doesn't she call us?

—She's all right. She'll call.

—You don't think she's called Carol?

He called Carol, who had heard nothing. She listened to his account of each call. I'm sure she's all right, she said.

—Does she talk to you? he asked Carol.

—Not much. All I know is what she thinks of the war. She's probably protesting somewhere. Or she got arrested. Dad, do you think she's in jail?

—She'd have called us, he said. He didn't know how he'd get through the hours. How's the baby?

—He's fine. He turned over from his back to his front—but I told you that.

—Did he do it again?

—Only once.

With a pile of change next to the phone, Brenda dialed her parents' number on her second night in Seattle, from a booth outside a pancake house she'd walked to. Her car was still in the shop. She had not yet decided what to tell Artie and Evelyn. They'd realize she was calling from a pay phone because the operator would break in after three minutes and ask for more money, but she might just say she had gone out to eat and wanted to phone before the time difference made it too late, which was true.

But Evelyn burst into tears when Brenda said hi, and now she was sobbing and calling, Artie! Artie!

—What is it, Ma? Ma? Is the baby all right? Are you okay? Brenda understood that she should have called sooner. There was some kind of emergency and she didn't know about it. At last, it became clear that she was the emergency. Now her mother sounded angry, and her father, even angrier, picked up the phone in the other room.

—Don't you have the slightest feeling for anyone except yourself?

—Of course I do.

He'd taken over the conversation. So where are you, may I ask? Your landlord says you left.

—My landlord! What right did you have to call my landlord?

—I didn't call your landlord. He was in the apartment when your mother called.

—Well, he shouldn't have answered. What did he tell you? Behind her was the driveway from the restaurant parking lot. Each time someone drove out, the noise of the motor made it hard to hear her father's voice. The operator asked for more money, and Brenda was tempted to pretend she had none, but she threw in some more change: it was good to hear his voice.

Now he was shouting about men. What had the landlord said? What did he know?

—That's simply not true, she said. I have friends, sure, and sometimes somebody came over.

—That's not what he seems to think. Where are you?

—I'm in Seattle. I'm coming home. You won't hear from me for a while because it's hard to phone when I'm traveling.

—Seattle? What are you doing in Seattle? Don't you have a job?

—It ended. You don't have to shout, Dad, I can hear you.

ALICE MATTISON

—I'm not shouting, he shouted. What do you mean it ended? They have summer vacation in April? What kind of a college is this? What kind of a lousy unaccredited joint did you end up in?

Again, she had to put in more money. It's a state junior college. You know this. Look, they fired me.

—They fired you? he said, and she heard her mother's sharp intake of breath. For what? Because you're against the war? Don't tell me you're another one like me—but why didn't you tell me? You think I haven't been through this?

She was on the edge of tears. If only she were a political martyr. She knew, in a way, she was—they'd been against her since her outburst at the poetry reading. She had told her parents that story, and her father had enjoyed it, while her mother found it frightening. Won't the dean be angry with you? she'd asked.

But she was as much to blame for losing her job as the college. She shouldn't have had the Christmas party at her house. She shouldn't have served beer and let the kids smoke pot. She'd played into their hands, and that was what had angered Richie. More than for anything, she blamed herself for Richie.

—I don't have any more change, she said, which was not true. Tell me about the baby.

They told her about the baby. The baby was perfect. I'll call again, she said, and hung up. Distracted, she put the remaining coins into her pocket and looked around for her car, then remembered she had to walk back to the motel. It took an hour. When she got back, she wished she had brought something with her, some sweet food to eat before turning out the light.

Brenda called her parents again in Chicago. She didn't want more details about her landlord's report—or that of anyone else in town he might have spoken to. She could never tell her parents the whole story. But it pleased her that they had worried. She'd forgotten that anyone, anywhere might be thinking of her, loving and worrying. And she was pleased that her father had been ready to welcome her to the club: people who'd lost jobs because they were true to their beliefs. This time she planned what she'd say before she called, and filled the time with an account of what she'd seen and where she'd been. Her parents had traveled little and were impressed with stories of stopping at the side of a river amid mountains in Idaho, of crossing the Mississippi.

—And I thought Idaho was just potatoes! her father said.

She answered their questions briefly: she didn't know where she'd live or what she'd do when she got back to New York. They didn't have a chance to ask more about her job: she had piled up only a few quarters. The baby was fine.

As she drove along the New York State Thruway a day later, through a landscape that looked more midwestern than eastern, she knew that no matter what it looked like, it would be transformed into her parents' kitchen too quickly. She was almost out of money, and she would have to live with them—fights every day—until she could make some more. They were friendly on the phone, but after a few days they would blame her for everything they knew of, and they'd be right, even if with luck they'd never learn about Richie.

A sign told her the number of miles to Albany, where she'd turn ninety degrees south, to drive the last hundred miles or so to New York. If only she could turn north, drive to Schroon Lake and out the road to the cabin, which didn't even belong to Harold anymore, but to his former wife.

Then it occurred to her that Myra didn't live in the cabin—she probably used it for a couple of weeks each summer, if that. It was Harold who had loved it—Harold and her father—and Myra had kept it, she'd always heard, just to make Harold and Artie feel bad. Maybe the cabin was empty. She could take a detour. She could stop and look at it, walk down to the lake and see how it looked in spring—it was spring, though she hadn't thought about that. Trees had new leaves, and one day her coat had felt too warm. Brenda had driven across the country looking around her as little as possible, but even in her present mood she'd noticed one or two things.

She couldn't afford to stay in a motel in Schroon Lake. To save money, she'd been buying food in grocery stores and eating sandwiches in the car. But she could look at the cabin, spend an hour or two there, breathing the calm, clear air. When she reached Albany, she turned north, imagining Artie and Evelyn shouting and gesturing: The other way, the other way! How they did love her, and how difficult their love was.

She remembered the route. The narrow road through woods, after she left the highway, gave her a feeling so strong she drove through tears. Nothing bad had happened to her in these woods, and in these woods she'd done no harm. The drive was longer than she remembered, and she thought she might be lost, but she wasn't. She drove down the long, bumpy, rutted driveway. The cabin, with an open area between it and the driveway, looked different but not very different. The living room now protruded toward the driveway, and the clapboards were tan with green trim, instead of green all over. There had never been noticeable trim. No cars were parked; there were no lights. Brenda stopped and got out. She walked around the back of the house—it was more of a house than a cabin now—and down to the lake. The ground was muddy. The lake and its surroundings looked messy and wild. The woods reasserted themselves, she saw, when people were gone. The last time she'd come, after her affair with Douglas, she had had no idea how much trouble was inside her, how much harm she could do. What a child she had been. Now she had done worse. She'd abandoned her students—she had lived in such a way that she had to.

It was too cold and wet now to crouch on the ground and stare at the lake, discovering unforeseen flaws in her own soul. She knew about her flaws anyway. She walked back to the cabin and sat down on the porch steps, facing the lake. At least she'd had the brains to come here, however briefly. The pine trees thrived, the houses receded, and the smell, as always, told her where she was. She was hungry. She had to urinate, and she walked a little way from the house to squat. The air was cold on her bottom, but peeing into the damp leaves was honest, valid. Pulling up her pants, she felt like a dog who had taken possession. She walked around the house and remembered where the key had been kept years ago, in a crevice in the stone foundation, near the ground, left of the door, inside a Band-Aid box. The box was rusted and battered. Myra didn't seem like the type to leave a key in a rusted box. She probably didn't come at all. The key stuck, then worked. Inside, the smell was the same, despite modernizing, and the air chillier than outside. In her coat, she lay down on a couch she didn't remember and slept.

When she awoke, it was dark. She brought in what food she had, and her bag with pajamas and underwear. The electricity and water were off. She found a flashlight and looked at the books on the shelf. Novels from a few years back, or many years back. *Lady Chatterley's Lover*, *The Alexandria Quartet*, Pearl S. Buck, F. Scott Fitzgerald, Henry James. She sat on the floor and read a short story in an old anthology of humor, but it was hard to read by flashlight. There might be a caretaker who'd discover her. If so, she'd apologize, say she was a friend of the family, and leave. She ate a sandwich and potato chips and drank from a warm bottle of grapefruit juice. She slept. In the morning she dug a latrine in the woods with a shovel she found. She wondered where the old outhouse had been.

Then she drove into Schroon Lake and, counting her money

carefully, bought more food at the Grand Union. She would arrive at her parents' house penniless, a further humiliation. Twenty-eight was too old for this. She called Artie and Evelyn, but they weren't home. It was a weekday. She'd have to return here and phone again in the evening. She didn't want them screaming at her again that she didn't care if they thought she was dead, and now that the idea of emergencies and death had been raised, she needed to know that they were all right, that Carol and her baby were all right. Back at the cabin, she chose a novel she didn't know—*The House of Mirth* by Edith Wharton—and lay on the couch reading. She heard nothing but the occasional scrape of branch against branch in the trees behind the house. There was a wind. She ate a sandwich and read some more, going outside only when she needed to use the latrine. The book was about a woman who spoiled her life out of vanity, and Brenda read it with interest for a while, then lay with it on her lap. Richie would have hurt her again if she had stayed, since she had no power to keep him away. At least she had run away. Like the number of dollars in her wallet, her supply of courage and brains was what it was.

Around five o'clock, she drove back to Schroon Lake in the cold, light spring air. Her parents would not be home yet, and she wandered around Grand Union, thinking how to conserve money, wishing she could afford ice cream—but she had no refrigerator—and fruit and meat. She bought corn flakes, then went to the pay phone.

—Where are you? said her mother.

—I don't know. I think I'll be home the day after tomorrow.

—Are you eating?

—I'm eating.

—Honey, are you all right?

—Sure, she said quickly, and got off before she'd planned to.

When she got back with her box of corn flakes in a grocery bag, in early twilight, the door of the cabin stood open. She was sure she'd locked it, and the key was in her pocket. Had she left it unlocked after all, and had the wind blown it open? No. She put her head down and breathed slowly, explaining to herself that there was no way Richie could know she was here. She saw no car. Before she could make up her mind what to do, a man's figure appeared in the doorway. Of course he had heard her car. She put her keys into the pocket of her jeans and got out of the car. She could leave in a hurry if she had to, abandoning her possessions inside. The man was young and looked familiar. He looked Jewish. Nelson? she said. His hair was wild and made his face hard to see, and she hadn't seen Nelson in years. But she recognized him by the way he stood, with a tentativeness that had infuriated her when she was a child. Of course. It was his mother's house. Walking closer, she said, Brenda Saltzman.

—Did someone send you to find me? Nelson said. Then he said, I thought you lived in California.

—I'm back, she said.

—Is that your stuff inside? He looked at her as if she could order him to leave, instead of the other way around.

She said, I knew where the key was. I needed a place to go.

—I don't care, he said. I wondered who was squatting here, that's all.

—You don't have a car?

—I hitchhiked from the bus stop, he said. Walked part of the way. So you have the key?

—Yeah. How'd you get in?

—The bedroom window. He fell silent, and then as if he'd belatedly figured out that he was standing in the doorway, he moved back, and she followed and closed the door. He sat on the sofa. He wore a flannel shirt and jeans.

—Why did you think someone would be looking for you? she said.

—I don't know. Nobody would. I need to turn on the water before it gets dark.

—You know how to do that?

—Sure. But he didn't stand up for a long time. She was hungry. I don't have money, she said. Do you? All I have is corn flakes.

—Did you put that bottle of juice in the kitchen? I drank some, he said.

—Yeah, that was me. He went out to turn on the water, and she followed. It was almost too dark to see the valve. She stood behind him. I don't suppose you know how to get electricity? she said.

—No, but I know where there are candles, and I've got matches.

—The comforts of home, she said. She was cold. He took a long time to figure out how to turn on the water. They went back inside. Do you have any food? she said again.

—I have some weed, and I have money, he said. He had stopped at the Grand Union but had bought only a package of cookies and some bananas. I have a sandwich too, he said.

—If you'd pay, we could go into town and eat, she said.

—All right, he said, but he didn't get up for a long time, and at last she put corn flakes into a bowl, and they ate them dry and shared his sandwich.

—Probably nothing is open, he said. He lit candles, and then he lit a joint. She was cold and wrapped a blanket around her shoulders. They sat at either end of the couch. He fiddled with something he'd taken from his pocket, some little thing. His face flickered in the candlelight—deep eye sockets, fleshy lips that seemed to change shape more than other people's when he spoke, which made his speech seem a little disdainful, with the elongated vowels of sarcasm. I sort of love this place, he said after a long silence.

—Me too. I love it a lot.

—Was California good? Lots of good people, right?

—Not where I was. They threw me out because I was against the war, Brenda said.

—No shit.

—Well, it was complicated, but that was the main thing.

—So you took off.

The grass was getting to her. I had nobody to talk to, she said.

—That's not how I think of California.

—How old are you? she said.

—Twenty-four. I never grew up, he said.

She remembered that he'd been in a mental hospital. I wish I had some wine, she said.

—There's nothing here. My mother hasn't been here in years, he said. She wants to sell it.

—I used to love to come here, she said. Maybe it's not so nice anymore.

—She never liked it, Nelson said.

—She should sell it to your father.

—She'd die first. He laughed. After a silence, he said, I used to be afraid of you.

—Of me?

—You weren't afraid of your father, Nelson said. I was afraid of you because you didn't seem to be afraid of anything.

—You mean if I wasn't afraid of my father, I wasn't afraid of anything?

—Something like that.

—In a way I was very afraid of him, she said.

—I'll never believe that. He got out his package of cookies and put them between them, and she took a few. They were
Oreos. The first one was delicious, but then the sugar made her
jittery. In the dark she could see that he was doing something to
his cookie. He separated the chocolate wafers and was licking
the icing off.

—I have to stop eating these, she said. I wish I had a steak
and some vegetables. Tomorrow we're going into town and steal
some. She felt happy to have this boy with her. She had been
alone for months.

—We could buy some, but we can't cook them, he said. Well,
I guess we could build a fire.

—I have to go back to New York, she said. How long are you
going to stay?

—Oh, man, I have to get my shit together, Nelson said. I can't
go back to New York. Or maybe—I don't know what I'm going
to do.

There was silence again, and he said, Would you mind if I
touch you? Sometimes I need so badly to touch someone, and
grass does that to me, especially.

—What do you mean, touch?

—Just touch. Your hair maybe.

Brenda's hair was still thin and short, nothing special, and
she hadn't taken a shower in days. But she stretched out on the
sofa with her head toward him, and he stroked it hesitantly. Do
you have a lot of guys? he said.

—No.

—Nobody? Do you have an old man?

—I had a bad affair in California, she said.

—You want to tell me?

—No.

She was freezing. She wondered what time it was. Nelson,

behind her, continued crunching cookies. You know about me? he said.

—You tried to kill yourself.

—I jumped in front of a train. The first time.

—There were other times? she said.

—When you're like this, you don't stop, you just postpone it. Nelson continued stroking her hair and her forehead, and then he left his hand on her hair. It was scarcely a weight on her head. She turned so as to bring her forehead and face into contact with this childish hand. It was the first time she'd been touched—except maybe by a stranger putting change into her palm—since Richie had hit her the last time. She'd done the only thing she could do. But she'd have liked to be someone who could do other things instead, and she wondered what a stronger, more adult woman would have done, and when. Each occurrence had followed, step by step. She'd never chosen to have an affair with a married man who beat her up regularly. But this cool, young hand on her face. She was crying and he was touching her tears, then began wiping them with his fingers. I need you! he said after a long time.

—I was in love with your father when you were little, she said slowly. I wished he was my father. I used to imagine that he'd come and save me. I was jealous of how you could stand near him and touch him.

—Weren't your parents okay? I mean, even with your father being like that?

—They're decent people, Brenda said. They just didn't know what they were doing. My father is surprised at everything that happens. Now he got his job back, and he's surprised at that. This was not fair, she decided, but didn't say so. She was surprised at everything too. She too didn't know how to do things so life worked out.

Nelson stopped speaking, and after a while Brenda thought

she'd get up and wash her face. How good to have water, even though it was only cold water. She sat down again next to Nelson. There were no towels in the bathroom and her face was wet.

—We could ball, Nelson said. Would that be incest?

—Maybe. She laughed. But maybe we should, she said. Then she said, The guy I was in love with was married. And he hit me.

—That's heavy, Nelson said after a long pause, and his voice sounded young again. She wasn't attracted to him in that way, but she wanted to press her body into the body of another person who would not hurt her.

She said, I found sheets. They made their way in the dark into the bedroom and for a long time lay holding each other in the bed she'd slept in the night before. Then in a sleepy, delicate way he moved on top of her, somehow without resting his weight on her. She perceived that he was naked and didn't know when he'd taken off his clothes. She stood and removed hers, then lay down next to him and slowly, awkwardly, he moved on top of her again and touched her breast. She lay still, stroking the vertebrae of his back, then brought her hand around his narrow hips to touch his penis. Almost immediately he entered her. Even on top of her, he felt tentative and light. Being with Nelson was sad but good. There were other beds in the place, but they stayed together in this one.

The next day he was moody and quiet. Brenda said she'd leave the next morning. She was awkward with him and envisioned them reading quietly together or going for a walk, but they did little. She walked a little alone, but he stayed in the cabin. They drove into Schroon Lake and found an open lunch counter, then returned there for supper. Nelson paid both times. They didn't make love again, and he had no more grass. In the evening, she wished she'd asked him to buy some beer and cigarettes. Early, he took some blankets from a shelf and went into the other bedroom. You're going in the morning? he said, turning in the doorway.

—Yes.

—Wake me before you leave, he said. Okay?

—You're sure?

—Yes.

She hoped she hadn't harmed him. She wasn't sleepy yet. She took one of Myra's books into the bedroom and tried to read by candlelight, wondering how literature survived the years before electricity. Maybe candles were better in those days. The lost art of candlemaking, she said out loud.

She slept well and long, and when she woke up, the light told her it was late morning. She got up and washed her arms and face and neck in cold water. She ate corn flakes with milk. They'd bought some milk and left it outdoors in the cool air. Nelson had drunk much of it. Then she began to gather her things and take them out to the car. It looked like rain. She went back into the cabin and into Nelson's room. He had put something over the window, and it was dark. He was solidly asleep, snoring lightly. She put her hand on his shoulder. Nelson?

—What?

—I'm going.

—No, don't.

—I have to, she said. She wanted to.

—Wait.

—What is it?

He sat up in bed and pushed his long hair out of his eyes. Would you do me a favor? he said.

—Sure. Well, if I can.

—Drive me to New York.

—But you just came. You said you wanted to stay here and think. You haven't had a minute, with me around.

—Is that why you're going? So I can be alone?

—No.

—I might come back here after I go to New York, he said, but there's something I have to do there.

—What is it? Can I do it for you?

—No, he said. I'll tell you about it. Just wait, I'll be ready in a minute.

They didn't turn off the water, but Nelson said it was all right, that there wouldn't be another hard frost. He had brought a large duffel bag with lots of things in it—maybe all his things. She had to work to get it into her packed car. I like my things, he said. She didn't think he'd opened it, except maybe to get a toothbrush. He was wearing the same flannel shirt and jeans he had on when she found him there.

They rode down the Northway in silence. Then Nelson said, When people ran away from the mental hospital, they called it *eloping*.

—That's funny.

—It was funny. As if they were getting married. You know where it is?

—Where what is?

—The hospital. It's right near the George Washington Bridge.

—Oh, right, she said. She was changing lanes behind a slow driver.

He went on. With her peripheral vision, she could see that he was gesturing. Nelson had long narrow hands and long oval nails, and his gestures were slow and beautiful. There was a girl I liked, he said. Her name was Susan.

—What was she like?

—Do you have anything to eat? I didn't eat.

She said, The corn flakes and a couple of other things are in a grocery bag, on top of the shit in the back seat. But we left the milk.

He turned around, and then she heard him crunching corn flakes.

—I still have just a little money, she said. We'll stop and get something.

—I have money.

—Do you sell drugs? she said.

—Sometimes. He reached into the box for more corn flakes. Want some?

—No. What was Susan like?

—She was little and she had long dark hair. She used to play the guitar and sing. She sang Joan Baez songs.

—She sounds like Joan Baez.

—A little. With curly hair, though. And—do you mind my telling you this?

—Of course not, she said. She thought he might mean she'd be jealous of this Susan. Are you going to see her? Is that why you're going into the city?

—Something like that. He seemed to have put the box of corn flakes down at his feet, in the space that was already cluttered. He was silent. Then he said, Susan eloped, and she jumped off the George Washington Bridge.

—Oh my God, Brenda said. Oh, honey. Do you want me to get off the road, so I can stop and hold you?

—No. I think about it all the time. Thing is, I have to walk out on the bridge and tell her I love her. I've loved her all these years.

—Did you ever do that before? Walk out on the bridge?

—No. Being with you made me know I should do it.

She considered. You want me to drive you to the bridge?

—I won't be able to do it otherwise.

—And it's so important, all of a sudden, after all these years?

—She was a really sweet girl, he said.

—Was she your girlfriend?

He considered. Sort of. We didn't screw, you know—that would have been hard to do there, and we were kids. I didn't have the nerve to say I didn't know how. But we used to talk and touch each other. It was touching your hair that made me know I had to go onto the bridge and say good-bye. I never said good-bye. They wouldn't let me go to the funeral.

She turned on the radio. Here she could find stations that played the music she liked. Over the sound of a Doors song they listened to together, she said, But how do I know—Nelson, you know what I'm thinking.

—You're thinking I'm going to kill myself.

She waited until the song ended. That's right. Another song began.

—What can I say? You have to trust me. Don't you trust me? There was a hint of a whine in his voice.

She didn't answer. They were still north of Albany. You jumped in front of a train, she said.

—That was years ago. I was shrunk and treated and given a million pills—I'm not that kid now.

She was silent. She wished the George Washington Bridge were farther away, so she could think. She calculated. Simplest would be to come at it from the Jersey side. But she wasn't going to do that, and she knew he didn't mean that. The girl would have walked out from the New York side. And she herself needed the drive through the familiar avenues of New York. She wouldn't be able to think until she was in New York. I hate this road, she said, and at her next opportunity she got onto Route 9, which would slow them down and would take her right into the city.

—This is the way we used to go when we were kids, he said.

—Us too. I'll take the Taconic State. She'd drive through the Bronx and onto city streets in Manhattan. Now there were things to look at beside the road. They stopped for coffee and dough-nuts. The small shabby businesses were cheering after the speed and mindlessness of the highway.

—What's your brother like these days? she said, when it be-gan to seem that they had been silent for too long.

—My brother. Well, he smiles all the time, Nelson said. He has tried marijuana exactly once. He's a kid, but it's hard to re-member he's a kid. He's like the mayor. He's taller than my dad and wider.

—He's fat?

—No, he's just got arms and legs like telephone poles. He does everything right. Somebody has to be like that.

—That's my sister, in my family. She has a husband and a baby.

—No shit. A baby. Do you like it?

—I've never seen him, Brenda said. That's part of why I have to get to New York.

—How old is he?

—Five or six months.

—You didn't fly east to see him?

—I should have.

—Your sister was nice to me when we were kids, Nelson said. I wasn't afraid of her.

—She's still nice.

The next time they spoke, he said, Are you going to take me to the bridge?

—Can't you take the subway to the bridge?

—You don't want the responsibility. But look, Brenda, even if I was going to kill myself—isn't that my business?

—You're going to kill yourself, I knew it. They were driving through a town, an ugly town. There were traffic lights at every corner, and they were all red.

—I'm not going to kill myself. But why should you care? Isn't it my business to choose the length of my life? I could get drafted. I could end up in Vietnam and not only die but kill other people. This way I wouldn't be killing anybody but me.

She missed a corner where the route turned and had to go back. They're not drafting guys your age, she said.

—At the moment.

—You could go to Canada.

—Well, the army might not want me because I was crazy.

—That's right, she said. They were finally out of that town. She would never know its name. Soon they'd be on the Taconic State and would be going faster again. The slowness frustrated her, but she didn't want to speed up.

—And we'll probably all be dead before too long, from some Russian bomb.

—Look, we survived the Cuban Missile Crisis, she said. We could go on for a while.

—But sooner or later—you have to admit that sooner or later . . .

—Nelson, she said, that doesn't have anything to do with it. It's not true that if you killed yourself, you wouldn't kill anybody else. You'd kill your father. I know it would kill your father.

—My father. Professor Father.

—Did you see that piece he wrote about being against the war? About trusting your opinions? I read that over and over. I love your father. She decided that Harold was the only man not related to her that she had ever loved. She clenched her hands on the wheel. Nelson, I forbid you to do this, because of your father.

—That pisses me off.

—Why?

—It's very establishment, Brenda. It's not what I thought you were like. It's like the rest of them. Why bother to be the kind of girl you are if you're going to say something like that?

—I don't know what you're talking about.

There was more silence. You have to trust me, that's all, he said.

—I trust you not to hurt me, she said. I trust you not to tell anybody what I told you about that guy I screwed. I don't trust you not to kill yourself.

—So you're not going to drive me to the bridge? I just need to walk out on the bridge. And I need you to be there when I come back.

She didn't answer for a long time. For a long while, nobody had needed her to do something she *could* do. Who was she to be such an advocate for life? I'll drive you there, she said. Okay.

She got lost three times and spent nearly all her remaining money on gas. They stopped for lunch because Nelson said he'd pay again, and she ordered a roast beef sandwich, the most substantial meal she'd had for a while. She and Nelson seemed to be children, unable to make judgments. She could turn around and drive back to the cabin—except that they'd starve there. She could drive straight to her parents' apartment or Harold's, finding an excuse to stop at a phone booth and look up his address. But she owed Nelson more than that. He was making a claim: that he wasn't a child, that he was making a judgment, that he should be listened to. She was older than he, but she was not doing much better at growing up. If she was wrong—if he jumped from the bridge into the Hudson—she could never justify her decision to anyone. But, at present, driving Nelson Abramovitz (he'd told her he had not changed his name when Harold did) to the George Washington Bridge seemed like the only possible expression of trust and friendship. His touch on her hair had been gentle—gentle by habit, gentle by conviction—and it made Richie less: farther away and less powerful.

By the time she reached the neighborhood of the bridge, it was chilly and windy, almost evening, with the sun just a white circle through the clouds. A line of poetry came into her head: *The sun was white, as though chidden of God.* There was no place to park anywhere near the bridge, though she drove everywhere through that neighborhood. She could see it above her, huge. She saw the hospital where Nelson had been imprisoned. He said nothing. Finally, he spoke. You could wait at a hydrant and keep the flashers on. If a cop comes, you could drive around the block. If I come back and don't see you, I'll wait.

She had thought she might go with him, whether he wanted her to or not. Now she was trapped. All right, she said. She pulled up to a fire hydrant. The bridge was several blocks north. She didn't know how he'd find the walkway. Will you be okay?

—I can find it from here. I just need to say good-bye, he said.

She turned, her hands still on the wheel. Okay. She didn't want to make it a farewell—partly because she couldn't, partly so he'd feel he had to come back. She would treat it as if he was getting out of the car to ask directions, or to buy a bottle of milk.

But he put his long arms and long hands around her and hugged her, pressing his long sweet hair—it had to be dirty, but it smelled good—into her face. She hugged him tightly. She got out of the car and hugged him again, and he walked away, his flannel shirt flapping and the wind billowing it in back. It was blue and green plaid, and she remembered what it was called: Black Watch plaid. It had been popular a few years before, and Carol had owned a skirt in that plaid.

Brenda got back into the car and turned on the radio. She couldn't concentrate on the songs and couldn't remember, when a song was over, what she'd heard. Soon the radio became intolerable because no matter what station she tried, the DJs kept saying what time it was, and she didn't want to know. It was getting dark. She didn't know where the walkway to the bridge was or how long it would take to walk there. It was not far. From where she sat, she could hear the rumble of cars on the bridge. The girl who looked like Joan Baez had found the will to climb over whatever barrier there was and let herself go. She didn't know what it would feel like, whether one would be unconscious before the killing slap of the water, whether death would be from trauma or drowning. She imagined Nelson jumping, his flannel shirt billowing like an ineffectual sail. She thought she should leave the car and walk until she found a pay phone and call Harold, who would take a taxi to this terrible place and save his son. What if she couldn't find a pay phone? What if Harold wasn't home? She reached behind her to find something to read, something to do, but all she had within reach was dirty laundry.

She wished she could call her parents, and for the first time she felt sorry for them, waiting to hear from her, becoming scared. Until now she had mostly been angry that they had talked to her landlord, that they had not respected her privacy and hung up. But here she was, respecting privacy, and what did it get her? Nelson might be dead by now, and she wondered if she'd hear anything—a splash, any sound, any commotion—if someone jumped from the bridge. Probably people who wanted to jump waited until there was a break in traffic and slipped down without being seen. Their bodies washed up days later— that's how people found out what had happened. If Nelson was dead, nobody would ever know that she had helped him die unless she told on herself, and she wondered whether she'd do that. It would be a hard secret to keep for a lifetime.

But it was his business, as he'd pointed out. She had loved that valley in California when she arrived there amid the peach and apricot harvest, and yet her life there had ended up valueless, maybe harmful to others. Why should she try to keep Nelson— or anyone—alive? She had spoiled her own life yet again. If she were braver, she'd jump with him.

When three hours had passed and it was completely dark— and maybe Nelson had been waiting for dark to jump, so it was less likely he'd be seen—she could bear it no longer. What she had been thinking made no sense, no sense at all. She got out of the car, considered leaving it unlocked for him but then locked it—it contained everything she owned—and set out for the bridge.

The walkway was hard to find from the place where she'd parked. She was frantic now, hurrying, confused. Maybe Nelson had not been able to find it either. Maybe he'd given up and had gone in search of a cup of coffee. Or a glass of milk. No. It was not that hard to find, and eventually she did find it. She was freezing. She walked out on the walkway. She'd been unprepared for the size of it, for how long it took just to be away from the land, over the water. But he would have gone out there, where Susan had gone. The wind was so strong she was afraid—afraid she might be blown in—and she clutched the railing. Cars swept past her. She saw nobody. Maybe she'd missed him in the streets around the bridge. Maybe he hadn't jumped but was trying to find the car again. She kept walking. It was dark. She saw nobody. He was gone. He had jumped.

Then she saw something, a bulge in the shadow of a cluster of the uprights that held the thick cables supporting the bridge. She willed herself not to get excited. It could be anything—or any-body. She kept walking, and then she saw that it was someone; it was someone with long hair. She was afraid Nelson would jump as she watched, climb over the railing and jump. If she cried out, that might give him the nerve he'd been seeking, the nerve to do it. She kept walking, keeping her head down so she wouldn't see.

Then she made herself lift her head because she had to see. He saw her when she was yards away and her legs trembled as she hurried, not knowing what he'd do. He did nothing, just stood where he was. She came up to him. She was larger and heavier than Nelson Abramovitz, and she knew that now, at least for the moment, he was safe. She put her arms around him and held him tightly, and after a long time Nelson raised his arms and put them around her too. She had done something right. She did know how. She would lead her life.

PART TWO

The Next Thirty-five Years:
Not So Many Arguments

A Fool and His Principles

7

1973-2002

1

Aman, Ted, had moved on. It was November 1973, and Carol's children were four and two. Brenda didn't live near them now, and sometimes her hands and arms ached with the wish to hold them. First, she had glumly followed Carol around, gingerly helping with Gabriel. She had a one-room apartment and a job waiting tables, sure she'd screw up anything in which she had to do with people for more than an hour at a time. She babysat Gabe and then his sister, Ruthie. A teacher left their day-care center without warning, and Brenda was hired part-time, then full-time. By then she'd met Ted.

She moved to Concord, New Hampshire, to live with him and work in the business where he had just gotten a job, and the business had come to interest her more than it interested Ted, more than either of them interested each other. So it was not terrible that he was gone. And not terrible—still hard to believe, though—that she was six months pregnant. A child she hadn't known about until weeks after he left now kicked steadily in Brenda's belly.

Her laundry luxuriated in gray suds, diving and rising on the other side of a round glass door framed in steel, and she had nothing to do but look at it. She'd forgotten to bring a book, and there were no magazines. She owned three pairs of men's overalls, and two were in the washing machine. The buckles clicked on the window. Her shoulders hurt after a day at work, wearing her third pair of overalls. Next time she did laundry, she'd wear one of the other pairs and wash this one, the time after that the third pair, and she saw that she could count out her life in the movement of overalls—or other clothing—into and out of washing machines. She'd worn skirts to teach in California, jeans or overalls at the day-care center, where she could get dirty at work: there was mud outside, paint in the art room, sticky children at meals and snacks. Maybe her present overalls wouldn't fit during her last weeks of pregnancy and she'd need a larger size. The baby would make a division in her life, a before and after. Still, whatever happened, as long as you had the wherewithal to acquire and wash clothing, you could describe a life as so many pairs of clean underpants, so many pairs of socks, washed and worn again, washed again.

The washing machine shuddered to a stop, and she moved her clothes to a dryer. It was hard to be patient, to keep putting in coins until everything dried thoroughly, but if she brought her laundry home damp, she'd live for days with clothing draped on furniture. She wished for a cigarette, but she'd quit smoking—for good, she hoped—when she found out she was pregnant. Next to the dryer was a newspaper she hadn't noticed, the *Concord Monitor*. Because of Watergate, there was always something new, but this paper was a few days old. *I'm not a crook,* Nixon had said. She knew about that.

She scanned the comics, the horoscope, the classified ads. The dryer stopped and she removed bras, a T-shirt, and three socks, then inserted more coins.

Ted didn't know and would not be interested. She would manage. She leaned on the table where people folded laundry, turning pages. A small item announced a talk to be given in a local church: "When Your Child Tells You He's Gay." Some of us are girls, Brenda said out loud. Wait a minute.

She put the paper down, walked to the front of the empty laundry, looked out at the wind-scoured street and a street lamp. She had heard herself speak, and she knew what she meant: the title of the talk should say *He or She Is Gay*, not just *He*. But she had said *us*. If someone had asked her whether she was gay or straight, right until this moment, Brenda would have said she was straight, not consciously lying. She looked at the street lamp. A scrap of paper blew sideways along the sidewalk, then, for some reason, stopped. Brenda ran her hands slowly up her sides, past her hips, up her overall bib and her breasts, over her cheeks. She would have been lying. She had always loved women. She walked back to the dryers, asking herself when she had known this. She was crying. Before Ted. She'd been lying to herself for a while. Well, I wanted a baby, she said.

—I'm a lesbian, she said tentatively to the rattling, shaking dryers, which looked as if they might fly open in astonishment, but they always looked that way. She wondered if the people at work would be astonished: a middle-aged owner, his son, and a woman older than Brenda who'd worked there for years. Probably not. They made wooden playground equipment, and Brenda had learned to use power tools on the lovely maple and oak, to shape the posts that held swing sets and climbing structures, to finish them so they were smooth and golden. Here she got dirty but in a different way. She had ideas about the equipment they built. She was thinking about an arrangement of uprights they had not tried, with crisscrossing pieces to give children another way to climb.

She looked around. Everything was different—*everything* was different—having said that she loved women, though here doing laundry there was no woman to love. All these years, into her thirties, she had poked her thoughts into the alignment they should have, constructing shapes more complicated than the clever climbing structures they made at Mountainside Playgrounds—she and Gene, his son (also Gene), Lydia—along with Ted, for a few weeks. Her ideas about herself had climbed up, down again, across, negotiated a little twist and then leaped over a barrier, all to avoid the knowledge she had just come to.

Her secular parents—her unconventional father—had not brought her up to think homosexuality was sinful or sick, but her parents and friends, and she herself, had believed, until recently, that it was not a good idea: inconvenient, frightening because illegal, not quite the real thing. She'd gradually learned that it was a good idea, as large and as real a thing as loving men. She'd understood this since gay liberation—the public declaration that it was all right to be gay, after the Stonewall uprising—made everyone who thought like Brenda acknowledge abruptly, with relief, that homosexuals didn't lead lesser lives or need to be fixed. It was fine to be gay, she had reasoned, but she had slept with so many men. Yet often, all these years, there had been a woman, some woman she wanted, whom she explained away. Just now it was a neighbor, a woman who'd come over with a basket of apples when she had extra, who had stood in the doorway, talking, after

Brenda took the basket. She might or might not try to seduce her neighbor—the woman seemed to have a boyfriend—but how much better even to know it was possible. Brenda was not religious, but what she felt at this moment was gratitude. Her laundry was dry and electrified, and she gathered it in her arms—overalls with flopping straps and hot buckles, flannel nightgown, pullovers, plaid flannel shirts, cotton underpants—transferred it to the table, smoothed and folded it, and stacked it in her laundry basket. Then she went out to her car to see if she felt the same way after the drive home or in the morning.

2

Wind blew March rain sideways and made Harold's umbrella a useless encumbrance. He needed one hand to hold the campaign literature, which he should have put into a plastic bag, and the other to press doorbells and insert brochures into mail slots and mailboxes. He also had a chart on a clipboard, on which he was supposed to note down a number for each person he talked to: *1* meant definitely voting for Senator Kennedy in the Democratic presidential primary that was now three days off, *2* meant leaning toward Kennedy, *3* was undecided, *4* was leaning toward President Carter, and *5* was definitely for Carter. It was a neighborhood of brownstones, shabby blocks in Chelsea, and his legs hurt from walking up and down stone steps. Why had he agreed to do this? A friend had asked. He was seventy and still a fool. Well, he had agreed to do it, as he had agreed to give any help asked of him in these last eight months, because Nelson was dead and had not asked for help before he took the pills.

A quiet death, Harold had said to himself more than once, and more than once he'd admitted that after all these years, despite his wild grief, there was some relief in knowing he no longer had Nelson's death to expect and fear. Nelson had left notes for Harold, for Myra, and for Paul. He had never learned to live, but after many tries he'd learned to die compassionately. And what was the benefit in that, Harold had asked Naomi, over and over, these months. Were they better off because Nelson had been kind in his death? He had left his notes, along with a list of telephone numbers of family members, in a sealed envelope in his apartment, and on the outside he had written the name of a friend, a coworker at the bookstore where he had a job. He had given this friend a key to his apartment and asked him to come at a certain day and time.

—Didn't you *know*? Naomi had asked the friend, who had phoned when he found Nelson dead and then delivered the notes. She barely kept back her fury. Didn't you know you had to go for help? Couldn't you have done that much for him? They were at the door of Harold's apartment. They had not asked the man in—he was a sad, shy man, a little older than Nelson, pained but resolute.

—He picked me because he knew I wouldn't, the man said. If he thought I'd have done that, he'd have asked someone else. Isn't this better than having the police break in and find his body, after none of you heard from him for weeks?

—It would be better if he was in a hospital, Naomi said.

—He knew the inside of too many hospitals, the man said, and Harold knew that was true. Even Naomi quieted.

He and Naomi had thanked the friend, eight months ago, and had gone inside. He had read the note, which was loving. Naomi sat opposite, her thin arms stretched on a chair that made her look even smaller than she was. She was undergoing chemotherapy for breast cancer, and her hair was gone. She had put on her wig to receive Nelson's friend, but it was uncomfortable, and now she took it off. Harold put down the note and studied Naomi's cherished bald head in the diminishing evening light. Its paleness seemed to draw what light was in the room.

—We should marry, she said at last. I've pretended too long that I'm not your wife.

There was and would be no comfort, but alongside the weight that made it hard to breathe, alongside this new, permanent pain, came something light and cool, lovely.

—You don't want to rush into something like that, he had said, smiling.

S̲ome people didn't know there was a primary; some didn't know that as Democrats—nearly everyone in this neighborhood was a Democrat—they could vote; and a few didn't know who was running against Jimmy Carter. When he said it was Senator Kennedy—Teddy Kennedy—they had seen that on the news, they now recalled, but one woman said, holding up her hand to block the offered brochure, I wouldn't vote for that scum. What he did to that girl!

—He isn't perfect, Harold conceded. None of us is perfect. He's strong on gun control. He'll deal with the economy. Get the hostages out of Iran—

Harold tried to keep the brochures from flying away as he walked down her steps and farther along the block. The next man was voting for Kennedy because Carter was bad for the Jews. Harold didn't think Carter was bad for the Jews, even though the United States had voted against Israel on the issue of Israeli settlement in occupied Arab lands, but he agreed because he was glad to mark down a *1*. Nobody answered at the next three houses, and then a woman said she was voting for Carter because everyone knew Reagan would get the Republican nomination, and Carter was more likely to defeat Reagan. She quoted a poll

Harold didn't know about. Carter would beat Reagan 63 percent to 32 percent. Kennedy would beat him too, Harold noted.

—But not as definitively, she said. The main thing is, Reagan has to lose.

—You don't think Ronald Reagan is a serious threat, do you? Harold said. She was a rumpled, brainy-looking woman, maybe in her fifties.

—Of course he is, she said. The only thing that matters is to defeat Reagan. He's an idiot. Did you hear about that joke?

Harold had heard about the joke. On the campaign bus, Reagan had told an ethnic joke: *How do you tell the Polish one at a cockfight? He's the one with the duck. How do you tell the Italian? He bets on the duck. How do you know the Mafia is there? The duck wins.* Edwin Meese, his political adviser, had said, There goes Connecticut.

—People will see through Reagan, Harold said.

—No, they won't. Kennedy won't ever be president because of Chappaquiddick. Who wants to win now so we can lose in November?

—But if you could just choose your favorite, Harold said, it would be Kennedy?

—Yeah, she said. It would be Kennedy. She took a brochure and closed the door. He put her down as a *3*. Next came a man who said, I hate Kennedy, but I'm voting for him because I hate Carter more. Harold looked at his watch. He had promised to meet Naomi at her old apartment. She had moved out, but there were little things to do. Real estate was getting so expensive they had despaired of finding an apartment where they could live together comfortably, but at last they had found a co-op apartment they could afford. Harold had now lived there for a month and Naomi for a week. He could hardly believe that something in his life, at this late date, could be new and yet good—a gain, not a loss. They were to be married the next day: Sunday, March 23, 1980—two days, as it would turn out, before Kennedy won the New York primary—and at first Naomi had said he had no business volunteering for the primary the day before his wedding. Then she relented because the wedding would be so simple. Really, there was nothing to do.

He quit early, tired, and took a cab to her old place. She was cleaning the kitchen. The furniture was gone, and he didn't know how to help but couldn't sit down. He stood and watched her. Her hair had grown back, dark gray, spiky, charming. I should help, he said.

—I'll tell you when I think of something.

He was tired and leaned on the counter. I should have brought coffee.

—I'd love coffee. He went into the rain again, leaving behind his clipboard and brochures, and found an open coffee shop. He brought back two containers, with two muffins in a bag in his raincoat pocket. Walking in the rain—again the umbrella was useless, and now he needed both hands for the coffee containers, but they were warm—he looked forward to the next day.

There was always a next day and a next, and each took him further from Nelson's life, each was a day that Nelson would not live, and each took Harold closer to his own death. But each took him further from the day of Nelson's death, and that was worth it, further from the moment of finding out. They would be a small, quiet group at the wedding tomorrow. He was being married by a rabbi—would wonders never cease? As he walked carefully with the hot containers, head down against the rain, it seemed that if he concentrated enough, it would already be that next day, which was predicted to be sunny. He would be unmarried and then, as if he went over a bump, married. Naomi had wanted a rabbi, and Artie had produced one: Carol's husband, Lenny, in midlife had gone to rabbinical school. Not too much God, Harold said to Artie.

—Are you kidding? With me for a father-in-law? He doesn't dare. Harold knew Lenny wasn't afraid of anyone, but so what? They'd be married at Paul's substantial home near Poughkeepsie—he taught history at Vassar—and Paul and his wife, Martha, were having lunch catered. The only guests would be Artie and Evelyn, Brenda and her little boy, David—who was six or seven—and her latest girlfriend (I try not to like them too much, Evelyn had told Harold, because they just don't last). Carol and Lenny had two children, but Harold had no idea how old they were or whether they were coming. His own grandchildren would certainly be there: Paul and Martha had two boys and a girl, Amanda, who at three somehow knew about weddings and had insisted that she would be the flower girl in Grandpa Harold and Grandma Naomi's wedding. So there would be no fuss—except that Amanda would carry a basket of petals and, if she could be persuaded to give them up, would strew them on the ground. Like Harold, Naomi was an only child, but two of her friends were coming to the wedding.

After Nelson died, Artie and Evelyn had sat silently with Harold for hours, then returned day after day. They sat near him, bent forward as if their chairs had no backs, as if they sat on stools, as Jews are supposed to in mourning, though they were not on stools.

D id you pick up your dress from the cleaners? he said, when he'd brought the coffee back and was leaning again on the sink.

—What do you think? Huh? Do you think I picked up my dress? Or do you think I just left it there? She finished cleaning the stove, drank more coffee, elbowed him away from the

ALICE MATTISON

sink and shook some cleanser into it. I've lived in this apartment all these years, she said, scrubbing. Decades. *Decades*, not just years. That stain in the sink. I clean it every week. It never changes. Oh my life, she said. What did I do with my life?

3

These days there were more homeless people in Grand Central Station than people taking trains. This was not true, Artie acknowledged to himself, but the homeless took up more room and were more noticeable than the people hurrying to or from the tracks, or even the people like him, waiting at the clock. A person who might be a man or a woman—in a woolen hat pulled down over the ears—sprawled against a wall, surrounded by battered suitcases. Artie's bum knee was bothering him, and he walked repeatedly around the information kiosk in the center of the station because walking was easier than standing. He had arrived twenty minutes early for David's train. Only eleven, the kid was coming by himself from New Haven, where Brenda had driven from New Hampshire to visit her girlfriend. The two of them would be alone for the weekend, while he and Evelyn got to keep David, which was good. But he didn't see why she couldn't have driven David into New York. Maybe the kid liked trains. He could remember being eleven, and he would have wanted to come alone, to come on the train alone. In a way, Artie was still eleven.

Or Artie could have taken the train to New Haven, said hello to the girlfriend, Jess, whom he liked, and picked up David. Well, Brenda thought the way Brenda thought, and there was no point in arguing.

Seventeen minutes until the train was due. Maybe Brenda

thought taking the train back and forth would wear Artie out—that he was too old. She'd given him a funny look the last time they were together, as if she was shocked at how old he was, all of a sudden.

Or maybe the kid insisted. Probably that was it. He enlarged his walk. No point in circling the information booth for seventeen minutes, giving himself the same circular explanations. He toured the station, studied the stupid Kodak ad, studied the homeless. The indeterminate person was a woman. Fourteen minutes. If you often showed up early to meet trains, life would not seem short.

Retired, he had too much thinking time. At the moment he was not worrying about the goddamn country four years after Reagan was elected or about Brenda's love life—Jess had lasted for a while; maybe she was permanent—but, more immediately, about whether David would get safely off the train and into his arms and whether Evelyn would be standing inside the entrance of Macy's closest to Sixth Avenue and Thirty-fourth Street when he and David arrived. What would Evelyn say if he couldn't find David? What would David say if he couldn't find Evelyn? Evelyn might get mixed up and go to the wrong place. He should have thought of something simpler. Macy's had a million entrances. Thirteen minutes. Did he have time to go to the men's room and get back before the train? He should have thought of that before. The impulse had been unexpected. Instead of wasting time deciding, he hurried down the stairs. He could still run. All that tennis. If everyone played tennis, the world would be a healthier place.

He got back with two minutes to spare. Now he circled the information kiosk again, but when the train came in, he couldn't help it, he went to the gate where David would come out. Then he thought that was a mistake, they'd miss each other, and he started back. Grandpa! called David, and Artie turned and opened his arms wide for a skinny boy and a fat, dilapidated backpack. David was wearing a Red Sox jacket.

—You come to New York like that?

—Like what? He smelled fresh and familiar, pressing his face into Artie's chest—eager, cool, aromatic—as if he'd been outdoors, not cooped up in a train. Don't you know better than to come to New York in a Red Sox jacket? Some Yankee fan will knock your block off. Don't worry, I'll protect you. I'll turn you into a Mets fan. Dwight Gooden. You know who that is?

The kid was trembling. Maybe he'd been frightened after all, alone in the train. Artie held his skinny shoulders. You want me to carry your pack?

He shook his head. I'm okay.

—What's the matter?

—Nothing.

—You know, Artie said, when I was eleven, I didn't have a grandfather. I *never* had one. They stayed back in Russia. Horrible, what happened. So I have no experience with how you talk to a grandfather.

David shook his head. I'm okay.

—We'll go find Grandma, Artie said. He'd taught children David's age for years and years, but he'd rarely thought about them one at a time. If there were thirty, he'd know what to do. But this was true for kids too: they liked being with adults if there were plenty of kids around. He remembered being eleven, being with adults at eleven—embarrassment, bafflement. He said, Do you have to go to the bathroom?

—No, David said. Yes.

Back to the men's room. David went into a stall. Artie stood watch. A homeless man washed clothes in a basin. Did you see that? David said as they left. They crossed the main concourse.

—You want something to eat? Can you wait for lunch? He could buy him a knockwurst. A place in the station had great knockwurst. We're having lunch soon—can you wait? I don't want to spoil your appetite.

—I can wait. David had straight, dark hair, like Artie's own before it turned white.

—I'll tell you what. We'll get one knockwurst and share it.

—Okay, David said. He seemed excited. Artie gave him most of the knockwurst. They walked to Broadway—Times Square—and down Broadway. Did you see that? David said again, after a silence.

—See what?

—A man in the men's room was washing clothes in the basin.

—Homeless, Artie said. Reagan's homeless. It's 1984 and we've got 1932 all over again. People with no place to live. Now they're throwing them out of the station. Soon that guy will be out in the street with dirty clothes. A woman got thrown out in the cold a couple of months ago and she died. You know what your friendly president says? He says they're homeless by choice. *Homeless by choice.*

—He's not my friendly president.

—Good boy. He's disgusting. And, you'll see, he'll be re-elected in November.

—My mom's not voting for him.

—I should hope not! Artie said. How's your mom, anyway?

—She's good.

—So this Jess—is she going to last? Is she better than the others?

—I liked some of the others, David said. I liked Karen. Karen had been Brenda's partner for two years.

—Everybody liked Karen, Artie said. A block later, he said, Hey David, you like limericks? Listen to this:

A woman in females delighted,
And by many of them was excited,
But they'd shout or they'd pout.
They didn't work out.
Would her troth ever be plighted?

David was silent.

—You don't like it? Artie said.

—I don't know, he said. They walked, and Artie looked for something else to talk about. The weather was warm, and he opened his jacket. You want to take your jacket off? Is that thing heavy?

—It's not funny, David said.

—What isn't? Oh, I know what. Artie didn't say anything for a while. Then he said, I know, kiddo. You're right. It's not funny. They didn't speak for a couple of blocks. He should have skipped the goddamned limerick.

When they were almost at Thirty-fourth Street, David said, Grandpa?

—We're almost there. Let's see if we can find your grandma.

—I was scared I wouldn't find you, David said, and burst into tears. He was almost a teenager, Artie saw, looking at him before he put his arms around him, skinny and short but with the beginnings of a man's face, a jaggedness. His cheeks no longer stuck out—that was the difference. David had had round little cheeks Artie liked to pinch. Now he had a bony face. He sobbed and trembled.

—She shouldn't have sent you alone! Artie said. I don't know why the hell she sent you alone!

—I wanted to, David said. But then I was afraid I'd be lost in New York.

—You're not a New Yorker, Artie said. He had almost never known anyone well who was not a New Yorker. A grandson growing up in Concord, New Hampshire! That's okay. I'll teach you to be a New Yorker. I'll teach you what to do. First thing, I gotta take you to a Mets game. I think they're playing tonight—I should have thought. Now Evelyn will want to make a big dinner, the whole bit. Well, we'll watch it on television. But I don't think Gooden is pitching.

If he could find Evelyn. The kid wasn't the only one who worried. Evelyn got mixed up these days. She'd worked at the nursing home for so long, and then one day, before she'd thought about retiring, they told her they were having a big party, a dinner to honor her years of service. I get the message, she said to Artie.

Holding David's hand though the boy protested, Artie went into Macy's and stopped just to the side of the entrance closest to Thirty-fourth Street and Sixth Avenue. He looked at his watch. They were ten minutes late. He didn't see Evelyn. He would count to a hundred and not say anything. He would count to three hundred. Five hundred. There she was, dressed up in a spring coat but with flat shoes. Evelyn had finally stopped wearing heels. A broken ankle I don't need, she said. She was getting shorter. She and David were the same height. I'm late, she said, after she hugged him. Don't say anything, Artie, I know I'm late. I bought you some shirts, David, and there was a line to pay. Wait till you see—very nice shirts.

4

Finding their way in an unfamiliar store, they forgot soup when they were in the soup aisle, so Jess went back. Brenda pushed the cart across the front of the store toward cookies but stopped when she found piles of newspapers. Here in the Adirondacks, they carried the *New York Times* but not the *Boston Globe*, which they read at home in New Hampshire. The Soviets were withdrawing from Afghanistan. What she wanted to know was how the Red Sox—in second place—had done yesterday, but New York papers neglected the Sox. Jess had grown up in New York and Connecticut. She rooted for the Mets, though now she'd lived in New Hampshire for four years. She'd moved in with Brenda in Concord when—weeping and hugging, arguing, teasing each other for their nervousness—they made up their minds after months of discussion to live together, even if David didn't seem to like Jess much—these days David didn't like anybody much—and even if Jess was a Mets fan. Brenda (who'd been away from New York for years and years, whose son had become a Sox fan the minute she let him out the door) liked the Red Sox.

Two years ago, in 1986, their relationship had survived Bill Buckner's error and the Mets' defeat of the Red Sox in the World Series. If we can handle that, we can handle anything, Jess had said. Now the Mets were in first place in the National League East, the Sox in second place in the American League East. Would they meet again? Could Brenda and Jess still handle it? When nobody was looking, Brenda leafed through the Sports section. Oh shit. Roger Clemens had screwed up early in the game and the Sox had lost.

They had lost in 103-degree heat in Fenway Park, and the paper said it was hot in New York, but here in the mountains it was raining. After weeks of heat and humidity, they'd packed for a hot weather camping trip, and it was cold. Now Brenda was restless. She'd have walked up a mountain, but Jess hated hiking in the rain. Brenda wore the only sweatshirt she'd brought, now grubby. But here came tall Jess down the coffee aisle, grasping the top of a can of Progresso soup with each long-fingered hand, her thin arms bare, her high round breasts discernible under her dark green T-shirt. Looking capable, looking happy. Nobody else in the store carried two cans of soup, one in each hand, and if they did, they would not look as if carrying soup was original and slightly scary. If the arm swung wide, a can of soup could become a weapon. But Jess was gentle. You are my sunshine, Brenda said.

—And it's all the sunshine you're getting, said Jess. What now?

—Cookies, bananas, bread.

—I mean when we're done.

—Let's go for a ride.

—Where?

Brenda said, The map's in the car. They found cookies, bananas, bread. They bought wine. She knew where she wanted to go, the reason she'd proposed the Adirondacks in the first place.

—At least we don't have David to amuse, she said as she carried their groceries to the car. David had a summer job this year, busing tables, and was spending the week back home in Concord with a friend.

—And to tell us our misdeeds, Jess said.

—I can't help it, I miss him, Brenda said, lowering the bag into the trunk, then stretching her arms and fingers. But I'm glad he's not here. This long-necked, complicated but essentially lighthearted woman lived with her and loved her. It was still astonishing, and Brenda was never sure Jess wouldn't change her mind. Jess was driving. She got back on the road. Look, Brenda said, pointing at the map Jess couldn't see, pretending she'd just thought this up. Here's where I used to go when I was a kid. The cabin. Let's look for it.

—You know where it is?

—I think so. I loved being there. My parents would quiet down and forget I existed. I could think.

—I love these roads in the rain, Jess said, but she sounded resistant. The dark green hills curved around them, two minutes away from the store. I don't care if it's raining. Here we are, not at work. We are *not* at work.

They drove. For miles, nothing but evergreens or clearings where wildflowers drooped in the rain. Then, abruptly, there would be a lake ringed with cottages, lonely with rain, a general store with a gas station outside. Or a break in the woods and a view of mountains, barely visible in mist. They both liked their work, but vacation was exquisite. Jess was a divorce lawyer. Brenda—with Gene Stearns, whose late father had started the company—supervised ten workers who built wooden playground equipment. Mostly they sold it in sections, to schools and community groups. They held workdays to put it together, and Brenda traveled with the equipment and taught people who'd never built anything how to make a playground. She'd been as far south as Maryland, all over New England and parts of New York State. Best and hardest were playgrounds in the backyards of women's shelters and residences for battered women. Those customers got a discount. She'd spend a week working with the women, showing them how to use tools, how to use their bodies, sleeping in an unoccupied room and eating with them, pretending to get their jokes. She might have lived in a place like that, she reminded herself. It could have happened.

Jess had always known she loved women. Hearing about Brenda's past troubled her. How could you? she had said.

—I didn't know who I was.

—I don't know what that means.

In Schroon Lake village, only a few miles from the cabin, they stopped for coffee, which always made Jess happy. There was decent blueberry pie. Then Brenda said, Let's walk down to the public beach. The village of Schroon Lake was the way villages ought to be: the stores were a block from the beach, and in between was the library, where Brenda had read as a child while her mother did the shopping. The little street, with shops crowded together—filled with tourists buying postcards and souvenirs, impatient with the rain—was unchanged. There was the Grand Union, the liquor store whose owner had given Brenda a ride to the cabin in 1969—incredibly, nineteen years ago. Nelson was dead, but it was as if she'd find him there, as if he might have escaped everywhere else to be at the cabin. They walked down the curved street and stood above a lawn and the beach, staring out at the big lake. Swimming was possible at the cabin, but Evelyn had preferred this beach with its clean sand, friendly women to chat with, and lifeguards, and Brenda had spent many hours here. Now the lake's surface was gray-green, rough with wind and rain. No lifeguards in the big chairs on the beach. They descended the lawn and walked in the sand to the edge of the lake. The smell of this country . . . what was the smell? The sounds and smells were not like anywhere, not like southern New Hampshire—what was the difference? Without knowing what she meant, she said, The sky has a different shape at home and here.

—No it doesn't.

—It circles differently. She'd lived in New Hampshire for something like sixteen years. The sky there curved back to David's long, difficult babyhood and a list of women: Roz; Karen, whom she'd loved too hard; scary Jean; Annie; and then the first hard year with Jess, when she couldn't believe she'd found, at last, the person with whom she'd grow old and kept trying to spoil things just to make sure. But the sky here in the Adirondacks made a larger curve, all the way back to her mother under a big hat calling to her and Carol, brushing sand off their backsides and pulling the fabric of their ruffled cotton bathing suits from where it was caught in the cheeks of their buttocks, telling them to stay out of the water because they'd just eaten ice cream. Evelyn was younger then than Brenda was now. How had she caught up to and passed her mother? A fragile, imaginary Evelyn, having seated her girls on the sand where she could see them when she turned her head to breathe, yanked her own rust-colored nylon suit down, tucked her hair into a white rubber cap with a strap under the chin, glanced at the sky—imaginary Evelyn saw sun, not rain—walked purposefully into the lake and swam back and forth parallel to the beach.

Jess looked bored, her arms crossed, and Brenda put her arm around her shoulders to turn her back toward the car. Okay if we look for the house?

—We have enough gas, Jess said.

Brenda made one mistake, then backtracked and had Jess turn down the right road. Nothing much had changed since she'd been there last. At last, came the long driveway. Jess turned down it, but said, What are we going to tell the people here?

—Maybe there won't be anybody, and we can walk down to the lake. It was a small lake, lost in the hills. She went on, Or we can say we're lost. Or we can tell the truth.

Nobody was there. The house looked much as it had when she'd been there with Nelson. The grass was high, and the windows were boarded up. A faded FOR SALE sign leaned on its pole near the driveway.

—Does it still belong to Harold's first wife? Jess said.

—I heard she sold it years ago.

Jess parked the Toyota and slapped the edge of Brenda's seat. Let's go, she said. Anybody asks, we'll say we might buy it.

They walked around the edge of the house. The rain had stopped, but the sky was low and dark above the lake. Brenda walked down to the edge of the water—the familiar round shape, a few houses close together on the opposite shore—then turned to look at Jess coming too. She put an arm around her and Jess leaned into her. She stroked the back of Brenda's neck and ran her forefinger down Brenda's back to just below her waist. It was good to be away from people, where they could touch.

—I'm cold, Jess said.

—At last, Brenda said. Let's go back into town and buy you a sweatshirt.

—Dark green, Jess said. Also—could we get a dog?

—Today?

—When we get home.

—What made you think of it now? Okay.

—I have a past too, Jess said. Brenda turned and took Jess's face in her hands, thrust her tongue into Jess's mouth. They both laughed but they prolonged the kiss.

Brenda wondered if the key was still in the Band-Aid box in the place near the door where it had always been. Probably not. The exterior had been painted since her time, though it was in need of paint now. Anyway, she didn't want to go in. Inside was Nelson's ghost. She touched Jess's arm. You still put up with me, she said.

—I like the way your head sits on your shoulders, Jess said.

—Unlike the heads of your old girlfriends, which stuck out of their asses.

—That's right.

—Maybe I'll call Harold, tell him the place is for sale, Brenda said.

—How old is Harold? Jess said.

—Same as my father. Seventy-eight. Not too old to answer the phone.

5

Harold—on a bright, cool Sunday morning in September 1995, after an insufferably hot, dry summer—discovered yet again, at eighty-five, that he was a pretentious idiot. When he'd retired from teaching, he had told Naomi, who was already retired, that he was going to write, that he'd write every day in the spare room of their apartment, which he'd made into a study, that he'd write even on weekends.

—A couple of hours on weekend mornings, that's all, he said. Otherwise, I'll stop believing I'm worth anything.

Naomi, as emotionally complete as ever—she was a tidy zippered case equipped with every tool—had readily agreed to leave him alone in the mornings, and she accomplished that all too well. On weekdays she took classes, taught illiterates to read, and went to a gym. On weekends she walked with a friend even older than Harold. Today, after that, she was going on to lunch with another friend. Harold usually wrote. Sometimes he couldn't. Since he'd retired, he'd published a study of Delmore Schwartz he'd worked on for many years and had written some reviews and articles. Nothing he wrote changed anyone. Walking with Naomi would have been appealing, but he had not yet said to her, I'm not going to write on Saturdays and Sundays anymore. I'm going to be with you. She'd probably prefer walking with her friend. Her friend was ninety-one. How long could she walk?

And he—he was about to start another book, though only a fool would start a book at his age. Well, he would be a fool, then. He had bought a computer a few weeks earlier, and mostly, this morning, he had been wasting time, stomping back and forth to the toilet, glancing at the paper (Bosnia, as usual). But he had also learned how to insert page numbers. The real job of the day was continuing to copy notes he'd been making for the last eight months, a plan for this book. Typing the notes on the computer was different from typing them with a typewriter because he was a messy typist, but the computer made everything look good. He disliked the finished look of what he'd typed: his plan, plainly set down as if an office full of assistants would carry it out, made him feel even more like a pretentious idiot. The book—for God's sake!—the book was an autobiography. A memoir. A memoir of doing things wrong.

And right. Also doing things right. Personally wrong, up to a point, politically right, mostly. Something like that. He had just typed *death of Nelson* in the list of events to write about. He got up and left the room, though he had three-quarters of an hour of his two hours left.

One reason he felt like a pretentious idiot had nothing to do with Naomi. Evelyn Saltzman had had a heart attack. Artie had been too upset to call, but Carol had called Harold, and he'd gone to see Evelyn in the hospital. Now it was a few weeks later and she was home. When he'd phoned the other day, Artie said, Come see us, it would cheer her up. Come Sunday. Maybe ten or eleven? I'm driving her to Carol and Lenny's for lunch.

—I write in the morning on Sundays, Harold had said. How about after lunch, when you come back? Artie and Evelyn had never moved out of Brooklyn, but now they lived in Brooklyn Heights and it was easy to get to them.

—Nah, she'll be worn out. And I want to watch the tennis. Then Evelyn had called to him, and Artie had gotten off the phone.

Now on Sunday, Harold—amazed that at eighty-five it was still possible to do something he regretted as much as he regretted having said he was writing this morning and couldn't visit Artie and Evelyn—picked up the phone. Can I come now?

—Sure, Artie said. We're just about to take a walk. She's supposed to walk.

—Where?

—The river.

—I'll find you, Harold said. He took a hat for the sun and left the apartment. All over the city, old people walked. Naomi and her friend, Artie and Evelyn. Well, he and Artie had walked when they were young too. As he hurried to the subway, he spotted a cab. Eagerly, he rode across the Brooklyn Bridge, back into Brooklyn. He sat up straight and looked at the river. The glint of sun hurt his eyes.

He had the taxi drop him near the Promenade, close to Artie and Evelyn's apartment. As he set out on the paved walk next to the river, he heard Artie call, Hey, you old bastard! and turned.

—*One-four-nine is the school for me, drives away all adversity!* Artie sang. He was elated now, after being terrified when he thought Evelyn would die. They were sitting on a bench, smiling and waving. Harold stood in front of them, leaning over to kiss Evelyn, who looked old, but whose eyes were bright with humor and pleasure. How do you feel? he said.

—I'm alive, she said, and what crossed her face for a second looked more like despair.

Harold made the choice to ignore it. And you're out of the hospital. You look wonderful. What a beautiful day.

The wind made crisscrossing lines on the river. There were sailboats.

—Sit, Artie said. We're resting. How's the work?

—I'm an idiot, writing about my life.

—From what you tell me, the point of the book is that you're an idiot. Artie had shriveled and darkened like a nut. His nose looked bigger than the rest of his face.

—I haven't started writing, Harold said. I'm making notes and typing them on the computer. Did I tell you I bought a computer?

—Who needs it? Artie said.

—No, it's terrific, Harold said. You want to add something, you just stick it in. With a typewriter, you retype the whole damn thing. I keep finding notes that belong somewhere else, and I just put them where they ought to go. He thought about typing *death of Nelson*.

—Ridiculous, Artie said.

—How is your wife? Evelyn said. I'm sorry, I forget her name.

—Naomi. She's fine. She sends regards.

—Where is she?

—With a friend, Harold said. Naomi had kept her friends when they married, and she only rarely saw his.

—She should live so long, Evelyn said. Startled, Harold looked at Artie, who shrugged.

Artie said, You need to walk. They stood and he took Evelyn's arm. Harold went around to her other side, and the three of them promenaded down the Promenade, part of a cheerful procession of lovers, dog walkers, children in strollers.

—You are so right, Evelyn said, as they set out. She wore a light blue sweatsuit and clean white sneakers.

—In the hospital, Artie said, they made her walk every day. We'd walk to the nurses' station and back. Then we did it twice. The day before she came home, we did it twice without resting.

—A good walk, Evelyn said, and Harold was relieved that this remark was not a non sequitur. She put one foot deliberately in front of the other, but she was steady. She smiled. I eat such smart food, she said. You should see.

—A lot of fish, Artie said. You want to know my personal recipe for fish? I broil it with lemon. Delicious. A little oil, no butter. But the trick is to know how long it takes. You have to take it out at the right minute.

—It's very good, Evelyn said.

—So is this Wild Card thing going to ruin baseball? Artie said then.

Harold shook his head. He knew there would be more play-off games this year. He hadn't followed baseball closely enough to have an opinion, but surely anything done for the benefit of the advertisers was bad. The sun was pleasant on his shoulders. He was a little chilly in a lightweight jacket. Summer was over. Funny how you looked forward to the next thing, even though each one brought you closer to the end. It had to be Darwinian: species survived when they found excitement in the renewal of the seasons. But you didn't have to be old to die. Nelson was dead. Myra had been dead of lung cancer for years. Thinking of Myra made him think of the cabin. How's Brenda? he said.

—She was here when Ev was in the hospital, Artie said, and she's coming back soon. The dog sitter—something. In a few days. She and Jess—they have money, who would think? Getting bought out was the best thing for Brenda's business. Jess makes a fair chunk of change too, with that law practice. They sent us some stuff to eat.

—Low-fat, Evelyn said.

—Brenda asked me, Artie said, Does Harold go to the cabin? God, I loved that place. Ev, when you're better, we'll go stay in a hotel in the mountains.

—Brenda was the one who told me it was for sale, Harold said. She and her partner drove over to see it. Can you imagine? The next day I made an offer—asking price, no inspection. I pay a caretaker so it doesn't go up in flames. But I've never once gone.

—That's a mistake, Artie said. You should go. You still drive? Take Naomi and just go, take a look. Just make sure the mountains are still around the lake.

Harold was silent.

—It won't bring him back, staying away, Artie said. And he didn't die there—I honestly don't know what that has to do with it.

—You're right, Harold said. Nelson never liked being there. Maybe if I had helped him have fun there, everything would have been different.

Evelyn spoke slowly, almost making it a chant, with pauses between each word, Honey, it . . . is . . . what . . . it . . . is. She patted his arm. Come on, I'll race you, she said, and walked a little faster, pulling her arm away from Artie's and pumping with both elbows, her hands in fists. Her short hair was white, fluffed by the wind.

Gulls screamed above the river, and a red dog stopped to sniff Artie's shoes. He leaned over and scratched the dog behind the ears, and Harold and Evelyn walked past him. Artie broke into a little jog to catch up. The dog's owner, a young woman, called, Great day for a walk!

6

Brenda's mother had complained for years that she couldn't sleep, and when she died, two months ago, in her honor Brenda had apparently become the new Evelyn Saltzman Insomnia Expert. Jess thought it was Evelyn's way of being with her.

—It's a visitation, she said. Brenda knew Jess would have liked a visitation from Evelyn for herself. Her own mother, still alive, was sometimes hostile and sometimes elaborately friendly but never relaxed about Jess's homosexuality. But Evelyn had been as matter-of-fact about women loving women as she was about everything else. Her only objection to Jess as a partner for Brenda had been that she smoked, but soon Jess quit and then she had no faults.

Brenda had pointed out that Evelyn was too considerate to keep someone awake; any haunting she'd need to do, she'd accomplish at some reasonable hour.

—Heaven is timeless, said Jess. No clocks.

—Jews don't go to that kind of heaven, Brenda said.

So now she was carrying out her recently acquired duties as an insomniac while Jess breathed steadily in her sleep beside her, lying on her side facing away from Brenda, her butt in flannel pajamas just touching Brenda's thigh. Brenda checked the red numbers on the clock at their bedside too often, glumly noting the passage of the next to the last day of the first year of the new millennium—it was 2:47 AM on December 30, 2000. Purists said the first day of the new millennium had not been January 1, 2000, but would be January 1, 2001, which didn't make anybody think planes would fall from the sky, as they had thought last year. Brenda had not worried about Y2K.

She rolled over onto her side, facing away from Jess, and now their rear ends touched. Jess stirred in her sleep and moved away slightly, and when Brenda reached back and just touched what her hand came to—a thigh, she thought—Jess grunted contentedly, as if to say yes. They had driven to Vermont one weekend this fall, with Abby the dog in the backseat, and had a civil union ceremony. Jess said she'd like to marry. Brenda didn't believe in ceremonies. She told Jess she was having this one because it was important to do everything possible to give other gay people the right to do whatever they wanted, but the truth was that she was happy that Jess wanted—as she herself wanted—to promise to stay together. Brenda saw it as for life; Jess was sure they'd be together after death as well.

—I have no *objection* to being your partner after death, Brenda said. This was in the motel the night after the ceremony. She lay on the bed flexing her feet. After the ceremony they'd taken a long walk. She'd been wearing the wrong shoes, and her ankles were sore. She said, I needed to make that clear.

—My grandmother must have been so surprised when she got to heaven and found gay couples, Jess said.

—Do you think she spoke to them?

—Oh, she'd *speak* to anyone.

Now it was 2:53. What was keeping her up, Brenda decided, was an e-mail she'd written to David. Maybe it had been a mistake. These days David was a technical writer in Silicon Valley whose work she didn't understand. He lived alone in Mountain View and had a long, narrow face and lank black hair. He didn't look like Brenda, but like her father—her father in a rare mood. David's face told you he could be hurt; her father's had more often expressed—less so lately—anger or defensiveness. She scarcely remembered David's own father's appearance (but she had supplied Ted's name when David had requested it as a college sophomore—he had found Ted living on Long Island, and they had met once or twice).

Brenda knew David had written fiction in college, though he'd never let her see it. But two weeks ago, she'd received a priority mail envelope from him containing a short story. This is some *real* writing I did, he had scrawled on an accompanying sheet of paper from a company scratch pad. The story was about a boy with a lesbian mother who has a girlfriend, Carrie. His babysitter is sick, and Carrie agrees to take care of him. She drives them to a nearby lake, where the boy talks her into giving him money for ice cream. His mother does not allow him to walk to the refreshment stand alone, at a distance, but Carrie doesn't object. He gets lost, and when he gets back, he can't find Carrie. Afraid she has drowned, he tearfully begs help from a lifeguard, who leads the boy to a boat shed, behind which is Carrie, making out with another woman.

Brenda had had no idea David could produce a story like this—or any story—and was as impressed by its length and number of characters as by anything else. She thought it seemed good enough to publish. She wondered if it was true, if he'd been afraid to tell her about an infidelity by one of the women she'd loved. There hadn't been anyone exactly like Carrie, but one— the one they lived with for two years—was Karen, a similar name. She didn't think Karen had cheated on her; they'd had plenty of other problems but not that. Karen didn't drive, though.

She wondered what David hoped she'd say, whether he might want her to critique the story, and when she read it again, she found she wasn't sure she believed the ending. That was what she'd written about, finally. She praised the story effusively, did not mention its similarities to their own life, but questioned the ending. Maybe Carrie should be making out with a man, she suggested. Would Carrie make out with a woman on a New Hampshire beach? And wouldn't the lifeguard be too embarrassed to lead the boy to the right place? She had written the e-mail several times and sent it three days ago. David hadn't replied. Maybe she hadn't praised the story enough. Maybe David hadn't wanted criticism or praise but something else.

Brenda got up, pulling her robe around her. Abby, who was floppy-limbed in all circumstances, part golden retriever, was a rag doll at night. She was stretched at the foot of the bed. Without noticeably organizing her legs, she rolled onto the floor and padded after Brenda, who went down the wide oak staircase— the first thing she'd loved about the house; it still needed to be refinished—and let Abby out.

A newspaper stained with coffee was spread on the kitchen table. Gore—it now turned out—had won the popular vote by more than half a million. Bush had picked somebody called Donald Rumsfeld to be secretary of defense. Jess kept up with the news, but after the Supreme Court had made Bush president, Brenda couldn't bear it, read little more than headlines. She bundled the paper into the recycling bin and opened the refrigerator. Then she closed it and ate a banana. Abby barked and she let her in.

She still wouldn't be able to sleep. She went into the living room. The computer was on a table in the corner. She got a blanket from the sofa, wrapped it around herself, and turned the computer on. It was 3:42 AM. She checked her e-mail. Something had come in just after she'd left the office. It was seven or eight years now since her company had been bought by a firm in Ohio that made similar playgrounds—also imaginative, also put together often by volunteers on the site—but made of steel. Brenda, now in charge of Mountainside and its finely crafted wooden products, kept an eye on design and construction at home, but she also traveled more. She supervised volunteer workdays for both parts of the operation, did some of the teaching herself, and had a staff of two for the rest. A school system in Iowa was buying three playgrounds and wanted to reschedule a workday. She'd deal with that in the office. But there was also a message from David—no, two messages from David.

Mom,

Thanks for the suggestion—it's interesting, though I'm not sure I agree.

What an astonishing boy. She could never have expressed polite disagreement to her parents. She would say, *How can you possibly think something so totally wrong?* Often in tears. David was almost twenty-seven. Did she still do that at twenty-seven? Yes.

He went on,

I think the story needs Carrie to cheat on Liz with a woman, and the lifeguard wouldn't have the nerve to confront them until the kid asked, but then he would. He'd be seething about their shocking behavior. If you're wondering about the time Annie drove me to the lake, by the way—I assume you are, and thanks for not asking if the story really happened, which is all anybody else I show my stories to seems to care about—she did not kiss another woman behind the boat shed or anywhere else. I don't think there was a boat shed. I've conflated our usual lake, which is where Annie took me, with another one. But I really did go for the ice cream by myself, which you didn't allow even at our little state park. I felt bad about that for years, but it wouldn't have made enough of a story.

Anyway, thanks for reading.
D

As so often, Brenda sat back in her chair, reminded that David was someone she could rarely predict. He had said, *stories*. This was not an isolated story. She deleted two spam messages and read David's second one.

Not to go on about this too much, but it's an example of something I think about all the time: I don't know other writers. I belong to a writing group, but they don't know shit. I'm thinking about grad school. There are programs where you can go for a week or two and then mail in work, so I wouldn't have to move or quit my job. More soon.

D
PS Happy New Year

It was past four, and Brenda heard Jess's footsteps on the stairs. The dog stood up. Sweetie, Jess said, what?

—It's okay, said Brenda.

—It's cold in that bed without you.

—I'm coming, Brenda said. I miss my mother, she added. She started to cry. Jess held her arms open, and they embraced awkwardly on the stairs in their two puffy down bathrobes—one blue, one green—which they'd bought each other a couple of years ago rather than replace the heating system. Jess, who also missed Evelyn, cried too.

7

A fool and his money are soon parted, but a fool and his principles are harder to separate, Harold wrote. He didn't know what came next. How long had he been writing this book? He'd bought his first computer in the mid-nineties and had made notes for months before he started writing. Now it was almost winter, 2002. A long time. When the initial draft—well, the fifteenth draft, which now seemed like the initial draft—was done, a year or two earlier, the editor who had published Harold's previous books had retired, but his longtime assistant had become an editor. She had accepted the book but sent a letter of suggestions, queries, and complaints that Harold had put aside for months, the months of a cardiac bypass. Whenever he looked at the letter, Harold got so upset he couldn't read it: it was three pages long.

Paul—author of two books on early nineteenth-century American history—finally persuaded him that they should sit down together and try to make sense of what Harold's editor wanted. Paul said, You like her, remember?

Harold had known the editor, Jennifer, since she'd started at the company, right out of college. Indeed, how had she become someone Harold was afraid of? Paul spent every free weekend and his long professor's summers at the cabin in the Adirondacks—after finally talking his father into letting him fix the place up and use it—and one Friday in spring, about a year and a half ago now, Paul had driven to the city, picked Harold up—Naomi was if anything pleased to be left alone for a weekend—and brought him, late at night, to the cabin with a trunkful of groceries, Harold's manuscript, the editor's letter, and a laptop computer. Paul took the luggage and said, Wait, but Harold—despite his dimming sight and stiff legs—didn't want to wait. He walked to the back of the car and around it, his palm flat on the roof, then the trunk. The chilly mountain air and the smell of the evergreens brought a catch to his throat, and he made a surprised sound that caused Paul, ahead of him with his arms full, to turn abruptly and put down the bags.

—Dad, stop, he said.

—No, I'm all right. It had made no sense not to come. It made him think of Nelson, but there wasn't anything that *didn't* make him think of Nelson. Once again, he had been a coward.

The next morning Paul sat at the kitchen table with the manuscript, the letter, and the laptop, while Harold sat and sometimes dozed in the rocker Paul had placed near it. Harold was delighted to be where he was, proud of himself for owning it, for providing a country retreat for Paul.

The sounds and smells were right. The cabin brought Nelson back, but it brought back the pleasure and oddness of Nelson as much as the pain—his quirky goodwill, his tense alertness.

—This isn't hard, Paul kept saying, looking over the editor's suggestions. You should have seen the corrections on my last book. Harold's book was autobiography—memoir—and so most of it came from Harold's memory and couldn't be checked. But facts about history could be checked, and Harold had to check them. He had never had trouble before. With this book, he couldn't begin to think what to do. But Paul knew. You've forgotten how to get organized, he said, halfway through the morning. That's all that's wrong with you.

—I was never good at that, Harold said.

They took a break and walked slowly to the lakeshore in fleece jackets Paul's wife had bought for both of them. They sat carefully on the dock. The surface of the lake glinted as it always had.

By the end of that weekend, much had been done, and Harold knew what else was needed. Soon the revision was accepted, but then Jennifer phoned with two more requests. Everybody hates the title, she said cheerfully. This was new! The title had always been *Autobiography of a Fool*. Think about it, Jennifer said.

—What's the other thing? Harold said.

—Could you write a little preface? It needs a preface, she said. She rarely sounded so firm. Harold knew at once that she was right: it needed a preface. It started with his birth, but why would anybody care if they didn't know anything about him? A month's thought had led to the new title: *A Fool and His Principles*. And that led—this morning, with not much time left before his deadline—to the new first sentence, the first sentence of the preface.

So that is where Harold Abrams was, that fall morning in 2002: he was writing a preface to his new book, *A Fool and His Principles*, and the first sentence of the preface was—he read it again and didn't hate it yet—*A fool and his money are soon parted, but a fool and his principles are harder to separate*. He still didn't know what came next, but Naomi was standing in the doorway behind him.

—What? he said. He wouldn't mind being interrupted. She hardly ever interrupted him, maybe a little more these days, when she'd become so intent on a thought that she'd forget they weren't already in a conversation about it.

—What? Nothing what.

He swiveled his chair. Small but with sturdy shoulders, Naomi peered at something in her hand. She said, I was just trying to see in the light, tilting her head toward the window in his study. The corridor was long and dim. That was why she'd stopped where she had.

—See what?

—My gloves. I got wax on my gloves last night. How can I get it off? I can hardly see it. White wax.

—Let's see. He got up. The night before, Naomi had worn black woolen gloves to a candlelight vigil to protest President Bush's plan to go to war in Iraq. He had stayed home.

—Standing still is harder than walking, she said when she came home. She sat down in the nearest chair, still in her coat. Harold, I can't believe it. I saw people tonight I haven't seen since the Vietnam years. I can't believe we have to do this again. Everybody got old. The kids with peace symbols have gray hair. Everybody my age is a wizened little troll, except for the ones who are dead or in nursing homes.

Harold was older than she was. He took the gloves and sat down, trying to flake off the wax with his thumbnail. Could you melt it?

—Wouldn't that just make it worse?

—I don't know.

—We didn't use to carry candles, she said. It's a nuisance, but it did look nice. What are you doing?

—The preface.

—Oh, she said, I'm sorry I interrupted!

—That's okay, he said. I'm stuck, after the first sentence. He read it to her. Before she could speak, the phone rang. There was a phone on his desk, but Naomi usually answered the phone—she had many friends—and she left the gloves and went into the bedroom. He heard her voice—surprised, excited, not faking it, but couldn't make out the words. Then he heard a tone that suggested Naomi was going to ask the other person to hold the phone while she consulted Harold. Sure enough. She made her slow way back to the doorway, while he worried that she'd trip on the cord. She had broken her hip a year earlier.

—It's Amanda.

—What's wrong?

—Nothing's wrong.

—The baby's okay? he said. Paul's youngest child, his daughter Amanda, had married young. Harold and Naomi had defended her decision on illogical grounds that Harold knew were illogical, but he wanted to be on Amanda's side.

—I didn't even think of marrying your mother until I was getting old, he had said to Paul. Young isn't so bad. If I'd been young, I'd have had the nerve to break her heart. It's not good to wait until your conscience kicks in.

—That only makes sense as a decision *not* to marry, Paul had said.

Amanda hadn't cared what either of them thought. She married and had a baby. Paul and Martha had hoped she'd go to medical school. She'd expressed interest in that, and she had the grades, but so far she just took care of her daughter, Nell. She and her husband—at least he earned a living; Harold had forgotten what he did—lived in Boston. Naomi said Amanda was in New York for a couple of days and would like to see them. Harold saved the sentence he'd typed and picked up the phone.

—Amanda?

—Grandpa. I'm in New York. Her voice was confident, a little raspy. She sounded like the boss of a small company or maybe a high school girl with a mild case of stage fright playing the boss of a small company in the senior play.

—So I hear. How's the baby, honey? She had interested him from the first—always a little more troublesome and unpredictable than her brothers.

—She's a monster. Aren't you a monster, Nellie?

—Where are you? he said. How long are you staying?

—Well, said Amanda, here's the thing. I should have called you before. I'm leaving in a few hours. I was going to call you, but things kept coming up. But I want to see you so much! I don't want to leave without seeing you.

—Where are you?

—I'm at my friend's house, but I'm leaving. I thought I'd take Nellie to a playground and hang around there until it's time for my train. Is there a playground near Penn Station?

—When is your train? Your friend—where does she live?

—Um, Astoria, but we're right near the subway.

—But you've got bags, Harold protested. And a stroller. Don't you want to take a cab? I'll come and get you. Could he do that? Which train went to Astoria? He knew there was a good train to Astoria.

—No, I got here fine. I've got a backpack for Nell and a suitcase with wheels—it's easy. But do you know a playground?

He wasn't hurt that she hadn't called before—he knew that Amanda liked him. She'd gone to NYU and had dropped in now and then in those years. She'd bring her friends and would pull Harold's books off the shelves to show them. He liked her independence—but he liked it even more that when she needed something, she turned to him. He couldn't think of any playgrounds near Penn Station. How should he know? He remembered a playground where he had taken his kids—or maybe he and Paul had taken Amanda and her brothers—near the southwest corner of Central Park. He directed her to meet him on Central Park South in half an hour.

—Let me give you my cell, she said. Do you have one?

He did, but he didn't remember the number. He hurried to find it while she stayed on the line. He rarely used it, but he did find it and it was charged up. We're in business, he said.

—We've got a date, he said to Naomi, but she had a hairdresser's appointment. Harold put on an overcoat and a scarf and set out alone for the subway station, elated.

He was a little tired when he came up the stairs, but only a little. He thought he saw Amanda at a distance and hurried toward the girl with the shaggy light hair and a big baby on her back. Yes. While she waited, she'd walked over to show Nellie the horses, waiting to pull tourists in carriages. She turned, saw Harold, and hurried to meet him, her wheeled bag clattering on the paving stones. She was tall and sturdy, and Nell bounced and frowned over her shoulder. She was named after Nelson. Nell and Amanda both had shaggy light hair.

When they reached him, Amanda threw her arms around him and he staggered. Oh my God, I'm going to knock you over and break your hip, and my dad will shoot me! she said, grasping his arms above his elbows, while the bag fell over. Nell cried.

—This is Grandpa, Amanda said. No, Great-Grandpa!

—Horsie! Nell wailed.

—We could go back, Harold said.

—No, let's go to the playground. She should run around before she's cooped up in the train.

He insisted on pulling her bag, and they found the playground soon enough, with an unoccupied bench in the sun. She complimented him on the kind of New Yorker he was. My friend

Steve's like that, she said, squatting to set the baby carrier on the bench and shrugging out of it. Steve moved here years ago and he knows everything. He told me all the stations we'd pass.

Harold noted, startled, that the friend Amanda had stayed with was a he. Well, maybe part of a couple.

Amanda lifted Nell out of the carrier and kissed her face, then settled her on the ground. Let's go on the swing. She carried the baby, and Harold followed, pulling the suitcase. The carrier was slung on his arm. Yeah, I guess we'd better keep an eye on that stuff, Amanda said. I never think of that.

Harold was a little out of breath. The swings would keep a toddler safe: rubber buckets with holes for her legs. Amanda stuffed her daughter into one of them and began pushing her vigorously. The day was bright and chilly, and the gray buildings around them surrounded this tiny light-haired child, her feet in little red sneakers with Velcro closers, her legs in pink corduroy. Harold wasn't dead yet and could still walk and talk and read and write. *After so many deaths I live and write*, George Herbert had written. I'll wait on the bench, Harold said, and once again hoisted the baby carrier and grasped the suitcase by its handle, then made his way back to the sunny bench.

Nell tried what the playground had to offer. At last Amanda led her back to him. She's cold, she said. I'm freezing. Aren't you?

—A little, Harold said.

—You're not hard of hearing, she said. My other grandparents can't hear me.

—I wear an expensive hearing aid, he said.

—They're afraid I'll say something they don't want to hear, Amanda said, still parked in front of him. You're not like that.

—I don't know, he said. Say something bad and see if I pretend not to hear you. Without much consultation, they started down Seventh Avenue in search of a place to warm up and have something to eat. Everything would be expensive in this neighborhood, but he didn't care, as long as it wasn't too crowded. Amanda bounced along at his side, seemingly unaffected by the weight of this big baby, who spoke inaudibly. She was telling herself stories, Amanda said. They found a Jewish delicatessen. Harold excused himself to go to the men's room, and then Amanda carried Nell off to change her diaper. They ordered lunch. With his heart condition, Harold couldn't order the pastrami he'd have preferred, but he didn't mind turkey. Then Amanda ordered the same—she didn't eat red meat. The baby would eat scraps from their plates, and they got her a bowl of applesauce.

—The people you stayed with, Harold said, as Amanda dug out toys to amuse Nell, who was in a high chair. Do they have children?

—What people? Amanda said.

—In Astoria, Harold said.

—Oh, you mean Steve—no, he lives alone, Amanda said. He's divorced.

A bowl of sour and half-sour pickles was on the table, and Amanda ate a pickle with her free hand. Her other hand danced a small plastic animal up and down to amuse Nell. She was looking at Nell, not at Harold, but her shoulder, the side of her face— something—looked self-conscious. How do you know him? Harold said, coming to the slow understanding that Amanda had phoned him not just because he knew his way around New York.

It hadn't occurred to him before to wonder what Paul had told his children about Harold's divorce from Myra. Myra had died when Paul's children were small, but they might remember her; in any case, Paul remembered her. Amanda knew not only that Harold wore a hearing aid because he preferred to hear, she knew how Harold had lived. He'd even written about it—well, tangentially, except for this book he was trying to finish. Which

Amanda might read. He didn't know what reader he'd imagined until now, but now he imagined Amanda reading about his infidelities, his uncertainties, his clumsy use of politics to guide his private life and also justify the private life he felt like leading. Harold had never concluded—he didn't conclude in this book either—that because he'd been a fool, he was sorry about his life. It seemed all of a piece. He didn't regret the politics, wrong as they sometimes were. Was it impossible for a lefty to be faithful to a woman? In the book he argued that it would have been impossible for him, that the nerve to break rules made many rules breakable, and made him understand and sympathize with rebellious young people in the sixties.

—Is Steve your lover, Amanda? he asked the side of her face. She focused more intently on Nell, and he wondered how much the little girl understood. But that didn't seem to be the issue.

—I kept asking myself if I was going to tell you, Amanda said. I don't know who else to tell—what a crazy thing to say to my grandpa.

He could think of no answer. The food came and Amanda fed Nell applesauce, then turned to her sandwich, offering the baby bits of bread and french fried potatoes.

—He was my professor at NYU, she said. He's nine years older than I am. He was junior faculty then. Biology. Now he has tenure. We had an affair my junior year—he was married then. I didn't break up his marriage. Are you shocked by all this? I was careful not to tell you at the time!

—I thought nowadays teachers didn't do that, he said.

—It wasn't sexual harassment, Amanda said, and though he hadn't been particularly shocked by her news, he was shocked at her easy use of the sociological, legal, distancing term. Then she said, Oh, maybe it was. How should I know? But it was harder on him than on me, that's what I mean. It wasn't like, I'm weeping in the dorm and he's callously making me go to bed or he'll fail my lab report. He was the one who did all the weeping. Now he weeps because it's the other way around—I'm married. He says to me, I'm a grownup; I should know better. As if I was a child.

—You are a child, Harold said, before he thought, and was afraid she'd say nothing more, as she shook her head in impatient dismissal.

—Sorry, he said. Of course you're not. You're a mother.

—Children can be mothers, but I'm not a child, she said. She faced him now, and he saw that her eyes were close together, not crossed but just slightly out of sync. They were not blue or brown—hazel, did they call that? Flecks of gold in them.

—Eat, he said. Shall I take the baby? Nell was getting fussy now, crying a little. He stood and lifted her out of the high chair. But he did it wrong, and her leg was caught and she yelled. Amanda reached to open the high-chair tray, but she didn't take the child. She put the tray back on the high chair and began eating her sandwich rapidly. He'd finished half of his. He stood Nell on the seat next to him, on the window side, and said, Look, Nellie, a baby! And a dog. Nell pressed her dirty hands to the glass and commented. He wasn't sure she didn't want to go through the window to the dog and the baby. Maybe this was the wrong idea. The little girl wriggled in his hands, firm and vigorous. His right arm hurt—it often did—holding her by the waist as she shoved against his grasp.

—So do you think I'm a horrible person? she said. I shouldn't have told you.

—Don't be silly. It was hard to think with this baby pulling so. Now she was trying to go under the table, and if he wasn't careful, she'd bump her forehead on the table's edge. Finally Amanda took Nell back. To his surprise, she twisted around in the seat and pulled up her sweatshirt to nurse her. He looked around, but nobody seemed to be watching, and Amanda's breast was covered by the sweatshirt. Now Nell was quiet and Harold was free to give a better answer. He hadn't had a conversation like this in years—a conversation in which it was this uncertain what would be said, what he and the other person would feel. He had forgotten about this kind of thing.

—Do you love him? he asked.

—Love Steve or love Zack? He'd forgotten her husband's name—the husband he'd been so quick to argue for, when Amanda suddenly wanted to marry, right out of college. I love them both, she said.

—That's too easy, he said. That's the sort of thing *I* said. He'd had a sandwich, he'd had coffee—coffee, not decaf for once—and it was as if his brain had wandered back into his skull. He knew who they were: a man and a woman who both had trouble with love. He remembered Artie's disgust, his unvarying disapproval of Harold's shenanigans, as he called them. But Harold had been seeing Naomi most of those years—not all, but most—not a flibbertigibbet but the love of his life.

—I can't leave Zack, she said. He's Nell's father. He loves me. We do all these things together. Steve's bored with a lot of stuff I can't do without. I don't mean in bed, just things like dancing. Partying. But Steve is the man I really love.

—You married Zack to stop thinking about Steve? he said.

—No, it's not that bad. I thought it was over. I honestly thought it was over. I didn't think of Steve for years. But the last time I came to New York—well, I knew where he was and I called him. Nell was tiny then.

She hadn't called her grandfather that time. Of course not—she didn't want anybody telling her not to do what she wanted to do. If Nell was tiny, it was a year or more ago.

He looked at his watch. We should get you to your train.

She looked at him, as she eased the baby away from her breast and smoothed her sweatshirt. You weren't wrong, telling my dad he should stop yelling at me about getting married. Getting married was right. It's just—

—Marriage should be different?

—Yeah, marriage should be different.

—Zack doesn't know what you're doing?

—No, and I don't want him doing the same thing, she said, and then she laughed, and her face reminded him of her—no, of Paul—as a child. I'm a hypocrite.

—You need a better grandpa than I am, Amanda.

—No, you're the best, she said. He hadn't meant she needed someone who was better at being a grandparent. He had meant she needed a grandparent who was a better human being. But he let it go. He held the baby while she flagged down a cab, and they were jostled down Seventh Avenue. He paid the cab, and they made their way into the station, now with him pulling the suitcase and the baby on Amanda's back. Her train was half an hour late, and they found a place to sit. Nell sat with her face pressed into Amanda's chest. If I'm lucky, she'll sleep all the way, Amanda said. If not, she'll yell.

—I'm glad you called me, Harold said. He patted Amanda's knee.

—Oh, so am I!

He wanted to come up with something wise—a resolution—but they sat silently, watching people drag their luggage by, eat snacks, study the arrivals and departures board, embrace. Commuters were rushing to Jersey Transit, though it was early. Trains were announced. He felt more like a grandfather now, benevolent and vague, competent to offer money and love. At last the train arrived—forty minutes late—and he kissed her at the barrier, as she scrambled for her ticket and bumped her suitcase behind her,

her daughter waving her arm in its white sweater toward everyone who passed.

Harold was tired and did not leave the station for a little, though he didn't like Penn Station and still missed the famous old masterpiece it had replaced. After he sat doing nothing for ten minutes or so, he had an idea and pulled out a little notebook and a pen. Amid the clamor of the station, its bright lights and hard plastic seats and mixture of sounds and smells, he wrote something else that might belong to the preface:

Certain principles are worth any amount of trouble, any error and pain. Many of us carry out a series of mistakes as parents and do terrible things—unwittingly, unconsciously—to our children. There's little to be learned from the way we treat our children. But though we're not much wiser when they come along, we usually do better with our grandchildren. The premise of this book is that even a flawed private life—my own life has been seriously flawed—can provide some guidance for living a public life, for deciding how to live the public life none of us can escape, as we form opinions, join groups, and vote, even if we don't run for office or work for the government. And maybe it is the way we treat our grandchildren that we should regard as a standard for living as citizens of the world. We must resolve to treat other people's grandchildren—in our own city or country or elsewhere—in Iraq and Afghanistan, for example—as we treat our own grandchildren. We may not do well even so, but maybe that's all we can manage.

8

The Look of the Lake

1

Brenda Saltzman picked her way barefoot over grass and pine needles between the house in the Adirondacks and the beach. Paul had put in a beach. Did one have sand delivered? She laughed at herself for thinking Paul Abrams's improvements fussy and tame. She was Paul's guest and happy to be comfortable: he and Martha were doing something important in Prague for the month of July, and he'd invited her in an e-mail to use the cabin whenever she liked, giving her the code to the combination lock that padlocked a little wooden box in an inconspicuous corner of the porch, where the key was kept. Jess had come only once, but Brenda owed herself vacation days and didn't mind the drive. She was glad to be near hiking trails, and that sand felt good on her toes. Now she seemed to be the only person at the entire lake. For the moment. In a little while David would arrive from New York—where he lived now—with her father.

Artie was sturdy but creaky, hard to talk to in the years since Evelyn had died. He lived in a little apartment in an assisted-living facility. She wasn't sure he understood from her phone call where David was taking him, and he might have forgotten about her call by the time David arrived. But she thought that once they'd packed some of his things and had driven here, he'd recognize the place and be glad to be back. Brenda had driven into Schroon Lake that morning and bought food for supper, and now she had time for a swim. They'd be another hour or two, depending on how long a lunch stop had taken.

She dropped her towel. It was hot enough that she walked three or four steps into the lake before she got cold and stopped, liking the chill circle of water around her thighs and the warm underneath, squeezing mud between her toes. She stood taking in the sun on her shoulders. Something, a memory, pulled at her, a memory from way back. Though Artie had rented or borrowed the place year after year, the two families had been here together only rarely. She remembered Harold floating serenely on his back, his fleshy chest above water, and Nelson, a little boy, shouting. During this month she'd often thought of Nelson, thought of their single quiet coupling, which was all kindness, without anxiety or need. Or that was the way she remembered it. It was the only time she'd been with a man without trying to be different from the person she was—and even with women, for a long time she'd wanted to seem other than she was: more beautiful, less needy, or better at waiting. She was exactly herself with Jess now, and their going to bed was full of laughter but maybe less romance. Did romance require anxiety? Turning that question over, Brenda walked in up to her waist, leaned forward, accepted the first cold shock, and began stroking toward the middle of the lake. The stretch in her arms, the thrust of her legs, felt good.

She had just finished her swim and was wiping water out of her eyes when she heard a car, and then the front of it pulled into view: David's green Honda. She put the towel around her shoulders—a big, cushy blue one, one of a pile she'd found in the linen closet—and picked her way across the rough ground in front of the house, where Paul and his wife had put in a bit of a garden that she was supposed to water and weed. David was already leaning over the opened passenger door, apparently listening to Artie, his arm outstretched as he grasped the top of the door, his legs in shorts. These days David shaved his head. The position of his back seemed amused—tolerant—and Brenda, as she walked toward her son and her father, tried to decide if that was possible: if a back would look different if its owner was impatient or tense or worried. Yes, it would. She knew what she saw. She had always known what she was looking at and what she felt.

David lived in Brooklyn. He saw her father more often than she did: one of the ways he'd changed his life in the last few years. He'd stopped writing fiction and, at the last minute, applied to graduate school in nonfiction. Brenda had asked what nonfiction would consist of. History books?

—Personal essays, David had said. Remember that story about the kid at the lake with his mother's girlfriend?

She wasn't sure. She remembered others better.

—It was partly based on something that happened. I made up the exciting part because I thought what really happened wasn't exciting enough. Now I want to learn how to make what happened exciting.

He'd begun to send her essays, and she'd braced herself—but they weren't titled *The Faults of My Mother*. David went to graduate school, two frenzied years. When he graduated, he quit his job, moved to Brooklyn, and began working in a coffee shop and dropping in unannounced on his grandfather. He'd published essays, some on the Web, some in print. Some were about his personal life, others about topics or people who interested him. Brenda wasn't even sure she'd seen them all.

Now the grandson backed up a little and let go of the door, shifting to support his grandfather as Artie stood up, grasped the top of the door in his turn, and stepped away from the car.

—Hi, Brenda said, coming up behind them.

—We made it, David said. He has to pee.

Calling Hi, Dad, how was the trip? Brenda scrambled to open the front door, and then said, Watch the step, Daddy, as Artie and David approached, David looking carefully ahead, Artie staring at the ground. Inside, she hurried to open the bathroom door. Her father didn't greet her. How are you? she said as he went by.

—Gotta go, he said.

While her father was in the bathroom, she excused herself and went into the bedroom to dress.

—We didn't have lunch, David said, when she came out.

—Why not?

—Too hard. He shrugged toward the bathroom door. Artie was still in there.

It was almost three. We'll eat now, she said. She was caught unprepared. It was too hot for the evening meal she'd planned: boneless chicken breast, boiled potatoes, carrots. A meal her father would like. But she hadn't thought of anything else, so that was what they'd eat. She was taking things out of the refrigerator when her father came in behind her. You're the daughter with the wife, he said. The other one's the daughter with the husband.

She let that go, except that she wondered if he'd forgotten her name. And was he attempting a joke or reassuring himself that he knew who she was? Do you remember this house? she said, her back to him.

—Do I remember this house! No. I never saw this house, he said, sitting down at the table. She started peeling carrots.

—Sure you did. We came here when I was a kid. You came here with Harold when you were young.

—Not the same house. Maybe the same lake, not the same house.

—It's been renovated, she said. Several times. She sliced the carrots, annoyed that she'd have to eat dinner in the middle of a hot afternoon.

David had quickly changed and gone for a swim. *That* wasn't easy! he'd said on his way out, shrugging toward Artie.

When everything was ready, Brenda was hot and frazzled. Several times, as she cooked, Artie said, Couldn't you have cooked something simpler?

—Harold owns this place? Artie was saying, as David came in again, rubbing a towel over his bald head. How come he never invited me before?

—I don't think he comes much. Paul uses it. She looked at him. Lately, he was always smaller than she expected. She said, It's the place where you came when you were young, Dad. Where we all came.

—No, that was different.

—Maybe he means it doesn't have the same feel to it, David said.

—Is that what you mean?

—It's completely different, Artie said.

—Let it go, said David. He took his clothes into the bathroom and returned, dressed. They sat down. Picking up his knife and fork, Artie asked, This is Harold's too? His hair was all white and hadn't been cut for a while, and it hung over his face as in photographs Brenda had seen of Carl Sandburg, someone her father had once admired.

—The plates? The house? she said. Yes. Dad. Wiping sweat off her forehead with her napkin, Brenda spoke more slowly and precisely than she usually did. This is the house you and Harold stayed at, during the Depression, when you were young. Later, somebody added this kitchen. Somebody put in a bathroom. You used to bring us here when I was a child.

Artie didn't look up from his plate, and Brenda became more expansive, nodding vigorously as she spoke. It had the kitchen, when I was a kid, but it didn't look the way it looks now. The counters. The cabinets. She gestured. Harold's son—Paul—put those in.

—A professor, Artie said. He grasped his knife tightly and sawed his chicken into tiny pieces, several at a time. Then he put down the knife, lifted his fork, and leaned over his plate to impale one bite at a time, and bring each to his mouth. He ate audibly, and bits of chicken spotted his lips and chin. Artie had an uneven white beard. He had begun growing it a few months after Evelyn's death, during a time of almost wordless misery, as if he thought he'd feel better if he made himself look different.

—What? Brenda had stopped speaking and was watching him. Oh, Paul. Yes.

—You should have married him, Artie said.

David let out a bark of a laugh.

—What? said Brenda. She decided to make a joke of it. She said, He never asked me. He's ten years younger.

—The girl can ask. Artie looked up and all at once could put words together. It's good if the girl is older. Women live longer.

It was silly to take him seriously, but Brenda couldn't stop herself. I'm gay, remember? I like women. Paul's nice—we're friends. He invited me to stay here. Again, she vowed to weed and water Paul's garden. Mostly marigolds. She noted that once more she was talking in overly simple, emphatic terms to Artie.

—If you married him, Artie said, this would be your house.

—Well, that's true, Brenda conceded. You could come here all the time.

—This is my point. Artie went back to his chicken. If my friend hadn't been so stupid, he said, partway through his carrots, then stopped. Brenda and David were silent; she was trying to think what she'd feed them all later. They'd need something at night. It was too hot for canned soup. She resented the fact that because of her father's presence she was cooking and eating differently, and she couldn't even say so: he was old, and this was what he liked. She had gray hair and should be used to him.

Artie continued. If he wasn't stupid in the first place, marrying that dame, he would have had this house all along.

Brenda thought this was not true, but she couldn't remember the history of the house and the history of Harold and his first wife well enough to be sure. Everything he did, stupid, Artie said. He has to go and join the party, we lose our jobs. I told him at the time.

—Wait a second, Brenda said.

—It's always wait a second, Artie said. That's what he tells me his whole life. Everything has to be his way, and all he wants is attention. Who told him, teach? I told him. And what does he do—he loses both of us our jobs.

—But you got it back, David said. He took more chicken.

—Aah, it was never the same.

—But Dad, it wasn't like that, Brenda said. Harold didn't cause you to lose your job.

—What do you mean? Artie's voice was raised. He's out in the street, calling attention? Of course he did!

—But you lost your job because that woman lied about you, remember? It had nothing to do with Harold, Brenda said.

—Let it go, Mom, said David. What difference? He was pushing his chair back, suddenly wanting to move. He'd eaten half of his second piece of chicken.

But Artie, eyes flashing, was shouting at Brenda. How the hell do you know?

—I was there.

—You were a kid. What does a kid know?

—I knew. Mother knew.

—Mom, forget it, David said.

—Aah! Artie waved away what Brenda said with his fork, dropping it on his plate.

—Let's go, Grandpa, David said. Let's go look at the lake.

—Don't rush me, Artie said. He picked up his fork, wiped it on his napkin, and left the napkin on the table. Now Brenda stood. Maybe she should give them dessert. She had ice cream. Artie sat alone, stabbing his fork at what remained on his plate, his head down. He looked old, unhappy. David stood behind his chair. Brenda, trying to think of something to propose, stood behind hers. But Artie stabbed his fork in the air toward David, not his remaining carrots. I asked you what's the rush! he said. You got something to do? Always rush rush rush. Rushing me out of the bathroom. No lunch. I'm supposed to eat, my doctor says eat.

—I'm sorry, Grandpa. I couldn't figure out a good place for lunch, David said.

—What's so difficult? You've got something better to think about, maybe something you're writing? Artie's voice, all of a sudden, was heavy with sarcasm, with rage. You write that trash—I read that thing. You think I don't read, but I found it on the computer and I read it.

—Yeah, I heard you read it, David said. Gabe told me. He told me he showed you it was there. He thought you'd just be proud it had my name on it, but you read it.

—Did I read this? Brenda said.

—It's the one about Julie. I don't use her name.

—Pornography! All that money. Graduate school! Where he learns to write trash—people going to bed, every goddamned detail. All those girlfriends of yours—you see what he learned from you? Sex, sex, sex, nothing else matters.

—Okay, Dad, enough, Brenda said, trying to keep her voice steady. You want to take a nap? You're tired. She began clearing the table. She was angrier than she'd been for a long time. Maybe it was because they were here together—there had been plenty of screaming matches between her and him, here in this kitchen, down at that beach. She used to wonder if people on the other side of the lake could hear. She'd finally take a book and escape into the woods.

Artie stood up. I am not tired! he shouted. I am talking about your son that you didn't bother to bring up so he could even get a decent job! No—excuse me. He had a decent job and he quit. Gave it up. And for what. Pouring coffee, that's what. *Do you want cream and sugar?* This is my grandson? His grandson is a lawyer, and this is my grandson! His son is a professor, and my daughter works in a factory!

—Stop it! Brenda screamed. She was screaming. Jess would hate it. She was screaming and starting to cry as she had forty years ago, fifty years ago. Stop it! Leave my son alone. My son is fine. He is doing fine. And you don't know anything about my business.

And David turned and faced her, speaking in a low, tense, furious voice. Mother, would you just stop it, please! I can take care of myself! He left the room, saying over his shoulder, I'll wash the dishes. Tonight. I'll be back. His backpack was on the sofa, where he'd have to sleep—there were only two bedrooms. As she watched, he dug hiking boots and heavy socks out of his pack.

—Where are you going? she said.

He didn't answer.

—David, what?

—I'm taking a walk. Now would you leave me alone? I can't stay in the house with the two of you, that's for sure.

—But where are you going?

—Giant.

—Giant? She'd expected he'd name one of the hikes near the cabin.

—Up 87.

—The High Peaks? It's too late. Are you crazy?

—Look, I'm not going to hang around here listening to the two of you screaming at each other.

In moments he had filled two water bottles. He dumped his pack out on the sofa—a book, clothes—and put a few things back.

—Wait a minute!

—Where the hell are you going? Artie said.

—I'll see you later. David waved lightly and was out the door. She heard his car start.

D avid had begun writing true essays instead of invented stories because he was disgusted with himself. Though he considered his life uneventful—at that time it consisted primarily of biking to work in Silicon Valley, sleeping late on weekends in the bed of a girlfriend, disliking an unreasonable boss, and failing to phone his mother—he experienced as much rage, shame, desire, and sorrow as if he was in the habit of hurling his relatives off cliffs or losing his women to murderous pirates. His stories were not dramatic, but they were more dramatic than his life, and that felt like cheating. He'd never be a good writer until he told the truth. Somebody else might become a writer by learning how to make things up, he conceded, but not he. He had to find out how to tell the truth and yet convey to the reader the feelings that were stupid to feel but that David Saltzman did feel. And so he'd begun to write essays, timid essays that got him into graduate school but had teachers asking, But what's at stake here? And then maybe better essays, true stories about himself or other people.

He drove up the Northway, not wanting to look at the dashboard clock because he'd be shocked at how late it was, definitely too late to start a hike, start one when he was already tired. But nothing could calm him except walking up a mountain. He'd hurt his mother; his grandfather had hurt them both. David had refused to see why she was angry when he knew perfectly well why—and at the same time, he scorned her for being angry, for never having grown up, for needing at sixty-two or whatever she was to squelch and silence her admittedly obnoxious father. Only fast driving followed by fast walking would help.

And in truth, it was July, when daylight lasted. He had decent hiking shoes, water, guidebook, a first-aid kit, and trail mix. He had a rain poncho and a warm jacket. Hell, he was as much of a worrier as his terrified grandfather, who had inherited the fears Jews had held for centuries without inheriting the rituals they used to calm themselves. David would not fall off the mountain, would not die, even though he had hurt his mother and probably his grandfather.

He'd picked out a few hikes at home, choosing them for proximity and promised views. A line of cars was parked along Route 73 when he got there, and even before he reached the trail, he met people coming down. It was hot even under the trees, but the glare of the day receded as David began to walk. The trail register showed that dozens of people had gone up this mountain that day. He'd imagined being alone. Many had descended, checking off their return. Some included a comment: Good walk. Nice walk. Nobody admitted to being tired.

Walking felt good, but the trail was steep. He didn't want to fail. Now and then he'd hear a descending party above him, and then they'd pass him with greetings. There were children and dogs, babies on their parents' backs. He was breathless, but it got easier. More people descended.

—You've got a long way to go! a woman said, but she looked as if she'd never hiked before—no pack, flimsy shoes. The woods were dense with heat, but they were *woods*, and he could scarcely believe he'd been in New York that morning. Finally, he looked at his watch: it was 5:30 PM. He couldn't get down before dark. Well, he couldn't get down before twilight. When he came to a lookout, he was disappointed to learn he'd gone only seven-tenths of a mile, but the next time he checked the guidebook, he'd walked a mile. He'd been walking through deciduous trees, but now he entered an evergreen forest, and as always it seemed quiet, strange. He saw fewer descending hikers. The trail became steep again, but now and then he had glimpses of distant peaks—clouds were coming in—and small ponds and lakes. He let himself drink some water. He climbed.

Artie returned to the bathroom. He'd been reluctant to make this trip—to this house that might or might not be the house they used to go to—because there would be only one bathroom, and when he needed to go, he couldn't wait. Now the door was open, so he went. Brenda was washing the dishes. It was hot, but he no longer minded that.

Once when David was three or four, Artie had taken him by the hand and brought him to the playground. He had to keep slowing his pace. David let him hold his hand the whole way, though he had to hold his arm up. They had to stop and look at every construction project or truck. Best of all was a garbage truck. Artie had joked for days about his grandson who came to New York and wanted to see a garbage truck. Broadway show? Nah. Radio City? Nah. Garbage truck.

He'd tried to teach David to play the recorder, but he was too little. Evelyn yelled at him to cut it out, leave the baby alone. She let David help mix cookies, and he ate the dough and wouldn't eat his supper. They kept him for a whole day, maybe two. Some dame his daughter was chasing.

No point sitting here anymore. Why was he sitting here? What had he been doing before he came into the bathroom? He remembered shouting at Brenda and David. He didn't remember why. Time and again, the last few days, he thought of the old guy in California, just last week, who put his foot on the gas instead of the brake and killed people in a market. Artie hadn't driven a car in a while and wouldn't try, but he had the strange feeling, at times, that he too, because he was old, could kill. He didn't think he had killed anybody. He stood, flushed the toilet, reassembled his pants.

Nobody was on the top of the mountain when David got there. Clouds were dense, but the place—one of the higher of the High Peaks—was spectacular. It had taken him three and a half hours, and it would be dark long before he got down. But now he could hear thunder and see what looked like a storm on a nearby peak. He stayed at the summit for only a few moments. Then a spit of lightning formed above the distant storm, and David hurried back down the trail. Rain overtook him a third of the way down, first only a few drops. It was dark, but he had a flashlight, and he could see the trail, different from the shrubs and trees on either side. He was drenched in sweat, hot, and rain was welcome. He didn't want to stop and take out his poncho. He was hungry and thirsty, bitten up—his bug spray wasn't strong enough—dirty. Happy. No longer angry.

Brenda wanted to follow David: take her car, her guidebook, drive to the mountain. But she couldn't leave her father. He managed in his apartment, but it was familiar and there were staff and alarm systems. She was furious with him at the moment, blaming him for being the kind of father who had taught her to manage by shouting. She heard him stumping around in the bathroom—the flush, the water in the sink. It had been her idea to have him brought here, where he and Harold had been happy in their youth, where she and her parents and sister had spent slow, hot vacations in her childhood, dawdling in and out of this lake or Schroon Lake.

She left the cleanup when she heard him come out. Let's walk down to the lake, she said.

—Too far.

—It's not far. It's right outside the door. She opened the screen door and held it.

—You're letting the bugs in.

Of course, that was what he'd say. She waited.

Shuffling the little distance from the porch to the lake, he tripped on a tree root. He fell forward before she could grab him and landed on his hands and knees.

—Dad, my God, are you okay?

He was silent. After a pause he rolled into a sitting position, knees up. He was stiff but also supple, if that were possible, still with a tennis player's sense of where his limbs were and what to do with them.

She leaned over and brushed the dried pine needles off his knees and each hand, taking his hands in her own, one at a time.

He didn't think to brush off his own hands. They were ten feet from the lake.

—New boat, he said. It was a red canoe, upside down on the shore.

Brenda stood over him. He shifted to face the lake squarely. It's beautiful, he said. She sat down next to him. It was still hot. Storm clouds made fantastic dark shapes over the lake. She knew that thunderstorms came up quickly in the mountains, and just because there was a storm in one place didn't mean there was one somewhere else. Still. The clouds moved over their heads. Her father didn't seem to notice.

It was impossible to know where David was right now or whether there was a storm there. She heard distant thunder. Dad, she said, with an indefensible feeling that if she could straighten things out between them—difficult as it would be to apologize to a man who never apologized—then everything would be well. David would make it up and down his mountain, and no storm would harm him. Artie didn't look at her.

—I shouldn't have yelled, she said. I know you don't think I brought up David wrong. You understand why he's working in a coffee shop, and it's so good that he's written these things and gotten them published. You didn't mean what you said.

Artie looked at his knees for a long time. I certainly do mean what I said. His voice had the rasp it took on before it got loud. Your kid gave up a perfectly good job. What kind of thinking did you teach him? It's the parents who have to do that. When there are parents. He paused. Par-ents, I said. Plural. And I have never been here before.

Rain began. Artie looked up but made no move to go inside. His hoarse voice sang, *One-four-nine is the school for me, Drives away all adversity . . .*

2

The sound Harold heard was the phone. The voice said, This is David Saltzman. David waited for him to remember who that was, but Harold was waiting in his turn: he was afraid.

—Your grandfather, Harold said. Did Artie die?

—Oh my God, David said. No. That's not why I'm calling. I'm sorry.

—It's my fault. I always expect bad news. How is he?

—Not too bad, David said. He's got some problems. I wanted to talk to you about your book.

—Oh, my book. Harold sat down. He was in the living room. Naomi was cooking, and he had been on his way to keep her company.

—Congratulations. It was early in 2004, and *A Fool and His Principles* had just come out. There had been two reviews. Harold hadn't asked about sales. He didn't like to think. What I wonder, he'd said to Naomi, is how many people bought it whom I have never met? My guess is two. And the people I know—I've outlived them.

—Not all, Naomi had said.

—What I'm calling about, David said, is I was wondering if I could interview you. I don't know if you ever look at Bad Weather?

—Bad weather?

—It's an online magazine—news, politics, arts. I write for it. We'd like to run an interview about the book.

Harold laughed. No kidding!

—So would that be okay?

—Sure. Want to talk now? I'm not so good on the phone. He had to strain to hear.

—Actually, I was thinking I could come over? Maybe several times? I'd like to run something substantial.

—Who's going to read it? Harold said.

—Who's going to read it? said David. Lots of people. If the book continues to sell . . .

—Continues?

—You know about amazon dot com? Your book has a low rank. That's good. Low is good. It's getting attention on blogs. It's kind of controversial.

As Harold tried to take this in, David said, So if I could come over, maybe three or four times in the next couple of weeks?

—Sure, Harold said.

Your father is abusive, said the director of the assisted-living facility. Brenda felt ashamed, defensive, and a little excited—vindicated. Carol's husband had become the rabbi of a congregation in Michigan, and suddenly she in New Hampshire was the local daughter. The director said that Artie shouted at the staff. They didn't want to keep him, but they would if the family hired aides round the clock. It would still be cheaper than a nursing home.

The daytime aide Brenda found sat in Artie's little living room, listening and talking. He seemed to understand her despite her Jamaican accent. The nighttime aide said Artie was rude. Artie insisted he couldn't understand a word she said, though her accent—also Jamaican—was less pronounced than the daytime aide's.

Artie was obsessed with the toilet and spent an hour at a time sitting there, trying to squeeze the last urine from his bladder. The nighttime aide, like Brenda, seemed embarrassed that when Artie's mind narrowed, it had narrowed to urination; the daytime aide smiled and nodded, surprised by nothing. Maybe that was kinder and maybe it was condescending. Brenda drove to New York and slept on David's couch once a week, and she always dropped in on the director of the facility to demonstrate that the Saltzman family was cooperative. She hated these trips. Jess wondered if they were truly essential, and David was too busy to spend much time with her.

Once, she didn't even see David, but he left an elaborate note: they had to get Artie's power of attorney, and he had consulted with a friend who was a lawyer and printed out forms he'd found on the Internet. The next week he met her in the lobby. The forms had to be notarized, and he'd arranged for a notary to meet them.

Artie was in the bathroom when they arrived, but he came out when cajoled by the daytime aide. He had to initial many pages of forms, and he did so with appalling meekness, signing away his right to sell property, pay taxes, or make decisions without the consent of Carol and Brenda. The effort was all in the action itself. His *A. S.* kept getting larger. The notary brought out her seal.

At three the next morning the phone rang in David's apartment, where Brenda slept. It was Jess. The nighttime aide had called. She says she called 911, Jess said.

—What's wrong?

—She just gave me her cell phone number. Honey, I don't know, Jess said. She said she couldn't tell me, only you.

Brenda dialed like a robot.

—He went crazy, said the nighttime aide.

—How did he go crazy? He's always been crazy.

—He screamed. I called 911. I don't have to put up with violence.

—What's happening now?

—They took him.

—They took him?

—He's at the ER. She named a hospital. Brenda hung up and asked David if she had to go now.

—You'll go in the morning.

She called Jess and asked the same question, and Jess too said she should go in the morning. Brenda slept.

B ad Weather: You call yourself a fool in your title. Do you really think you're a fool?

Harold Abrams: Yes.

BW: That's all?

HA: Well, I suppose in one sense I am not a fool. I have a doctoral degree. I supported myself for many years. But I trust the reader will understand that someone who writes a book who calls himself a fool does not mean he is too stupid to write a book.

BW: Then what do you mean?

HA: I mean [coughs] . . . I mean that in most instances I am less kind, less sensible, less unselfish than I would like to be.

BW: What do you regret most in your life?

HA: I was going to say, marrying my first wife, but then I would not have had my children, so I regret being unfaithful to her, but then I would not have my second wife, so I regret nothing.

BW: What are you most proud of?

HA: Proud? I don't know. I should have done everything a little differently, you know what I mean?

BW: Do you believe in God?

HA: No.

BW: What world event had the greatest effect on your life?

HA: I have to think. The Depression, of course, but I managed. Not the war. The killing of the Jews—that had the greatest effect on my thoughts but not my life. I would have to say McCarthy.

BW: Because you lost your job?

HA: Because I got to start over.

BW: What is your hope for the 2004 presidential election?

HA: It looks like it will be Kerry. I don't care much, as long as we get rid of these idiots.

BW: So they are worse than fools?

HA: I'm a genius compared to George W. Bush.

BW: And do you think he'll lose?

HA: [coughs] [long pause] I think he'll lose.

B renda found her father under a white blanket, his face looking shrunken. She took his hand. Hi, Daddy, it's Brenda.

—Bathroom.

—You need to go to the bathroom?

—Bathroom.

—Did they bring you a bedpan?

—Bathroom.

—Did they give you breakfast? Did you have something to eat?

—Bathroom.

No, the nurse told her, he didn't mean he had to go to the bathroom. Sometimes they just say the same thing over and over, she said. They don't know what they're saying. Brenda tried to distract him, talking about David.

Artie said, Did he go to the bathroom? Did you go to the bathroom? You have to go to the bathroom.

Hours passed. Nobody looked at her. Maybe they were giving her privacy, which was not what she needed. Nobody could tell Brenda what was wrong, nobody seemed to understand that it had happened all of a sudden. But had it happened all of a sudden?

B W: Looking back, why do you think you joined the Communist Party?

ALICE MATTISON

HA: I joined to impress my friends. But sometimes we do the right thing for the wrong reasons.

BW: Why was it the right thing?

HA: Things were different. It was the right thing. Later, *Communist* turned into a dirty word. The Russians didn't do it. Stalin—you can't imagine.

BW: What can't I imagine?

HA: Ideals turning to blood. The loss. We have never regained—maybe in the sixties, for a minute—the optimism. There's no protest without optimism. You protest—do you understand me?—when something could change.

BW: But we still have antiwar marches—protests . . .

HA: No, nothing like that. Nothing. When I lost my job—

BW: As a teacher?

HA: Nobody knew why. We should have been heroes, but the time was over. We were just dirt to be mopped up. Later, they said, Oh, you weren't the dirt; we made a mistake. Big deal.

BW: Is that why you didn't go back to teaching?

HA: Didn't go back? I was a teacher all my life.

BW: In college. I guess you weren't going to give up a college teaching job to go back to teaching high school.

HA: I suppose I should have. I'm not a good person, never was. I had to do what I could as an essentially selfish person. That's what I should have called the book. Fool has nothing to do with it. I should have said, *A Selfish Man and His Principles.*

Artie was sent from the emergency room to a nursing home, then back to the hospital two weeks later when he seemed to be having a heart attack and dying. Carol flew in from Michigan, and she and Brenda sat by his bed. After three hours of silence, Artie said, There's no question the reduction of problems will increase.

Brenda laughed.

—He's alive? Carol said, looking at Brenda. He's going to stay alive? Carol was slim and blond; her hair was dyed and curled, and her tears were more touching, Brenda felt, than the tears that fell down her own square face, under her short gray rumpled hair. Artie didn't die, and the doctors decided it hadn't been a heart attack after all, but an infection. Carol left.

He lay in a sunny hospital room, where Brenda spent day after day, phoning Jess each night. One morning Artie said, I want to be that same old age as Harold.

Harold's birthday had already happened. Artie's would come in a week. She said, Ninety-four?

—Yes. Then, enough. Living like this is no fun.

B W: Was there anything you could have done to prevent your son Nelson's suicide?

HA: When he was two. When he was ten. Sometimes you shouldn't tell yourself there was nothing you could have done. Sometimes there are things you could have done. I can say I didn't know it would happen, but from the time he was a teenager, I knew it would happen.

BW: Do you have advice for the parents of children with mental illness?

HA: Such as, don't beat up on yourself? My advice would be, Beat up on yourself. But nobody needs advice to do that. Everybody can do it already.

BW: In your book, you say that the best thing in your life has been your wife, Naomi, but that falling in love with Naomi caused Nelson's death.

HA: Do I say that?

BW: You imply it.

HA: So what do you want from me?

ALICE MATTISON

Clothing that's halfway between theirs and ours, Artie said to Brenda. She'd gone home for a few days and had returned. Then, When your women and my women are together, what is the relationship?

She was baffled. What do you think?

—What do *you* think, and what do the girls think?

She decided they were combining their staffs, like King Lear and Goneril, but perhaps with less friction. She said, I think they'll get along, and we can deal with problems as they arise, and he nodded and quieted. The days were boring but pleasant. David came when he could. She and her father conversed—how urbanely and politely!

He said, All night it came to me that I was going between Evelyn and . . . trigger finger. Do you know who trigger finger is? Trigger finger is Brenda.

That afternoon he was tired and petulant. The room felt small and stuffy. Artie said, Confusion, confusion, confusion.

Later, Why did they play so many tricks on us?

Later still, Green paper, green paper, green paper.

—Do you want green paper? Brenda said. Do you remember something about green paper? She hushed herself.

—Sick, Artie said. No sick. Sick. No sick. Sick. No sick. Confused.

—You're confused.

Time passed. Brenda, he said. Brenda, Brenda, Brenda, green paper Brenda. Green paper, green paper . . . really happened.

Then, Yellow paper, yellow paper . . .

A nurse took his vital signs. I don't want to live, he said.

The next day he said, Yellow, yellow, yellow, and circled his hand in the air as he said it. Brenda Saltzman, he said then. Pink paper. Carol. Green paper. No release. Green medicine in red paper. Must bus. Green paper.

—Who are you? Artie said abruptly, looking right at Brenda. David had stopped by after work and stood near the window.

—Brenda.

—Who?

—Your daughter.

He said, Daughter has *d, g*.

—Yes, *d-a-u-g-h-t-e-r*.

—So why didn't you give me the *d g* medicine?

—I don't know how, Brenda said.

He laughed weirdly.

—Are you laughing?

—It's funny. David, take over. Be smarter.

The next day there were more words. What do I do now? Artie said.

—Just rest.

—Where do I rest? How do I rest? My right foot is locked up. Then, No, he said. Terrible feeling. Oh, my God. This is the worst.

BW: You are primarily interested in political life, but you taught literature and wrote books about literature. Why is that?

HA: I am interested in literature. I hate public life. As citizens, we must pay attention to public life, just as we must pay attention to private morality as human beings, whatever our interests.

BW: You hate public life? Really hate it?

HA: Yes.

BW: Does literature relate to politics?

HA: Literature is dangerous. It tells us things are more complicated than is convenient. You can't make policy if you think all day about literature. Literature professors who won't sign the petition because they don't like the semicolon.

BW: But doesn't literature teach us how to be moral?

HA: No.

BW: That's not true! You're not telling the truth about what you think.

HA: How do you know what I think?

BW: I read your book. I read all your books.

HA: I am tired.

BW: Is it too much? Should I come another day?

HA: How is my friend?

BW: My grandfather? He's in the hospital.

HA: What does literature tell me to do when my friend is sick?

BW: You could go see him.

HA: Does literature tell me to do that?

BW: I don't know.

HA: Are you crying?

As Brenda walked through the corridor toward Artie's room, a nurse said, He's pretty wild.

—Could I tell you something? she said, when she came in. It was his ninety-fourth birthday.

He said, No, no—not now. I'm in a very difficult game.

Artie had been taken out of bed and put into a lounge chair with a tilted back. A tray table crossed his lap, maybe to keep him in one place. His legs were stretched out on the footrest, and Artie flexed his feet alternately, rhythmically, with the agility and control of an athlete. He said, I want to tell you how I got into it. It's very bizarre.

Brenda sat opposite in the straight chair. Artie never stopped flexing and straightening his legs and feet, alternately. Then he said, Quarter.

Then, You can make a day's pay out here. I saw five quarters.

She understood something. You're picking up quarters?

—Yeah. He paused, concentrating. Then he said, Look at that fish!

Finally, Brenda understood. He was in a pedalboat. What's the fish doing? she said.

—Not that, the way it looks. So tempting, he said. But after a while, he said, Well, I want to get out. Suppose you wanted to go somewhere right now, what would you do?

—I'd take the subway to David's and pick up my car.

—Forget I asked you. He called to invisible people to his left and right. Do you want a boat? Do you want this boat if I get out?

After another pause, he said, I had no idea this was competitive—but they're scoring.

—Is it a race? Brenda said.

—No, but they're always counting time. People were watching. One gave me a white paper, one gave me a black mark . . .

When a nurse came in, he demanded to get out of the boat.

—It's a chair, Mr. Saltzman.

—So how can I get out of this *chair*? A minute later it was a boat again. You want this boat?

To Brenda, Is this boat riding or staying put?

Brenda said, It's tied up.

He said, Let me sit on it for a while. His feet stopped. Then, What do they charge for it? Is your boat sitting or perched on a small boat? I seem to see something underneath.

It was compelling. She said, Do you think we're in a lake or a river?

—A pond, but I'm just wondering if those little boats are going to move. Rapidly and lucidly, he explained that it wouldn't be a problem if the boats were going to stay where they were, but if they were going to move, he needed to know so as not to collide with them. What is the usual ride? he asked.

—An hour, Brenda said.

—How are my touches?

When she asked for an explanation, he said, One boat touches another. Is the guy going out behind me to the left?

—He's at a good distance, she said.

—This is comparable to playing tennis on Sunday morning. Brutal. Absolutely brutal. As a matter of fact, I think I wouldn't do this on Sunday. She could see the pond, the boats going back and forth, the difficulty of moving without colliding with another boat. When the aide came in with lunch, she seemed to be from another plane of existence, but her father said agreeably, I had orange juice and Jell-O and a combination of a sandwich that was quite good.

Next he said, Try to move a boat over and open up a space for boats. It would be good if you could take yours and move it over.

Suddenly, after a silence: The number of faces I recognize but really don't know just who they are—but I know they're from New York—is unbelievable.

After another silence, he said, I don't have the patience for this. Then, I don't understand this peculiarity. When it's very warm and I'm speaking a lot, my voice goes down and I can't whistle.

—Try, Brenda said. He pursed his lips in the old way, but there was no sound.

She had worked out that the game was something like bumper cars: he had to avoid being touched by other people's boats. But it was good to be on the lake. She said, Remember the lake in the Adirondacks?

—Oh yeah. Those were lovely years . . . The look of the lake . . . Why don't we move a few of the boats? There's a big space here.

At last, Brenda agreed they should move the boats. He tried to get up, and she suggested that he supervise while she did it. She said, Okay, I'm moving the first boat. Now I'm moving another boat . . . He was calm. They discussed the weeks at the lake. The most refreshing feeling, Artie said.

Someone knocked at the open door. It was Harold. Brenda jumped up to kiss him. Shall I leave you two together?

—Oh, no, Harold said. I won't stay long. He carried a newspaper and a book, and he put them on Artie's bedside table. Brenda saw that it was his new book, *A Fool And His Principles*.

—Artie, Harold said, leaning over the lounge chair that was a pedalboat.

—How are you? Artie said.

—How are any of us? said Harold. How are you?

—Who needs it? said Artie.

—I know what you mean. Harold took his hand and held it with both his hands. Happy Birthday, he said. I brought you my book. He moved Artie's hand up and down, then leaned forward and held it to his cheek. When he let it go, he sat down on the bed. His head was down, and he brought out a small package of Kleenex from his pocket and blew his nose.

BW: What do you want people to remember about your life and your ideals?

HA: No one will remember them.

BW: But if they did?

HA: I'm sorry. You make me think of my dear, difficult friend, your grandfather, and I become difficult because he no longer knows how. I will give you a straight answer. I would like to be remembered as someone who was worth the trouble. I would like people to read Henry James and the rest. I would like people to think about trying to make things better, even though it's complicated and there is another way to see everything. People suffer. We must end suffering, when we can. When we can without lying.

Tentatively—experimentally—Artie died. It was as if his body had rolled off the edge of a cliff, then come to rest on a short ledge over water. Something might have brought him back; he even knew as much. Desire was gone, anger was gone, but knowledge (without words for what he knew) continued. Nobody came, nobody touched him, and after a time his body tipped off the place where it had paused, and he was nowhere.

3

We could stop for coffee, Brenda said.
—Do you want to? said Jess.
—I don't have the energy to get out of the car.
—I'll bring you some, Jess said. She was driving. Brenda knew every place between New York and Concord, New Hampshire where you could get a decent cup of coffee not too far from the road. I think at the next exit, she said. They were somewhere in Massachusetts.

When they stopped, Brenda wanted to get out. It was a cool day for July, and a damp wind blew into her face. They walked together through the parking lot. Then she said, I need to get back into the car. Is that okay?

—Sure, Jess said. Brenda had imagined someone asking them what they wanted. She couldn't speak to one more person.

Jess brought coffee and an enormous cookie. They broke off chunks, handing it back and forth. Brenda said, Harold is so sad. He had spoken, that morning, at her father's memorial service, looking as if any touch could knock him down. His wife handed him into and out of his chair, but his voice was sure. He told stories about Artie that Brenda had never heard. She said, I didn't think there was anything I didn't know.

—I thought even I knew all the stories, Jess said. Artie used to call her Daughter-in-law, as if it was her name. Hey, Daughter-in-law. He had never stopped finding it interesting that he had a daughter-in-law, though he had no sons.

Jess put her cup into the holder and pulled out of the parking lot.

—Do you want more cookie? Brenda said.

—You finish it.

—It'll make me fatter.

—Medicinal purposes. She signaled to return to the access road and then to the highway.

They were silent. I thought he'd be there, Brenda said. When I pictured my father's memorial service, I imagined him at it.

—That's funny.

—Or at least I thought there would be trouble—people quarreling, misunderstanding each other on purpose.

—*Mmm*, Jess said. That he'd be there in spirit. She changed lanes. They were in the part of Massachusetts where the traffic thinned out. She said, It was a tame gathering. A little boring.

—That's all the family I have left now, the nice ones, Brenda said. My perfect sister and her perfect husband and children and grandchildren.

—David's another one, Jess said.

—I'm the only disreputable family member left, Brenda said. But even I was good. I was good to all those cousins.

—I love your family, Jess said. I want family. Jess's parents were dead. She had a brother she rarely saw. She hardly knew her cousins. Brenda got e-mails from cousins whom she liked. They'd turned up; they'd spoken politely to Jess. What did she want, criminals insulting one another? I don't know what I want, she said.

—You want your dad.

—Oh, I don't think so. It's a relief. She couldn't put it into words, what was missing, what she couldn't do without. I don't feel alive if nobody's yelling, she said, though that wasn't it.

Before going home, they picked up the dogs at the kennel. Brenda waited in the car. There were three, big old Abby and two middle-sized, younger dogs, one brown, one yellow. They bounded into the car, licking her and thumping their tails at her face and breasts. Okay, guys, okay, she said, but she was smiling and crying, her sunglasses knocked off into her lap.

At home, they carried their bags into the house, the dogs running ahead. Brenda set her bag down. They'd been gone for two nights, but the house felt as if it had been empty longer. She sat in the chair nearest the door. Jess went through the house and opened the back door so the dogs could go into the yard, which was fenced. While they were outside, she brought her bag upstairs. She came down again. Her footsteps on the stairs sounded old. Then she went out the front door to the mailbox. Brenda was hungry. Jess returned with a fist of mail, catalogues and flyers. One of the dogs was barking: Lulu, the young brown dog. Jess didn't go to the door, and Brenda didn't get up. Lulu barked some more, and then the other two joined in. Still Brenda didn't get up, and Jess leafed through the mail, brushing her hair off her face. Jess had worn a suit to the memorial service but had changed into shorts for the drive. As she grew older, she was bonier, rangier, like an old New England farmer's wife. At last, Brenda stood to let in the dogs.

—You don't have to do that, Jess said.

—They're barking.

—So they're barking. Nobody cares. Brenda and Jess lived in town, but there were only three houses on the block.

Brenda opened the door and the dogs shouldered their way in. She liked the look of their muscular bodies coming forward almost as one body, their different colors and textures. She returned to the same chair. They had a little dining room and she was there, but the dining room led into the kitchen. Jess was still at the counter, gathering envelopes to recycle. It made Brenda desolate that Jess didn't turn and look at her, didn't say something affectionate, didn't offer to feed the dogs or go and buy takeout for their own dinner. This was unfair: Jess had driven home. Jess had brought in the mail. Jess had let the dogs out. Jess had put up with months of Brenda's absences.

Artie had not done well at noticing other people's needs, so it didn't make sense to miss that today, but she wanted, at the moment, not a lover, not a wife, but someone who'd let her be a child.

Jess put the empty envelopes and the catalogues into a wastebasket they kept in the kitchen for recycling, and went upstairs again. Now Brenda heard her tread crossing and recrossing their bedroom. Was she unpacking? How compulsive was that? Then she heard Jess take a shower. All she needed was for her longtime lover and wife to come down the stairs and say, Are you hungry, sweetie? Or even just, Are you hungry? Maybe even just, I'm hungry.

It was a long shower. Brenda continued sitting where she was. When Jess came down at last, she was wearing a robe and her hair was wet. She came into the dining room and sat down in the chair she sat in at meals, which meant her back was to Brenda. She pushed the chair back and began rubbing her head with a towel she'd brought down. Jess had shoulder-length hair,

ALICE MATTISON

blond, not gray, because she said she'd look old at work. She said nothing.

Brenda stood up and moved to where she faced Jess. Don't you care about me? she said.

—What are you talking about? Jess said. I drove to New York. I was friendly to your relatives. I drove *back*. Now I am worn out. Taking a shower felt great. Go take a shower.

—I took one this morning. Aren't you hungry?

—We had that cookie.

—That was hours ago. Don't you want dinner?

—I don't know, Jess said. Maybe some cold cereal.

Brenda walked to the window and looked out. The yard was a mess. The grass hadn't been cut in too long. I cannot bear this, she said.

—Bear what?

—You think my father dies and that's the end of it?

—Oh, for heaven's sake, Jess said. She went upstairs again with the towel. This time she was gone for a long time. When she came down, she was dressed in shorts and a T-shirt again, with sandals on her feet. She put her arms around Brenda, who had been turning the pages of a catalogue from which she would never buy anything. You are an impossibility, she said. You want me to go pick up food?

—I don't know, Brenda said.

Jess went to look in the refrigerator. Leftover chicken, she said. I forgot this leftover chicken.

—Is it still okay?

It was okay. Brenda washed her face. She said, Okay, I'll cook. Now she wanted to. She cut up the chicken and put water on to boil for pasta. She went outside, and there were ripe tomatoes—the first ones. They were warm to touch. She brought them into the house and cut them up. It was night. Jess poured

red wine, and they carried their food into the living room and turned on the TV. The Democratic National Convention was on, but everybody knew that Kerry and Edwards would be the candidates. Now it was time for the keynote address, and the commentators were talking about the man who'd give it. Brenda sat in an old upholstered chair near the TV, her plate on her lap, her wineglass on the arm of the chair, though she'd spilled wine on that chair before. Jess was on the sofa, her plate on the coffee table. One commentator said the speaker's name, which was something like Baracco Bama—an Italian pol from Massachusetts or Rhode Island? No, he was running for the senate from Illinois.

—Oh, yeah, Jess said. He's black.

Barack Obama was a good speaker, and nobody would forget how to spell his name because suddenly the whole convention waved signs with it.

—You think at every session each one gets a bunch of signs with instructions? Brenda said. I never heard of this guy until one minute ago.

—He's gotten a lot of press lately, Jess said, but yeah.

Brenda ate her spaghetti and drank her wine. We've got some gay friends in the red states, Barack Obama said, and Brenda said, over her shoulder, He said *gay*.

—I heard, Jess said. Then she said, Honey, I care about you!

—I know, Brenda said. Oh, sweetie, I know. She abandoned her spaghetti and Barack Obama and went to sit next to Jess, squeezing her shoulder. Jess's fingers just grazed the back of Brenda's neck.

Now the speaker was saying something about Iraq. I read a book recently that put it well, Barack Obama said. This writer—his name is Harold Abrams—

(Brenda gasped, and wine spilled on her shirt.

—What? Jess said.)

points out that though we mean well, we don't always do the best thing for our children—we're young, we're inexperienced—but by the time our grandchildren come along, most of us are pretty good at looking after others. We've learned some wisdom. Abrams says we should resolve to treat other people's grandchildren—in our own city or country or anywhere in the world—as we treat our own grandchildren. Maybe it's that simple.

The speech ended and the commentators talked.

—What was that book? one said, and a photograph of Harold's book—black letters on white background—flashed on the screen. Brenda glanced to her left, where the book itself—the copy Harold had inscribed to her father—sat on a lamp table. For a second she thought it might not be there, as if there were only one copy, and to appear on TV it would have to disappear from her living room.

—Harold's famous, Jess said. What would your father have thought?

—Oh, he'd be mad. And excited. He'd buy ten copies of the book and give them to everyone he knew. He'd show them his name in the index. That thought made her pick up the book and turn to the back, checking for *Arthur Saltzman*, who apparently appeared many times in the book. She stopped and turned off the TV.

—Are you looking for the quote? Jess said.

Brenda looked up *grandchildren* in the index but it wasn't there.

—It sounds like something from the first page or the last, Jess said, and she was almost right: there was a preface, and Brenda looked at the first page of the preface, and then the last page of the preface, and there it was.

—This will sell copies, Jess said.

—It will please Harold, Brenda said. Will it make him less sad?

—About your father? Jess said. No. Sadder.

—They can't talk about it, Brenda said.

—Argue about it.

—Argue.

Brenda's cell phone rang. She took it out of her pocket and looked at the screen. David, she said. She took the call.

Acknowledgments

Thanks first to Edward, who got well, and who makes a toast to literature whenever we eat out. He and Douglas Bauer, April Bernard, Susan Hulsman Bingham, Donald Hall, and Susan Holahan read the manuscript of this book and offered helpful suggestions. Warm thanks to them and to others who steadily gave help, wisdom, and companionship: Ben Mattison, Lisa Yelon, Andrew Mattison, Jacob Mattison, Jill Mulvey, Sandi Kahn Shelton, Anita Taylor, Ann Leamon, and Jude Stewart. Thanks, too, to Naomi Tannen and Joe Mahay for quiet time in the mountains.

Thanks to the Crossett Library at Bennington College, and to my colleagues and students in the Bennington Writing Seminars, who remind me with their work and passion why we read and write.

Thanks to my loyal and ever-surprising agent, Zoë Pagnamenta, and her associate Sarah Levitt. Much gratitude to my brilliant editor, Claire Wachtel, to Elizabeth Perrella, and to all the clever people at Harper Perennial.

Thanks always to the MacDowell Colony and to Yaddo.

Many books were useful in the writing of this novel; I'd especially like to mention *The New York City Teachers Union, 1916–1964*, by Celia Lewis Zitron, New York, 1968.

About the author

About the book

Read on

Insights,
Interviews
& More . . .

A Note by
Alice Mattison

WHEN WE ARGUED ALL NIGHT is set in
Brooklyn, where I grew up. It was after
the time of immigrants from Europe
and their politically radical children, but
before the borough acquired its present
lively cultural life. In the Brooklyn of my
childhood—the late forties and fifties—
the Dodgers played in Ebbets Field, the
Brooklyn Public Library in Grand Army
Plaza smelled new, and each year school
closed for Brooklyn Day, with a parade
including scout troops and mothers (no
fathers) pushing baby carriages with
crepe paper streamers wound around
the spokes of the wheels.

I grew up near Highland Park,
at the northeast end of the borough.
Intellectual life was in Manhattan, where
my college friends and I saw films at the
Thalia, believed that the paintings in the
(free) Frick Collection and Metropolitan
Museum were our personal property,
and walked the island late at night.

Living at home, I commuted to
Queens College. My spare time was
spent not with fellow students in a dorm
but with relatives who loudly said what
they thought whether or not it made
sense, and who stuck to positions so
outlandish that anyone listening who
cared to write would eventually write
about people like them. While living
the heartbreak and comedy of family life,
I studied English literature, Latin, and
Greek. The disparate parts of life had to

be made to connect, and figuring out how could be a life's work.

After earning a doctorate in English literature at Harvard, I taught composition, mostly in community colleges; I was no scholar but loved to teach. I now teach fiction in the Bennington Writing Seminars, an MFA program at Bennington College.

With my husband—who directs a project employing people with a history of mental illness, addiction, or homelessness—I live in New Haven, Connecticut, where we brought up our three children and where I am a longtime volunteer at a soup kitchen. My fiction, I believe, reflects a life spent in close touch with others, always—paradoxically—seeking time alone for writing. It's about urban people with close bonds. My characters are often of my parents' generation, and their concerns are not quite those of the present day—but are ours with a difference. I return to certain questions: How can we live morally in private life? How can we live private life at all, given history's ravages? What are our responsibilities to the larger community? How can we endure the people we love?

When We Argued All Night *is Alice Mattison's sixth novel. Her others include* The Book Borrower, Nothing Is Quite Forgotten in Brooklyn, Hilda and Pearl, *and* The Wedding of the Two-Headed Woman; *her four story collections include* In Case We're Separated: ▶

66 My fiction, I believe, reflects a life spent in close touch with others, always— paradoxically— seeking time alone for writing. 99

A Note by Alice Mattison *(continued)*

Connected Stories. *Mattison's stories, essays, and poems have appeared in* The New Yorker, *the* New York Times, Ploughshares, The Threepenny Review, Ecotone, *and elsewhere, and have been anthologized in* The Pushcart Prize, Best American Short Stories, *and* PEN/O. Henry Prize Stories. ⌒

An Interview with Alice Mattison

by Ann Leamon

Your earlier books have primarily dealt with women—women's friendships and relationships between mothers and daughters. What was different in writing about the friendship between two men?

It didn't occur to me to write from the viewpoint of men when I was younger. I remember hearing that Jane Austen never wrote a scene in which no woman is present—presumably because she'd never been present at such a scene, so she couldn't say what might take place. One day, on a bus, I overheard a frank conversation between two men and realized that contemporary life gives us chances to guess what it's like to be people different from ourselves. Jane Austen might never have overheard two men she didn't know talking to each other. It's easier now for a woman to imagine what a man might think or do than it used to be—or for a man to imagine being a woman.

Still, though I wanted to write this book, I postponed it. It seemed daunting—maybe because the main characters would be men, maybe because it would cover so much time. But at last there was no other book to write except this one; I had to write this one. All writing projects are potential disasters, after all. It isn't as if everything will be ▶

5

An Interview with Alice Mattison (*continued*)

fine if you just write about what you know firsthand—and sometimes it's harder to write what we've experienced; we become shy, or self-consciously awkward. The hard projects demand to be written eventually, and really, they are no harder than anything else.

Once I began writing, maybe because I'd had the book in the back of my mind for many years, it came readily. Or maybe it came readily *because* I was writing about men. When the book was done, I happened to say in an e-mail to a former student that it was easier to write than my other novels, and she wrote back and asked why. All I could say was that the characters wanted to be written about, and some of my other characters had been reluctant, slower to make themselves known. That's not something one can say about imaginary people and sound trustworthy—although we know that for many authors, characters seem to take on life as one writes. The men I know in real life seem to have, on the whole, a greater willingness than the women I know to take up space, to be visible—or maybe it's a greater sense that they have a right to take up space and be visible. It was as if Artie and Harold were urging me on. Whether I felt this because of the era in which they grew up, because of their particular personalities, or because they are men, I can't say.

Some of your earlier books—particularly **The Book Borrower** *and* **Nothing Is Quite Forgotten in Brooklyn**—*deal with an episode in the past and the impact of a moment in history on the characters' later lives.* **When We Argued All Night** *takes in almost the entire sweep of the twentieth century. We meet Artie and Harold when they're twenty-six, and they're ninety-four at the end of the book. What challenges did this pose for you in conceptualizing and writing the book?*

When I set out to write this book, I'd just finished a novel (*Nothing Is Quite Forgotten in Brooklyn*) that takes place in two weeks' time—two weeks that are fourteen years apart but are narrated in detail, day by day, morning, afternoon, evening. I didn't feel like doing that again soon. Writing that book, I had to keep in mind whether the characters had eaten meals yet and make provision for them to do so; I had to put them to bed, get them up in the morning. Now I wanted to write a novel in which the characters would eat lunch on their own time.

That gave me the opposite problem—writing about long stretches of time. In some chapters, decades pass. I'm more at ease describing a moment in time than several years all at once, and the chapters in which many years passed took the most work. Gradually I saw that I had to dip into a year and find the right moment in it, narrate that, and pull back again.

My characters ate lunch only when that seemed to contribute to the story, but maybe every novel includes a certain amount of housekeeping—the kind of careful attention to not terribly interesting detail that doesn't feel creative at the time but is essential. This time I had to keep track of how old the children were in any particular year, and since their birthdays are not all in the same month, I couldn't just add the number of years since they'd last appeared. I suppose all novels present difficulties—it's the nature of the form.

As for writing about the whole twentieth century—or most of it—I am no historian, but I can read. I read newspaper stories to know what my characters might be thinking about during particular weeks and months. I also came to the task with some first- and secondhand experience. Some historical events are occasions I remember, like the war in Vietnam. Some I heard about. I knew from my parents and aunts and uncles, and my husband's parents, that although some people were embittered by the Great Depression, others, with little to expect or hope for, became adventurous and resourceful. I knew that not everyone in the "Greatest Generation" served in the war, and that in the fifties not everyone lived in the suburbs in households consisting of stay-at-home women and men with boring corporate jobs. Artie and Harold don't resemble my parents in detail, but like them they are urban, they are not surprised when women work, and they are more threatened by the ugliness of McCarthyism than by corporate jobs or the need to conform—issues I never heard about growing up in Brooklyn in an opinionated family, with grandparents who worked in the garment trades, and aunts and uncles who did everything from driving a taxi to breeding ▶

German shepherd dogs, but who never ever conformed. There's much about the twentieth century I don't know, but I tried to be faithful to what I did know.

How did the Depression, World War II, and the Holocaust affect people in your family? How did those events and your family's experience of them affect you?

During the Depression my mother's degree from Hunter College, one of the free city colleges, didn't help her get a job: she said that to be a Macy's salesclerk you had to have gone to a fancier college than that. She worked in a factory for a while and later qualified for a WPA job and became a teacher of the homebound—children with disabilities who couldn't get to school—and she did that all her life. My father, like Artie, sold photographs to newspapers; then he worked for the welfare department; eventually he learned stenography and became a court reporter. My parents were engaged for five years before they could marry—they couldn't afford rent and lived with their families.

I think my father was more troubled by the Depression than my mother was. He remained a worrier; she came out of the experience optimistic: I don't think she'd have thought of teaching the homebound on her own. The WPA changed her life.

When the war started, my father was not drafted because of a minor physical problem. The war meant Hitler to my parents, and they could barely speak of it, though my mother mentioned hearing Hitler's speeches on the radio, listening with horror though she didn't understand what he was saying. My grandparents were in America, but some relatives had stayed behind in Europe, and nobody talked about them. The exception in my childhood was a visit of two cousins who had escaped to Israel. My grandmother's Yiddish was now almost English—nobody understood the visitors, they didn't understand us. If I came across a photograph of other European relatives and asked my mother about them, she'd just say "Hitler." I never heard the term *Holocaust* until I was an adult.

My mother spoke of learning about the death camps when they were liberated in 1945, and it wasn't until I read about the period so as to write this book that I understood that people who read the newspaper carefully, and could bear to believe what they read, knew about them as early as 1943. Alfred Kazin wrote of what he knew in one of his three memoirs, *New York Jew*. (The others are *Starting Out in the Thirties* and *A Walker in the City*, parts of which I read aloud, as a teenager, to my illiterate grandmother because it was about East New York, where we lived.) The *New York Times* didn't give the extermination of the Jews the emphasis one would expect, but if you look for the old stories, they are there—and in my book, Harold knows about it.

Growing up, I thought of the thirties and early forties as a period when my parents had something they'd lost by the time I knew them. In their stories, they seemed more passionate, more adventurous. I've often written about the years when they were young, maybe trying to recover what was lost.

The history of the Communist Party in the US is not widely known. How did you become interested in it, and in the impact of the McCarthy investigations on teachers?

I wasn't what was called a "red diaper baby," but my parents had friends who were or had been Communists, and I knew a girl named Joan, after "Uncle Joe" Stalin. My parents were ardent Roosevelt Democrats, but it was ordinary for people like them to feel positive toward the ideals of the Communist Party, and my mother talked about going to a Communist Party meeting in the thirties—like Artie, she was put off by the coercive discipline. After the last few decades, in which we've heard so much about communism as a horror, it's hard to remember that the party represented a plausible and progressive way of thinking in the thirties.

During the McCarthy era, I was old enough to be aware that something was troubling and frightening the adults in my family. A family friend, who had never been a Communist, lost his teaching job. I scarcely knew him, and my parents believed that children should be protected from hearing about trouble. ▶

When children are kept from knowing facts but sense feelings, they are more affected than if they were told everything. I found the event unforgettable, and I've twice written about New York teachers losing their jobs because of McCarthyism—in an earlier novel, *Hilda and Pearl*, and now here.

Teaching runs through the book—Artie and Harold are teachers at various levels, Brenda is a teacher before she starts building playground sets. How has teaching (good and bad) informed your life?

My mother, as I've said, was a teacher of the homebound— children whose disabilities, in the days before ramps and elevators in schools, kept them home. She traveled from house to house, teaching children in grades one through six. She and my father seemed to assume I'd become a teacher, as so many girls did, and they expected me to live at home during college and attend one of the (then) free city colleges, as they had. I did. My parents were not ambitious, but they were slightly ambitious for me: they hoped that I might go away to a university after college, earn a master's degree, and become a high school teacher. I grew up wanting to teach (as well as write) and have taught all my life, but in community colleges and four-year colleges. However, I absorbed my parents' admiration for high school teachers and still feel it. The high school I went to, Franklin K. Lane in Brooklyn, was full of gifted, serious teachers, men and women of astonishing depth and learning. Best of all was an English teacher, Agnes Jaffe. I love to write about teachers—I'm still trying to thank them.

The cabin on the lake is an important location for the characters even though they identify strongly as city people. Do you have a "cabin on a lake"? What role does it play in your life?

There is no cabin on a lake, and there have been many cabins, some on lakes. Many summers, my parents rented cabins in the Adirondacks or New England for a few weeks, often in bungalow colonies. Years later, my husband and I discovered we wanted to take the same kind of vacations—though we like more remote cabins than they did, with as few people around as possible.

If you could, would you buy such a cabin, or is part of its magic that it's not yours?

I've never wanted to own a cabin—one would always be worrying about the leaky roof—and in my book, the people staying in the cabin, experiencing something important there or thinking about it, usually don't own it. The cabin in the book represents—as such vacations represent in my life, I suppose—respite: physical and imaginative freedom. You can't take that for granted: no one can own that. People have always written stories in which characters from cities or towns come to understand a truth when they go into the woods, into the wilderness. It's in the Bible, in *King Lear*, and in books as different as *Pride and Prejudice* (Elizabeth Bennet understands that she's in love with Mr. Darcy when she meets him by chance on his wooded estate, which she tours with her aunt and uncle) and Toni Morrison's *Song of Solomon*. The cabin—the woods—is where my characters, too, learn who they are. I'm one of those people for whom letters of the alphabet and numbers have colors in the mind and, at times, so do books. This one, long before it was written, was "green book." ◡

Have You Read?
More by Alice Mattison

**NOTHING IS QUITE FORGOTTEN
IN BROOKLYN**

Constance Tepper is staying in her
mother's Brooklyn apartment while
her mother is out of town, and her week
turns frightening when she wakes to find
someone has entered the apartment and
taken her purse. A series of revelations
jeopardizes her marriage, her job, and
her love for an older woman who has
mesmerized Con all her life. Years later,
now living in Brooklyn, Con is brought
back to that week when reminders and
discoveries lead to grief, love, and the
unraveling of the past—personal and
historical—as she crosses the city,
from Coney Island to the Metropolitan
Museum of Art, from Prospect Heights
to the traces of a lost elevated train line:
a forgotten, century-old attempt to make
sense of Brooklyn's peculiarities once
and for all, through public
transportation.

"A generous, empathetic writer,
[Mattison] believes that the human
connection, while imperfect and fragile,
takes precedence over any abstraction."
—*New York Times*

IN CASE WE'RE SEPARATED

Spanning the length and breadth of
the twentieth century, Alice Mattison's
masterful *In Case We're Separated* looks
at a family of Jewish immigrants in the
1920s and 1930s and follows the urban,
emotionally turbulent lives of their
children, grandchildren, and great-
grandchildren against a backdrop of
political assassination, the Vietnam
War, and the AIDS epidemic. Beginning
with the title story, which introduces
Bobbie Kaplowitz—a single mother in
1954 Brooklyn whose lover is married
and whose understanding of life is
changed by a broken kitchen appliance—
Mattison displays her unparalleled gift
for storytelling and for creating rich,
multidimensional characters, a gift
that has led the *Los Angeles Times* to
praise her as "a writer's writer."

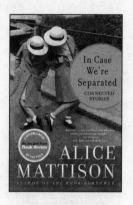

"Radiant. . . . A book filled with
felicitous writing and ferocious
insight."   —Susan Halpern,
New York Times Book Review

THE WEDDING OF THE TWO-HEADED WOMAN

For years, following an early first marriage, Daisy Andalusia remained single and enjoyed the company of men on her own terms, making the most of her independent life. Now in her fifties, she has remarried and settled into a quieter life in New Haven, Connecticut. She's committed to a job she loves: organizing the clutter of other people's lives. Her business soon leads her to a Yale project studying murders in small cities. While her husband, an inner-city landlord, objects to her new interest, Daisy finds herself being drawn more and more into the project and closer to its director, Gordon Skeetling.

When Daisy discovers an old tabloid article with the headline "Two-Headed Woman Weds Two Men: Doc Says She's Twins," she offers it as the subject for her theater group's improvisational play. Over eight transformative months, this headline will take on an increasing significance as Daisy questions whether she can truly be a part of anything— a two-headed woman, a friendship, a marriage—while discovering more about herself than she wants to know.

"Bracingly serious but without pretension, Mattison's voice is like that of no one else writing today: the demands she makes of her readers are difficult but exhilarating."
—*Kirkus Reviews* (starred review)

To Frances, an only child living in McCarthy-era Brooklyn, her mother, Hilda, and her aunt Pearl seem as if they have always been friends. Frances does not question the love between the two women until her father's job as a teacher is threated by anti-Communism, just as Frances begins to learn about her family's past. Why does Hilda refer to her "first pregnancy," as if Frances wasn't her only child? Whose baby shoes are hidden in Hilda's dresser drawer? Why is there tension when Pearl and her husband come to visit?

The story of a young girl in the fifties and her elders' coming-of-age in the unquiet thirties, this book resonates deeply, revealing in beautiful, clear language the complexities of friendship and loss.

"Accomplished poet, novelist, and short-story writer Mattison adds to her laurels with this quietly suspenseful, psychologically penetrating novel, which is both a perceptive study of adolescence and a dramatic exploration of family relationships."   —*Publishers Weekly*

THE BOOK BORROWER

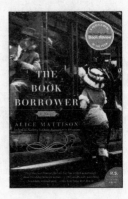

On the first page of *The Book Borrower*, Toby Ruben and Deborah Laidlaw meet in 1975 in a playground, where the two women are looking after their babies. Deborah lends Toby a book, *Trolley Girl*—a memoir about a long-ago trolley strike and three Jewish sisters, one a fiery revolutionary—that will disappear and reappear throughout the twenty-two years these women are friends.

Through two decades, Deborah and Toby raise their children, embark on teaching careers, and argue about politics, education, and their own lives. One day during a hike, they have an argument that cannot be resolved— and the two women take different, permanent paths—but it is ultimately the borrowed book that will bring them back together. With sensitivity and grace, Alice Mattison shows how books can rescue us from our deepest sorrows; how the events of the outside world play into our private lives; and how the bonds between women are enduring, mysterious, and laced with surprise.

"Extraordinary."
—*Washington Post Book World*

"An ambitious and original novel."
—*Wall Street Journal*